The Cleaner of Kastoria

Jacqueline Paizis

PUBLISHED BY JACQUELINE PAIZIS
Hove, UK, http://www.jacquyp.blogspot.co.uk/

All rights reserved

All material © Jacqueline Paizis

This book is in copyright. Subject to statutory exception and to provisions of relevant collective licensing agreements, no reproduction of any part may take place without the written permission of the author.

Printed by Lulu, www.Lulu.Com

This book is distributed subject to the conditions that it shall not, by way of trade or otherwise, be lent, re-sold, hired out, or otherwise circulated without the author's prior consent in any form of binding or cover other than that in which it is published and without a similar condition including this condition being imposed on the subsequent purchaser.

ISBN 978-0-244-96763-5

About the Author

Jacqueline Paizis (@slenderbeak) was born in Hythe, Kent but spent many years living and working in London and Athens. She now divides her time between Hove, East Sussex and Greece.

The Cleaner of Kastoria was a runner up in the 2007 Literary Consultancy novel competition.

Jacqueline was a contributing editor on the Queenspark Books publication Backstage Brighton and was a runner up in the 2007 Bluethumbnail competition with her short story Albanian Mothers.

Jacqueline is currently completing her second novel set in contemporary Greece at the beginning of the socioeconomic crisis. She also writes a blog www.jacquyp.blogspot about Greek life, politics and literature.

AUTHOR'S NOTE

This book is a work of fiction but it is about real people, places and events. It was born from stories I heard told by Greek villagers, from my memories and from interviews I conducted with women like Dina. The experience of the Greek Civil War is here written about from the point of view of one woman and therefore it does not claim to be a work of 'objective' history. Dina could be any one of the women who shared their stories with me.

I have tried to be as accurate as fiction will allow in my description of Kastoria and its surroundings but none of the characters portrayed are based on any person, living or dead. Rather, they are a kaleidoscope of people I have known and places I have been.

When I began my research I was working towards a doctorate but for various reasons I abandoned my study. When, ten years later, I opened the tin that contained cassettes of my interviews with real Greek women who had fought in the Civil War I decided to write a novel that would be enriched by their stories not only of war but their lives after war.

A Note on Greek names

Greek masculine names ending in os, as and is lose the final s in the vocative case e.g. 'Makis, Dimitris and Nikos are having an argument' but 'stop arguing Maki, Dimitri and Niko.'

Feminine surnames are formed differently from masculine ones e.g. Spiros Venetiados but Vassiliki Venetiadou.

The consonant transliterated as 'dh' e.g. Dimitris, fasolada, is pronounced 'th' as in English 'these'

FOR THE READER

Most historians date the Greek Civil War as 1946/47 until 1949.

> *"At the present moment in world history nearly every nation must choose between alternative ways of life. The choice is often not a free one."*
> Harry S. Truman, Speech before a joint session of congress, March 12 1947

1947 The Truman Doctrine – the turning point for US foreign policy and in the escalation of the Cold War. The year in which America steps into the shoes of the British in Greece.

President Truman addresses the US Congress on the subject of aid to Greece and he has words to say about the women and men who are fighting in the Democratic Army (DA).

"A militant minority, exploiting human want and misery. They've been allowed to create political chaos. We're not going to stand for this state of affairs any longer. The home of the brave and the land of the free will show them who is boss and in the process rescue all those innocent, law abiding citizens."

A Greek woman answers: *"Mr President. Just because we're fighting with belief and enthusiasm it doesn't mean we like war. That we are warlike. It is not our choice. We have been obliged to choose between dignity and humiliation. What would be your choice Mr President?"*

By the end of 1947 four-hundred thousand villages have been evacuated often as a tactic to prevent the DA from recruiting. Despite this the armed struggle led by the DA is rapidly developing into civil war. Government security battalions begin to appear. These are Para-military bands whose task is to inform as to the whereabouts of partisans and prevent recruitment to the DA in the countryside.

Dec 1947 – The Communist Party of Greece (KKE) is outlawed by Emergency Law 509.

1948 – Tito-Stalin split. Yugoslavia is expelled from the Cominform by Stalin. This has devastating effects on the DA because they rely so heavily on Yugoslav support in terms of supplies and movement across the border from northern Greece. Yugoslavia does not accept their expulsion and hope to find an ally in the KKE. But this is not fulfilled. Zachariades supports Stalin and the leadership of KKE aligns itself with the minority Bulgarian claims to Macedonia, instead of with Yugoslavian claims. By 1949 Slavo -Macedonians probably outnumber Greeks in the DA.

Women comprise at least thirty per cent of fighters in the DA by this time. But Stalin already has his eyes on Eastern Europe. The women and men of the DA are being abandoned.

August 1949 – The last battles of the civil war are fought on the mountains of Grammos and Vitsi, close to the Albanian border and close to Kastoria. Many DA fighters are forced to retreat into the People's Democracies of Yugoslavia, Albania, Bulgaria, Czechoslovakia and USSR. Some never return to Greece, while others have to wait until 1980s. The DA has little chance against the Hellenic airforce and its US reinforcements including a new bomber known as the Helldiver.

But the most devastating new weapon that finishes off the DA is called Napalm B. The Greeks call it sticky fire because it sticks to the skin and causes severe burns when on fire. It is developed in a secret laboratory at Harvard University in 1943 by Louis Fieser. This is the first time this weapon has been used. It is supplied by the USA for use by the government army against the DA fighters and the first attacks using this take place on the mountain of Grammos.

The Marshall Plan or the European Recovery Programme (ERP) is the invention of George Kennan or 'the father of containment'. The USA sees Greece and Turkey as the front line in the battle against communist expansion so these countries receive the first offerings of aid. European countries are required to become wealthy enough to later import US goods.
In 1948/49 Greece receives only $175 million in aid compared with West Germany's $510m and Italy's $594m. Some dissident American voices notice the disparity. *"Say, President Truman, we thought the fight was against fascism in Europe. How come we're giving the fascists a lot more than the poor Greeks? Has Kennan got his figures wrong?"*
By the end of October 1949 about eighty thousand Greeks have fled their country. Many homeless peasants migrate to the growing suburbs around Athens. The war has turned Athens into a metropolis and it will take until the early Nineteen Fifties before Greece can reach the living standards it enjoyed in 1938.

In the Nineteen Sixties, Greece is recovering economically but political instability persists so that when their chance comes on 21st April 1967 the Colonels, like eagles, swoop down from the wings and make their coup. The following years until 1974 are to be ruled in accordance with Hellenic-

Christian Ideals – a New Democracy of New Men and New Ideas – a golden dawn?

PROLOGUE
Civil War 1947
PANIYIRI IN NESTORIO

> *"Just because we fought with belief and enthusiasm it doesn't mean that we liked the war, that we were warlike. We were obliged to choose because they hunted and tortured us – in that way we travelled along the mountain road."*

On the eve of August 15th the whole village squeezed into the square to celebrate the Feast of the Assumption. On one side the butcher had set up his stall. He was proud to be able to offer meat to his village after weeks of near starvation. A fourteen- day fast before the Paniyiri was usually observed by everyone except the few village atheists but this year government troops had enforced their own fast on the people by stealing goats and chickens to feed themselves. Between swigs of wine the butcher dodged from one spit to another. On the first two skewered suckling pigs were stretched out end to end crisping up to the colour of burnt honey. The butcher smiled as he looked at them but the smile developed into a frown as he used all his strength to rotate the lever on the second spit. This one was a heavier beast. Children licked their lips at the sight of the fat dripping and hissing onto the coals.

Great grandparents, grandparents, mothers, fathers, sons, daughters, uncles, aunts, first, second and third cousins vied for the juiciest cuts of pork and the most sure-footed dance partner. Dina Konstantinou's eldest brother Takis had taken the first dance with her and then nodded his approval to the man who was now making her so giddy.

The young man's eyes were resting on her as he rubbed the plump green basil leaf between his forefinger and thumb. He placed it carefully behind his ear, the signal that he meant to keep her close as they danced. Taking her hand he swung her round before she could tell him her name and they were swallowed up in the crowd of sweating bodies, pressed together in one rhythm. Dina could see her sister in the arms of tall, fine-looking Thanassis. She felt pleased for Artemis but it was a bad time to fall in love. Government troops were increasing their raids and seizing all the younger men. Any village that had been loyal to the Resistance could suffer the same fate. If her unit came for her Dina knew she would have to leave at a moment's notice but this man who held her so tightly and stared into her eyes so intensely gave her reason to want to stay forever. She felt endangered and at the same time excited. I am going to die, she thought. I could die because of what I feel for this man with strong arms and blue eyes. What if I can't concentrate when I go back to the front and forget my training? I'm going to be thinking of this. Oh brother! What a gift you've brought me. I'm crazy. My knees are wobbly. This didn't happen when I was facing my first target. My legs held me steady then.

He whirled her round until she was dizzy, hot and thirsty but she wished the dance would never stop. Strands of her long auburn hair had freed themselves from their black ribbon and stuck to her breast and neck. The young man blew on them to cool her. She couldn't help noticing his full lips and blushed. They still hadn't exchanged names.

After the dance he sat Dina on the edge of the well while he lowered an old dented bucket into the depths of the water. With a flick of his wrist the bucket clattered against the sides of the wall as he pulled on the rope.

"It's very low." He balanced the bucket on the wall beside Dina. "Let's hope there's some rain before winter." He dipped the tin mug into the water and passed it to Dina.

She gulped without taking breath. "Another problem! Where will it end?"

At the butcher's stall he chose her portion carefully then led her to sit on the churchyard wall. He spread out his jacket for her. "I'm Maki. I'm from Kerkira."

"Ah! I thought so from your accent. My name's Dina but you probably know that from my brother."

He nodded maybe with a grin that showed uneven, white teeth.

There was a silence as they quickly unfolded the greasy brown paper and bit into the chunks of tender meat.

"Some wine? It's your local damson. Much better than the stuff we make in Kerkira." Makis passed the flask to Dina. She hesitated, embarrassed because she had only tasted wine once before at her cousin's baptism. But she was a soldier now. She took the flask from Makis's hand with conviction. To her surprise the thick syrupy liquid flowed easily down her throat and left a pleasant warmth.

"The occupiers tried to destroy our village but they didn't succeed. After that I had…" She paused. The village postmaster appeared, on his way to the dance and dressed in smart grey trousers and jacket. The left half of his body bent sideways as he walked because of the heavy postal bag he carried on his daily rounds. He nodded good evening and went on his way.

"*Prodotis,*".Dina mouthed but Makis pressed his forefinger to her lips. They waited until he had disappeared.

"I know, Dina. I know you've joined up."

"Yes. I guessed my brother had told you. Is there anything he didn't tell you?"

"Uhm. The red- head lives up to her hair colour." Their eyes locked. Never was a truer word spoken. She wanted more sparring. "And he didn't describe to me the green of his sister's eyes or the shape of her mouth." As he spoke Makis edged closer to Dina.

Thank goodness she was sitting on the wall. Her body felt heavy. "And you? What about you?"

"Yes, I also had to leave my village. Do you know Gastouri in Kerkira?"

"I've never been over to Kerkira. It must be a beautiful island."

"I'll take you there one day when all this is over." He took her hand. "I joined up about six months ago. Now I'm a Captain in the Fourth Battalion. I'll have to leave in a little while. Where are you based?"

"I've just finished training camp at Agrafa, can't you tell?" She giggled, sipping more wine. Makis answered with a smile and took the flask. He didn't want to risk the wrath of her brother and father on the same night. As they wandered towards the music he took her arm.

In the square the musical tension was deepening. Three litres of wine later the band struck their chords with more drunken confidence. Dina saw her brother hurling himself down, bending his knee, arms outstretched on either side, his head flung back in pleasure. The outer circle of dancers clapped at his agility and roared approval when the butcher's son pounced into the centre to join him. Petros gripped the blade of his knife between his teeth while he danced, forcing his mouth into a devilish grin.

Makis was pulling her back into the wave of dancers. The stem of basil was still stuck behind his ear. Dina put her nose up to it and took in its perfume. "It works."

"What works?"

"The basil. I haven't left your side since the dance started." They held each other's gaze for what seemed like hours and from that moment she felt that the course of her life would take a new direction. This taste of passion was sweet but she also felt a premonition of pain. The night was close but Dina still shivered.

"Dina, I have to leave you for a while. I need to make some arrangements with your brother but I'll be back as soon as I can." He squeezed her shoulder and kissed her on the cheek. When he had gone she pressed the place with her fingertips.

Then Artemis was suddenly at her side. Dina turned round to meet her wide grin.

Encircling Dina with her arms she kissed her on the cheek. "Guess what, Dina?"

"As if I need to guess! You're in love."

"He's asking *Babas* tonight so he'll be sure to be in a good mood and won't say no." Her face saddened a little as she pulled at a stray cotton thread on her button. "But we can't get a ring yet, he's got to go back to the Front tomorrow. But in two weeks he'll come back and we'll go to Kastoria to buy it."

Dina put her arm round Artemis's shoulder to steady herself. She was beginning to feel the effects of the wine. "Artemis, you know I love you dearly. I want you to be happy and I don't want to spoil the night for you, but what if *Babas* says no?"

"Have you been drinking Dina? " She linked Dina's arm through her own. "Has that *levendi* been getting you drunk on purpose? Who is he? Does Takis know you're with him?" She supported Dina to a chair outside the *taverna*. "Now sit down. Why should *Babas* say no? He'll be glad to get one of his daughters off his hands. Won't he? He can't keep us forever and things are getting so bad now in the fields. You know what Angeliki told me the other day? Panos Theofilos was shot by a soldier. He probably thought Panos was an *andarte*. Just think of that! There he was stripping leaves from his plants, packing the sacks and then bang! Dead. And the soldier just turned and ran away. Angeliki said nobody was brave enough to chase him in case there were others hiding. Our men are cowards. Why didn't they go after them?"

"Why d'you think? Our men don't have guns, do they? That's one of the problems." Dina imagined the scene. Baking hot tobacco plant. Panos Theofilos doing what he'd done for thirty years, working his fields, bothering nobody, trying to feed his family. Who would have taken him for an *andarte*? He could hardly stand up straight on those skinny legs. She didn't believe it was an accident. It was a provocation to the village, a scare tactic to prevent the Democratic Army from recruiting. She felt her stomach tighten. Why had they surrendered their weapons at Varkiza last year? If only more of them had listened to Velouhiotis their farmers wouldn't have ended up like Theofilos. "Ah well, Artemi, that's exactly why I'm not sitting around here any more, waiting for them to destroy us. But getting engaged isn't going to help is it? You won't have time to marry; he's enlisted and this war has only just started." Her sister needed protection. But who was she to preach? What had she been doing tonight? Getting drunk and letting down her unit. For the second time that night she had to remind herself that she was a soldier. But surely soldiers could be forgiven for falling in love.

"Why do you always ruin it for me?" Artemis shook her arm free and disappeared into the crowd. Dina felt guilty. Perhaps she was being unfair, envious even, pointing out the pitfalls when her little sister was so happy. Tonight wasn't the night to dwell on what might or might not happen. Leaving her village and becoming a fighter had taught Dina that nothing was certain any more.

The snake of dancers weaved in and out of the crowd. They were led by a bearded elder, baring still white teeth that stood out in relief against his brown face. Stretching out his right arm and waving a red kerchief, he crouched and straightened up repeatedly, egged on by the applauding bystanders and the haunting oboe. His wife broke free from the crowd and slapped him across the back. "Useless!" She cried in a piercing voice. "You'll be useless tomorrow...and what then? Am I to go to the field as well as everything else? Useless husband!"

Dina's father had told her about the man. His wife was right. He was useless at everything except what he was doing now but these were her people and she might be called on to defend them. Her fear rose when she thought about leaving for the mountains. She hadn't rested enough, she wanted to stay and be with Makis, to bathe in the little pebble cove near her house, feel his arm caressing her waist and watch her skin change colour under the summer sun. She studied her palms. Hours of rifle practice and trying to dig out trenches in the baked uplands of the Pindus had given her calluses. Her hands looked like those of an old woman. The first weeks of training had been tough on her body and she had cried for home like a baby. Lack of sleep meant that on some days she staggered from one drill to the next, aiming her rifle at imaginary figures. Her captain punished her in front of the whole company and forced her to do extra guard duty one night because she had missed her target. They had gone to bed hungry, only dreaming of the rabbit they could have eaten. But from somewhere inside herself she found the stamina to keep going and in the process it was not only her body that hardened, her attitude began to be that of a soldier. She learnt to rely on her eyes and ears more than she had ever done before.

An old path ran between the church and the doctor's house. The cobbles were slippery, polished by years of tread. By day it was a busy path, used by the locals to take their vegetables and tobacco to the waterfront where they bundled them into the boats. As she made her way down, carefully placing one dancing shoe in front of the other, Dina felt her strength sapping. The neighbour shot in his tobacco field was a warning. The troops would be back. She worried especially for her brother Takis. He was too headstrong, never considering the consequences of his words or actions. It was best that he was leaving soon, but Makis would be going with him.

At the bottom of the path the streetlamp lit up the magenta bougainvillaea trailing over the railings of the doctor's house. Village gossips said that Doctor Nikos was drinking because he had time on his hands. Government troops were blocking the roads, so the medicines weren't getting through. Doctor Nikos couldn't bear watching children sicken with tuberculosis so in company with the priest he consoled himself with the congregation wine.

She could hear the fireworks beginning in the square above. A bright purple plume shot whistling into the night sky and stray dogs stopped and howled. As a child Dina used to long for August 15th. It was the one time in the year when they could all eat a little more, drink a lot and dance all night. But now there were few animals left in the pastures and chickens were often snatched from their yards by wild dogs.

Down at the jetty the boats were nestling together, bobbing gently on the black water. A moonbeam picked out a little carmine caique, shiny with new paint. Its nameplate MAKIS. His name again. Her spirits rose. She sat down on the steps, taking off her shoes to let the water tickle her toes. A second shower of pink sparks broke out on the hill behind her then sprinkled away into the depths of the cypress trees. Dina shook the droplets of water from her feet and slipped them back into her shoes. It felt good to have her blistered feet free after months of wearing heavy, badly fitting boots. A young couple had appeared. He took her hand as she stepped into his father's boat. It was Alekos, the cobbler's son. He lifted the oars and slipped them through the rough pieces of string that rested round the pegs. Then he rowed rhythmically out into the bay, the oars creaking in time to his pull. Dina felt envious. She wanted to be in a boat with Makis, lying back against the stern. He must have strong muscles in his forearms and he would be rowing her out beyond Broken Nose Point. She was reluctant to leave her place on the steps, where she watched the water gently swelling under the moon, but Makis might be looking for her. She climbed slowly up the cobbled path. The night was too warm to hurry.

Re-entering the square Dina bumped into Artemis, who clutched her young man's sleeve and greeted Dina with a wide smile. "He said yes, Dina. *Babas* said yes."

"Ah Artemi! I'm so pleased for you and I'm sorry about what I said earlier." She squeezed her sister's hand. Dina was wondering if her father had agreed because he was drunk. He was always easy to get round when cradling a glass of his own wine. After the Papas he was considered the best glass in the village - a dubious compliment according to Dina's mother.

"It's forgotten. I know your mind's busy with more important things. I do admire you, sister."

Dina turned to acknowledge Thanasis. "So, congratulations to both of you. I really hope you'll be happy...that you can be together, at least for a while." He nodded solemnly. The crowd engulfed them, still for dancing and singing. They linked hands and Dina picked up the rhythm as if she had been dancing all night. Small children darted between adult legs. Elder brothers stood against one end of the school wall like sentinels while younger sisters sat together at the other, fluttering their eyelashes and looking down whenever a boy caught their glance.

Suddenly Makis was behind her and guiding her away from the dancing. They had to step over the sleeping oboe player, propped against the Rigas Ferraios monument. His right hand still clutched an empty bottle of cognac to his breast like a baby after its milk.

"Not this way. I want to go back down to the jetty where it's quiet and we can put our feet into the sea. Come on." She pulled them both into a gentle run that became a race as the slope steepened and they released hands. Makis overtook her and won. She ran into his arms and he scooped her up.

"What if someone sees us? They might tell *Babas*." And at that moment the priest appeared round the corner, holding a small plate of watermelon." Here my children. Eat this. I've had enough, enough." He waved his free arm in the air and lost his balance. Makis tried propping him against his own body. Dina took the toppling plate but his body slid slowly away from Makis's side and slumped in front of the doctor's gate. They left him in peace, a contented smile stretching his old creased face.

Makis held a slice of ripe watermelon up to Dina's mouth. Juice ran down her chin and as she began to wipe it off with the back of her hand Makis was there with a handkerchief, dabbing gently.

"I can never eat this without getting it all over myself. It's delicious. Have a piece."

But Makis only watched and stroked her hair. "It's turning red from the sun. Beautiful." He then laid his head on her shoulder.

Of all his movements and touch this was the one that thrilled Dina the most. It was intimate and yet it could have been a gesture of endearment made by a friend or a comrade. But this man would become more than a comrade. She dared herself to meet his gaze.

Makis took her small, trembling hands between his. "Swear by the August moon above us that you will be mine."

"I swear. I will follow you and I will find you again," she hesitated. "Captain."

***

That night, some traitors took advantage of the village revellers and secured positions in the hills above. They gave safe access to the government security battalions. They waited in hiding until the dawn of August 16th when the musicians and dancers had fallen into their beds. Then the traitors, whose names were Adonis Vlavianos, Panos Dimitrios and Giorgos Vendouros, led the soldiers through Fotis Konstantinos's little vegetable garden and into the house. They dragged Konstntinos by his hair, out of his bed, along the road and into the square. They sat him up against the Rigas Ferraios monument and each of the men aimed their precision carbines, supplied by the British S.O.E. and left three gaping holes in his forehead. Around his neck they had tied a cardboard label that read 'KKE *prodotis*'

Dina and her brother and sisters woke to their mother's wailing. They followed the bloodstains on the gravel. They got to the monument and the people already there tried to shield the sight from them. Dina's mother screamed. "*Thee mou*, why have you punished us like this?" The villagers parted and she fell on her husband's body, still in his bedclothes and still warm.

Afterwards, with the help of Father Gerasimos, they laid him out on their parents' bed. Artemis wrapped a sheet round his head. Then they watched as their mother tore up the wedding photo she had kept in her bedside table for forty years and let the pieces flutter onto the body. Dina still couldn't cry. Yannis cursed their brother for bringing such tragedy upon the family. "Where is he now, when his family needs him?"

Dina sat down. Artemis had taken their mother to lie down. "Don't blame Takis for this, Yannis. He didn't know. How could he know! He's been away too long." She understood her brother's eyes, which brought no comfort. "Do you still believe we have a choice? Now can you see what we have to do to protect what's left of our villages?"

Yannis stood tall over her. She sank to her knees but he pushed her away and left the room. She never saw him again.

Without disturbing her family she collected her knapsack, changed into her boots and closed the back door quietly. One second, two seconds of hesitation as she leaned against the door. She would follow Makis to the fourth battalion and share her grief with him but until then she would contain it in her heart and carry the weight with her. Then she took off, running down the lane, eerily quiet for that time of the morning. No birds sang.

CHAPTER ONE
Kastoria N.W. Greece 1974

"They pounced; they jumped on us on 21st April 1967. They witchunted those of us who'd fought the Occupiers of our country and then they imprisoned us like criminals. They were the criminals. Some of my friends escaped to other countries. I still have friends in London."

"On November 17th 1973 I was a Law student at Athens Polytechnio. They sent in the tanks and they murdered my best friend. But the public supported us. They took courage from our bravery. Without us I don't believe the Junta would have fallen in 1974."

Dina had been on her knees for more years than she cared to remember. She was in demand – a good thing for the family purse, but her knees disagreed. As she stretched forward she swung her wrist in circular motions and the sleeve of her nylon overall rose above her elbow to reveal a sinewy forearm. Dina hated people seeing her arms.

Marble floors were Dina's speciality. They sparkled in response to her efforts. She skated on them to get the best shine. Every week Dina followed the same rota of apartments and houses. Monday was Miss Dabas, twenty four and still not married, Tuesday Theophilos, Wednesday the Styllou family, Thursday the Panayiotou's with four children who left a trail of unwashed clothes. Then it was Friday, poor old Mr B, a widower all on his own. Dina always called her employer Mr B because she had trouble pronouncing his name. It was one of those long Greek names that never seemed to end so she asked his permission to call him plain Mr B and he said that was fine. "In fact I like it," he said. "It makes me feel more mysterious, more interesting."

On her day off Dina took her granddaughter shopping, ironed the clothes and cooked. Her daughter Rena worked nights in a washing powder factory.

On Sundays Dina rested, letting the family take care of her. She wasn't very good at doing it herself. Propping her right leg on the stool she rubbed her knee, easing the ache a little. This was the weak leg. It had caught the shrapnel and screamed ever since. Dina had a good relationship with her right leg because it always let her know when the pain was coming, giving her chance to take the weight off. Even five minutes helped. If she heard a song that reminded her of the unspoken years a tear would squeeze its way into her eye and stain her cheek. In spring her heart ached as she breathed the perfume of the jasmine flower. How practised she had been in warfare and yet how innocent in love. When she remembered her first kiss she felt her cheeks redden. Even if she was alone.

Wealthy Kastorians were always pleased with Dina's work. She cleaned devotedly for these families and if they moved house she went with them like a piece of the furniture. Her strong hands transformed their floors into mirrors that beamed back as she knelt on her kneepads as if in prayer. Her reputation went before her duster. There was even a waiting list for her skills. Kastoria was a town built on the fur trade and that meant generations of families, like Mr B's, had become rich, originally as trappers but later as fur importers. Their wives paraded the beautiful furs in their daily appearances around the town while poor women looked on and shivered with cold. But chance was part of Dina's philosophy of life and she felt lucky that she had found herself in Kastoria at the right time. She was never without work.

Friday was Dina's favourite day because she cleaned Mr B's magnificent mansion. His house sat majestically in front of the northern lake-shore. Dina often imagined how it must have looked centuries before when it was inhabited by some aristocratic family. High-born women would have stepped up and down the sculpted marble staircase in their full embroidered skirts. Her predecessors would have polished those same steps in threadbare overalls and darned stockings. "It's pleasing to the eye," she used to tell her neighbours in Kalithea. "When you walk by the lake next time take a look at those wonderful wooden balconies. Ah! It's a handsome house is Mr B's."

The view from the veranda was the most splendid in the town and when she was out there beating rugs or sweeping, Dina was a queen in her castle. People would glance up, "kali mera Dina" and she would wave her duster back as if it was her own house.

Mr B had a heap of steel greying hair that resembled Dina's cleaning mop. His hair had rapidly whitened after the shock of his wife's death. Dina knew too well how shock could do that. She knew the woman who had been the cleaner before her, a woman who had been devoted to Mrs B but after her death she said she couldn't bear it anymore, cleaning where Mrs B had kept the house so beautifully only to see Mr B wreck it with his drunken soirees. She had explained to Dina – either he was in a foul mood and then forgot to pay her or he shouted at her when she dusted around his late wife's ornaments that he refused to put away. In the end he had scared her off and Dina stepped in to face the chaos and dirt.

But Dina made her conditions of work clear to Mr B from the start. She expected her wages every Friday when she left; she would not demean herself by having to remind Mr B. She would not be shouted at. She was a cleaner but she was no man's slave. In return Dina would make Mr B proud again that he had such a beautiful house. Mr B never shouted at Dina and he never forgot to pay her. She subtly reminded him what a joy his house was and how he must really love it. How anyone would love to have such a family home. But she had learned to be careful about mentioning the word home because he became morose. He and his late wife had never been able to have children, a tragedy in Greek eyes. So, although Dina listened and empathised with Mr B's laments she never indulged them; as a result he sensed her empathy and then he wanted to know more about her family. She always rationed this information, not wanting to appear rude to her employer by being completely secretive but the snippets of Dina's life were like bait on a hook to Mr B and he always seemed to want more than she was prepared to give.

When Mr B came home from his business, Dina would be on her knees cleaning the marble floors. . At first she refused his offer of a glass of wine but before long she became used to their ritual and looked forward to it. "But I'm still working Mr B," she would object weakly and ignoring her, he would hold out a small glass so that she was obliged to rise from her knees, reach out her arm and receive it She felt a little guilty allowing this interruption but she saw Mr B needed her company. After all it wasn't such a sacrifice. But if he trod too close to her past Dina always remembered an unfinished job and disappeared into the kitchen.

Dina was skilled at disappearing. She had had enough practice. When she returned to Greece from Yugoslavia in 1969 Dina with her daughter Rena it was at great risk to them both. An old comrade had sent word that her mother was dying. They were smuggled across the border where she came face to face with the shores of the Prespa lakes. She couldn't appreciate the beauty, the wildlife, because she could still only see her sister's dark curls before her head plunged into the water and emerged white like a ghost. Dina and Rena were disappeared into a remote village north of Florina where comrades had brought her mother to spend her last days with her daughter and the granddaughter who she had never seen. In 1969 the Greek Junta was only two years old, an infant monster, paying desperate villagersto inform on their neighbours so as to root out communist partisans and sympathisers. Even the elderly village men, lifelong kafeneon friends, began to mistrust one another. Their daily pleasure of tavli and coffee was embittered by the uncertainty of who had already been bought or who was up for sale. So trusting Mr B was a scary thought for Dina. But she couldn't dislike him.

When they swapped stories Dina imagined she was his equal. Their differences seemed to melt into Mr B's floors like Dina's polish. They had built reputations for themselves at opposite ends of society but somehow this united them in a common understanding: they shared the pleasure of not just being good at their work but excelling in it. Dina understood that crafting a fur was a slow, meticulous business. Mr B had shown her some of the mink pelts and photographs of tradesmen putting their furs out on the street to stretch and dry in the sun. "We had beavers in those days but not any more. They've gone now."

Even so, when Dina was putting all her strength behind her many-layered cloth and feeling angry with the world, she found herself resenting Mr B and laughing at the idea that they were equals. Mr B had inherited his wealth from his father, who, in turn, had benefited from his father. Building up a fur export business hadn't exactly been hard labour. That had probably been done by those who worked in his factory treating and manufacturing the furs. Dina's only inheritance would have been her dowry, two goats and a rug. Instead she had received a leg full of shrapnel, a souvenir from the Epirus mountains in 1948. Every twinge and ache brought back the shock of seeing the metal shard jutting out above her knee. The cold winters of northern Greece were not kind to her leg. She had thought of moving to the drier climate of Athens but it was far away from everything she knew and everyone she cared about. She couldn't return to her village. No work and too many memories to haunt her. Here in Kastoria she had built her reputation as a hard worker but even here she hadn't felt free to open her mouth about her past life. The Junta still had its spies everywhere. They bought the hungry and desperate just as others bought their daily bread and when they were no longer of use, tossed them aside like apple peelings.

"Our house was small but we could walk out our back door into the fields. I miss that. Here never feels like a home; it's just a cramped basement and there's no light. I hate the dark."

Mr B stared into the depths of the living room and sighed. " Dina, I wish I could make that better for you."

"I don't want your pity." His manner annoyed her.

He ignored her outburst. "I know things aren't easy for many of our people. I know what you mean. A house is what, four walls? But a home is the people who live in it. A home means somewhere you matter to someone. They make it live and when they go it's not home anymore." Mr B was back in his world of loss and despair.

"Alithia," she said. "It's true. But it will get easier, the loss I mean." Reassuring him was pointless but she did it anyway.

Only his eyes spoke. You know that's not true. You know this void never leaves you.

They sat together. In her floral housecoat Dina made a small, colourful dent in the settee; he was a dark suited bulk perched at the other end. The living room was like a stage on which each of the actors was absorbing the emotions of an unseen audience. Dina was aware of the car horns on the lakeside road, across the square market stall-holders shouting bargains at people as they made their way home, **a** grandmother coaxing her grandson away from the edge of the lake. She did not feel any awkwardness between them. It was as if each gave the other permission to just be in the space.

The phone rang. Dina took the opportunity to scurry back to finish off her kitchen duties. She wrung out the floor cloth, hung it over the back balcony and put away the broom and mop. She loosened her housecoat strings, unwrapped herself and stepped out of her work clothes. In the bathroom she washed her hands with Mr B's luxurious lavender soap and applied some red lipstick for her journey home. As she ran the comb through her thinning hair she was aware of a feeling of lightness in her stomach and heart. She turned away from her reflection. She didn't need a mirror to know what she looked like. Why did she always regret looking in a mirror!

Dina walked into the hall, preparing to leave. Mr B was putting down the phone.

"That was the hospital. They want me to go for more tests." He slumped into the armchair still holding his wine glass.

"Ah." She couldn't think of anything else to say. How was she supposed to respond at such moments? So many thoughts were rushing into her mind.

"Are you really leaving me like this?" asked Mr B.

He looks like a sad old dog, Dina thought to herself. " Come on Mr B, don't be dramatic. It's probably just routine. They're being thorough."

"Bloody needles in you everywhere. I've seen enough of hospitals. I'm not going!"

Now he sounded like a spoilt child. "Don't be crazy Mr B, you have to go. It's for your own good. They know what they're doing; you need to trust them a bit more and then if, if you need, you know, anything doing, they'll have all your notes and put you right. Isn't that what hospitals are for?" Dina was irritated. She put her bag down and approached him. "And anyway, you don't have to put yourself in the state hospital. If you don't mind me saying you've got enough money to go into the best clinic in Athens if you wanted to. I don't really understand what all the fuss is about." Had she really said that? She wished it hadn't slipped out.

He looked up at her. He had tears in his eyes. "Would you go into the best private clinic Dina?"

"No, of course not, I wouldn't be able to afford it would I?"

"But even if you could, you wouldn't would you?"

"Why do you say that? What's this got to do with me? It's you we're talking about Mr B." She was becoming wary.

"Oh, something about my little wiry bird that tells me she despises the idea of buying privilege, that's all."

"Wiry bird. Well, I've never been called that. And I thought I looked bad in the mirror just now. But I don't despise you Mr B. You know that. You're a very kind employer and I appreciate the salary you pay me. I hope I never give you cause to complain about my work "

"Is that all I am to you Dina? Just your sad old employer? At least you go home to your family at the end of the day."

Dina hesitated. She wasn't exactly sure what Mr B meant. She almost felt guilty for having a family. "Mr B, I do understand how you feel. I've also lost family. I've lost brothers and sisters and…I can't begin to tell you how much I've lost in my life but I have to go now or the bakery will be closed."

Mr B hauled himself out of his armchair and placed the empty glass on the coffee table. As he did so his legs wobbled, sending him back down into the chair.

Dina frowned. "There, Mr B, you've drunk too much wine on an empty stomach. Aren't you going for lunch at your sister's today?"

He snarled. "No, definitely don't feel like it today. She'll just try and squeeze more money out of me for Theo's business. That's all she cares about, that and her fat grandchild!"

"Come on Mr B, don't talk about your family like that. Be thankful you have them all."

He studied Dina's face. "Why are you such a wise owl Dina? Cleaning the houses of the rich has turned you into a philosopher. Well! I'm not so naïve. I suppose I can see how that could happen, spending hours alone in empty houses."

"So the wiry little bird is also a wise owl. God what a picture I'm getting of myself. But don't go believing it's just cleaning houses Mr B. I wasn't always a cleaner you know!" She hesitated before opening the front door. "Now let me pass or my family won't have any bread with their meal."

CHAPTER TWO

Winston Churchill: *"Now Joseph, as far as Britain and Russia are concerned, how would it do for you to have ninety per cent predominance in Rumania, for us to have ninety percent of the say in Greece and go fifty-fifty about Yugoslavia?"*

Joseph Stalin: *"I'll go along with that Winston. Here, let me give it a blue tick on your paper."*

As usual on a Friday, Dina stopped at the local street market to buy freesias for Mr B's dining table. They were her favourite spring flowers. It was a quarter to eight in the morning. The market was rapidly filling up with housewives and grandmothers carrying baskets full of vegetables and fruit. An argument had broken out between a stallholder and a toothless black widow. The woman was holding an apple in the air and complaining about its poor quality. The stallholder made a swipe for the outstretched apple but the widow was too quick for him. She dodged out of his way with the agility of a much younger woman and disappeared into the crowd cackling her victory. Dina laughed. The widow reminded her of the women in her own village; women who she had feared as a child. They had the smell of death about them with their dirty black dresses, smudged with food, their nails clogged from potato picking.   Will that be me in twenty years time? She asked herself as she jostled her way through the bodies. She was stopped on two occasions by neighbours eager to know about Mr B. Dina learnt he had been on another of his drunken evenings at the local taverna where the eves dropping flowed as easily as the wine. She politely avoided answering their questions. Discretion was required. She kept walking.

The Friday ritual began. She hung up her jacket on the door. She was already looking forward to her cigarette and coffee break on the kitchen balcony.

Mr B returned early and found her there. She was startled to see him.

"I couldn't stand any more today. It's all getting too much." He leant over the balcony, coughed and then spat down into the orange trees below. Dina hated seeing men do that. She was reminded again of the widow at the market that morning and realised it wasn't only men. Old widows in her village had the same habit. Mr B walked back into the lounge.

Dina stood up and stubbed out her cigarette. She followed him. "Maybe you should try and get to bed earlier Mr B. After all, we all need our beauty sleep especially when we're getting on in years."

Mr B dismissed her comments with a wave of his hand. "Bah. I'll get enough sleep when I'm gone. Now, are you ever going to tell me about yourself Dina?"

"How was Yanni's baptism? Did he cry?" Yanni was Mr B's great nephew, the grandson of his sister Vassiliki.

"I ask you about yourself and you want me to talk about the damn baptism!" Mr B was pacing in front of the door, his hands deep in his pockets. "You never want to answer my question Dina. Don't you trust me by now? You've been working for me for a year now. Don't treat me like a stranger."

She flinched at his raised voice. She didn't consider a year to be a long time and she couldn't believe he was genuinely interested in her life. She shifted uneasily. "Why d'you want to know about my past Mr B? I'm a fifty year-old grandmother who cleans houses for a living. Who on earth would be interested in someone like me?"

"Me! You've never told me about your past. I know you have Rena and little Evy so I imagine you were married when you were young. But clearly not any more."

"Your imaginings are more like questions Mr B. But they won't get you anywhere."

"When you're young love is your whole world, don't you think?"

Dina hadn't intended any reply. One part of her was determined to dive back into the kitchen to start on the floors but the other part won. "Go on with your imaginings if it pleases you Mr B. It would be a boring old world if we didn't have our imagination and dreams I suppose."

Mr B stopped pacing and turned to face Dina. He came very close. "What I'm thinking is that you must have had a difficult time, being a young, unmarried mother. They will have treated you harshly." He emphasized the unmarried word.

"I didn't say I was an unmarried mother. You assume too much Mr B."

Silence between them, punctured only by a distant car horn. Dina surveyed the room in which she was now sitting. She knew every inch of this space. It was massive. She could smell the polish she had put on the oak table that morning; she listened to the table creaking as the room temperature rose. Her whole family could get lost in that one room. She pondered the extremes of life; her own tiny basement with its cheap curtains and kourelou rugs. Petamena lefta (wasted money) they called the rent they paid to fat, greedy Alekos. On the same day of every month they could hear him puffing down the stairs, almost smell his foul breath through the apartment door. Dina sometimes studied his grotesque form through the spy hole, keeping him waiting.

Christ, had it come to this? Had they given their lives for nothing? It often felt like that. Living cooped up in hovels while others lived in luxury? Her shoes caressed the Persian rug spread out in front of the black marble fireplace. They're trespassing, she thought, pulling them back with a jolt.

"You're torturing me with your silence Dina."

"Torture? And what do you know of such a thing Mr B? Have you ever been tortured?"

"Only by my sister's tongue." He grinned.

She should have been relieved by his attempt at humour but instead it stirred her anger. "Don't joke about it. If you'd seen what I have...if you'd been hunted out of your house, your village, had your brother die at the hands of monarcho-fascists, spent nights and days half frozen on mountain-sides, no sleep or food for days. If you'd seen the ground full of corpses, children, girls, all young, shattered to bits by the fragments of rock, you wouldn't joke about such things." Tears of anger glossed Dina's eyes. She was shaking.

Mr B stood still. "You have wonderful eyes. They've seen a lot. I've never seen you so impassioned. I take it you mean the bandit wars."

His choice of word stung her. How dare he insult the men and women who had fought in the Emfilio only to have the likes of him call them bandits. She struggled to stop herself telling him more. But he hadn't given up.

"Were you a partisan? When are we talking about? 1947/48?" He moved towards his drinks cabinet.

If I continue to pour out my memories like he pours out his drinks I will regret it. Better I just ignore him now and get on with my job.

"Did he even propose marriage to you?" He turned, offering her a glass. She shook her head and prepared to leave the room but he stood in front of her, laying his hand on her shoulder.

Dina glared at Mr B. "You mean could Rena be the result of some wartime fling? Now, please Mr B, take your hand away so I can get on with my job. I'm already behind."

He did as he was asked and stood aside. "I'll take your silence to mean she is your husband's then."

"You take it any way you want Mr B."

Back in the kitchen there were last night's dishes to wash up and Friday was rubbish collection so Dina would have to make sure she took all the bags down to the street.

But he was there again. "So you won't tell me more about

him Dina? And tell me about yourself. I want to understand you better."

If she stopped scouring the saucepan Dina knew she would scream. She rubbed it even harder. Still, as his cleaner, she felt obliged to answer her employer. It was never her intention to be rude. "There's not really much to know Mr B. I'm your cleaner and I come here on Fridays and I do my job. Then I look after Rena and little Evy and I go to sleep tired out. Then I clean my other houses and sometimes on name days or other celebrations I gather with old friends at the *taverna*. Then I drink too much wine and dance and sing. I have my memories but if you don't mind, they're private." The saucepan in her hand was finally clean so she rinsed it under the cold tap and began the next one. "Did you have company last night? I don't normally find this many saucepans."

"Yes, sorry about the mess in here. Vassiliki cooked for me and Aris and he brought Thalia so we were four in the end."

Yes, thought Dina, I bet she loved piling these up for me. She banged the pan down as she pictured Mr B's sister prancing around the kitchen leaving a trail of filthy pots and pans that she hadn't even bothered to soak. Then, as she pulled out the sink plug a thought occurred to Dina. "Tell me then Mr B where were you during the *Emfilio?*"

"Maybe you give that period more respect than it deserves."

"And what were you doing then?" She insisted.

He gazed out across the orange-tiled rooftops to the distant foothills where little frothy clouds were gathering. He patted his jacket pocket with his free hand while his other held a newly poured glass of cognac.

He's preparing to speak.

"I had responsibilities then – the family business. I was the eldest son so they fell on me of course and I had other commitments."

"Such as?"

"Public duties. I have a social conscience Dina even if it isn't very evident these days."

Dina glanced at the hall clock. She really wanted to hear more from Mr B but she had to get on with her work and most importantly get the rubbish out before the truck was due. So she darted back into the kitchen, collected up the assorted plastic bags and struggled down the back steps with them. The warm sun was a welcome break from the smoky rooms. Dina tossed the bags into the old dented bin and decided to take a quick walk through the orange grove before returning to her work.

And she could conjure him up, standing under the sweet almond tree, hands digging into deep pockets, head bowed. A tuft of fair hair flopping over his brow. Smiling through his eyes.

But back in the kitchen it was Mr B who was there waiting for her. Waiting for more. Everyone wanted more. Nobody was content with their lot. She busied herself but he was in the way. "Please Mr B, let me get on. You say you have a social conscience well then show a little of it towards my need to get on and make your house shine."

He smiled. "Ah Dina, your words are so precise and always so direct. I know I'm an old drunkard now and you don't approve but once I was respected. People looked up to me. Some even said I should go into government."

"But you didn't?" Dina was curious. What she saw in front of her was a man embarrassed in his own house.

"No. Not exactly. I believe I saw what was coming and wanted no part in it. Even now I feel shame that we Greeks let ourselves down with those bandit wars."

"Your words, not mine. Your words belittle our struggle. There was no such thing as having no part in it. Just who were the bandits, Mr B? Tell me that! Was it government soldiers who bought into government lies about a future free of fascists and informers or was it us? Without us that lot would never have been able to liberate our country. Don't people have the right to defend themselves when their country's occupied and they're hunted? "

Mr B shifted his feet on the Persian rug. Dina's feet hovered around its edges. "So where d'you stand now? You kow-tow to those bastards round Karamanlis I suppose!"

Mr B flinched. He had never heard Dina swear. "I don't agree with everything our government does Dina but you must understand that at that time I was running the family business. I had responsibilities. I thought I was doing the right thing for Greece. Don't forget what a state the occupiers left us in."

"The occupiers you colluded with! You and the British, our so-called protectors. Some protection for us tobacco workers' kids. What choices did we have, eh? Tell me that. No, better I tell you! We could run to the mountains or stay hungry and unemployed because we were blacklisted or go to prison where many of us died."

"Dina, I believed that bringing our king back would mean a fairer, more democratic Greece. Of all nations we are the ones who should take a lead in that. I'm a democrat at heart!" He placed his hand on his heart.

Dina listened but his words were hollow. Her effort to keep calm wasn't working. "At heart! What about in deed? So you sided with the enemy. You helped evacuate our villages so that we couldn't recruit into our army. D'you know how close we were to taking this town?" She ran her fingers through her hair in exasperation.

"Well, I'm glad you didn't Dina and I'm sure a lot of other ordinary Kastorians would agree with me."

"Bah! What would you know about ordinary Kastorians?"

"It was never in our interests to become a Communist country. Look at Russia. Is that what you would have wanted for Greece?"

"But that's not what we were fighting for…Ach, what's the point?" The argument was making Dina hot. Her mind was dizzy and tired. Exhausted, she flopped back and the armchair immediately swallowed her up. She was no more a Stalinist than she was a Karamanlis supporter. Why did they always assume that they had fought for Stalin? They fought for their lives. They didn't have time for big names and dogma when their families were being murdered. Dina realised she had spoken too much, and revealed far more than was wise for someone in her situation. She had argued with Mr B as if he were one of her own. Never, in her cleaning life, had she spoken to an employer like that, so impassioned, so angry, disrespectful even.

"You have my word this won't go any further. Please trust me." Mr B tried to reassure her. Then he crossed the room, opened his drinks cabinet and poured two glasses of cognac. He handed one to Dina. "Here, drink this."

She took the glass from his hand without question and stared into it. Mr B carried his drink onto the veranda and leant against the carved wooden balustrade where he could position his glass. A man shouted from the veranda of a side street diverting their conversation.

"Eh, Pano, are you watching the game later?"

"Probably. I'll give you a ring."

"Come on now…don't stay there moping all by yourself."

"What makes you think I'm by myself?" Gut laughter rang across the street between the two houses.

"Eh.... you dirty old bastard and here's me thinking you're done with all that. Is she from Mikael Voda?"

Mr B swept his hand downwards dismissively and re-entered his lounge. "Excuse him Dina, he's very crude but he tries to look after me since Maria died."

That makes two of us.

Mr B took the empty glass from her hand. "I feel I understand you a little better now."

No. You don't.

"Will you talk with me again next week Dina?"

She moved towards the kitchen to collect her things. " I think I've said too much already. I'm not here to entertain you Mr B. I'm your cleaner. I can't forget that even if you can." She found Mr B following her as she picked up her bag and hung up her housecoat. She moved into the hallway and paused. "Until next Friday then, have a good week-end Mr B."

Dina closed the front door quietly, shaking her head. Why had she allowed herself to become involved in such an exchange? She couldn't blame him for that.

I'm not obliged to tell anyone anything, I don't owe him anything. But on the other hand his questions were tempting and perhaps she did need to talk. He had told her how Maria's illness had suddenly taken her away from him. That would have been painful. But he had asked her about Rena's father. He shouldn't have done that.

CHAPTER THREE

"In July 1974 Turkey invaded Cyprus. The slogan 'Karamanlis or the Tanks' was everywhere. Some choice! We nearly went to war with Turkey. They appeased those in KKE by legalising it but I don't even trust the Party anymore. It's hard to trust any political Party."

When Dina arrived back at home she was faced with another, more pressing problem.

Rena was pacing the floor, hands in pockets. Dina could tell from her face that something was very wrong. She could also smell something wrong. The potatoes were burning on the stove.

Evy came bounding in from her room to greet Dina.

Dina put her bags down on the kitchen chair and bent down to kiss her granddaughter. Then she turned to Rena. "What is it my love? What's happened?"

Rena was a thin, pale twenty five year old who resembled her father in every way. She was Dina's treasure. When she looked at her daughter she saw Makis. Rena had the same blue eyes and fair hair but she was tall for a woman and so she caught the eye of many men. One of them had managed to get his own way four years earlier so a hasty marriage had been arranged followed by little Evy in 1970. They had moved to Kastoria where Dina found work as a housecleaner, supporting the family and sometimes even Rena's new husband. Nikos who was a building worker from Thessaloniki and came from a family of strong Party supporters. His union and political education had largely taken place on the various construction sites that were dominated by the KKE. So it wasn't surprising that he still came across as a hard faced Stalinist. He had been imprisoned during the early years of the dictatorship and subsequently blacklisted and now had to take any work that was offered. If he seemed defensive and angry Dina could understand why. Still, she didn't really accept that her Rena, who could have become a brilliant engineer in Skopje, had ended up a mother working in a washing powder factory. When Rena had protested that she couldn't work in a factory owned by an infamous Junta supporter Dina had reminded her that in that case she might as well give up looking for work altogether. The dictatorship might be shaking under the workers and students opposition but they still held onto their power. They owned the workplaces. They sent in the army to Esso-Pappas in Thessaloniki when the workers there revolted. They were still controlling their lives.

Rena looked down at her shoes and back up to meet her mother's worried eyes. "I've been sacked mama. That's what."

Dina dropped into the armchair. Evy leapt up beside her, a childlike awareness that all was not well today.

"Ach! What next?"

"That bitch of a supervisor caught me talking with the union rep when I should have been at my section. She went straight to Lianthos. Then I was called into his office."

"Just for taking time away from your machine? No warning?"

Rena laughed. "They knew I was agitating the other girls about the masks. They knew I had support but mama, it's all too soon. Everyone's still scared to say or do anything because they just don't believe this government will be any different."

"And they'd be right." Dina cuddled Evy, a small bundle of warmth to melt her frozen fear. Dina knew from her old comrade Dimitri that the trade unions hadn't even begun to assert the strength they once had before the dictatorship's heavies started their cleansing programme in all the unionized workplaces.

"Even though the doctor's letter says so, Lianthos refuses to accept there's a link between respiratory disease and the dust particles."

"But your miscarriage! That was in your hospital notes. *Thee mou*, all you're asking for are protective masks. You'd think you were asking for a massive pay rise."

"Well now I won't be asking for anything, not in OMEX anyway."

Dina was quiet. She was thinking that the power really didn't lie in parliament so much as the workplace. What would it matter to those fascist lovers if they weren't actually in government? They ruled the places that mattered and it was going to be a long hard road to change that. She wasn't even part of all that. Housecleaning was a lonely job. Dina often went without speaking to anyone apart from the stray cats from morning until she reached the bakery each day. But she'd never known any other job and right now she would rather be scrubbing the floors of the rich than slaving in one of their factories. Housecleaning had its perks. You had control over your own time with no sneaky supervisor breathing down your neck. Mr B always said how lovely she left his house. That mattered to her.

Rena was trying to rescue the burnt potatoes but in the end she threw them with force into the bin. "We'll eat pasta instead. From tomorrow I'll have all the time in the world to cook proper dinners for us."

Dina pulled a face. Rena's cooking skills were not her greatest asset.

"*Ella* mama, I'm not that bad am I? You taught me how to cook *iouvetsi* and I'm good at that now."

"Yes, the only trouble is we can never afford the lamb." Dina was feeling strangely guilty because Rena seemed to have inherited her fighting spirit and in the factory that had proved dangerous. Rena could end up being blacklisted very easily.

"When we lived in Skopje we had everything we needed mama. Life seemed easy compared with here in our own country. Why are we treated like dirt by our own government when the Yugoslav government showed us respect? I could've studied and qualified as an engineer. We should have stayed there mama."

"And left your grandmother to die alone without her family close? Not ever having met you?" Dina knew what Rena meant, though. They had left a working state democracy and been propelled into a malicious dictatorship and once they had returned there was no way back. They would have been arrested and sent to one of the prison camps bulging with ex partisans and communists. "I made that choice for both of us Rena. My mother needed me. Maybe I should have left you there."

Rena put her arms round her mother. "For me never to see you again? No, mama, you did the right thing because you acted out of love and compassion. I don't mean to blame you, after all, I have Evy now." She took her daughter's curly head in her arms and held her tightly. "And we're with our countrymen. We have to fight together for a better Greece."

Dina had heard that said so many times in her life and she was still waiting for it to happen. Her daughter had been becoming more involved lately in one of the student groups but that meant travelling to Thessaloniki and they rarely had the cash to do that. She had Dina's love of spontaneity, of action not reaction and because she had received a full education until she was eighteen Rena was a bright, well-read woman. Dina could see she was respected. When she watched her daughter speak at a trade union demonstration Dina closed her eyes and heard Makis's voice carried out over the megaphone. And it felt like another war was happening all over again.

Later that evening, when Evy was in bed and Rena and Nikos were listening to a record by a foreign group who Rena called Iron Butterfly, Dina pocketed her cigarettes and went out to sit on the park bench opposite their apartments. She didn't see what was wrong with their own Greek music. She would be happier to hear Theodorakis or Rebetika any day. But these young, long haired tourists they saw on television who seemed to just wash up on one island or another every summer brought with them a different kind of enjoyment. Still, as long as they were spending drachmes what did it matter? They were harmless enough. Some of them never went back. Dina liked that. She liked the idea that someone would love her country so much they couldn't leave.

The night sky was rich with stars and the air warm enough for her to sit there without a jacket. Zephyros, god of the gentle west wind is bringing spring, she said to herself. She heard men's voices coming from the *souvlagidiko* on the other side of the park, a moped struggled up the hill, its exhaust popping with the effort. Dina spotted two stray dogs barking at each other in the childrens' playground and a cat fight going on under a budding Judas tree. Dina's hopes of sitting alone faded when she saw Eleni, her second floor neighbor, suddenly appear from round the corner.

"*Spera* Dina. How's things?"

Dina slumped back against the bench. It looked like Eleni wasn't in a hurry. "*Spera* Eleni. I'm fine. How are you?" Eleni was always sharp and lively and kept herself in good shape for her years. "I haven't seen Maro lately have you? I hope she's alright."

Eleni smoothed her skirt and looked up to the stars. "I went to see her on Tuesday. Her knee's still painful but they've told her it will heal in time as long as she does the exercises they gave her."

Dina immediately felt guilty that she hadn't been to see her but the two of them didn't exactly see eye to eye. Still, Dina thought, that's no excuse. I should visit her. It's only neighbourly.

"You came out for some peace and quiet and instead you've got me and those damn cats and dogs." She rattled some keys in her cardigan pocket.

Eleni chatted away about her children and grandchildren but Dina only heard half of it. Eleni's talk of hospital had sent Dina's thoughts back to Mr B and his prognosis. And he was a poor patient. He didn't seem to be coping a year after Maria's death. He was drinking far too much cognac and in the mornings, before lunch it was easily two ouzos. His health wasn't good and the hospital tests were worrying. She wouldn't tell him but she feared he would need treatment. He had a sister, nephews and nieces, his business, friends, wealth. He had all that, she thought, but of course none of it could make up for his wife's absence. He was lonely and he wanted Dina's companionship. Vassiliki, his sister, didn't qualify as a companion and Dina could sympathise with him there. She took a deep drag on her cigarette. He still didn't want to put away Maria's little ornaments and personal trinkets so Dina had to take extra care when she dusted them and make sure they were always returned to the exact same position. Sometimes he even watched her doing it, not, she thought, to make sure she did her job well but perhaps because he liked to imagine it was his wife doing her housework and taking care around her beloved possessions. But lately Dina had sensed that Mr B was watching her more closely than he had done previously. He had become more attentive and she knew it wasn't to check on her work. She always left his house spotless. She had to admit she was flattered by his interest in her but she didn't really know anything much about his past apart from what he had told her about the fur business. Maybe she should start asking him some questions and remove the focus from herself. Yes, she would do that in the future.

Dina turned to Eleni. "I'm sorry Eleni. I've been miles away tonight. What were you saying again?"

Eleni stood up. "Eh, nothing important Dina. Our Christos has finally found some work in Saloniki. His uncle Stelios put a word in for him. You remember he came to visit last year. He's a political engineer, in partnership with someone else and Christos says the business is doing well."

"That's good news Eleni. I'm pleased for you. He'll be moving there then?"

"Ah yes. It's too far to drive every day. I'll miss him but it's for the best. So, I'm off now. I'm looking after Fotoula tomorrow so I need an early night."

"*Sto kalo* Eleni."

When she went back into the apartment the television had taken the place of the record player but Nikos and Rena were in the same position on the settee. Dina saw pictures of the uprising at Athens Polytechnic the year before, thousands of marchers heading up Akadimias Street from Syntagma Square towards the Polytechnic and down Pattission and 28th October Streets. The voiceover warned: *Fellow Greeks, Greece of Christian Greeks, do you want this again? Do you want to see your futures, your children become corrupted by the threat of the Communist agitators still in our midst? Make no mistake, they will be dealt with. We, your committed government promise you, our people, that we will root out the ringleaders and restore our country to stability.* Nikos jumped up and down in his seat. *Look carefully at what these ringleaders did.* Cut to film of overturned trolley buses being dragged by the demonstrators to make barricades.

Dina let out a sigh. "Why are they showing us this now?"

"Because they're getting desperate mama. There are rumours that Papadopoulos is going to be dumped. And they're trying to get us on their side now that there's trouble brewing in Cyprus."

Dina was surprised. She had forgotten about Cyprus. "What's happened?"

"It's to do with Archbishop Makarios. Ioannides doesn't trust his allegiance to *Enosis* and get this," Rena put her hand on her mother's shoulder. "He thinks he's a communist sympathizer."

Dina smiled. "Well, you know Rena it's not such a mad idea. We had a fair number of priests willing to give their lives when we were fighting in the mountains and you've seen pictures of the ones who were caught and hanged. I hope Makarios is a communist sympathizer but I suspect he's just on the side of peace. Our Cypriot brothers and sisters lived happily alongside Turks until the British messed things up."

Nikos walked towards the kitchen. "I'm having a cognac to stop me getting angry. Anyone want to join me?"

"Yes please." Dina's bad leg was moaning. She shifted it onto the stool. "Ach, that's better. I swear this leg has a mind of its own."

Rena reached for a cushion and slid it under Dina's leg. "Here, this will make it happy mama." She stood up and sighed. "I have a feeling we'll have a new government before too long."

"Yes but the trouble is, a change in military leadership can't deal with the growing economic crisis. Prices are going up by the week. We've got empty pockets and we can't get jobs. You can change Generals like you change your mood Niko but it won't solve that problem." Dina took her glass from Nikos.

Nikos scratched his beard. "Uhm, true. But we need leaders who can look after the interests of the whole country before we try anything more radical."

Dina laughed loudly. "Huh! Who would you believe in enough to elect though? Say you elect Karamanlis or even young Papandreou. You still leave the police and army intact, ready to crack down on us whenever we dare ask for more. The Party's been talking about returning to normality but what d'you mean by normality? You didn't even support the actual occupation of the Polytechnio!"

Nikos paced the small floor space before coming to a stop beside Dina. "We argued that it would scare away good people who opposed the Junta."

"Yes and in the process you managed to confuse workers and students who would otherwise have thrown themselves wholeheartedly into the struggle. Don't think it's something new. I've seen it all before and I know the KKE leadership is capable of betrayal."

"You'll always have age and experience over me Dina and I respect you as my mother in law but you were idealists and see where that got you."

Rena stood up and faced her husband. "But mama is right. When I went to that meeting at the university in Thessaloniki there were some students who'd been in Paris in 68' and do you know what one of their demands was?"

Nikos sighed. "No but you're going to tell me aren't you?"

"Be a realist, demand the impossible."

Dina was heartened by her daughter's intervention. She could count on her to understand how important it was to dream and hold on to your ideals. She waved her arm in the air. "I call a truce. We're a family and we have to live together. Now, isn't there anything but propaganda on television?"

CHAPTER FOUR

"By the end of 1947, the year in which I became a soldier in the Democratic Army, 400.000 Greek villages like mine had been evacuated by government security batallions.
I remember how hot it was that summer. And then we had the harshest of winters."

Mr B offered Dina one of his cigarettes. She accepted out of politeness but really didn't like the strong Sante brand he smoked. He put his own out and lit another.

Dina's face flashed disapproval.

"Oh, come on. Don't be so hypocritical Dina, standing there accepting one and telling me that I can't."

"But I don't smoke sixty a day Mr B and cough my lungs out every morning and I didn't start smoking when I was ten."

"No, I bet you started when you met that levendi of yours. I bet he led you astray when he stole you from your village." Mr B's eyes twinkled.

"Nobody stole me from my village. I chose to leave because the alternative was worse. I would have been hunted out if I'd stayed. For God's sake! I was twenty three years old."

A small goldfinch landed on the veranda railings in front of them and began delicately pecking at some breadcrumbs that Dina had shaken from the tablecloth. The bird lightened Dina's heart. It was a harbinger of spring and she loved the spring more than any season. "Your face is grey Mr B. It doesn't match the beauty of the day. You should get more exercise, fresh air, take some time off work and go to your summer house or spend some time with your brother."

Mr B's bushy eyebrows sent the skin on his forehead into deep furrows. "What? Go to Volos? Are you kidding? What would I do in Volos? The air's better here."

"Well anywhere then – just a break, a rest." She stubbed out her cigarette and returned her attention to the plants she had been watering when Mr B interrupted.

He watched her with tender eyes as she plucked the dead leaves and heads from the geraniums. As she stretched out her arm the sleeve of her nylon overall rose up above her elbow. Dina could feel Mr B's eyes studying her but she said nothing. She was absorbed in crafting the plant into the shape she wanted but her knees said no, forcing her to stand upright to ease the pain.

"Leave that work for now and come and talk with me."

"No Mr B. I've already said too much. I'm here to clean, nothing else and I'd appreciate it if you let me do what you pay me for." She tried to brush past him but as she did so he stretched out his hand to touch her bare arm. "Dina, my little bird, what would I do without you? All this time you have helped me in my sorrow and asked nothing in return. I pay your wages and you fly away until the next week."

She was embarrassed. What was he getting at? "Is there...something you're not telling me? I feel a little uncomfortable Mr B."

"I don't mean to do that – only I'm afraid you won't give me the answer I want and I'll be forever sad and sorry."

"I thought I'd made myself clear Mr B. I don't want to talk about that any more."

She opened her mouth to continue but Mr B cut in. "No Dina, I don't mean that. Don't you see I..." He swallowed. "I have feelings for you. I haven't had these feelings for any woman since Maria died. Come and live with me Dina, marry me." His words gushed out, filling the room and then nothing, silence. Dina sat down on the settee to steady her trembling legs. She flushed with embarrassment at Mr B's words. It hadn't occurred to her that he thought of her in that way. She looked at him and saw a widowed, lonely old man who wasn't used to looking after himself. He liked the bottle but it seemed he also liked her weekly visits.

"I'm shocked Mr B. I mean I'm flattered, I really am but I can't and anyway, cleaners don't marry their employers." She really couldn't imagine such a thing. "I know I spoke out of turn earlier but I do respect our relationship for what it is. You're the best employer I've got but I never forget you are my employer Mr. B. I hope I didn't abuse your kindness in hearing me out. I don't expect you to see me as your equal, of course I don't. And it's not that I don't care for you; I do very much care for you and what happens to you but..." She twisted the duster between her fingers. This was so awkward. Not wanting to hurt Mr B's feelings, impatient to get on with her job where she belonged. She just wanted to be in that safe place again.

Mr B turned to face the drinks cabinet, his left hand agitating the coins in his pocket, his right already reaching for the cognac bottle. "But you don't want me like that!" Liquid gurgled into an empty glass. "And why would you want an old drunkard like me? I'm a good twenty years older than you and worse for this." He raised his glass. "No. Why should you be interested in me!"? He paused as if reconsidering his words, tapping the glass with his index finger. "Then again what's twenty years when two people have a good understanding between them? We've both suffered loss. We have that in common at least. That's not such a small thing is it Dina? It's not as if you're twenty."

Dina screwed up the duster and jammed it into her overall pocket. She didn't need reminding of her age. He had made it impossible for her to give the table the shine it deserved right now. "No, I'm fifty, which is why I know better. The time for marriage is when you're young and fresh and in love and the whole world is there before you and you have no fear, and." Dina's tears finished her sentence. She was crying for both of them at that moment. A surplus of sorrow flooded her.

Mr B moved nearer to her and rested his hand on her shoulder. "Then just come and live with me and enjoy my wealth with me. What's the point in me having all this?" His hand swept the room. "If I don't have anyone to share it with?"

Dina retaliated. "What do you take me for? If that's what you need you only have to walk a couple of streets and you'll find a woman cheap enough. With your money you could afford to keep an upmarket mistress! I don't know what all the fuss is about." Dina scrambled her overall pockets for a tissue.

"I didn't mean to offend you Dina. My first choice was for you to marry me."

"And your second was lousy!"

Dina's life had been a constant battle but now she felt locked into a battle of a different kind. "Do you really think I could live off your wealth? Well, here's the problem. In my humble opinion, it's not yours to give away in the first place. It belongs to all those who scrimp and save and cough their guts out every day, like my Rena, because washing powder dust got on her lungs. And even if they wanted another child the doctor says don't, it might be deformed. D'you want me to go on?" Her breaths were shot with anger.

Dina saw Mr B's face redden - from cognac or shame, she thought. Either way she'd said too much. Again.

"I'm sorry about your daughter Dina. I truly am. I can't really help my wealth though, can I? Who in their right mind would give up the family business? My father would have disowned me. Family inheritance was everything for us."

"For your class, that's for sure. But my people never seem to inherit anything but debt."

Mr B appeared to reflect on this. He poured himself another drink. His face brightened as if this was the first time he had considered the possibility. "I could change all that for you."

"By me agreeing to marry you! I have to admit it's tempting Mr B but it's also insulting. Don't you see that?"

"Ach! What's an insult or two when I'm offering you a life you will never have otherwise? Just think, your daughter will have the best doctors. And you won't need to worry any more. And the most important thing, Dina, is that I do really care for you."

Dina listened. Despite her resistance she weakened for a moment. She was being told someone cared for her. That didn't get said very often. She could imagine life as he had described it. But then a great fury took over and all she could feel was the insult again.

He moved closer to sit on the arm of her chair. Dina shrank in response. "I know you're a poor Kastorian. I mean to say, you've suffered the disadvantages of life but now I'm offering you a chance to be a rich one. You deserve it."

"What people deserve and what they get doesn't often match up. Haven't you noticed?" Dina rose from the chair. Something about Mr B's attitude really irked her. Good that he would never know how close he had come to convincing her.

Mr B waved his glass towards Dina. She ignored his offer. "It's time I went. I'll have to finish off the plants next week. Rena's not well again and there's the dinner to cook."

"Will you at least give marrying a rich old capitalist some more thought? And Dina, will you call me Pano?"

It was her habit to straighten the mat with the toe of her shoe as she opened the door. "I apologise for speaking out of turn to you today Mr B but you took me by surprise and hit a nerve. I'll see you next week and, Pano, try to go easy on that." She
 touched his shaky hand as it clutched the glass. Then she

respectfully closed the door.

CHAPTER FIVE

"I was married for three months in 1949. Three months! They napalmed the whole mountainside. It looked like burnt jam with the bodies stuck to it. My comrades and my husband among them. He was in one of the camps on Grammos. Trees were on fire. You can't put out napalm, not with anything. It burns even without oxygen. No, I don't really know marriage."

When Dina opened her own front door she heard two sounds. Her daughter coughing in the bathroom and the newly-weds next-door having a fight.

What is marriage? She asked herself.

I was married for three months in the summer of 1949. I don't really know what it means to people. Listen to them, they've only been married for a fortnight and already he screams at her for being late with his meal and she moans because she doesn't have a new fridge. My Rena and Niko never pass a day together without arguing – over what? Some trivial thing or other. People are never contented. What was it all for? Maybe if Maki had survived the war we would have been like them, bickering over this and that. How simple it all was before.

She thought of the old Papas standing in front of them in his filthy black robes, blessing their heads with the *stefania* entwined with tiny white jasmine flowers. Then he made them man and wife and she tasted that perfumed kiss that could never, ever be compared with any other. And they all piled back to Dimitris's store. And Makis's arms whirling her round the tiny floor space between cardboard boxes full of evaporated milk. Dimitris had jammed their bags full of rice, lentils, bandages and dressings and popped a special bar of honey soap into Dina's bag as a wedding gift. And those two hours respite from the front line seemed like two minutes when their commander called time and she was heading back to the mountain, a married woman.

Dina was jolted out of her reverie by Evy tugging at her shoulder.

"*Yiayia*! Mama couldn't cook. She's too ill. What are we going to eat?" Dina decided that if there was a god he definitely wasn't on her side and that prayers wouldn't satisfy the hunger of her five-year old grandchild. She began preparing the family meal, sifting through the lentils for stones before rinsing and boiling them. Banging the knife down into the garlic she winced as it sliced her finger instead. "*Na pas sto diabolo.*" She sent the knife to the devil but it landed on the chopping board. Dina held her finger in the air and watched the blood trickle towards her wrist. She let the tap run until she could feel the icy water numbing her wound and sending her into another spring when blood and pain had been everyday occurrences.

***

"Dina, Dina wake up, we've got to leave now." She heard the urgency in Makis's voice and someone was slapping her cheek. She had no feeling in her right hand and she couldn't prop herself up. Her bootlaces were untied. Her head ached.

"Give her some water. She can't move yet, we need to bandage her hand. Look! It's rigid. Is it broken?" She saw faces bobbing in front of her like balloons on strings, dissolving into the hillside; disembodied voices faded away and everything went black.

"Come Dina, you must drink. Come on, just a tiny sip – for me." It was Makis pleading with her.

She floated back into consciousness with a searing pain on her right side and immediately gagged. Makis sat her upright against the rock and offered the water canteen up to her burning lips.

"What happened Maki? Was I asleep?"

She could make out a smile, feel his lips impress themselves on her forehead. She began to feel the throbbing in her right hand and looked down to see the crimson bandage.

"Yes, you were out for an hour."

She gagged again.

"We need to move Dina. The fourth battalion is trapped in the ravine with many wounded. They need our help. Can you stand yet?"

She looked from Makis to the depths of the ravine. Her courage was buried under an earthquake of pain. She wanted to be strong but her body was failing. "You go Maki, leave me here. I'll follow as soon as I can stand up."

"We can't leave you here Dina. You need help. I think your hand may be broken from the bullet and you're losing a lot of blood. Kosta has the medical supplies and he's gone down. Come. Lean on me. Put your right arm over my shoulder and hold your hand up." So she did as commanded by her captain and they struggled towards the drop but before they could start their descent they heard the eerie whining of an enemy plane circling above them like a vulture and then they were rolling, rolling down, clasped together, tumbling through thick undergrowth, bouncing like rubber off outcrops of rock and all the time the darkness gathering as the sky shrank and the tree tops closed in like a curtain from both sides of the ravine. Separated from Makis by the fall Dina now lay on the valley floor, her pain so immense that she passed out.

She woke up on a stretcher to the moans of her wounded comrades. Her hand still throbbed but the pain had eased and the bandage was drying. She felt her body retaliate in a million places when she tried to move it even slightly.

Little Nikolaki arrived, carrying a plate of porridge for her, his fourteen year-old face ruddy and proud. "Come Dina, you can eat this. It'll be edible now. I managed to steal some salt from the platoon leader's store before anyone spotted me." She looked at this child standing beside her, his ragged trouser legs billowing in the breeze and his skinny little ankles all red and chapped and she felt her heart wanting to explode. Positioning himself on the rock next to the stretcher he lifted the spoon to Dina's lips and even though she was not hungry there was nothing in the world that would make her disappoint this boy, who six months ago was still an innocent fishing in the lake next to his house.

Dina's eyes rested on the scraggy yellow crocuses poking out from the ground in the sheltered valley but they were deceptive. It was not yet spring. They still had to cross the icy river if they wanted to reach the camp by dark. Running like a bird on wiry, unsteady legs she felt herself moving forward without really knowing where she was going, her small frame buckling under the weight of the heavy gun slung over one shoulder.

Then she was embracing a girl called Frosso. A sixteen year old. "They will catch me and torture me," the girl gasped, clinging on to Dina's jacket.

"Don't be afraid. They won't get us here."

"Kill me!" She screamed.

Unbuttoning her shirt, Dina saw the stomach wound. A bullet had splintered inside her and produced a rose. She held the girl closely, rocking her, so that the last thing she would feel would be the warmth of her comrade. Dina's head nodded forward onto the girl's breast. Her cap fell off and she felt the girl's blood warming her jacket.

Then someone was pulling her away from the dead girl. No longer Frossso. Just the dead girl. And they were helping Dina to get up. She heard the front row of comrades gasping as they waded into the river. Instantly, the water numbed her up to her neck, she followed, still unable to speak or shriek like the others. The waters reddened around her as the blood seeped from Dina's jacket. As soon as they began climbing up the opposite bank their clothes froze on them. Makis ordered them to keep moving. They must keep moving. So they walked on and on uphill, their badly fitting boots tripping them up on the ridged concrete track.

Dina's teeth chattered with cold. The muscles in her arms were burning from the weight of the stengun she was forced to keep swinging round to cover herself from all angles. They were passing a house with broken panes of glass in its windows. Fragments of the glass lay splintered on the road in front of their boots and old blood stained the jagged edges that framed the windows. Probably smashed from the inside, as if someone was trying to get out in a hurry. The door must have been barred. Dina had seen it all before. An unwelcome memory. The house was a traditional stone build, once the pride of some Epirean family now home to rats and wild kounavia. Ketty and Maria climbed through the window and reappeared with bags of rice and flour. Ketty carried two blankets in her arms. "Here, Dina. Catch these. The moths haven't got them yet." There was always something left behind they could use. Ice lodging in the creases of her sleeves cracked as Dina stretched out her arms.

The track opened out into the village square. Here, if anywhere there should be the coming and going of daily life but they found only a sinister silence. They had reached a deserted village with no apparent name. The inhabitants had left in a hurry and some hadn't managed to leave at all. Unfinished bowls of food lay on tables in some abandoned houses. In those places they fell on the chunks of stale bread and tipped the bowls to their mouths. In others they picked their way between the mutilated bodies of whole families who had not been spared by the passing security battalions.

The little whitewashed church sat in its courtyard dwarfed by tall plane trees. The wall was spoiled on one side where machine gun holes had punctured and flaked the white paint. Dark stains trailing down from each hole told the rest of the story. Dina sent the young ones into the church to bring candles. The ground was frozen so they couldn't bury the dead but at least they could light a candle and place it in the snow beside each body. Then they gathered in the empty kafeneon drinking from the bottles of ouzo and cognac and singing away what they had just seen. Here, where they could finally rest, they peeled their socks off together with pieces of flesh.

The lentils tasted bitter and some were still hard. Dina had not cooked well today. Her thoughts had distracted her to the point where she had even forgotten to add the carrots. She was too eager to get out onto the street to smoke. It was the smoke that buzzed her into the present like pressing a bell and then walking through a door. And here she was back from the past, on the other side but the dark thoughts clung on to her. Her secrets took her away from everyone who loved her and she could never admit to them that sometimes those memories reminded her of a time and place that she preferred.

CHAPTER SIX

OMEX HELLAS

"I asked about these things they call enzymes and apparently they were first added to washing powders in the 1960s. But they said the effects of these enzymes, especially problems like breathing diseases and conditions were not recognised at that time. There have been three women I know of who have all suffered miscarriages since they started working here. But they can't prove anything."

It was Friday 13th April. Dina had a heavy feeling inside her stomach as if a magnet were pulling her downwards. Her footsteps, usually light and nimble, felt solid and lumbering as she rounded the corner of Nikis Road and pushed open the wrought iron gate of Mr B's house. She didn't need her old winter coat on today. At eight in the morning the sun was already warm. The yeasty smell of rising dough hung on the breeze from the nearby bakery. A small child, held in its grandmother's arms, waved goodbye to his mother from the balcony.

"Mama!" The child called. The mother turned her head in response and smiled as she crossed the street, smoothing her coat over her stomach in a gesture peculiar to pregnant women.

No such luck for Rena. The sadness must have shown on Dina's face as the woman joined her on the pavement.

"Morning Dina. How are you today?"

"Good morning Maria. I'm okay. What about you? Not long to go now is it?"

"Middle of next month they say. I say end of this one, the way I'm feeling and I tell you this Dina, this is the last time. Four's enough!" Dina's smile belied her envy of Maria and her comfortable life. Oh that it could be so easy for her Rena.

As if she had read her mind, Maria asked. "How's your Rena? I heard what happened at the factory. I hope the union will do something."

"I don't think much will happen. From what Rena says that union rep is in Lianthos's pocket. How else do you afford a new car on those wages?"

The two women walked together until their paths diverged.

Dina found Mr B sitting at his kitchen table. In front of him his third coffee of the morning and an ashtray already filled with cigarette butts.

"Morning Mr B. Thee mou, there's no air in here. Why don't you open the windows? It's a beautiful day outside." Without waiting for his answer she flung open the window and unlocked the door. He made no movement.

Strange, she thought, after his passion last week, he's certainly cooled off.

"It's my heart Dina."

A smile flooded her face. "Ah! Mr B, you old softy. Don't tell me I've broken it by refusing you?"

Mr B did not return her smile but planted himself in front of her. "No Dina, it looks like I've broken it by years of abuse. I'm dying Dina, that's what I meant."

The test results. Dina remembered. How she wished she could take back her flippant remark. She came forward to touch his arm.

"I'm so sorry Pano. Is it? Can't they operate?"

"No point. It's too weak and I'm too old. With my lungs I probably wouldn't be able to take it."

"But there must be a chance?"

"Yes, if you call thirty per cent a chance. That's not enough for me Dina and anyway I would be an invalid afterwards. I don't want that. I'd rather die as I've lived."

Dina saw his eyes watering and averted her gaze. She sat down at the table, contemplating the gravity of his news, laying her hand on his arm.

"They give me six months if I'm careful." He snorted. "Careful...what does that mean? When have I ever been careful? What's the point of telling someone to be careful just so they can last two weeks instead of one?"

"You're upset Pano. Don't talk like that. It will matter to you when you've got over the shock."

He puffed smoke in her direction, cocking his head back and laughing. "Oh, I'm over the shock alright. I've had all last night to get over it." Observing her alarm he seemed to reconsider. "Well, perhaps you don't need to hear that after all..."

Dina challenged with her eyes.

"Ach! My big mouth. Just forget I said that Dina. I don't want you thinking even worse of me than you already do."

"I don't think badly of you Mr B. At least you're honest. News like that is always going to be painful and when people are in pain they lash out and do stupid things. I can guess what you were going to say."

"Go on then guess! If you guess right I'll double your wages this week."

Dina hesitated and then looked him in the eye. "Mikael Voda." Did she detect a hint of a blush on his pale cheek?

"Okay. You win!"

"Was she worth it?"

"It seemed so at the time, after you rejected me. I needed it. That's all that matters."

Dina felt both pity and disgust. She understood why he needed the comfort a prostitute could offer him after being given such news but she felt ashamed of her sex. How could they sell themselves like that? Give up their honour and respect?

Dina looked at her employer. So, she thought, he can look after himself. He knows what he needs and really, this is good even if I don't like how he gets it. It doesn't matter because he's a man with very little time. I would hate to know I only had six months to live. At least my comrades never knew their fate. Dina carried his coffee cups to the sink, ran hot water over them and emptied the ashtray. A fly landed on the sticky strip hanging from the ceiling, trapping its wings.

Death and endings. Her whole life seemed to revolve around them. How welcome a new life would be, a new baby for Rena so that they could laugh and sing again. But she was fooling herself believing that would happen. Instead she was probably looking at an early death for her daughter as well. Rena was only twenty five years old but the damage was done. She may not see her fortieth year. At least Mr B had lived a comfortable long life.

Draping a small rug over the balcony Dina wondered if she should swallow her pride and marry Mr B. It would solve some problems for her famil. Rena could study and they might even be able to afford specialist treatment. She attacked the rug, her anger transformed into particles of dust carried on the gently gathering breeze.

"Easy, you'll burst a blood vessel at that rate." Mr B was suddenly behind her on the balcony. Dina was sweating. She could feel the tiny droplets trickle down her forehead. Before she could wipe them away with the back of her hand Mr B had traced one of them with his finger.

"There my little bird." The feel of his flesh on hers made Dina blush but she was olive skinned so she hoped he wouldn't notice. It had been a very long time since Dina had been touched by a man. It was an alien feeling. His hand dropped to her shoulder making contact with the heat permeating through her nylon overall.

Dina considered his eyes, candid as always. She gently removed his hand and gathered up the rug from the balcony. "D'you want me to put this away now Pano? I don't think we'll get any more cold spells this year."

Mr B nodded with disinterest. "I suppose I've ruined my chances now I've confessed to that, not that they were very strong anyway. Have you thought any more about my proposal Dina?"

She considered how to respond but decided that the best thing would be to just get on with the housework. She sidled past Mr B out onto the balcony where she tied up the plastic bag full of rubbish. Down below in the garden some cats were skirmishing over discarded fish skeletons ravaged from the bins. Dina hissed them away and stamped her foot. She felt she owed Mr B the same sincerity he was offering her.

"Given my condition, you'd only have to put up with me for six months wouldn't you?" He was beside her again on the balcony.

"Oh Pano, don't talk about yourself like that. You're a generous man and you know I would like to see you happy but that's just....I couldn't Pano. Can you imagine the gossip? Your family? My daughter? And they'd be right. I would be your wife for six months and then your widow. I don't want to be another man's widow. Once in a lifetime's enough." It was out of her mouth and she couldn't take it back. So now he knew. But he wouldn't know why or how.

"Ah! So he died." Mr B had sat down at the kitchen table. His erratic breaths alarmed Dina.

"How did he die Dina?"

She drew up a chair beside him. "That is not something I will ever tell you." And she offered her compromise. "But I could come to see you more often…you know, say three times a week, if you like!"

He appeared to think about this. "Only if you let me pay you for it."

Dina considered. "I don't want you to pay for my company."

"Why? Because you have a guilty conscience?" Mr B chuckled.

"No Pano. I don't say it because I feel guilty…it's because that's all I can offer you. But you could tell me more about your life couldn't you?"

"I could agree to that but I insist on paying you. I am your employer as you keep reminding me, so I will pay you. Have we reached an agreement?"

Smiling, Dina placed her thin, veined hands over his and breathed calmly as if coaching him. They remained like mute accomplices trying to solve a riddle, until the doorbell rang. Mr B made no attempt to move but stared at the blue checked formica tabletop. A small stain had been left by his coffee cup. He traced the encrusted circle with his forefinger.

Dina decided to answer the door after the third ring. Making a mental note that the hall table and mirror were in need of a polish, she straightened her overall and opened the front door. There stood Vassiliki. Immaculate. A grey suit caressed her wide hips and minimised a large bosom. A cluster of pearls joined itself around the folds in her neck. Vassiliki's smile narrowed at the sight of Dina's slight form.

"Ah! You're still here Dina? I forgot my keys! Is my brother here or has he gone out?"

"No, Kiria Vouyoukas, he's here. He's..." Dina considered alerting Vassiliki to her brother's condition but decided it was not the business of a cleaner to be the carrier of such tragic family news.

"He's in the kitchen. Please come in." Dina stepped aside to allow Vassiliki to pass the threshold. Vassiliki's heavily mascared eyes made a wide sweep of floor, sideboard and coffee table and she didn't forget to look at herself in the full-length mirror.

"Panouli." She croaked. "Panouli *mou*, where are you? Not at work again? What keeps you here when your business needs you?"

Dina glared at the marks left on her shining marble floor by Vassiliki's heels.

"What's going on with you?" She bent over to peck her brother's cheek, securing her snakeskin handbag on the table. She received no reply. She drew up one of the small straw bottomed chairs that disappeared under its burden, its legs creaking and swaying. Vassiliki changed her tone. "Are you ill Pano? What's the matter with you?"

Mr B raised his head. "Stop. Stop all the bloody questions woman. You interrogate me just like those doctors."

Smarting from his words, Vassiliki wriggled uncomfortably. "Is that the way to speak to your little sister now? What d'you mean doctors? Have you been to the hospital?"

Dina could hear the conversation between brother and sister as she put her weight behind polishing the hall table. She couldn't avoid passing through the kitchen to put her bucket and dusters away before leaving. "Excuse me. I'll be going soon." She said as she rushed towards the balcony.

Mr B reached out and caught her arm as she passed. "Will you come to me Friday then Dina?"

Annoyance showed itself on Vassiliki's face. "I asked you a question Pano!"

"Yes Vassiliki. I've been to hospital." A deeply inhaled breath followed by a cloud of smoke engulfed Vassiliki's face and head. "I've been given six months to live. It's my heart.

"Give me one of those." Her hand shook as she pulled out a cigarette from the packet lying on the table, pushed it into her rubbery mouth and lowered her head towards the outstretched lighter.

"That's shut you up." Said her brother.

CHAPTER SEVEN

Song
"You will say, 'never mind, a brighter day will dawn for us.'"
"Θα λες, 'δεν πειράζει, θα έρθει άσπρη μέρα και για εμάς'

Dark, rich curls swung sideways as Evy darted from one corner of the room to the opposite end, her child's excitement infecting the family mood and illuminating the drab basement. It was Evy's fourth birthday. She had been born on 1st May while her grandmother marched in celebration of Mayday. Dina had returned home to find she was a grandmother. The celebrations continued throughout the night. This child was an agile, alert miniature of her grandmother; identical green eyes and olive complexion. Her features seemed to have skipped a generation.

"Here my love. This is a present for you from one of the houses yiayia works in." Evy stretched out her little arm and placed the parcel gently on her lap as she sat on the floor.

She looked up at Dina with wide-eyed surprise. "For me?" Dina felt so much love for this child that her simple question brought tears to her eyes.

"Yes, my heart, for you, from Mr B."

"Who's Mr B?" Evy had begun to tear off the wrapping paper to reveal a shiny covered book.

Rena had come to sit beside her, looking as surprised as her daughter had been. She studied her mother, trying to make sense of the unexpected gift. "The Child's Book of Birds of Kastoria Lake." She read the title for Evy. "Oh, what a beautiful book Evy. Look, that's a stork." Evy pointed her chubby finger at the bird and repeated its name after her mother.

"He must be very fond of you mama. He seems to know a lot about our family!" Mother and daughter studied each other's faces for meaning. Dina sighed and stroked Rena's hair away from her forehead. She was fairheaded like her father had been, with blue eyes and pale skin but Rena's face showed an unhealthy pallor and her clothes hung on her body as if she was their coat hanger. Dina remembered Makis's thick shock of fair hair, his big blue eyes and his Kerkirean accent that made them all laugh. As she remembered their laughter she began to laugh herself and then found that she couldn't stop. "What's funny mama?" Rena and Evy looked up from the book and smiled with Dina.

"It's like when you haven't laughed for a long time you can't stop." They all laughed together. "You're a lot like your father, especially when you laugh. You might think we couldn't laugh during the war but we did you know. We used to get issued with these terrible clothes. Mine always seemed too big for me but we had to wear them or freeze. Maki put on a woman's vest once. How we howled! And some of the men were small enough to wear women's trousers but they had no fly in the front and you can imagine what problems that caused."

"Why does a fly want to be on trousers?" More laughter as Evy tried to join the conversation. Three generations of women rolling about the floor and settee failed to hear the doorbell. Rena's husband emerged still wet from the bathroom shouting and cursing all women. He jerked the door open.

"Yes? What d'you want?" A young boy hovered behind a huge bunch of red roses, his head invisible and his words muffled.

"Flowers for the lady, Sir."

"Lady? Who d'you mean? My wife?"

"I don't know Sir; the label says for Kiria Constantina, that's all I can see." Clearly, the boy feared being attacked by a jealous husband. Dina had made her way to the door when she heard her name.

"Ah...then they must be for me my child. Thank-you." She waited for Nikos to tip the boy but he just turned his back and returned to the bathroom. "One minute." She grabbed her purse from her handbag and pressed a coin into the boy's palm.

"There. Have a good day." The boy smiled his thanks, pocketed the money and sprinted up the stairs two at a time. Dina studied the handwriting on the card and realised that she had never told Mr B her family name – to him she was just Dina.

"What beautiful roses! Uhm…smell these Evy." Dina lowered the flowers to reach Evy's nose. The child closed her eyes and fluttered her lashes as she inhaled their scent.

"Who are they from mama?" Rena was busying herself in the kitchen, filling plastic containers with cheese, salami, pieces of yesterday's spinach pie and roast potatoes. Dina filled her biggest and best glass vase with water and carefully arranged her flowers. She carried them through to the lounge table and bent over to smell them again. Instantly her head was filled with their delicate bouquet travelling down her throat and engulfing her heart. Their perfume had already begun to compete with the stale, humid air of the basement. "Mama…I asked you who they're from?" Dina walked back into the kitchen and began chopping up the lettuce.

"They're from Mr B."

Rena snapped a lid closed and swivelled round to face her mother. "So, present and flowers all on one day…well, well. This Mr B's very keen isn't he?"

"He's a very kind man Rena. I think you'd like him – he's not like the rest of them. He's different. The understanding sort."

"And what about the rest mama?" Rena paused in her picnic preparations to give the conversation her full attention. "Why is he sending you flowers today? Because it's Evy's birthday? Or is it because he celebrates Mayday too? Since when have the likes of that sort celebrated our victories?" Rena raised her voice, which brought on a coughing fit. Her narrow shoulders heaved as she gasped for breath.

"Now look what you've done – making yourself ill over nothing. Sit down and drink some water. You talk like you resent me being appreciated." Dina sat beside her daughter, "He meant well. He has a big heart." She reflected. "But not a strong one I'm afraid." Rena laid her head on the back of the settee, allowing her mother to dab her moist forehead with a tissue.

"Are you telling me there's nothing more to it then? How old is he?"

"About Seventy."

Rena's coughing had softened her mood and she managed to smile at the thought of her mother being fancied by her boss. She noticed her mother's blush.

"He thinks a lot of me. As I said, he appreciates my company as well as my cleaning. It's good to know someone does."

Rena rolled over and nestled her head on her mother's neck. "He does fancy you doesn't he? That's it! Have you, you know..? "

"Rena, how could you ask me that? Do you really think I would do that?"

"No, I suppose not but if he likes you so much and he's as decent as you say then why hasn't he done the right thing and asked you to marry him?"

"He has."

Rena's eyes opened wide. "*Thee mou*! All this is going on and you say nothing to us. Your rich boss asks you to marry him and you say nothing to your family. I can't believe it"

"Well don't let it bother you because nothing will come of it. I'm not marrying him and he's accepted that. In any case, he's only got a few months to live. His heart is very weak."

"Oh, that's too bad for him." Rena hesitated. "It's bad news for him mama but just think, you would be a rich widow instead of a poor one."

Dina's anger drove her to tear a cigarette from the pack and light up in front of Rena. "How dare you speak to me like that? Aren't you ashamed?"

Rena paused and hung her head down. "But why not mama? What have you got to lose? Think what it would mean."

"Don't you think I've thought about it? Yes, it would make our lives more comfortable but you can't marry someone you don't love. Who does that?"

"A lot of people, royalty do don't they? They marry their own kind and that's all that matters to them isn't it?"

"Well I don't sell my principles like they sell their daughters and it upsets me to think you would." Dina stubbed out her cigarette and noticed Evy standing in the doorway.

"Come here my love and let *yiayia* tie your hair back."

The child protested. "Why are you and mama shouting? Can't we go for our picnic now?" Evy wriggled under Dina's hands and pulled at her mother's skirts. "Come on mama. I'm hungry! I want to go to the lake and see the birds. Come."

Rena collected the food from the kitchen. Nikos lifted his daughter up into his arms and swirled her round. "Stop your arguing women! Come on, let's get out of this dingy place and enjoy the day."

Okay. Sorry children. She spoke to herself but she also spoke to Makis. I'm guilty because I deny my family an opportunity to improve their lives but this just seems one sacrifice too many and most of all I would be betraying you Maki, the love of my life. I don't love Panos.

Out on the sun-bleached pavement another world was waiting for Dina. Blinded by its blaze she collided with her old comrade Dimitris, his huge bear-like arms outstretched towards her, one hand clutching a bunch of brilliant red poppies.

"Dina! Good morning. How are you today? Here, these are for you from one old comrade to another, in remembrance of times past." They hugged and kissed.

Dina took the flowers and pressed them close to her heart. "Dimitri, my friend! Thank you, such precious flowers."

"Are you coming to the march?"

Dina frowned. Torn allegiances. "No, Dimitri, I can't. We're going on a picnic to the lake and it's Evy's birthday."

"Of course, how could I forget she was born on Mayday! Well, enjoy the beautiful day."

"Why not come and join us later, we've got plenty of food and you know you're always welcome."

"Thank-you Dina, maybe I will if I can escape the speeches."

"Well you know I'm with you in spirit. Give my regards to the others, won't you?" Dina watched him with fondness as he turned and walked briskly off in the opposite direction but her thoughts stayed with him…

I remember you. You gave me hope. You with your long confident strides coming towards me, bringing our battalion the vital back-up ammunition when we most needed it, when we thought we were as good as dead. Huddled there in the trench all night, waiting, watching, listening to the night sounds, listening for the hope you brought with you, hearing the throaty hoots of the night owl perched on the pine branches. And the hunger that wasn't there anymore because your stomach had forgotten what it needed. And the hallucinations from lack of sleep, when it felt like your body was leaving your soul behind to fend off the dark shapes of mountain creatures that turned into mist the next minute. You appeared like a vision out of that mist and you emptied your pockets of bread and sugar and we fell on you like vultures.

The old blue and white bus trundled to a stop, belching out oily black fumes and drowning all other neighbourhood noises. Dina was reminded of a scene she had caught on a television news item. It was rooted in her memory. Catholic women in a Belfast street kneeling down and banging dustbin lids on the ground, protesting against British occupation. The scene comforted her; people making their own noise, being heard above the lies.

They clattered up the metal steps of the bus, their feet fitting into the moulds made by generations of shoes. The bus was buzzing with the expectation of a good day out, plenty to eat and drink and respite from the drudgery of the working week. The adults laughed, argued, dozed, and read the Sunday newspaper. Children and babies were wedged between grandparents to make room for picnic baskets and rugs. One young man had brought his guitar that he cradled in his arms, politely refusing any offers to mind it.

Dina loved these neighbourhood outings. They brought people together for a day and helped everyone forget their problems. She greeted her neighbours and sat down, taking Evy onto her lap.

"Ready?" The driver shouted, checking in his mirror.

"*Figame*"! (We've gone!") Came the united response from the passengers.

The driver released the handbrake and once again the exhaust from his tired old bus polluted the street as it pulled itself sluggishly up the incline, swaying from side to side under the weight of the neighbourhood.

Once the bus had come to a standstill at the lake there was an almighty scrum to disembark. The driver shouted and waved his arms. "Stop! Stop the stampede children. Let the two expectant ladies off first. Where are your manners?"

Their husbands escorted the pregnant women down the steps but as soon as their feet had touched down the crowd surged forward again. Grandfathers steered their grandchildren in front of them. Grandmothers clucked their tongues at the lack of manners displayed by their husbands.

Dina took Evy's hand and swung it backwards and forwards as she walked towards the lake. The child skipped her joy across the grass, clutching her new book in the other hand.

"Here. Here is good." She pleaded, throwing herself down on the grass and opening her book. Dina put down her basket and called to her daughter and Nikos. They settled themselves on a large woollen rug. Rena spread out the food on white plastic plates while Nikos uncorked the bottle of wine and poured himself a drink.

"Mama, did you come to the lake for us? Didn't you want to go to the demonstration?"

"No. I wanted to be with you, of course."

"But your heart was with your comrades mama!"

"If only we could be in two places at once." Dina sighed and looked at her daughter. "Then we could please everyone."

"Dimitri was always very fond of you wasn't he mama? Did you ever think of getting together with him after *babas* died?"

Dina considered this as if it was a suggestion new to her. Of course, she must have thought about the possibility. Dimitris was an attractive man. But hearing her daughter ask the question now caused her to hesitate.

"We didn't have time for things like that then and after he met Artemis and married her." Poor Artemis.

"But she died too! God, your generation mama, you had so much death. What about happiness for you mama? You deserve some happiness too. Why d'you make yourself a martyr? For what? A battle that can never be won! Not by the Party at least. No Party ever stuck to its promises and if your lot had got into power you would've been just the same."

'Maybe you're right. Who knows? But what's your solution? To do nothing? Just accept it as if it was fate? Isn't that why we've just had another dictator beat us down, because we did nothing to stop them?"

"But we couldn't have known there was going to be a coup. If the government didn't even know, how should we?"

Dina scoffed. "That's just the point Rena. We elect crap governments. They say people get the government they deserve. Do they really believe New Democracy will be any better for us than Papadopoulos?"

"Neither of them cares what happens to people like us. People vote because they don't know what else to do. I'm not going to bother to vote if there are more elections. It's a waste of time and it just gives people false hope. Anyway, enough of that, just think mama, you could be the rags to riches story if you married Mr B."

"Ach, not that again!" Dina closed her eyes and rolled over onto her stomach, feeling the sun's rays on her back. She had no intention of going over the same ground with Rena. As far as she was concerned the marriage matter was closed.

Rena nestled up to her mother. "Ah mama! Father must've been some catch for you to stay faithful to him even in his death."

Dina studied the backs of her hands, smoothing their lines with her thumb. "It's the little things you remember, like someone who can make you laugh when you really need it so you forget your pain. He could do that to everyone in our battalion. When the children cried from hunger or when they were hurt we used to say 'go to Maki, he'll make you better' and they trotted up to him and he would pull some funny face or other and in seconds they would be rolling on the floor clutching their sides. He wasn't so handsome but his face had a lot of expression in it."

"I wish Niko could make me laugh like that."

"He has other good points Rena. He's not a bad husband and father. Look at him. A lot of men wouldn't play with their daughters like he does." Dina could see that she had failed to convince her daughter.

"O.K. but he wanted a boy. He pretends he's playing with his son…"

"Come on now. He loves Evy and he loves you. Stop this discontent, this constant searching for something better from him. Leave the man alone. You could do worse Rena."

"Yes, yes I know mama but how did you feel when you realised you were pregnant with me? It wasn't great timing was it; in the middle of the Emfilio and you fall pregnant to your captain. It's quite romantic really, when you think about it like that. I bet I was conceived on mount Vitsi in some deserted village house. I'm unique really aren't I?"

Dina hugged Rena and felt a surge of love in her heart. "Of course you're unique my love."

"Did you tell my father straight away, when you realised?"

"Just about. It was the last thing I ever said to him. Next morning we were fighting a battle and he was organising our front line. He never let me stay on the front line when he was in charge. He told me that I was to sort out provisions for both our battalion and another one that was expected that evening. 'Maki' I said, 'I've got something to tell you. Stop what you're doing for two seconds and look at me.' I remember him looking straight at me like I was giving him an order. I think he knew you know – something in his eyes. He said, 'tell me now Dina or it will be too late.' I sat down. I was nauseous anyway. I didn't like those last words of his. They frightened me, and I said, 'Maki, I'm pregnant.' His eyes sparked just for a second, 'I thought so.' He wrapped his big arms round me tightly and as we let go of each other because his name was being called, I thought I saw tears in his eyes. And then he was gone and I never saw your father alive again."

"You've never told me this mama. Why haven't you told me before? It's a really romantic story. You could write your story, our story mama, and then people would know what all of you went through, what you lost." Rena stopped. She could see her mother was trying not to cry.

"That's it Rena." Dina sniffed and wiped her cheek with the back of her hand. "That was your father and then he was gone, gone for good and twenty-six years later I still cry for him and you tell me to marry someone else. I can't. He's still with me."

Dina watched the lake sparkling under the warm spring sun and listened to the sound made by clumps of reeds as they rubbed together abrasively under the weight of the wind. A white stork, its pink legs poised like a ballerina, hovered at the edge of the lake. Dina put her forefinger to her lips and beckoned Evy to creep forward. She saw the bird and immediately recognised it from her book. Delight coloured her face as she silently mouthed its name to Dina. Pe-lar-gos.

Rena approached with the spinach pie and potatoes, tucking a napkin around her daughter's neck. "Come on now Evy. Eat your food."

Evy placed her hand over her mother's mouth and continued to study the stork. "Shush. Be quiet mama or the stork will go away." Rena left the plate of food beside Evy and went to serve her husband. Dina crumbled her feta into the oil on her plate and dipped in her bread. The only sounds were those of the west wind lapping the water at the lake's edge into little foothills and the laughter coming from the bellies of old men and children. The women surveyed their surroundings silently.

CHAPTER EIGHT

"The 1973 Referendum asked us, the Greek people, to choose between Monarchy or Republic. The King was still in exile in Britain. They let him make his case for returning to Greece on television. Nice of the British to stay so impartial. But when it came to the vote only 30% of us were for the monarchy and they were mainly from the traditionalist areas like the Peloponnese."

When Dina arrived at Mr B's house she found him waiting for her on the doorstep.

"Hello Dina. Good morning to you. My sister is coming to cook a meal for me today."

"Oh, so you didn't really need me here today."

"Of course I need you here Dina. I always need you here." Mr B sat down. "I thought you might like to give Vassiliki a hand with the cooking?"

Was he being sarcastic? She hesitated, not enthusiastic about sharing the kitchen with his sister. "But I'm not employed to cook. It's not my strongest point." She objected, aware that her real reason was all over her face..

"Ah, she's not all that bad! I know I curse her but she's been nicer since I gave her my news. She's softened.'" Mr B fanned himself with a magazine while Dina began sweeping up discarded fistikia shells and cigarette butts from the floor.

"Judging by the state of my floor it looks like you made another night of it last night. Your aim wasn't very good was it?"

"We got a bit carried away I'm afraid and now I'm paying for it. I lost a thousand drachmes last night." Mr B rubbed his forehead.

"Is it aching badly? I don't have much sympathy I'm afraid." Dina disappeared into the kitchen and returned with the dustpan and brush. "God, they're everywhere! Were you having a competition?"

Mr B smiled and then winced. "Something like that. Dina, you're a diamond. I don't want Vassiliki to see the room looking like this. She'll start haranguing me again."

No change there then, Dina thought to herself as she dropped two empty whiskey bottles into a rubbish bag. He won't like this.The clanging of the glass sent Mr B into the depths of his study where he slumped into his old leather chair. Dina noticed him staring at the mound of invoices from his Scandinavian importers. Approaching the walnut desk Dina ran her forefinger along the panelled edge, double checking her work. "You still have some on the hall-stand Pano. I'll bring them in to you."

Mr B raised his head from his hands and smiled. "I'm grateful to you. Yes please do that before eagle eye sees them. I'm going to sign all the cheques at once so that I don't have to look at these again, and then, by the next time..." They exchanged looks. Dina took herself off to the hall and was just picking up the envelopes when she heard the rattle of keys outside the door followed by a burst of turquoise. It's arrived! Just in time. Almost caught red-handed.

"Morning Dina. Beautiful day isn't it?" Without waiting for a reply Vassiliki brushed past and headed for the veranda. She expects to find him there and she's going to blame me now for not getting him to sit in the fresh air. Dina took the opportunity and dived into the study.

"Here Pano! She thinks you're on the veranda." Dina handed over the envelopes.

"Secretary, conspirator and cleaner all in one day." She laughed at her momentary self-portrait.

"A woman of many talents." Replied Mr B. "And you forgot cook."

Dina's smile faded. "Ah, d'you really think that's a good idea? Why does it matter to you?"

Mr B frowned and blotted a signature onto the desk pad. "I just thought it would be a good opportunity for you to get to know each other a little, that's all."

Dina remained unconvinced but she didn't want to upset Panos's plans. "It's nice to see you, sitting here at this beautiful desk. I've often thought what a waste to keep polishing it when it never gets used."

"A shadow of my former self you're thinking, I bet." The veranda doors were open and the incoming breeze was sending the voile curtains into little undulations. Mr B took a handkerchief from his pocket and mopped his brow.

"You've become tired Pano." She watched him as he ran his hand through his thick silver hair. It glistened at the hairline. He pushed it back revealing a pallid face. With his other hand he took up the fountain pen. Dina watched him sign a cheque, his signature florid.

Maybe people think life's pointless once they know their time is running out. They get intolerant, irritable. It's not so much his physical deterioration as his mental state. Dina's diagnosis was interrupted by the smell of Chanel No 5.

"Panouli, my brother. How are you today?" Without waiting. "And why aren't you out on the veranda getting the air? You know what that doctor said." Turning to Dina, "he should be outside, you know that."

Mr B sat with a red lip smudge on his forehead. "It's okay Vassiliki, Dina does look after me, only not in the same way you do." He winked at Dina. She studied her toes in embarrassment.

"I've bought beef for kokkinisto and some heavenly pasta from that new shop on Koumanoudi street and what excellent lettuce you have in your market. Ours isn't a patch on yours."

Dina made a quick exit into the lounge and as she crossed in front of the coffee table she spotted some more scattered shells. Bending down, she scooped them into her hand. She rose to find Vassiliki's eyes burning through her housecoat. "Are those nut shells you're picking up?"

Dina opened the palm of her hand for Vassiliki to see. She felt like a naughty child, showing the stolen sweets. What a stupid question! "Yes, it looks like it doesn't it?"

"So, he's been partying again has he?

"I don't know what he's been up to Kiria Vouyoukas."

Vassiliki lit a cigarette, hissing out the smoke through the side of her lipsticked mouth. "Oh, come on. I know my brother chats to you."

Dina headed for the kitchen. I'm not giving her the pleasure of telling her she's right and she's not cornering me like a frightened animal. Anger welled up inside her. She felt like having a cigarette herself but resisted. Instead she went out onto the back balcony, shook her duster and watched the leaves of the eucalyptus tree as they scraped edgesr in the wind. It was June and the grounds of Mr B's house were coloured with beds of orange and pink geraniums and white chrysanthemums. Jasmine crept delicately up the white walls and threaded itself through the balcony railings where Dina stood. The lemon trees twinkled under the angled sunlight that picked out the fruit. She smelt the pungent damp rising from the newly watered soil and gave in to her urge to smoke. She fumbled in her overall pocket and pulled out her lighter and pack of cigarettes. The first draw was always the best. Leaning herself over the balcony and scanning the grounds, she inhaled deeply. A stray cat shot out from behind an oleander bush pursued by a larger version of itself. Dina chuckled.

The cat from next door was curled round the base of the holm oak. This tree claimed centre stage in Mr B's back garden. Dina watched the cat stretching stiff her front legs and paws, playing with the generous amount of shade offered by the plump summer leaves. There were many cats in the area. Dina's favourites occupied the steps of the taverna across the road. Depending on size they sat in varying positions on the steps. The ginger king sat at the top. Immediately below him, flanking the sides were the black and white and the three-legged. Twin kittens cowered on the bottom step, so small they appeared to be one cat. Here they waited patiently every day until late into the afternoon when fish-heads and bread were tossed into a bowl at the edge of the steps. None of them moved until the king had inspected and eaten most of the offerings. Dina often wondered at the deference these cats showed to the king and his routine. If there were any scraps from Mr B's kitchen Dina would put them in a secret place only known to the kittens. And when she saw them dash from the steps she was pleased that she had helped them rebel in a small way. *If we don't rebel, we die.* These thoughts remained with her as she headed back, leaving the natural beauty below her to face the manufactured one in the kitchen.

She heard Vassiliki busying herself, rustling plastic bags and banging saucepans down. "Can I do anything to help?"

"Yes, tell me where the cinnamon sticks are."

Dina crossed the kitchen and retrieved a small plastic box from the back of a cupboard. "They don't look very fresh. I don't know how long they've been in there."

Vassiliki opened the lid and sniffed. "They'll do. I'm not going out again, it's already hot and it's only June."

Dina took this as a hint. "D'you want me to go?"

Vassiliki put her latest hairstyle through an apron and tied its strings hurriedly around her waist. "No, no. You stay here and keep me company. You can chop some onions for me."

Dina obeyed. She wasn't keen to go to the shop either. The kitchen clock struck eleven. For a while the two women went about the food preparation in silence. The sweet smell of the cinnamon mingling with Vassiliki's perfume began to permeate the room. Dina preferred the cinnamon. She stirred the contents of the pot vigorously. Vassiliki produced a bottle of wine and settled it on the work surface. She rummaged around in a drawer. Once again she turned to Dina. "Dina, where does he keep his bottle opener? Knowing him it can't be far away."

Dina had seen a corkscrew on the coffee table. "Do you want me to open it?" She asked.

"Yes, do that. I'll put just a little in here and then we can drink the rest."

Dina began to wash the lettuce under the tap.

"Here, have a glass with me. It's Botrys best. You won't get another opportunity to drink such fine wine."

Dina was on the verge of declining Vassiliki's offer but took the glass, more in amazement than anything else, wiping her wet hands on her overall. "Thank-you Kiria Vouyoukas. That's very generous of you." The two women stood in the middle of the kitchen and studied each other, holding their glasses in mid air, each waiting for the other to go first.

"To our health and more so, to my dear brother who, it seems, doesn't share our good fortune."

Dina raised her glass. She was in an odd situation. She followed Vassiliki out onto the balcony and accepted a cigarette from her. They sat either side of the round wrought iron table. As Vassiliki inhaled her cigarette smoke her large bosom expanded even more. Dina imagined all the buttons flying off her blouse and scattering across the balcony.

As if her thoughts were transparent Vassiliki looked across at Dina. "Ah. I know what you're thinking. Believe me, it's a pain to have such a large bust. I have to go to Thessaloniki to find a brassiere my size. Don't envy me. I'd much rather be like you."

"Ah, I've always been on the skinny side." Dina was embarrassed by the familiarity of the comment.

Vassiliki took a gulp of wine and stubbed out her cigarette. "Have you? Even when you were pregnant? You do have a child don't you? I thought Pano mentioned it once. Why only one?"

Dina could feel the effects of the wine hitting her head be she was unruffled by Vassiliki's questions. "Yes, my daughter Rena."

"And when was she born?"

"49." Dina sipped her wine.

"1949! So…at the end of the troubles. It must have been tragic for you to lose your husband with such a small child and it was such a difficult time for us all."

"He died before she was born. He never got to see Rena."

Vassiliki refilled their glasses. "Ah, that's even worse. So, how did he die? Was he ill?"

"Very ill."

Vassiliki's eyes widened but she said nothing.

Dina took another sip of wine. "Shouldn't we see to the food?"

Vassiliki rose from her chair and wobbled into the kitchen. She shook the saucepan several times, stirred its contents and returned to the balcony.

"It needs longer to soak up the juices. But more importantly, tell me more…"

Dina relaxed into her chair and rested her head against the wall. "More?" More. People always wanted more from you. What if it's more than I'm prepared to give? I shouldn't tell her anything else. I mustn't let this wine go to my head. "He died and that's all there is to be said."

Vassiliki's lips tightened. "Very strange. Why so cautious about your husband's death Dina? It makes one suspicious to hear you clam up like that."

"He died in the mountains."

"Where?"

"I doubt the names would mean anything to you."

"I did do geography at school you know."

Dina grinned. She found the woman was really quite simple despite her airs and graces.

"Did his death have something to do with the bandit wars then?"

There it was again. That insulting word. "I don't know what you mean by bandit wars. When was that?"

Vassiliki puffed out her chest as she exhaled. "Oh come on now. You know what I mean. You said your daughter was born in 1949 so the end of the troubles. Those wars in the mountains that disgraced us to the whole world."

"I really don't know what you're talking about Kiria Vouyoukas. I only know about the Occupation and the *Emfilio*." She saw from Vassiliki's expression that she had finally rattled the woman.

"Well that's the one I mean but we don't call it that."

"And why not? Didn't brothers and sisters kill each other? Wasn't it a war only happening here in Greece? That's what civil war means." Dina had succeeded in diverting the conversation and it looked as though she had confused Vassiliki in the process

"So were you one of those andartes? That makes you a communist then."

Dina smiled. A knowing smile. There it was again. They had to put a label on you to make sense of anything.

She found greater confidence from the wine and stood. She thought of the world and its natural beauty as she looked down on the bright flowered gardens beneath her but it was ugly pictures of the war that sprang out at her most boldly.

"So, my brother has been employing a communist all this time eh? I bet he doesn't know that."

Vassiliki stood up so the two women were square. She planted her feet widely. She rested her hands on her ample hips.

She looks like a gladiator in a coliseum. My silence is agitating her and just think, an hour ago we were managing polite chitchat, now look at the gulf between us! A great idea Pano, putting us together in a confined space. "I think the food's burning." Dina removed the saucepan lid and stirred the contents with a wooden spoon.

Vassiliki strode forward and took control by seizing the spoon from Dina's hand and in the process spilled sauce on the floor. "Wipe that up will you."

Dina retrieved the floor cloth from under the sink, bent down and removed the stain with a circular sweep of the cloth.

Vassiliki began crashing dishes and banging cupboards. "Ah!" She noticed her brother who stood in the doorway holding his head. "I'm not surprised you're holding your head Panouli. Did you know your devoted cleaner here is nothing but a filthy communist – her and her type who thought nothing of rolling their tanks into those poor innocent Czechs a few years back."

"Curb your tongue sister. You're out of order. D'you think I don't know who I employ?"

Dina jumped at the anger in Panos's voice. Vassiliki seemed to be on a roll. She wasn't stopping for anyone or anything at that moment. She was also not stopping with one bottle of wine. This time she managed to uncork the bottle herself.

"I bet we have you lot to thank for that abominable taken in our name! To think that our dear King was kept from us by a rabble."

"It was a free and fair referendum. What more do you want?"

Vassiliki grunted as she shook the pan of roast potatoes and slid it back into the oven. Her cheeks were hot from bending over.

Mr B slumped down into a chair. "Dina, could you give me some water please. I don't feel very well."

Dina poured cold water into a glass and handed it to Mr B. "You look pale. Better take your pills and go and lie down Pano."

"Huh, so you're on first name terms now are you? I don't understand why you do it Pano!"

"No I don't imagine you do. I'll go and rest till lunch time." Dina watched him survey the situation between herself and his sister. She judged him too depleted to try appeasement.

Dina caught the disapproving glance levelled at her by Vassiliki and raised her hands. This meant she had had enough. I've probably compromised my own safety for the sake of a couple of glasses of wine in the company of a right wing monarchist. What madness. She slapped the palm of her hand against her forehead. Why? What did I expect from her? That I would really be asked to share some wine with the sister of the biggest fur importer in Kastoria, all out of the kindness of her heart? Acting like I was born yesterday. But then her second voice butted in and suddenly she didn't care any more if people knew. Let them come and get me for all I care. The wine had worked its powers through Dina's veins. She unhooked her jacket from the kitchen door and began to make her way to the hall but Vassiliki was on her heels like a snapping dog.

"Do you deny you were under Stalin's orders then? Is that all a lie and we're supposed to believe you would have returned us to a democracy?"

Dina sighed. There was no point in continuing to make herself sick with anger. She summoned up a stab of politeness towards the woman who now barred her exit. "Kiria

Vouyoukas," She looked her directly in the eye. "Your idea of democracy and mine aren't the same. Let's leave it there if you don't mind." Dina hesitated. "Please say goodbye to your brother for me and say I'll see him next week. I don't think I'm needed here any more."

"But we haven't finished our discussion yet." She protested. Her hands found their default position on her hips.

"You mean you haven't had your fill of abusing my values." Dina's own voice scared her. She wanted to escape now, get back home to her own people.

"How dare you speak to me like that? Just remember who you're talking to. Your type are all the same – show them some generosity and they think they have all the same rights."

Dina's was opening the door. "Ah but don't misunderstand us Kiria Vouyoukas. Our type, as you say, aim higher than that. And by the way, the wine was very average. Good day."

CHAPTER NINE

"There was a special interrogation unit of ESA (Greek Military Police) and in addition to the usual brutal torture like sleep deprivation and beating the soles of our feet they played music that was popular at the time but they played it repeatedly from loudspeakers, over and over. That damaged us mentally and ESA liked it because it had the advantage for them that it didn't leave any visible scars"

The August heat wrapped itself round Dina's body like a clammy cloak. Each step she took towards the bus stop was laboured. The argument with Vassiliki repeated itself in her head. It soured her mood. She was angry with herself for vealing her past to someone who she could not trust. She felt resentful towards Mr B for putting her in that situation. Dina did not see herself as the blaming type but on this occasion she was at a loss to understand why he had put the two of them in the kitchen together. What had he expected would happen? That they would become best friends? Maybe he just wanted peace and happiness at the end of his life.

Dina let herself into Mr B's house. "Good morning Pano". There was no response from the lounge. He must be in the kitchen. But there was no sign of him there either. She was surprised. It was unlike him to be out at this time of the morning and he was in no condition to go to his office. She peeped round the bedroom door and saw him asleep, bedclothes strewn across him as if he had been in a hurry to sleep.

Dina checked his bedside table.

His heart tablets are here, so, no worries, he hasn't done anything stupid.

She tiptoed back to the kitchen and opened the back door onto the balcony. Then she swept the kitchen floor in preparation for washing it. Coffee stains were dotted across the tiles. The sign of an unsteady hand.

Dina's arms began their backward and forward movement.

He looks thinner. I don't think that medicine is doing much good. I wonder if he's giving up on everything? I can't even smell cigarette smoke.

Dina emptied the bucket of dirty water. She had only finished one job and she was already hot and thirsty.

Feels like I'm giving up as well today.

Wiping her brow with the back of her hand she caught sight of herself in the mirror.

You could do with a rest too. She pulled a hair forward on her head and examined it. And it's time to renew the colour. I can't stand any more grey.

Returning to the kitchen she ran the cold tap and filled a glass with water that she then gulped down without pausing for breath.

Ach, it's going to be unbearable in August if it's this hot already. Wouldn't it be wonderful to go back to the mountains and breathe that air?

Mr B's kitchen looked out onto the back balcony. A door lead down into the rich garden. Dina had nurtured all the pot plants dotted across the balcony and down its wrought iron staircase but she took particular care of the large pot of basil. It reminded her of being young again. She rubbed the basil leaf between her fingers and smelt the perfume that sent her back again to her village. Closing her eyes she was dancing with Makis again but when she opened them it was just her mop and bucket at her side, waiting like devoted guardians.

Attacking the lounge, Dina found none of the usual signs of Mr B's revelling the night before. Everything seemed too clean and tidy. Unlived. Not a good sign; Was Mr B's body succumbing to his heart disease? Dina knew that if he couldn't be bothered to gather friends around and play cards until the early hours then the illness was taking its hold on him in ever more desperate grasps. She squeezed and twisted the mop into the bucket putting all her weight on its handle so that she was almost lifting herself off her feet.

"Good morning Dina. I'm afraid I'm not fit to get up today. I'm feeling weak. Can you hear me?" Mr B's voice was faint.

"Good morning Pano. I'm on my way. Can I bring you some water or anything?" She tried to sound cheerful.

"No, just come and sort this contraption out for me would you? It's driving me crazy."

Dina heard a crash and rushed into the bedroom to find Mr B entangled in his oxygen mask. "Here, let me help you." She unwound the plastic tubing from around Mr B's neck and chuckled. "How on earth did you manage to get into such a state?"

Mr B bent his head forward to allow Dina to slip his head out of its noose. "Perhaps my subconscious was willing me to end it all now"

Dina frowned. "Your what?" But Mr B had slumped back into his pillow, out of breath from the exertion of conversation.

Dina placed the mask over his nose and mouth, smoothing his brow calmly. "There! You just lie still and breathe slowly Pano. Remember, don't try and take in too much oxygen at once. This isn't cognac." She saw his smile beneath the mask and his old eyes twinkling and felt a deep compassion and sadness welling up that she quickly smoothed away with the bedclothes. She tucked them in on both sides. Mr B had closed his eyes again.

Let him sleep. He's not up to conversation much anymore.

Dina hated admitting it to herself but she knew Panos was deteriorating rapidly.

What would her weekly routine be like without him? It would continue, of course, as sure as day follows night but her week would lack the easy banter, the respectful understanding they had for each other. Her other houses were foreign to her compared with Mr B's. When she went to them every week they didn't shine back at her like Mr B's did. Kiria Styllou had few words to share with Dina and when she had they were usually words of criticism. Kiria Dabas was never there, the ghost house. God knows why she needed her apartment cleaned every week when she was only there half the year. No, Mr B was a rare find. Why did rare things always seem so fragile?

The phone rang in the lounge, interrupting Dina's reflections. She pounced on it to prevent him being woken. "Hello, Mr B's house. Can I help?" Dina held the handset away from her ear when she heard Vassiliki's voice.

"Hello Dina. How's my brother today? D'you think it's necessary for me to come only I'm very busy with the business. Someone's got to oversee it now Pano's ill and Theo has his own worries and…"

"I'm sure it's okay if you skip today Kiria Vouyoukas. Pano's asleep. He's had his medicine and taken some oxygen but I think it's time to consider a full time nurse. I can see him worsening."

"Yes, yes Dina. We'll come to that I'm sure but right now do you think you can do an extra day this week only I'm so…"

"Busy?" Dina cut in. "I'm not sure if I can Kiria Vouyoukas. I have other commitments. I…"

"Give me your telephone number so I can ring you to let you know exactly what arrangements need to be made for my brother. I've got a pen in my hand."

Dina could hear Mr B snoring. "356-91-86494".

"Fine. I'll ring you with my decision."

Dina stared at the receiver in disbelief.

"Don't tell me. It was my sister wasn't it." Mr B had woken.

Dina came towards the bed. "Yes, she's very busy and can't call in today."

"Thank God for that then, that's one more day of freedom."

"Pano." Dina hesitated.

"Come on Dina, get it off your chest. What has she said to you now?"

"No. It's not that…it's…I think it's time for you to consider having a full-time nurse here. You need more care than I can give you, someone who can be here twenty-four hours. Someone who's qualified. I'm not a nurse. I don't like leaving you alone."

Mr B pushed himself up onto his pillows while Dina plumped them up. "Alright Dina. Don't worry. I know what you see. It makes sense. I'll speak to Vassiliki tomorrow and we'll hire a professional nurse to live in. Will that satisfy you?"

"That would put my mind at ease Pano, to know you were in capable hands."

"I am already. What better hands than yours?" Dina smiled, aware that such a remark in the not too distant past would have made her blush.

Returning home, Dina was greeted by the smell of sweet onions that Rena was slicing into a large bowl of salad. Her daughter and granddaughter had been on a short visit to Nestorio where a great aunt still lived.

"Hi Mama, I'm glad you're back. Aunt Hariklia gave us courgettes, potatoes, beans and some honey. Old Fotis is still making it himself, at niney two! The phone's rung several times and then when I answer there's nobody there. Is this your Mr B again flirting with his cleaner?"

Dina frowned. She was confused, knowing that it was not Panos ringing her. She put down her basket and kissed Evy. Then she remembered the phone conversation with Vassiliki and decided it must have been her. She didn't know anyone else rude enough to do such a thing.

Dina flopped down in an armchair and fanned herself with the newspaper. Rena brought her a glass of water and placed a bowl of olives on the coffee table beside her."The chicken's nearly done and I'm just waiting for the water to boil for the pasta."

"It smells delicious my love and it's good to see you looking so well again with an appetite. You should go to Nestorio more often."

"Have you ever thought of going back mama? I mean, going back for good and settling there."

Dina smiled. "Yes, many times but we couldn't make ends meet there. Can you really see yourself on a tobacco farm Rena? Or harvesting olives? You're not strong enough I'm afraid, my love. There's not much other work and producing and selling your own olives wouldn't feed a family. That's why people pay others to do it for them when they can."

"But it would be a better life for us, for Evy."

"I think you've got a romantic idea of life in the villages Rena. Didn't you see how people struggle when you were there?" Dina gave the knives and forks to Evy who carefully placed them down on the tablecloth.

"I know they work long hours but so do we here. It's just a different kind of work and it would take some getting used to but I think I could do it."

Dina studied her daughter's face and wondered if she was right. She was also aware of a persistent nagging in her own head. She had a strong reaction against returning to her family village and she wasn't sure why.

"Maybe you could but for me it's out of the question. Every corner turned would be a reminder of what happened to your pappous. No. We need to live our lives looking forward not back. Here Evy, put these down." Evy danced around the table positioning the straw place mats. Rena brought the steaming chicken to the table and Dina began ladling it onto the plates. "Just wait Evy and I'll cut up your meat for you. Mama is bringing the pasta now. Careful it's hot." Dina saw the child's eagerness to begin and was happy that she had such a healthy grandchild.

The door opened and Nikos appeared. His clothes brought with them the smell of midday July heat mingled with cement and tobacco.

"Good timing baba. Hurry up and wash. I'm starving." Nikos kissed his daughter. Rena and Dina sat down to eat.

"In Anna's house they say a prayer now." Evy wriggled in her chair as Dina cut up her chicken. "They do it every meal."

Dina and Rena looked at each other and grinned.

"Well that's fine for them if that's what they want." Rena replied.

"They make me do it too, when I eat there."

"Well, I suppose that's okay too since you're a guest in their house but when Anna comes to us she won't be expected to say prayers."

"Why don't we say prayers mama?"

Rena looked pleadingly at her mother. "How did I know this was coming?"

"What was coming?" Evy banged her fork impatiently. "Come on baba. Hurry up. I'm hungry."

"Stop that Evy. Remember your manners or they won't invite you back to Anna's." Rena glared at her daughter. "We don't say prayers in this house because we don't believe there is a God up there."

"So what is there?"

Nikos walked towards the table and pulled out his chair. "There's people Evy, us, you and me and mama and yiayia and all your friends and neighbours. Now, let's eat!"

Evy dived into her food, her need for answers forgotten. Her grandchild's innocence left Dina thinking about belief.

I suppose most people in our country feel a need for it but praying to God hasn't solved our money problems has it? Dina had no time for people who were always deferring to a higher being. Why didn't they take responsibility for their own lives?

After the deep silence brought by siesta Dina phoned Dimitris. His animated voice told Dina of the forthcoming meeting being organised. He wanted her to be there. She nodded to herself, thinking how long it had been since she had attended any rallies or meetings. She wanted to be there. As their conversation finished and Dina was about to replace the receiver she heard a distinct click on the line.

"Dina, are you still there? I thought you'd put the phone down."

"And I thought you had." Neither spoke.

"Have you got an extension in your house?"

Dina laughed. "Don't be ridiculous – you know the size of this place. I can practically reach the phone from every room." Another silence.

"Have they been working on the lines outside your block?"

"No."

"Has it happened before?"

"Not as far as I remember but maybe with Rena or Niko. I'll check with them. What about your end?"

"No."

Dina studied her nails. Badly in need of a manicure. "But hang on a minute Dimitri, when I came in Rena said the phone had rung several times and when she picked it up there was no-one there."

"Leave it with me Dina. I don't like the sound of this."

Dina sat down on the end of her bed. She realised they both suspected the same thing.

"And be careful what you say Dina. If they're tapping your phone they know all about the meeting. Thee mou, they still can't leave us alone, hounding us like animals!" They both hesitated to replace their receivers, waiting for the click but it did not come.

That night Dina dreamed that Makis had taken her back to Kerkira. When she woke she was looking into her daughter's eyes. "Rena! It came back."

"What mama? What came back? You scared us all with your screaming."

"The nightmare. The one I used to have. It's come back." Dina stared through sleep-glazed eyes. Rena wrapped a shawl round her mother's shoulders and glanced at the clock. It was five.

"Mama. It's okay now. I'm here." Rena smoothed Dina's wet brow with her hand.

"It's that same dream again. I'm in Kassiopi. There's a fishing trata that won't go away and it's black and too big and it's night -time and there's huge waves drowning the beach. Then we see a spotlight and we all run for it but I can't run, my feet won't lift off the pebbles; they're stuck and I look down and all I can see is more black,thick sticky tar all over my feet. The others are all shouting, 'come on Dina, hurry. They know.' And I don't know what they mean and I'm beginning to cry and stretch out my arms and another great foaming wave crashes onto the beach and washes all the tar off my feet and I can suddenly run. I'm free and I scramble along after the others but they've disappeared into the water. And when I look into the water all I can see is fish, strange fish. I smell the sea. I feel the heat on my back. I'm in the spotlight. It's blinding me and my arms are being pulled back behind me so much it feels like they're being wrenched from their sockets. And my head is being pushed deep into the water and held there before they yank my hair and leave me spluttering and choking and the pebbles have turned to cold concrete and that's when I wake shaking and screaming." Dina sobbed in her daughter's arms, consumed by her nightmare.

Dina and Dimitris met in the grand old kafeneon on Venizelos Street. The round metal tables and chairs were uncomfortable to Dina who had never understood how the men could spend so many hours putting up with so much discomfort. They were extremely small chairs as well, not built for the likes of wide hipped grandmothers. In fact, the more Dina studied the furniture the more she was convinced it was a plot to keep women away from such places.

"Men will put up with a lot if it means an hour less with a nagging wife," commented Dimitris.

"You old cynic." Dina chuckled then checked herself. "But this feels like old times, having to come to a place like this to talk. Aren't we exaggerating things a bit Dimitri?"

"Better that than another spell in Averoff, wouldn't you say?"

The elderly men watched the world passing before their eyes, Dina jumped at the sound of tavli chips being slammed down at the next table and felt the accusing challenge from the eyes of some men. She wouldn't be there without Dimitris.

Inside, the ceiling fans whipped up the animated conversations and spun them round the room randomly. Dina spotted two other women. The kafeneon was a male domain, thought Dina. Even now in 1974. Come in here and you could be back in the 1940s.

Behind the counter the café owner and his wife boiled the coffees, occasionally stirring the thick dark liquid, adding sugar, rattling spoons onto saucers and joking with the slim black haired waiters who swept up their trays and glided across the floor with them like ballroom dancers holding their partners.

"I'm glad you brought me here. It gives me the chance to watch the men who watch the world and make silent judgements while their wives make the food and manage the chaos."

Dimitris grinned. "That was almost a speech. You're good Dina. Why don't you use your talents and help the Party?"

Dina sipped her coffee. "We didn't come here to discuss my level of commitment Dimitri. And you and I know we have differences there that can't be smoothed over by me rejoining. Have you found anything out?" She was very prickly when it came to the subject of her rejoining the Party.

Dimitris bent forward and rubbed his hands together. He sighed. "It seems like they're on to you. Who have you been talking to? Is there anyone new in the neighbourhood?"

"In our neighbourhood? What would an informer be doing in an area like ours? It's solid. They wouldn't stand a chance. We'd sniff them out. No. I think I know what I've done."

CHAPTER TEN

> *"You ask me about the priests during the Emfilio. Personally, I never came across a priest who wasn't supporting us and the Party condemned any disprespect for the church and clergy. We accepted their authority in things like marriage and divorce. Some priests were later prosecuted for their support. But I know that in camps like Makroniso they sometimes encouraged our comrades to sign declarations denouncing KKE. They stood by and watched while they were forced to humiliate themselves as if they had behaved like idiots when they chose to fight fascism or nationalism."*

She had let the wine go to her head and it had loosened her tongue. She felt foolish just thinking about it. The trouble was she knew she did need to talk to someone. It was 1974 and she had kept quiet since the colonels took over seven years before. The most embarrassing thing about her stupidity was that she couldn't have chosen a worse person to tell. Even Dimitris had opened his mouth and stared at her in disbelief. She let out a long sigh and decided to smoke a cigarette. Dina didn't usually smoke in the street. She had been brought up to believe it was common for a woman but it wasn't far to her bus stop. She would be standing still there. Why that made any difference she couldn't really say. But a cigarette was necessary. That was all.

The bells of Agios Konstantinos were chiming. Dina smoked so quickly that by the time she reached the bus stop she had finished her cigarette. The bells made her headache worse. She stood waiting and watching groups of people moving up the broad church steps in a procession- like wave. Young and old women, brightly dotted between the black worn by their widowed and bereaved sisters, men in smart suits, little girls in cheerful colours, the boys, miniature replicas of their fathers, all flowing through the great open doors.

Religion. What was it about religion that gripped hard working people? She leant against a crumbling old whitewashed wall; some of its hairline cracks sprouted green fronds of liquorice smelling fennel.

I suppose we all need something to believe in, something to cling to in hard times. Those of us who believe come together every week to keep the faith. Was she losing her own beliefs? Maybe political beliefs were the same as religious ones. Her questions bothered her. She found Dimitris had entered her head, uninvited. I want to have this out with you Dimitri. You always have the answers and that knack of explaining the most difficult ideas in a way that even Evy could understand.

Well, Dina, if something can't be explained while riding on a bus then it isn't worth explaining. And so the words went round in her head as she waited for the bus. She looked across to the hill opposite where the town met the fields. A motorbike was a black speck climbing up and away.

Although it was Sunday Dina was on her way to clean for Mr B. He had gone to close up the family home for winter and she was sad for him. It would probably be his last visit. In the last two months his health had worsened. He needed a live-in nurse who could tend to his failing old body. Dina thought he should be in a clinic but Mr B hated institutions. "Don't let them take me away." He had begged her. "I trust you." She was a little scared of him putting so much trust in her. "I understand how you feel but I don't think it's part of my job Mr B." He was right to be wary of her intentions. "And it's none of my business." She had blurted out. She would love to get some revenge for what that sister of his had done to her but she didn't want to spread the news any further. She suspected Vassiliki of telling her policeman husband about their conversation. Dimitris had told her it was him who had tipped off the security police.

Who else would have done it? What have I ever done to her except look after and clean for her brother and listen to him – more than she's ever done from what I can see.

At last the bus arrived. August had made way for September – a balmy heat bathed Dina's face. When she closed her eyes she was lying on a beach with that same gentle warmth nurturing her whole body, unlocking her bones. She peered over the veranda. The old adjoining mansion was derelict but its overgrown garden grew green and strong. A fig tree had broken through a window and taken possession inside. Dina tutted to herself. What a waste! She stretched out her arm and managed to pluck a fig from the branch. Her mouth watered. She split the fig's skin with her nails. The inside was sticky and sweet. Afterwards she threw the smooth green skin down into Mr B's garden hoping it would be spotted first by her favourite chaffinch.

She was thinking to herself how peaceful it was here on a Sunday. How the church walls must be very thick because she couldn't hear a single voice, not even the priest's. She was used to being at Mr B's on weekdays when the streets were bustling with people and traders. Today it was quiet except for the gentle tap tapping of the sun canopy against its iron pole. Yacht masts made the same sound. She had heard them once in Kavala harbour when her parents had taken her to visit aunt Frossini. You could always tell the people who came from yachts. They wore the same brown-laced shoes and long shorts and they all had the same ruddy, bronzed faces.

The heavier jobs had to be done first, while Dina had the energy. The lighter, fluffier jobs like dusting could be tackled after a rest, a coffee and a cigarette. The clock on the mantelpiece struck ten. Dina hauled Mr B's mattress out onto the veranda. It needed airing.

Pausing before attack was always a wise move. She drove all her strength into the mattress with a wooden beater, releasing her anger. Better on the mattress than that woman. She would need to be calm or God knows what she'd do to her! Between beatings she unbent herself, supporting the bottom of her back with her hands. The melody of popular music drifted across from the lakeside. Two long haired young men had turned up the volume on their cassette player as they sat on a bench enjoying the sun. Dina began humming in time with the tune. Then it erupted into the unmistakably strident beats of Theodorakis.

'Paidia sikotheete na voume stous thromous. Yinekes kai Andres me opla stous omous.'

Dina shivered.

There were Dimitris's words again. Come back to the Party Dina. Join us. We need you. What can you do on your own? We're your family.

Are you? I'm not so sure Dimitri. Too many mistakes and betrayals. Zachariades, I cannot forgive. It would be hypocritical for me to rejoin. The music had stirred her up. She came back to her job staring at the mattress. That blasted song. She was all goose bumps now

Dina dragged the mattress back into the bedroom.

We all deserve better than New Democracy. They'll never deliver. We feel grateful that we're allowed to vote again. No. I don't trust this government. They're just placating the generals waiting in the wings. Let them walk their own tightrope. If only people realised their power. Ach! Then the world would change.

Dina sighed. In the meantime there was a bed to make and floors to clean.

The thought of Mr B dying on the starched white sheets came to her as she was making his bed. She smoothed and folded back the top sheet before tucking in the edges. She laid his favourite bedspread on top. Then she patted each corner to finish off. It was just her way of telling herself that the job was finished. The bedspread had been hand woven by Mr B's late mother in law for her daughter's dowry. Every Friday Dina was reminded of the handsome dowry Mr B's wife had brought with her when she married him. The drawers were full of the whitest Egyptian cotton sheets and hand knitted blankets, linen and lace tablecloths, pillow cases with heart shaped edges embroidered in red satin. Ironing those needed patience.

By midday Mr B's bedroom was finished. The antique bedstead and side-tables smelt fresh. She wanted the room to welcome him. After all, he would be spending most of his time there. She had placed a vase of white carnations on his dressing table. He would appreciate these little touches. They would remind him of his wife. It wouldn't harm him to be reminded of the good things in his life.

They say it's not possible but I believe he's a man dying from a broken heart. Why didn't I die? At least he had nearly fifty years with his wife. Fifty years! Just think of that. I didn't even have a year with Maki. Was it fate? Do I believe in fate? I don't know what I believe anymore. But it's a lot of years to spend with one person. Maybe I'm better off on my own.

White muslin curtains fringed the rich wood- block floor. They quivered in the gentle breeze like the skirts of ballet dancers, screening the strength of the sun's rays and creating a veiled sanctuary. A faint smell of incense seeped in through the balcony doors. He's been swinging that censer again like it's a discus. Dina had no time for the priest at Agios Anaryiri. He had been a known collaborator.

That's my floor, Dina beamed proudly as she left the bedroom to begin work on Mr B's study. What a mess.

Mr B's beautiful walnut desk was almost hidden beneath his scattered papers. She couldn't understand why he had left it in this state but then remembered Vassiliki had probably been sorting out unpaid invoices incurred by her reckless brother. Dina sat down in Mr B's big, heavy armed chair to gather her thoughts and decide which piece of furniture she could tackle instead. She wasn't supposed to touch anything on the desk. Vassiliki didn't trust her like Mr B did. If it had been up to him he would have used Dina for his secretary as well as his cleaner. She would have enjoyed that. It would have felt like a promotion; recognition that she had other skills. Her thoughts travelled down to her hands. She imagined how she would describe them if she was a novelist and this prompted her to pick up the pen that was lying among the papers. But there was nothing to write on. She considered writing on the back of one of the invoices but thought better of it. Her shopping list was in her overall pocket. She turned it over and began writing.

The hands of a small, sinewy woman (apparently birdlike) who has remained the same weight, pregnancy apart, since she was twenty five years old. Knotted, raised blue veins, small hillocks for knuckles. She paused, her pen in mid air but quickly continued, now with some aggression. *Reddened from years of being plunged into hot water. Surprisingly delicate nails,* she studied them, *still showing the cuticle moons. No wedding ring, no band of gold.*

She stopped writing, her memory frozen in mid air. Where would Makis have found a wedding ring at the top of a mountain during a civil war? Then a romantic villager had come to their rescue, dismantling her only curtain to offer up the metallic ring that miraculously fitted the fourth finger of Dina's right hand. That too, lost in battle just like Makis.

Replacing it would never have felt right somehow. In any case it got in the way when she was aiming her rifle.

She was surprised at how much the act of writing had stirred up her emotions. She vowed to try it again sometime.

The front door slammed. She heard Vassiliki's heels click into the hallway. Dina jumped to her feet, pushing the list back into her pocket. She could hear her own words to herself. 'You know what she's going to say now, don't you?'
'Ah! Dina. Having a break are you?'

Vassiliki deposited her snakeskin handbag on the desk. Dina could smell her expensive perfume seeping through the sleeve of her intricately embroidered white blouse. "Ah! Dina. Having a break are you? I'm pleased to see you haven't disturbed my work here." She nodded her new hairstyle towards the desk.

Hideous.

Dina managed to be defensive when really she had no need. "Good morning Kiria Vouyoukas. I haven't touched anything on the desk I can assure you. I didn't know you were coming today."

"Ah, I can't sit and watch the business go under can I?" She raised her plucked eyebrows to the ceiling. Dina's eyes followed them and spotted a small cobweb. "He's got us into debt and now this place to sort out. I'm going to make a start on this room as soon as I've sorted out these invoices. I can't believe he's let them mount up for three months without saying anything to me. Get me a coffee would you? Straight, don't forget. I'm avoiding the sugar this week so that I can fit into my new Jaeger suit for Irini's wedding."

Dina had no idea who Jaeger or Irini were. She was more interested in what Vassiliki meant by sorting out the house. As far as Dina was concerned it meant getting the house to sparkle; to look its best for when Mr B came back.

Vassiliki rummaged in her handbag, retrieved a pack of cigarettes and lighter and snapped the bag shut. She pursed her red lips and frowned as she lit up. Dina watched. Vassiliki was one of those smokers who exhaled the smoke through her nostrils, in two jet streams. Dina headed for the kitchen to fill her bucket. Vassiliki was close on her heels. "Yes. I'll start in Panouli's study I think. Could you fix that coffee now please?"

"What are you going to start?" Dina banged the bucket down and turned to the stove. She levelled two teaspoons of coffee into the *briki* and switched on the small hob.

"The inventory of course! There's no point waiting until he's gone. There'll be too much to do then and I've got my own business to think about as well."

Dina stared at Vassiliki. "You mean an inventory of all Mr B's furniture and things?" She was astonished.

"Yes. We'll need to sell the contents separately from the house." Vassiliki paused and Dina noticed a mocking smile cross her lips. "Maybe you would like to buy some of the furniture Dina? I'm sure we could come to some agreement on price."

Dina brought the coffee to the boil and tipped it into a small cup that she set before Vassiliki on the kitchen table. "This table alone would take up my whole flat Kiria Vouyoukas and as for the price, I couldn't afford any of this. Mr B has some very fine pieces. They must be worth a lot but shouldn't it stay with the family? I'm surprised you're not keeping it."

Vassiliki sipped her coffee and tapped her cigarette ash onto the floor. Catching Dina's glare, she chuckled. "Well, I can see you haven't cleaned it yet. It looks like it needs a jolly good scrub. So you see Dina, even if we wanted to keep the house we couldn't afford to. Panouli's business is bankrupt and we'll need the cash for other things, my boutique for example. I'll need to get some of the new autumn collection from Milan. That costs money! The hotel, the food. You have no idea how expensive everything is in that country. Still, none of this is your concern is it Dina? I'm sure you'll find another employer soon enough."

Vassiliki's provocation was testing for Dina. Don't react, she told herself, that's what she wants. She felt rage scorching her body. She had rarely come so close to lashing out with her fists at another woman but somehow she held back. Lucky to be a cleaner. Always a broom handle to clench as if it was a gun. But why give this woman the pleasure? Dina's anger subsided into shock. She had not thought Mr B's fur business was in such serious trouble. He had never mentioned it to her. She suspected Vassiliki was exaggerating the amount of debt. "I hadn't even thought about that. I'm concerned for your brother. He looked very frail when he left for Perdikas. I would have thought the last thing he wanted would be for this house to be sold." That's it, she thought, as soon as the words were out. I've overstepped the mark again! This is none of my business.

"What he wants and what needs to happen are two different things. Not that it's any of your business but my brother expects the house to be sold. It's not a surprise. He tells me everything. You don't seriously think he would confide in his cleaner rather than his sister do you?"

That's one insult too many. It triggered Dina's tongue. "By the way Kiria Vouyoukas, is it true that your husband is in the security police?" Dina's short, direct cut had been well aimed. She could see the woman's cheeks darken and her bosom swell. She hadn't been expecting this.

"I hardly think that what my husband does is relevant to anything and…"

"So, I can assume it was you who organised to have my phone tapped because of what I was telling you last week."

Vassiliki's hand hovered as she momentarily realised she had left her handbag in the study.

Dina read her mind. "Have one of mine. Cheaper and stronger for times like this." She pushed the packet towards Vassiliki.

"Who told you this?" Vassiliki fumbled with the packet and drew out a cigarette.

Dina was flicking the plastic lighter in her face angrily. "It doesn't matter how I know and as you're so fond of saying, it isn't your concern who told me. You had me checked out didn't you? After our conversation, you realised what you could do to me. You must have thought how stupid I was for telling you those things about myself and you'd be right. I was."

The cigarette did its work. Vassiliki was calmed. She stood up and the rickety wooden chair that had been holding her weight, fell backwards in relief. "I'm proud of my husband and his family, a lot prouder than I am of my own useless brother who drinks himself to death and ruins the family business. Does he drink with you as well? God, our mother would turn in her grave if she thought her eldest son was cavorting with his cleaner. When I think of what he could have been and you don't know about my brother's past do you? He was no angel you know. I bet he hasn't told you. You imagine you have some kind of special relationship with my brother but let me remind you of this Dina Constantinou. I'm his sister. He's my family and you're just an overpaid cleaner."

Dina left the kitchen. It was the safest option. She knew enough to be sure that it had been Vassiliki's doing that she was now under surveillance and she couldn't bear to be in the same room with her any longer. She collected her duster and polishes and went back into Mr B's study to face the bookshelves.

Dina loved being near books although there had never been many of them in her family home. She stroked their spines with her duster. "Always treat them gently", *Barba* Stefos had advised. His crooked old bookshelves spilt out all kinds of pamphlets and novels. It was *Barba* Stefos who taught Dina her alphabet at four years old and helped overcome her fear of the village teacher. After twelve hours of physically exhausting work in the tobacco fields he could always find time to help Dina prepare for tomorrow's test. Then it all changed when he was dragged away one summer day in 1932. He never returned to his family. The Metaxas collaborators had robbed another family of their father and with him went their livelihood. This left seven year old Dina trying her best to make reading progress but somehow the joy had been taken out of it. Nobody could take the place of her uncle. Dina remembered her aunt Marika's disconsolate face when she stood in line with her two cousins, Katina and Giorgos to be told their father had been taken and may never return. The cousins consoled themselves by playing with newly born kittens, enough for one each. Dina's was black with two white feet. None of them had names because in their sorrow naming them didn't occur to the children.

Dina wished she could read faster like other people so that there was only ever one or two books waiting for her. She had such an appetite for the history and literature of her country. But reading books wasn't a requirement of a good cleaner. Prospective employers wanted their cleaners to be thorough yet speedy, invisible but polite, discreet but a source of local gossip, willing to work overtime but for no extra pay.

Vassiliki was behind her, breathing deeply. The depths of the smoker. "I'd like you to collect up all those invoices and put them in that top drawer for the time being. I can't face them now. The conversation with you has given me such a headache I need to lie down. When you've done that I want you to make a start in the second bedroom. Make sure you pay special attention to the appearance of the bed surround and side tables. I've got a man coming round tomorrow who's interested in buying it for his daughter. Top drawer don't forget." She had taken her shoes off. Holding one in each hand Vassiliki waddled into her brother's bedroom. Dina gritted her teeth. She's going to put those feet on that beautiful bedspread.

Back in Mr B's study Dina scanned the desk and sighed. She didn't really understand the workings of the fur business, only that Mr B was an importer and he clearly hadn't been paying the companies that sent him the pelts. She scooped up the papers. The names were all foreign but she could see the amount of money added up to thousands of drachmes. So Vassiliki hadn't been exaggerating.

Ach. The poor man! What a way to end your life.

Dina opened the drawer. It was empty apart from a few old black and white photos of the Vouyoukas family in their seaside home. She could easily pick out Vassilki. The same affected pose, right leg pointing forward, chest puffed out.

She was a lot thinner in those days. The years haven't added weight to my body like that but I wouldn't mind having legs like yours.

The last photo she turned over was different. At first she didn't recognise him. He was a lot thinner and he stood upright, smiling ahead. But it was from his hair that she really knew him. That same good thick head of hair, not yet grey. He must have been about forty. A small crowd were gathered round and looking up at him. He stood higher up on some steps – the town hall? Dina turned the old frayed photo over. It was dated 1948, nothing else. She pictured herself on Grammos in 1948. He must have been making a speech. Their faces showed they were listening. Several people had their hands raised together in what looked like applause. She held it in her hand and peered closely at the crowd again, mainly men but a scattering of women, all with the same gaunt stares and grey skin.

    She recognised the hunger when she peered closely at their empty eyes. It was winter. They wore heavy coats that hung loosely over their hungry bodies. The camera had just caught the corner of a placard and two letters 'VE'. Dina wondered if Mr B had once been Mayor of Kastoria, maybe this was his inauguration. She thought the clue was in the placard. Then she realised that the first letter was missing and if it was a Y then it could have been YVE, *Yperaspistai Voreio Elladas.* Them! That lot! She nearly lost her balance and had to steady herself against the desk. But just because they were there that didn't mean Mr B was one of them. Did it? She was unsure. Was he really so right wing? What did she really know about him? Vassiliki's words came back to her. She replaced the photo, laid the invoices on top of it and closed the drawer, pushing away the image. The photo didn't prove anything but what was clear was that Mr B had played some kind of prominent role in Kastoria while she was fighting for her life in the mountains not far away.

CHAPTER ELEVEN

Civil War
1948 Epirus Mountains

Combating the freezing cold was as much a mental thing as it was physical. Ririka focused on a single shoot of grass poking out from the snow. She couldn't stop shivering. "Aye! My stomach feels like it's being put through a wringer."

"Rub it. Make your hands move Ririka. Get some warmth to it!" Dina was crouched over, trying to avoid spilling any rice from the small sack as she aimed it at the saucepan. "Aleka!" She looked up losing her concentration. A handful of grains showered the grass. "Panagia mou!"

A tall, skinny girl with plaits down to her bottom looked to Dina for direction and went down on her knees when she saw the rice escaping from the sack. "I'll get don't worry. My eyesight's better than yours." She pincered the tiny grains between her forefinger and thumb and dropped them into the saucepan.

"Get some water for the rice so we can put something warm inside us." Dina's voice betrayed her frustration and hunger. She was very afraid that these girls would be so weak from hunger that they wouldn't be in a fit state to fight the next battle. They were already moving too slowly to reach Malimadi camp by the next morning but Dina had to weigh up their priorities. Soldiers couldn't move quickly if they were too cold or hungry. It was imperative to get one meal inside them while they still could. Tomorrow was always the unknown.

Unhooking an aluminium flask from her knapsack Aleka edged herself sideways down the steep riverbank. She bent forwards cautiously, dipping the flask into the fast flowing current that threatened to drown her boots.

I am going to get this fire going if it's the last thing I do. Dina spoke to herself and as if coaxed by her thoughts the flame flickered into life. She had sent a firewood search party out an hour before and now the light was fading like her spirit. She might have to make a sacrifice tonight, if there wasn't enough rice to go round. The younger ones must not go hungry. Her comrades were late. Without dry twigs the fire would die. Ririka rested her head on her shaking knees.

"Ella. Come on now Ririka; don't let it get to you so much. Once you've eaten you'll feel warmer. Do you still have the pains?" Dina put her arm round Ririka's shoulder.

"Oh Dina, you know, I haven't had a period for two months now. It's not right. I'm never going to be able to have children now am I?"

Aleka looked up from greasing her boots, shaking her head. "Me neither. Nothing. But it makes things easier doesn't it? It means we can be better soldiers every day, every month and then the men can't accuse us of being lazy!"

"If any man, comrade or not, accuses any of my unit of being lazy I will personally send him a bullet. Ella Ririka. Try to think of it positively and don't worry about the future. Who knows what's ahead of us? When this war's over we'll go back to our villages and settle down then our periods will come back and we'll be women again."

What villages? There wouldn't be any left.

Aleka abandoned her boots and joined Dina and Ririka. "Then we'll have to be careful they don't stop for other reasons!" She giggled and twisted one of her plaits

round her forefinger. "I'm not going to marry, Dina. I don't see what they all go on about. My parents always look so miserable. They never have any fun, only when Paniyiri comes round, then my father drinks so much he falls down and sleeps in the square and we find him like that every year on August 16th."

But Ririka was not amused. "Eh! What do you know child? You're only fifteen. You'll be married by the time you're twenty, just like the rest of us. Won't she Dina?"

"With hair like that, of course she will and we'll all be at her wedding won't we girls? With flowers and dancing and beautiful satin dresses. And you'll have the best made bed strewn with handpicked rose petals. I can just smell them now."

Yes, she'll get married. If she reaches twenty.

"But what's the point of getting married when your husband just ends up like my father? I want to have adventures and fall in love. From what I've seen marriage stops all that and then you can't stop having babies. It's endless."

Dina chuckled at Aleka's innocence. "There are things you can do you know, to stop yourself getting pregnant." Then she added. "Not that I've tried."

Ririka raised her eyebrows. "Eh Dina, don't give her ideas if they're not true. I wasn't supplied with anything when I joined up, were you?"

The flame was beginning to strengthen, lighting up the women's faces as they crouched round. They stretched their arms towards the flames, fanning out their frozen fingers. Dina began to break twigs in half over her knee. It kept her warm. She fed them into the flames. "No, I think they just assumed that we were virgins and for most of us that was probably true but they warned us not to get intimate with the male comrades in my battalion."

"Our company commander always seemed to have a supply if anyone ever dared to ask." Ririka laughed. "I was never that brave and I was scared word would get back to my village then I would never find a husband."

Aleka sat beside Dina. "I know what you two are talking about, I'm not that stupid. I'm nearly sixteen. You're talking about kapotes aren't you?"

Dina and Ririka grinned at each other from opposite sides of the fire, their mouths exaggerated into uneven shapes. Dina stroked Aleka's head. "Yes Aleka and we know you're not stupid. Come on girl, d'you think you would have got through your training if we thought you were stupid? Look." Dina swallowed and paused. She was hardly an expert herself but Aleka's curiosity needed an answer. "If…if you ever want to, you know, give yourself to a boy, then come to me and I'll sort something for you. Don't take any risks, you're too young to be a mother and your village would disown you."

Young girls advising even younger girls of the dangers of a life they may not live to see. The thin line between some knowledge and a lot, between being a plain simple village girl and a soldier. The body adapts and the mind follows.

Aleka shrugged. "Who cares? I've got my knife and rifle. They're my lovers."

From the darkness that had begun to hang among the trees there was the sound of twigs breaking and muffled voices. Dina rolled over, reached for her rifle and motioned for the others to lie low. They waited in silence until they heard the familiar melody that was Poppy leading the firewood party home, their arms laden with kindling and tree branches. Poppy was an islander. She sang in her beautiful rich voice. 'Wake up, wake up the dawn is breaking. Don't you hear the little birds that are chirping? Wake up, wake up because they will see that we spent all night together.' She dropped the wood in front of the fire then collapsed weeping. "My mother used to sing it while she was making the beds. It must have reminded her of when she and baba were engaged. I might never see them again and I never had the chance to explain. I couldn't just stay like an ordinary village girl." She looked up at Dina like a small child, her tear tracks lit up by the fire glow.

Dina balanced the small saucepan of water between two burning branches. When it was steady she buried four potatoes in the ashes. "At last! I was getting worried about your safety comrades. I thought you'd gone to Kastoria without us. It's getting late Thosia."

"We had to go further than we thought to get the dry stuff. A lot of the outer trees are soaked through. It's been snowing for so many days now. D'you have any tobacco Dina?" The tall skinny girl dug her hands into her pockets and shivered. She had carried a heavy load of pine branches without gloves. She had no gloves. None of them did. Some of her comrades wore woollen socks over sandals to stop them slipping where the paths were icy. They had to wait until they came across a dead body with the right boot size or at least one that closely matched.

Dina raised her chin. "No Thosia. No tobacco. Maybe Poppy has some left. Are you okay?"

"Yes apart from nearly losing my footing and ending up at the bottom of the gorge. Did you know that forest ends suddenly and there's just a drop, you wouldn't know. If we'd been on the mules we would've gone over the top. It was nearly too late for me."

Dina could see her hunched shoulders were shaking slightly as she remembered the fright. "I wish we did have mules. Come, sit down by the fire. With your wood it'll be roaring soon. Be careful of your hands though. Keep them away from the fire.

Thosia crouched towards the fire. Her knees cracked like the firewood.

"Did you see the bridge from where you were?"

"What bridge? Is there a bridge through that pass? I thought our orders were to pass over Mitsikeli not go south."

They exchanged glances; their cheeks blushed orange from the glow. Thosia's hollow cheekbones scared Dina. She hadn't started out looking like that. "They were but how can we go that way with this weather? It would be madness to try. We're waiting for a wire to confirm. If the bridge is blown we'll be wading through the Arachthos. See if Ririka's got the wire yet will you? Then you need to eat. We all do."

Poppy returned. Her woollen cloak was wrapped round her body by invisible arms. When she saw Thosia she opened the cloak and engulfed her. "I found some kalabokia at the bottom of my knapsack but it was still frozen. We can boil it when the rice is done"

"Fantastic, we'll grow fat on such a feast. Did you find any tobacco?" Poppy produced a battered tin from her pocket and handed it to Thosia.

"Okay Thosia now you have the tobacco please go and do what I asked." Dina was irritated but she also felt uneasy. They might lose some of the weaker girls if they had to enter the waters in this temperature.

Please, please let the Arta bridge be intact. If I look up to the sky I see the darkness and snow clouds and I don't see any stars to wish on.

Thosia's unsteady hand held out a thin roll up in front of Dina's face. She took it without turning her head in Thosia's direction and offered the tattered end to a flame. She wanted to inhale and feel the prickle in her throat before listening to what Thosia had come to say. The nicotine buzzed in her head then travelled down her throat.

Thosia stayed standing while she delivered the news. "The bridge is blown."

Nausea swam with the nicotine in her stomach making Dina retch suddenly. She immediately handed the cigarette back to Thosia, still looking at the fire, not wanting to face her because she had been the bearer of bad news. "Here. Take it back. I was never very good with smoking on an empty stomach."

Thosia stood still and put the roll up to her lips. "And the third battalion have lost twenty more at the Metsovo pass. Orders are for us to continue. We may get some reinforcements from Agrafa in two days, when we reach the pass."

Dina shook her head in disbelief. "In two days! How the hell are we going to get there in two days with this?" She raised her chin towards the clouds. Snow had begun to sprinkle. I mustn't shout, she told herself. It won't help. Stay calm. Think only of the next priority. She checked the fire. It was strong. She scrutinised the clouds. They were broken shapes. "Now. We need to eat. All of us."

The girls gathered round the fire holding out metal cups for their rice. Aleka scooped some snow into the empty saucepan and placed it back on the fire. She then emptied in the kalabokia and sat back on a rock to eat her rice. For some minutes nobody said anything but the gathering wind spoke with authority over the girls. They pulled their jackets tightly around themselves in response and stamped on the snow-melted earth. The fire was now blazing high and the pine resin had begun to hiss as it seeped into the flames.

The kalabokia were soft enough to chew. Aleka took command and ladled a small cup for each of the girls and they continued in silence as before. Dina said she didn't want her portion and to give it to Thosia. She had most need. The wind began to blow the snow into great gusts, thickening around their feet and threatening the fire. Aleka laid more branches. The dark had descended on them. Dina must organise their shifts for the night. She looked around the circle of girls. There were twenty-four of them if she counted herself. It was now eight o'clock. They wouldn't see daylight for another twelve hours. "Okay comrades which group want the first shift?"

"I don't mind Dina. I'm not tired. I'll take the first with Eleni and Fotoula. Come on girls let's get our guns."

The others organised themselves and began scraping away the snow from the edges of the fire. They prepared the ground by laying beds of twigs on which to spread their sleeping bags.

"Dina, I'm going to the deeper snow to get my sleep."

"Okay Aleka but make sure you dig in properly." She looked towards the remaining girls. "Two of you, make sure you put poles next to Aleka and any other comrade sleeping between the snow. By morning it will be a lot deeper."

Two older girls picked tall sticks from the pile and watched as Aleka tunnelled

herself between top and bottom layers of snow until she had disappeared. Poppy ran up to them, her mouth open in amazement. "Does it really work? Won't she freeze?"

"No. She'll sleep fine. It'll be steaming hot in there when she gets up for her shift and then whoever's next will have a warm igloo. D'you want to try?" But Poppy wasn't convinced.

By the time the girls had organised the shifts it was nine. Dina curled up under her cloak next to the fire. Although she was taking first shift she could rarely get any sleep later. Lack of food didn't help. Her eyelids drooped at the thought of her mother's halvopitta.

Night came on black and cold but the moon still managed to tint the valley. Heavy bellied snow clouds hid the peaks of Smolikas and Metsovo. Positioning herself on her stomach Dina rested her elbows on her knapsack as she peered through the binoculars. Her cartridge belt dug into her ribs and the bar of olive soap her sister had given her was jabbing her in the breast as she leant forward. She removed it from her pack and just for a minute couldn't resist putting her nose to it. She settled back, wriggling into position again but still it was uncomfortable. This time she emptied the whole pack. Out tumbled her sewing kit followed by a rolled up bandage and some rags for that time of the month. Her nail scissors pierced a minute hole in the snow and disappeared. She plunged her hand into the icy depths, hooked her finger round them and brought them to the surface. Too useful to lose. Nail scissors could spear lice in hair, press their points into infected wounds to release the puss and cut hand and toe nails of course. Dina slid the binoculars back into her pack and looked at the sleeping girls. They ought to move now when there would be least risk of an ambush but she knew how much they needed sleep after their last long, tough journey. What should she do? Her training told her to rouse them but her heart wanted to let them recoup but they could be heading into an American ambush – their worst fear. They had encampments all along the railway line. Their engineers were dynamiting the bridges. But they couldn't stay where they were. The risk of attack was greater that way. Her mind was made up. Dina stood up and walked to the fire. Little short bursts of snoring came from the youngest girls. One of them was crying in her sleep.

Dina scraped some snow away with her hands. "Aleka, come on, wake up now. We have to move. It's time." The surface snow broke and Aleka slithered out from her igloo. She stood up rubbing her eyes with her fists. Dina remembered her younger sister doing the same when she had to get her up for school. The other girls began rolling up their sleeping cloaks. Ririka put a pan on to boil and threw in some shreds of chicory. The coffee they had been given at Exohi had finished and the next village was a day's march. That's if there was anything left of the village. If the Americans hadn't got their first. Would they even make it to the next village?

In the EPON training camp Dina had been taught that an army was most vulnerable when it left its camp and marched. They were prey to ambush. Hidden in the dense underbush behind hilltops and steep river banks the enemy could mount the surprise attack. They must be prepared to use their eyes to see everywhere, all the time. Ririka handed round the tin mug of boiled chicory but there were few takers. It left a bitter aftertaste on the back of the tongue. Dina took a gulp, swilled it round in her mouth and spat it out.

They set off at 4 a.m. and the snow was still falling through gaps in the pine trees. To their right the mountainside was a blue bulk rising from the ravine. Their path through the trees was lost so they relied on Poppy's memory. The snow helped them in their silent march but it also tired them because they had to take high steps, their knees up to their chests and still their trousers were sodden in minutes. Dina took the lead with Poppy. "There's no way of knowing if they've laid any tripwire. We'll just have to take our chances."

Poppy started humming and shook her head. "I'm not even thinking about it Dina. I'm just concentrating on getting there." Over her left shoulder she balanced a shovel, the right her pick. She's a strong girl, thought Dina. She will survive. It took the unit an hour to reach the edges of the forest. The wind had weakened to erratic buffets and it seemed to be driving the snow away from the women. "God's hand." Poppy crossed herself.

"Bah! *O theos sou na paei sto diabolo* (your God can go to hell.) Don't you know child when the wind does that it means change. Something's going to change for us. Be vigilant now. We're coming out of the forest."

Where the trees ended the ground fell at a sharp angle like a slice of icing on a cake. The top layer of crystals twinkled under the moon that was now overhead. Dina looked ahead but she couldn't see any path. They would have to single file along the top of the ridge. She waved them on behind her. They didn't need to raise their boots so high as the snow was only ankle deep here. Dina gripped her rifle too tightly. She was frightened. It was too quiet. She looked to her right and could make out the snow covered shapes of boulders and as her eye moved across the width of the ridge it twitched in response to something. It had been a very quick flicker. Orange colour. Then black again.

The sky was lightening with the approaching dawn but down there it was still black. Her eye stayed focused deep into the ravine and there it was again, orange and gone. She gestured for the company to crouch low as they moved. They must not even whisper. Dina's heart thudded and each thud was like someone hitting a bruise. All the while they moved in a winding huddle around the edges of the pines and they were losing height. Dina stopped, stood upright and sighed as she understood. It was the flame from a match, no sooner lit than extinguished but not fast enough for her eyes. So they were there waiting to ambush them at the bottom. Whose surprise was it going to be? But that meant they had sent scouts ahead, on their way up the same incline to block them. Dina's next thought was that they didn't have enough rounds of ammunition to fight off an ambush. Not without reinforcements. But they were nowhere near Agrafa and wouldn't be for several days. This was what her training had really been about.

Without hesitation weigh up your options, take stock of your ammo, morale, numbers, position, route out or sit and wait. It was all too much at once. Her palms were now hot and slippery on her rifle while her fingertips were numb.

Poppy pulled Dina down. "You said to stay low. What's going on? What's the matter Dina?"

"I saw it. They're down there smoking, waiting for us."

"*Panayia mou.* You were right. I give up God."

"Pass it back Poppy, down the line. I need a couple of minutes to decide what we do. Tell them that for now we stay still." She looked once again to the valley floor.

According to her map the railway line ran alongside the river and that was where the Americans had their working camps. A plan began to form in Dina's brain. Her breath quickened when she realised what the consequences would be if it failed. She sat down on the clumped snow, laid aside her rifle and unbuckled her kit bag. "Poppy, when I tell you, shine the torch where I point." She handed Poppy the torch and unfolded the map. She struggled to locate what she thought was their position. "We must be about here." They studied the ragged map. Dina's forefinger travelled along the black railway line and then moved northwards. They were above the bend in the river which gave them the advantage of being able to hear the oncoming train before it rounded the bend where the Americans were almost certainly encamped. If they could find their way down to the point before the train reached the bend there was a possibility they could jump onto the expendable front wagons unseen by the Americans and that way reach Agrafa. But wait, not so simple. She would be risking all their lives if there were mines planted along the line. Then they would all be blown to pieces. What was the alternative? To stay and freeze up here with no food, no extra supplies of ammunition and the enemy scouts on their way up.

"Turn off the torch Poppy." She looked deeply into Poppy's eyes.

"Your look is frightening me Dina. What is it?" She gently folded the map and slipped it back into Dina's bag.

"We have to decide. We have to make a decision very quickly. We either stay here and freeze but they'll probably get to us first and then we might as well be dead. Or we head down there." She indicated with her thumb over her shoulder. "And jump onto the front wagons of the next train."

"Why does it have to be the front ones?"

"Because we won't get into the closed ones behind on a moving train."

"But I thought…"

"I know the risk but it's our only chance. Are you with me or not? We have to tell the girls and get moving."

Poppy shivered under her cloak. "Couldn't we fight them off here? I mean, we've got ten rounds of ammunition left."

Dina grinned. "Poppy, d'you really think that's enough to defeat a party of American engineers who've probably got a seventy five mm gun hidden somewhere?"

Poppy shook her head. "Okay. You win, well, not a good thing to say at the moment but if we're going to do it let's get them moving."

They headed east back into the depths of the forest. Dina was worried that she was leading an ignorant army of women and girls to their deaths.

I should have taken time to explain to them what we're doing.

But she mustn't think like that. Stay positive. Stay in control. Focus.

In that part of the forest the trees grew more densely together making the way darker. Although it was now five little light penetrated the trees.

We have no idea when the next train will come but we've no chance up here. We wait it out and if we freeze in the waiting so be it.

They could hear the rushing waters of the Arachthos echoing along the valley floor before it became visible. Dina's feet suddenly disappeared from under her and she found herself sliding to the bottom of the hill now beyond the tree line and exposed. Her right shoulder slapped against a boulder, stopping her freefall. She groaned.

She wanted to cry out so badly. "Help me up Poppy. My legs feel a bit weak." They tumbled over the last few ridges that levelled down to the flat river-bank, tripping on the blackened railway track that threaded its way along a ridge above the river. The rails intermittently disappeared under mounds of drifted snow then reappeared as dark wavy snakes.

"If we shelter here under the trees we can still see it coming before it hits the bend, It might give us enough time to throw ourselves onto the wagons." Dina began clearing away snow with her boots. The noise of snapping wood sent her spinning round. She tried to swing her rifle but it was too painful. But it was only Ririka leading the girls. Everyone was so tense. She must jump last to make sure they were all on board. Dina's throat was tight and dry. This sense of duty was making itself felt all over her body. She glared at Aleka and another young girl who had collapsed on the line. They've seen my look and understood.

"Start draping the canvas over these trees. I don't know how long we'll be here."

I can give orders like a general if I have to. These could be the last I do give.

No. Don't think like that. The train will come. It will come before we freeze and before they ambush us. They are close by. I can feel it.

How will they treat us if they find us first?

Are the Americans like our compatriots, all smiles then whack. They hurt us and they don't care that we are mothers and sisters and daughters.

Are the Americans like that?

They might be worse.

Could they be worse?

They can hurt us from a distance, that's it. They can bomb us from their planes and then we have no chance at all.

But our Greek traitors can hurt us close up and do things to us. They are animals. Americans aren't interested in forcing brothers to kill each other and raping their sisters. Our comrades would never do those things. Or would they? It seemed to Dina that in a war like this all certainty was lost.

Dina crawled over to Poppy who was lying in the snow, her ear against the tracks. "It's a long way off but I can hear a rumbling. Put your ear there." She indicated a piece of track jutting out from the snow.

"You're right. I can hear it too."

"Maybe it's a tank." Poppy crouched beside Dina.

"Not here. They can't put tanks on this terrain. There's too much forest. No, I think it's our train. I want it to be our train."

"You didn't answer me before Dina. Is it true what they say about the front wagons? Are they really put there in case there are mines so they get blown first?"

She would make a bad job of it if she lied. She just looked into Poppy's eyes. "Do you think my decision is wrong?"

"It's your decision lieutenant. I respect your decision."

Dina raised her eyebrows. "I'm not used to being called that."

"Eh, you know. You'll always be Dina to me but I know how much you feel the responsibility. You deserve to be called that." The two women embraced. The sound of a whistle pulled them apart.

Dina moved cautiously towards the rest of the company. She gave the girls their orders in a lowered voice. "Make a line and listen to me now." They shuffled obediently; a band of teenage girls, hair strands poking out under the sides of their caps "I want you to jump as soon as you can onto the front two wagons. Anywhere, just jump. Your aim is to get yourself onto the wagon. Once on the wagon you have no protection. Lie flat and the rest is out of your hands." From their eyes she saw they finally understood. Her breathing was too fast.

"*Eleftheri Ellada.*" They whispered in unison.

The train wheels kept to a rhythmic click as they rolled over the tracks. Click. Click. Louder. And just as she had been told, there in front were the expendable wagons. The noise dwarfed every other sound. She saw them jump, banging onto the hard wooden floor, immediately flattening their young skinny bodies. Then she saw Aleka frozen at the edge of the track. With one desperate rush Dina pushed the girl in front and jumped with her, landing on top. Aleka let out a scream of terror. Dina cupped her mouth. But they were all on board.

If she had to die now she wanted the mine to take her. Not the Americans.

Their bodies were shaken and bounced by the movement of the train. They clung on to the wagon floors with bleeding fingernails. Dina opened her eyes. Without lifting her head she saw the steepening river bank above them. They were gaining height, their bodies sliding towards the back of the wagon, their arms flailing in a hopeless effort to grip what wasn't there. Then from the frozen heights, a shot, echoing through the trees.

The train laboured alongside the river bank. Down below, the remains of the dynamited Aarta bridge.

Dina calculated they were at least half an hour from Agrafa. They were coming out of the forest now. Bouldered uplands gradually took the place of trees. Anyone could be behind those rocks. A second shot twanged against the metal of the track. A third punctured the old wooden wireless box. Now they were cut off from any other unit that might be in the area. But why are they such lousy shots? She was still lying on top of Aleka. The girl had actually fallen asleep. Amazing. Only babies and teenagers could do that at such a time. Here they lay, prone, two open wagons of DA girls and the marksman hadn't managed to hit anyone. She made one guess. She needed it to be right. The bullets were a signal. She raised herself and when she did she spotted him moving out from behind a rock. The man was too far up for Dina to see what he wore. His arm swept downwards, left to right. He shook his head quite violently backwards and that was the signal confirming Dina's suspicion. She struggled to stand up. Balancing was tricky. "We're jumping off when I say three." She had to shout over the noise of the engine. "One, two, three."

Ririka jumped late so her right leg caught the splinters of flying wood. The front wagon exploded first, sending debris high into the air then down into the river below them. They were pinned together against the frozen hillside. Fire burnt holes through their clothes. Sometimes there was a hissing where fire met flesh.

Dina felt a warm stinging above her knee. She looked down in shock at the heavy, crimson blood.

She found herself in a bed. Pinewood smoke curled between the roof beams A poem floated down and rested on her pillow.
On a high mountain, on a rocky crag
Sits an eagle, poor bird,
With his wings all frozen through
And asking the sun to rise
Rise sun, sun rise and melt my frozen wings *

It was a man's voice that brought the words of the eagle to her ears and the same man was offering the soup spoon to her lips. When she found her focus his eyes were the first thing she recognised. Blue eyes on a Greek. They'd all laughed. Bah! What do they know? They've never been to Kerkira.

CHAPTER TWELVE

"I knew of a girl from our neighbourhood, from Ghizi, who ended up in the port, in Pireus I mean, making enough to live on from the sailors. Even today I can't bring myself to call her a poudana because that word is so shameful. She did it to stop her family from starving after the Germans left."

The words spun round in her head. Rise sun, sun rise and melt my…

She woke to a thin slice of sun projecting onto her bedroom wall. She dreamed of leaving this dungeon. Tired of waking to the ration of sunlight from the small basement window. She needed coffee, thick and strong but Evy's little feet were already pattering along the corridor towards Dina's room. Dina rubbed her eyes with her knuckles, blinked and yawned.

Here she comes, the brightest light of the flat. Who cares about dreams of living above ground when this gem shines!

Her granddaughter bounced into her bedroom, trailing her security blanket behind like the train of a wedding gown.

"Good morning my love. You're early today. Has *baba* gone to work already?" Dina gathered the child in her arms and planted a kiss on her forehead.

"Yes." She sucked her thumb and laid her head against Dina's shoulder. "*Yiayia*, I'm thirsty. I want some juice." She scrambled free of Dina and rolled over the bed humming, in the sweet certainty that her grandmother would deliver.

Dina stood up and wrapped her bathrobe round her.

"Come on then my child. Let's go to the kitchen and I'll make your drink."

Evy darted ahead of Dina, collecting her doll on the way. She swung it by its leg as she took giant strides. "I'm doing a march like a soldier and this is my gun."

She clearly has other uses for her doll than playing happy families, thought Dina. "Her leg might snap off if you swing her so hard Evy. Use something else if you want her to last."

"Did your leg snap off? Did they put it together again? Is that why it doesn't work properly *yiayia*?" Ignoring her grandmother's advice the child came to a stop at her kitchen stool and promptly dropped the doll on the cold tiled floor.

Dina laughed and felt her leg. The child had such an imagination.

"Did you march when you were a soldier *yiayia*?"

Dina's smile faded as she took the carton of *visinada* from the fridge and poured Evy a glass. "Here. Drink this child, so many questions all at once and this early in the morning!"

Evy gulped down her cherry juice while studying her grandmother. "But you didn't answer me *yiayia*. Shall I show you again, so you remember?"

The child stomped up and down the corridor bending each knee in turn and flinging her arms forwards and backwards.

"Yes. Very good my sweet. Now let's forget soldiers and stomping and think about today. What are we going to do today?"

Evy thought about the question. She perched herself back on the stool and followed with her big green eyes as Dina spread some damson jam on a slice of bread and cut it in half.

"*Yiayia*, can we go to the playground? I want to go on the swings."

The children's playground was opposite their apartment block in *Plateia* Kalithea. Enclosed by metal fencing and entered through a safety gate, the children's joy consisted of rusting metal swings and a see-saw. The magic roundabout needed painting and the monkey bars were in the same condition. A small red and blue, riderless rocking horse still bobbed up and down on its spring. Surrounding the playground, dark green plane trees stood to attention, tall and straight, like sentries protecting their young wards. Motherless twin kittens stretched out their bodies in the shade of the trees. Rolling into one another the smaller of the two made a swipe with his paw, bringing his brother onto all fours and sending little clouds of dust swirling round the base of the tree. Evy's squeals frightened them into the bushes.

Dina led her granddaughter to the swings. Mothers and grandmothers were gathering for their Saturday morning ritual before shopping. Clustered around the peeling green benches, their chatter dominated the playground. Every now and then they cast protective glances towards the children (as if they had forgotten them).

Eleni, Dina's neighbour from the second floor, had a lot to say. "And let me tell you all," she was admonishing, pointing her painted index finger at each woman in turn. "Don't tell me later I didn't warn you. And another thing, I'm not exaggerating when I say there are more than two of them doing their business from over there. I've seen a third". She opened her perfectly lipsticked mouth to say more but the woman perched precariously at the end of the bench, cut in on her. Maro, another of Dina's neighbours was waving her arms in the air. One hand still held her granddaughter's rattle that jangled in tune every time Maro raised an arm. Up and down it went until the jealous screams of her granddaughter lying red faced in her pram, caused the gaggle of women to tell Maro to give the rattle back for God's sake. But Maro continued without the rattle. "It's true." She backed up Eleni, "I've also seen a blonde, dyed of course, and two with dark hair and the blonde came home in the early hours, at least four this morning and she wasn't alone. You know what I'm saying." A collective head nod answered her and a clucking of teeth on tongues was so loud that several of the children mistook this for a sign that they were doing something wrong and looked at one another in confusion.

The conversation amused Dina. She imagined what they must look like from above – an array of different coloured dyed heads; heads that still wore the bouffant style from the sixties. There was not a grey head among them yet they were all grandmothers whose collective age must have been near three hundred. Eleni and her sister-in-law wore black in remembrance of Eleni's brother. Even so, observed Dina, Eleni's dress was very smart - all black with little white flowers like daisies and her waist looked thinner because of that belt. You'd never think she was seventy kilos and the length looked right on her. It was only just below her knees but then she had good legs that didn't need stockings, even at her age. Lucky.

Another woman joined the group, having overheard their conversation. She was eager to give her opinion. Dina admired the newcomer's beige trouser suit. She was looking at a much younger woman who flicked back her long fringed hair as she laughed. Dina could see from the expressions of her neighbours that they were not amused by the woman's comments. She stood, one long leg in front of the other, hands on hips, big round sunglasses hiding most of her face. "And keep your views to yourselves, you old busybodies. Don't we have a living to earn any way we can in this godforsaken town? We don't bother you. We don't make a noise."

"That's not what Kiria Kondoglou said to me. She lives next to you. Walls have ears and apparently her walls aren't thick enough to bury the noises coming from your side when you're earning your living, as you put it."

Dina and Eleni exchanged glances and their laughter soon infected the bench. "Come on, Kiries, give the lady a break will you! Some of us don't have much choice about how we earn a living, she's right. There are people out there who earn their living by far worse means than our neighbour here and they reward themselves with little envelopes and pensions while the rest of us have to depend on our families in old age." There was no denying that, the bench agreed. "But no", implored the deeply religious Kiria Manakas, "they are sinners and there should be no room for sinners in *Plateia* Kalithea or any other neighbourhood in Kastoria, come to think of it." She was clutching at the large gold crucifix hanging at her throat. "Athens? Well, Athens is beyond salvation, "but here in Kastoria we can pray to God to cleanse us of our wrong doings and women like you should repent, before it's too late. And what about your child over there? What kind of life can she look forward to?"

The young woman planted herself in front of Kiria Manakas. Dina thought her proud and dignified. "She isn't my child Kiria. Do you think I would bring a child into this world and watch it suffer the way I have? Don't be so stupid! Come on Georgia. Your mama will be waiting." She turned her face towards Kiria Manakas. "I'll repent Kiria. I'll repent when our politicians and judges and policemen repent because then I won't be able to make a living!" Her parting words silenced the women momentarily. Georgia was marched away across the *plateia*. The woman's black hair bounced against her back as she walked beside the child. Then, as in the first rumblings before a gathering storm the women started up again, animated, getting their teeth into new prey.

Dina promised Evy a *koulouri* from the bakers if she stopped her wailing. Newly baked bread was the smell of her village and a thousand other Greek villages. It had been missing when she had staggered into those same villages, eerily deserted, their people dead or fled. Then the only smell coming from the baker's had been the bitter fumes from the charred remains of his building.

Dina handed over the drachmes for her two loaves and *tiropites*. The young assistant skilfully slid a large, heavy baking tray of sweet smelling bougatzes out of the metal oven and deposited it on the counter in front of Dina. He wiped his sweating brow with the back of his hand before rushing back to repeat the exercise with a second tray. Working long hours, for little pay, surrounded by oven temperatures of 250c and breathing in flour dust. Dina's uncle had been a baker and she had sometimes helped out in his shop, eager to learn the skills of kneading and sculpting, imagining herself to be producing a work of art as she stole bites, so hot it burnt her fingers. But the heat and lifting had made her dizzy and her mother had found her other less creative ways of being useful.

A woman came in carrying a large ceramic dish of vegetables that she handed to the assistant. It quickly disappeared to one of the ovens. The woman greeted Dina and bemoaned the fact that she had both her parents and the in-laws for dinner and her own oven couldn't accommodate so much food. The assistant returned with her dish and pointed out that she had forgotten to mark her name on the side of it. He handed her a black marker. Too many times, he warned, he'd seen forgetful women take home the wrong food because they hadn't written their names on their dishes and then come back and blamed him for the poor quality of cooking. Why, they'd had near fights between women right here.

He's decided to take an unofficial break, thought Dina. Good for him.

On the other hand, he continued, lighting a cigarette, in this way women and their families had been exposed to dishes they may never have attempted themselves, transforming the shop into a centre for exchanging recipes.

Dina would have stayed longer to learn about these unknown recipes. She wouldn't have minded 'being exposed' as the baker had put it but Evy was tugging at her arm. After the dark heat of the bakers the bright sunlit pavement was blinding.

Later that same evening Dina was crossing the square on her way to meet Dimitris. She nearly collided with a man in a smart suit. He appeared flustered. Then the same young woman who had confronted her neighbours earlier in the day was running across the street, into the square, holding a briefcase. She called a name but Dina couldn't hear clearly over the traffic noise. The man turned and stopped to allow her to catch up. Then he grabbed the briefcase from the woman's hand and walked purposefully out of the *plateia*. The woman stood looking after him.

"What can I get you Dina?" Dimitris stood up to greet Dina.

"Just a coffee thanks." She sat down, taking her cigarettes out of her pocket and placing them on the table.

"So, how's things?"

Dina leant forward in her chair. "I just witnessed a strange scene over there." She nodded towards the *plateia*. "I saw the young woman I'd seen earlier today. She gave my busy body neighbours quite a talking to when they started on about her business."

"And what is her business?"

Dina smiled. "The oldest."

Dimitris nodded, smiling.

"He looked wealthy in an expensive suit and he was clearly uneasy about being seen with her."

"Well that's not unusual. Most of their customers are married men and not a few of them are probably Junta lackeys."

"I hadn't thought of that, Junta I mean. Obviously it's common knowledge that most men that visit prostitutes are married."

"Sad isn't it?" Dimitris smoked a cigarette.

"It's sad that marriage doesn't seem to be enough but some of the women just see it as another kind of job. They don't have any shame."

"And why should they? If there's any shame then the men have to take their share of it too."

Dina stirred her coffee. "I agree but it's also about difference between generations. Our generation wouldn't have behaved like that. Marriage was something special."

"But Dina you were married for such a short time under such harsh circumstances. You can't compare it."

Dina nodded and lit a cigarette. She wasn't going to allow herself to think about Makis. "I wonder what's in the briefcase?"

"Something to do with his work no doubt. Probably plans for tapping more phones. Has it happened again?"

"No, not that I've heard but then our phone doesn't ring very often anyway and we make as few calls as we can, you know, the cost and everything." Dina looked down at her hands. "Dimitri, there's something else I wanted to ask you about. Last week, when I was cleaning one of my houses I found a photograph of my employer way back in 48'. He was addressing a small crowd of people outside the town hall."

Dimitris waited for more.

"He must have held some position to be talking to them like that and I could see part of a placard in the audience and it could have been YVE. I'm not sure. I couldn't see all of it."

Dimitris raised his furry eyebrows and nodded. "Well, you know as well as I do that they were active here. Were there many of them in the photo?"

"Maybe a hundred or so. I couldn't tell but some of them looked like they were clapping."

"So they were clapping his speech. Is that so surprising?"

"Dimitri, if I confide in you, you won't say anything." She didn't know why she was asking the question. He was the one person, outside her family, who she trusted. "I suppose he could have been a member of YVE. That worries me and..." She hesitated. "To tell you the truth, disappoints me. I never thought he would have been with them."

"What do you have to worry about Dina? Why do you care what this employer of yours was? YVE, EDES, the whole lot of them were natural homes for rich collaborators like he probably was. Is there something special about this man?"

"Not exactly special but he's always been the best employer, kind, generous. He pays me much more than the others and he sort of..." Dina was searching for the word, "respects me."

Dimitris looked irritated. He shifted his arm slightly away from where it had been resting on Dina's shoulder. "Ah! Now I see. You have a little soft spot for this dirty collaborator."

"Well, put yourself in my position, Dimitri. Cleaners don't get treated with respect very often."

Dimitris called the waiter and ordered some wine. "Yes of course I understand you. Does he have a weakness for you?"

Dina blushed. She wanted to tell him. "Yes and more than that. He asked me to marry him back in the spring. He's a widower, gets lonely, ghastly sister. I refused of course. Well, I don't love him and anyway the poor man is dying. His heart. He's got heart disease."

Dimitris let out a sigh. "You never said anything about all this. Do you think you would have accepted if he wasn't dying?" His tone had become more inquisitive.

"No, but he knows I was an *andarte*. I've told him a lot but he's never told me exactly what he did and now I've seen the photo I can't help wondering if it was him that put his sister up to the surveillance."

The music had been turned up in the café. Dina recognised it as a group calling themselves Led Zeppelin. She only knew because Rena loved it and stopped everything when it came on the radio. Dimitris had to raise his voice. "Christ! What a row. I'm close to agreeing with our late dictators to ban noise like that."

Dina laughed. "Yes I know what you mean but Rena likes it and so do a lot of our young people. Have you seen the length of their hair?"

"No and I'm not interested. Now, as I said it was Alekos Vouyoukas who was responsible for putting you under surveillance."

"That's his brother in law."

"So, yes. He could have been in on it with them but it sounds more like he was too taken with you to do that. But you know what they say, once a collaborator…"

The music drove them onto the street.

Dina listened to the sounds of the night. They were far more beautiful than the café music. Even a dog howling on the hill above the *plateia* was better than that noise. Laughter was coming from the balcony of the apartment above the café. The mad buzzing of the cicadas added weight to the heat. She looked up at the massive expanse of black, starry sky, feeling very small in comparison. The only movement came from moths flitting across the moonlight. Dina disagreed with Dimitris. "So you don't believe people can change? Can't you be a good person but just choose the wrong side?"

"Of course not Dina. Being on the right side is what makes that person a good person." Dimitris offered Dina a cigarette.

"I'm not sure Dimitri. So, people make mistakes in their past that they can never be forgiven for. Is that what you're saying?"

"You can't divorce the person from the deed." Dimitris was adamant. "If you believe this employer to be decent, honest, then ask him. Ask him outright. Then you'll know."

Dimitris hadn't convinced her. She thought of herself as a wise old woman now and she didn't have to accept everything he said, as she had done when she was young.

CHAPTER THIRTEEN

"Penelope loved the colour red but of course we had to wear our andartiko clothes, camouflaged for the mountains. When they executed her she took out her red kerchief from her pocket and held it out proudly."

"She said you'd be here."

Dina paused, her duster suspended in mid air. She was looking down at a young woman. The stranger was looking up to the balcony where Dina stood.

Dina frowned and leaned forward, her hands resting on the top rail. "And who is she?"

The woman put her hand to her forehead to shade her eyes from the sun. "Your daughter. She said I'd find you here. What a beautiful house this is."

Dina continued to peer down. She wasn't inclined to have a conversation about Mr B's house with someone she had never seen before. Although her Greek was impressive Dina could detect an accent. Was she German maybe? She had light brown hair with fair streaks. Could be German. Why would she want to speak to a German? Or perhaps, on second thoughts, she could be English.

The two women remained looking at each other for a few more seconds.

"I'm English. I was given your name by an old comrade of yours in Athens. That's where I've come from. Eleni Koutsouvelis, she's a friend of a relative of mine. Your daughter said you'd be working here now. I'm doing some research about women like yourself who fought in the civil war."

"My daughter can have a loose tongue sometimes."

Dina watched the confusion spread across the woman's face. *She's understood all right but she didn't expect my reaction. Why didn't Rena think before she spoke?*

'I'm sorry. Have I arrived at a bad time Kiria Konstantinou?"

Dina puffed up her narrow chest so that the floral pattern on her housecoat appeared to be a growing garden. "It's nothing to do with the time. I'm at work anyway so whatever it is you want you won't be getting it while I'm at work. I'm paid to work till two so work is what I do. Not talk. Not gossip. Work." There! She had said all she intended to. But the woman below didn't seem to be moving. Rather, she was putting down her bag.

It looks heavy. I wonder what's in there.

"I understand Kiria. It's just…would you be willing to give me a little of your time. I'd love to know about your experiences in the *Emfilio*? I could come to see you at your house at any time you say?"

Dina shivered. She didn't trust this foreign creature standing below her. *This woman who should have been doing her own job of work, minding her business in her own country. Why did she want to come meddling in her affairs?*

"Why d'you want to meddle in my affairs for God's sake?"

The woman hesitated before answering. "Because, from what I have read in books and from what some of your old comrades have told me, your story is one that people should know about and something you must be proud of. I don't think many people know about what you did in the war."

Dina listened. "That may be the case but I'm not digging all that up again. It's too painful. Go and find other women. I'm not giving any interviews. Now, if you don't mind I have a house to clean." She turned away from the balcony.

"But please, just think about it some more. I beg you. I understand it's painful but if we don't record your experiences they will be lost forever. At least let me come to your house after you've given it some thought."

Dina turned back, thrusting her hands deep into her pockets. She would be stubborn. "You can come to my house any time you like dear but you'll get the same answer."

She gave the cushions an unnecessary brutal plumping.

When Dina peered over the balcony ten minutes later the woman had gone. She felt a little disappointed not to see her still standing there.

I let her go. Well, it looks better if I refuse. I shouldn't appear too eager to blab about things. Anyway, I don't even know what she's going to do with that sort of information.

But then Dina's second voice took over and started its own conversation with her first. You feel quite flattered by the woman's request, don't you?

I suppose I do, if I'm honest.

Go on, be honest. Why not be honest?

Because, being honest has made my life hard. Harder than it would have been if I'd lied. Honesty hasn't made me rich.

No but you can respect yourself.

Is that supposed to comfort me?

Maybe. It's not necessarily about comfort though is it?

Maybe not. I don't know. All I know is that my past won't leave me alone. It trails behind me wherever I go like a child's blanket and now, just when I thought things were beginning to get a bit easier, along she comes with her pleases and thankyous.

Ach! You're being too hard on the girl. She's got some courage turning up like that and she's been very polite.

Too polite. She'd never have survived a war that one. You can tell she's never known hardship.

Bah! Are you going to blame her for that as well?

Why not?

Because you've seen where blame gets the world.

Dina sunk onto the kitchen chair and rested her head on her arms. Her right elbow knocked her lighter off the table. It skidded across the tiles before coming to rest beside her shoe.

There, said her first voice. Now you're going to smoke a cigarette aren't you? If that hadn't happened you wouldn't have thought of it now.

Maybe not now but the ebbs and flows of our lives depend on such small coincidences. She was already lighting the end before she realised her action. The nicotine helped clear her head to think. She thought. She still didn't see the point in reliving the past by telling the girl all those stories; all that dying and pain.

But was it all pain?

You know it wasn't.

Why not give the girl some of the good times; some of the joy and laughter you shared with your comrades? Are you ashamed?

No, of course not. That's one thing I'm not.

Well then, go on. What have you got to lose?

A job, maybe problems for my family if the secret gets out.

And do you think you're the only one with secrets?

No but I don't trust this government and its spies. They may call it a democracy but behind the scenes they're keeping watch on people like me because we'll be the first to be picked out when the trouble starts.

Trouble? What trouble is that Dina?

Well, you know. When we don't get paid or when they lay workers off and we don't have enough to eat. Then, what are people supposed to do about that? Just sit at home and hope it'll go away and meanwhile not even afford a piece of meat. They'll always be able to lay the blame on those of us who've got a reputation won't they?

And did this kind of fear stop you in the past?

No.

Then why now?

She scratched the cigarette stub round the ashtray. Her head hadn't cleared at all. It ached with doubts.

The doorbell rang. It was laundry day. Dina went to the door and was dwarfed by the plastic bundles of sheets that she dropped into the arms of the waiting delivery man. In return he handed over packs of laundered clothes and starched whitesheets.

The man smiled. "Ours is a fair exchange."

Dina noticed the gaps where teeth had once stood. "Indeed, Kirios Mazos. If only the rest of life could be so simple and fair." She dug in her pocket and produced the notes in payment. "Thank-you. Good day. See you next week."

Kirios Maza nodded. "Thank-you Dina. Next week."

Dina carried the laundry into Mr B's bedroom. She broke the plastic, lifted the pile of pressed sheets like a baby and placed them neatly down into the big trunk that stood at the foot of Mr B's bed. Two little pockets of lavender finished the job. She looked at the bedside clock and realised she was running late. It was that girl's fault, keeping her talking and confusing her. The baker's shelves would be empty.

Dina squatted and the oven came level with her face. It smelt of stale, burnt pork. She went onto her knees and scrubbed the inside with the repetitive rhythm that she reserved for her most hated household jobs.

"Last loaf, seeded batch." Manos indicated the lonely loaf with his eyes. Dina took it from the shelf even though she didn't like the way the seeds always lodged themselves between her teeth and Evy spat them out when nobody was looking.

The baker whistled as he pounded and moulded two dough balls that surrendered themselves to his big sprawling hands.

"What can I do eh Manos? There's always something to delay me. And is this really the only loaf left?"

"Yes, that's it. So who was it holding you up today Dina? Old Mazos? You know why he's always late don't you?" The baker winked. "Makes a little unscheduled stop. Over the road at Kiria Tsokas."

"I'm not interested in your gossip Manos. I'm in a hurry. Good day." She took her loaf and left the shop. Everything irritated her today.

Rena had made a pot of beans. Dina could smell it as she unlocked the door. Evy abandoned her dolls in favour of greeting her grandmother. She held up her arms to Dina, opening and closing her little fists in anticipation.

Dina put down her basket and scooped Evy up, whirling her round so that her little curly head drooped back and she giggled uncontrollably in the way of all small children. Dina buried her nose in Evy's hair, taking a deep breath. "Ah mama's been washing your hair in that nice smelly shampoo hasn't she?"

Evy touched her curls. "Yes and we're having *fasolada* and feta and mama said you would bring the bread cos we don't have any left from yesterday and *baba* didn't leave us any change to get any."

Dina threw a glance at her daughter. "Still no work then?"

Rena turned down the radio. The usual government propaganda. New finance legislation would provide a generous security package for all hard working Greeks.

"No. He went again to the site but they took on only two this morning and they decided it was fairer if they took the two who hadn't had any work yesterday. It doesn't matter how good they are at bricklaying." Rena let out a sharp rattle like cough and went into the bathroom. Dina watched her daughter and thought about the dubious logic of what she had said. She removed her headscarf and hung it on the door before taking control of the soup, testing its flavourings and consistency.

"It's fine mama. Don't meddle. I'm old enough to know how to make *fasolada*!"

Dina put aside the wooden spoon and sat down. Evy dragged the stool towards Dina and gently placed her grandmother's foot on it. She pulled off Dina's shoe and patted the foot that remained.

Dina smiled and rested her head against the chair. "Ach, you're an angel my love. That was just what *yiayia* needed."

Evy perched herself on the arm of the chair and giggled. "That stops *yiayia* from meddin mama."

Dina and Rena laughed at Evy's mispronunciation. "What a sharp little angel you are though eh?" Dina tickled Evy's toes.

"Sharp! That doesn't even come near what she came out with today. When that English woman came round earlier she asked her if she was from the German police and said we hadn't done anything wrong and to leave." Rena came to join her mother.

Dina frowned. She had pushed the issue of the researcher to the back of her mind. Not forgotten it. Just put it away until she could think about it clearly. But now Rena had brought it up she was forced to think what it meant again. Her mind was resisting being hurled back to that time of her life. The woman may well be nice. That didn't matter. What she wanted to know would wipe the smile from her face and then she wouldn't look so nice. If she decided to tell her.

"Did she find you then mama?"

"Yes she found me. What gives you the right to go telling a stranger where to find me and giving her hope like that?" Dina stamped the floor with her good foot – the foot that was still shoed. She watched her daughter's reaction.

"Ach mama! She was innocent enough for God's sake! She's an English academic who loves us enough to learn our language. I call that pretty impressive so why not give her an interview? She wants to publish your story, what you gave your lives for will never be known about to most of the world if someone doesn't do this. Are you ashamed?"

Dina's propped up foot had heard enough and it swung involuntarily off the stool to join the other so that they both stamped in unison. "Of course I'm not ashamed! How could you even suggest that?'

"Just to get you thinking about it seriously. What did you tell her?"

"I told her that she could come by my house any time she liked but I didn't say I'd give her an interview." Dina pushed herself out of the chair and paced the floor.

That evening the researcher came back.

Here's one that doesn't give up easily thought Dina. Maybe she had misjudged her. She was surprised that she had returned. She'd hardly been welcoming on her first visit. She still kept her at the door before admitting her.

It was Rena who showed her a seat. "Can I get you a coffee?"

"Oh yes, thank-you. *Metrio.*" She put her bag down beside her and crossed her hands. Dina saw how nervous she was and she softened towards the woman. She sat opposite the researcher and studied her face. "I'm Dina and you are?"

"Anne. I'm doing a doctorate at the University of London."

"A doctorate? Does that mean you are interested in the medical side of my war experiences?"

"No it doesn't mean that but yes I'm interested in all your war experiences. A doctorate is just the level of the study."

Rena stuck her head round the door. "*Didaktoriko* mama. That's what I would have done if we'd stayed in Skopje."

Dina nodded her head. "Ah I see. So, Anne, how long will all this take?"

"You mean my doctorate?"

"No, I meant how long will the interview take but I'm also interested in how long your studies will take you. You never know, our Rena might still be able to study one day."

"I have a set of questions but we don't have to stick to them exactly. They're just a guide really. In the end I have to come up with a hypothesis and produce original research for it to have any hope of succeeding as a doctorate."

Dina felt herself becoming more involved the more she heard about the researcher's interest. "And do you have any ideas for that at the moment?"

"Yes I have one main idea and I'd like to see what you think of it Dina."

Dina smiled. She felt flattered that her opinion on such an academic matter was being sought. "Okay, tell me."

Dina noticed the way Anne looked nervous before she started.

"I'd like to find out how equal women and men were in the D.A. during the period of the *Emfilio* "

"A couple of hours will never be enough for me to tell you about that I'm afraid but I'll tell you what I can in the time we've got." She looked towards her daughter. "Rena, can I spare two hours from everything I have to do tonight?"

Rena smiled. "One *metrio*" She placed the tiny cup and saucer on a round wooden table next to the researcher. "And you have no need to do anything else tonight mama."

Dina was beaten. She had run out of reasons to oppose what the researcher was doing and in any case she was fed up with fighting her own thoughts. Those damned arguments that kept happening in her head, just ignoring her as if they had a life of their own.

"My father was on the workers council. He wasn't just a worker. He and my uncle taught me to read serious books so I understood what was happening in our villages and in the rest of Europe at that time. You see just because we were villagers it doesn't mean we were uneducated. Some villages, yes, they were illiterate, most of them, but not ours. So when we were occupied we were ready. Then we formed EPON."

"EPON?"

"National Panhellenic Youth Organisation. We fought against the occupiers"

"The Germans."

Dina sipped her coffee. "The Germans and also the Italians. They were nicer but still our enemy. You know sometimes a nicer enemy is worse. You begin to trust them because they're more like you. The Italians of course are more like us Greeks but they did unforgivable things as well. That's how I joined EPON. And you know that EPON was the youth wing of EAM. That means Greek National Liberation Front."

The researcher checked her tape recorder and made a note on her pad.

"EPON was a broad organisation that had about sixty thousand young people. We had so many victims who were executed, beaten, tortured and in EPON there was no difference between boys and girls. We had equal obligations and we were all tortured, the girls probably worse than the boys. They raped them, cut their hair – things that they couldn't do to men." Dina put her head back against the chair and sighed.

I was the eldest daughter and I had two younger sisters and two brothers, all dead now. In 1947 they executed my father so I made the decision to leave our house and fight.

About me, how I found myself in the Democratic Army? I wouldn't have imagined it but the situation drove me there. Either we should have surrendered, in which case as EPON cadres they would have imprisoned us or they would have executed us. I ran to the mountains. That was the beginning of the *Emfilio*. I joined the Democratic Army. My mother and sister's lives were spared then but not their honour. My mother survived all that only to see all her other children die at the hands of their own countrymen. Imagine that if you can."

The phone rang, interrupting Dina's thoughts. She looked at the tape recorder that was still spinning and whirring. "You haven't asked me many questions."

"No Dina. It hasn't been necessary. Your story doesn't need questions."

Dina liked the researcher's reply. "So do you find my story interesting? Will it be of any interest to anyone now? It was all so long ago."

Rena was speaking on the phone. Then Evy began crying.

Dina pushed herself up out of the chair. "Excuse me dear but my granddaughter needs something. Please use the bathroom if you need to. It's the door on the right there."

Rena was having a heated argument on the phone and ended it by slamming down the receiver. "Sorry". She apologised as she disappeared to her crying daughter.

"In the D.A. we had women soldiers who were officers, lieutenants. I was a lieutenant. Women soldiers who commanded platoons; women who fought at the front line and they didn't fight any worse than the men. We had all the respect that men had; all their consideration. They never behaved in a way to devalue us, nor exploit us as women. No man could put a hand on any woman because they knew they would be punished. But it was also the psychology of the *andarte*s." Dina paused. She remained on her feet "Don't mind me standing dear. If I sit too long my hip starts complaining."

"It sounds like the men and the women had a kind of mutual respect for one another."

Dina nodded. "Yes. That's true. I can admit this to you dear because you're an outsider. No offence but it's something I could never say to my family. I feel like I need to get it off my chest." Dina looked round and lowered her voice. "My family wouldn't understand but sometimes I think I preferred my life in the mountains. We were always looking out for one another. Nowadays everyone's out for themselves. Of course, we're all individuals but there doesn't seem to be much goodwill. People aren't so generous even though, now, we have so many luxuries compared to then. Do I sound mad to you?"

"Nothing you've said sounds mad Dina. I can see why you wouldn't want to say it to your family though."

Dina continued. "Our struggle was very difficult. We waited for whole weeks. We were confronted with hunger, battles, thirst. It was my luck to be in battles where we couldn't find water and it was August. The sun was burning and there was not one tree. Our lips had split. For the first time I knew what thirst really meant. And all this without complaining."

"Was it all bad?"

"When you ask a question you ask a good one. I like that! It's a welcome one my dear. Of course we had some happy times when we laughed a lot. I spent some months working with the children who'd been evacuated from their towns and villages. We taught them to light campfires and cook. We sang songs together because sometimes they cried a lot for their families. The girls were the most difficult because we had to cut their hair short to get rid of the lice. In one camp, I forget the name now, we had a small calf. It was so sweet, like a toy for them to play with. Those children were angels. They cheered us up. Duties with the children were the best! Endless summer days with the dazzling heat when we kept the children in the shade. In our camp we had a couple of old tambourines and the goatherd had donated some of his bells so the children could make music. Some of them weren't too keen on goatmilk but they had no choice and we had to make them drink it. Then if we were in an area lower down in one of the valleys we sometimes managed to get them cow's milk. Have you ever tried milking a cow?"

"No. Never."

"It's not easy. The older ones tried but even their fingers were too skinny to get the pressure you need." Dina had tears in her eyes. She shook her head from side to side. "I often wonder what happened to some of those little angels."

The phone rang again. This time Dina had to answer it. She lifted the receiver impatiently and barked at it. "Yes. What is it?" A pause. "Can you speak up? I can't hear you very well." A second pause. "No. We haven't noticed any problem with the line. Uhm. Very well. Yes but not tomorrow. There won't be anyone here then. Yes. Tuesday morning. Fine. Thank-you." She returned to her chair. "Now where was I?"

The researcher had restarted the tape. "You had been ill…"

"I sheltered in Vitsi and Grammos during the *Emfilio*. The villagers helped us of course. The people were with us and that cost them a lot because whoever they caught helping us they executed them, they tortured them, they suffered a lot of persecution. Also, if one's relatives had sheltered or helped *andarte*s they wouldn't give them work. My sister was blacklisted. The same for me. I had a very good name but when someone offered us work and then the police came, they told them to get rid of us or they would have trouble. I wanted to be a teacher, you know, with the little ones. I always loved children but the war has hardened me and now, I can give my love to our little Evy but that's enough. I don't have the patience anymore. Then they tried to force us to become beggars or worse so that they could say to people 'look at these girls who went with the *andarte*s!' "

"What do you mean when you say 'worse'?"

Dina thought the girl might like a glass of beer as she was English. She was glad she wasn't German but both nationalities drank beer anyway. Dina wanted a smoke. "I'll explain but let's go out to do that."

They walked round the corner to Dina's local *taverna*.

"Evening Spiro. How are you?"

"Eh, Dina how are you? Come and sit down. I haven't seen you in here for some time. What have we done to you?"

"Time is what I don't have much of Spiro."

The bartender looked long at the researcher. "And who is this lovely lady?"

Dina put her cigarettes and lighter on the table. "This is Anne. She's a researcher come to hear all about the things I did when I was young." She winked at Spiros.

He smiled and extended his hand. "Of course. How do you do. What can I get you to drink?"

The researcher chose beer. Dina ordered her usual. She lit a cigarette and pushed the smoke up and away.

An iron pipe running across the ceiling from the stove was jointed and secured with tape in several places before it exited through a hole in the window. Faded posters were stuck to the bar informing customers of meetings and concerts long since past. Some old and some ancient men were playing *tavli* at a large corner table by the window. The men were silent but the chips screamed as they were slammed down onto the board.

Dina nodded to one of the men and waved hello to another. They were the only women in the bar. A cantata was playing from two speakers perched high up on the wall. A sombrero hung lonely on its peg, the ribbon, once red, now washed out pink, a donation from a passing tourist.

Dina waited for Spiros to bring their drinks before she resumed. The researcher started the tape.

"Now where were we?"

"I was asking you what you meant by worse?"

"I meant they were rounded up and taken to the nearest port and put into prostitution. Shocked? Yes I know. I don't like remembering those things. If I hadn't enlisted I could very easily have ended up like that." Dina watched the researcher's reaction.

The two women sat in the *taverna* until late, talking long after the tape had stopped. Dina was full of questions. What would happen with all this information? Where would it end up? Would it become a real book? Would it take a long time?

The researcher didn't know the answers to Dina's questions. "It depends if they like it or not."

"Like it? What is there to like? It's the truth. You don't have to like the truth. I hate it most of the time."

The researcher drank from her beer. "It's the way these things are done. They often say it's just one person's point of view of what happened."

"Well, it is one person's point of view. Mine! Isn't that good enough?"

"I think it's more than good enough Dina but I'm not the one who'll reject of accept the work once it's finished."

Dina flopped back against the little wooden chair. It creaked in sympathy. "So all this could be for nothing? All this work you're doing?"

"It's never going to be for nothing. What I've learned from you and the other women I've met is priceless. That experience alone is worth more than any book. Dina, you have my word that I'll do everything I can to get your stories told. But I'll be back before then. Can I come back and see you again. I'm not sure when it will be. It could be a long time."

"Of course you can. Don't leave it too long or you may find me in the cemetery. And next time you'll get a better welcome. I hope your hard work comes to something especially since I wasn't easy on you at first. Here, give me a piece of paper and pen." Dina bent over to write. When she had finished she thrust the paper towards the researcher. "Here. Take this. Can you read my wrting? I've got terrible handwriting. Tell Maria I sent you. It will be worth your journey to meet her but you'll have to go to Florina."

CHAPTER FOURTEEN

"We knew there were German collaborators in YVE and some were well known. They recruited army officers and called themselves patriotic – as if we didn't also love our country"

Dina stepped out into her street at eight in the morning; an early autumn wind blew across the Northern lakeshore, fanning the falling leaves into spirals along the promenade. Fancy that. She was thinking about the researcher's visit and the idea that what she and other women had been through could, one day, be written into a book. She would hardly be famous. No. That wasn't the word. But somehow the visit had lightened her heart, as if she was being relieved of a heavy load. She wondered what Maria looked like now. She hadn't seen her old comrade for twenty-five years. She hoped she would give Anne an easier time than she had. Maybe she would take a trip to Florina one day. It wasn't so far.

Wrapping her threadbare black coat round herself, Dina decided that this would be its last winter and if this one was as cold as the last she might even have to dispense with it sooner. Away with this black; it wasn't as if she was obliged to wear it. She'd had that dubious pleasure more than enough for one lifetime. Maybe she could replace it with a nice new suede one or even – no! How would she ever afford a fur? Absurd to even think about it.

Dina stopped at the kiosk to buy cigarettes. Her resolution to give up the day after the celebration had lasted a day. She was already buying her fifth packet. Plenty of reasons to give up. The cost of course. Her health. But most important of all, Rena who was ill enough already without having to worry about her mother's stupidities. Dina reproached herself. Something she always seemed to be doing lately. She carried her guilt until she was way past her bus stop and her bus was ploughing on ahead of her. No matter. She needed the walk to clear her head and she could probably do with the exercise.

Dina walked fast. She began to warm up, enjoying the change of routine and noticing details that she missed when she sat on a moving bus. Kalaitzidis had closed up, the old shoemaker's window now plastered with Rigas Ferraios posters. She'd never realised how 11th November Street was changing. A new dressmaker, Kaliope, had opened up next to the dry cleaners. Useful, Dina pondered. She can sew the dresses then pass them onto Diamante's for pressing. Maybe they're in business together. Diamante! With that name they should be in the jewellery business not steam cleaning. The sickly sweet fumes from the cleaning chemicals seeped out from the open shop. It mingled with the sharp disinfectant that Kaliope had recently swilled out over the pavement and was now trickling its way down the drain at the kerbside.

By chance, Dina found herself in Metropoleus street staring into the window of Lakounis furs. Her eyes rested on the centre manikin draped in a mink coat. She pictured herself in the coat doing her same walk to Mr B's, though, of course, that wouldn't be for much longer. Sadness welled up inside her. Well, anyway, she wouldn't wear it to work would she? Then again if she didn't wear it to work when would she? It wasn't as if she went out much. Ah! This must be Kirios Lakounis, all hungry for business, hoping he's made a catch with me. The man's stomach sagged sadly over his suit trousers. Business must be good, Dina thought.

"Isn't it beautiful?" She heard him say. He had followed her eyes and spotted their desire. "And if I may say so, how much better it would look adorning your slim physique Kiria."

Dina was tempted to say, 'you flatter me' but the words that came out were very different. "How much are you asking for it? There's no price tag."

Mr Lakounis hesitated and beckoned Dina into his shop. "Would you try it on Kiria, before we discuss price?"

Dina was already late for work but she followed the owner into his shop like a child smelling the promise of sweets. He relieved the manikin of the fur and held it out for Dina who threaded her arms into the sleeves and instantly felt her body melt under the weight of its warm caress.

Mr Lakounis studied its shape and pinched its seams in several places. "As I thought, just a few alterations here." He side -stepped around Dina. "And here. It will be…" Now standing in front of Dina. "It will be perfect for you."

Dina looked into the mirror and saw a different person. She turned up the wide, rounded collar and the coat swallowed her. Laughing at the image of herself thrown back by the mirror. Here she stood,

I'm like a puffed up peacock.

"I can see you like the feel of it Kiria."

Dina began sliding the coat from her shoulders. "Oh yes. I like it all right. I like myself in it but I'm late already. I must go. I don't know what I was thinking even letting you put it on me."

"But Kiria, we haven't discussed price yet!" The man was looking anxious.

Regretfully, Dina replaced the fur with her black coat. "Look at me! Do I really look like the kind of lady who could afford that?"

He cradled the mink in his arms like a curled up cat.

"Your customers don't come from my side of the town, do they?"

He opened his mouth to reply but Dina had already opened the door and was stepping out onto the pavement. "Just out of curiosity though…"

Dina smiled. More than two year's wages!

Arriving late at Mr B's Dina felt doubly guilty because she had indulged herself in a momentary pleasure. What if Mr B had been calling for her? What if? She wondered why she could fall so totally in love with the fur when she couldn't fall in love with Mr B.

"Mr B was asking for you Kiria Konstantinou." The voice of the live-in nurse, calm but curt, invaded Dina's world.

"Straight away." Dina pulled on her housecoat and still buttoning up, walked respectfully into Mr B's bedroom. There he lay, a strangely shrunken shape almost buried under a huge eiderdown so that only his grey head stuck out against the pillow. Dina saw a smile light up his face when she neared the bed.

"Ah! I know those footsteps like I know my favourite cognac and I've missed them both as much." Mr B tried to manoeuvre his way higher on the pillow but the struggle was too much for him and he sank back down.

Dina smiled. "Good morning Pano and welcome home. We've missed you too." Drawing up a chair Dina rested her hand on Mr B's forehead. It felt hot. She studied his face. It was sallow, gaunt. His once twinkling eyes were dull, no lustre to them. They had reflected more life after a hard night's drinking than they did now. These were bloodshot and this hangover was terminal. Dina was so shocked by the change in Mr B that she couldn't speak. Tears were threatening.

"Well I'm pretty much finished Dina, my little bird. Will you miss me? Will you take on another house and make it shine the way you've done with mine?"

Her tears won, dampening a patch of blood red camellias embroidered on the eiderdown. She rummaged in her pocket for a tissue. What was this premature grief? Was she really only crying for Mr B?

"Come Dina. It's my turn. You're no stranger to sorrow and loss, we both know that."

Blowing her nose Dina composed herself while the nurse placed the oxygen mask over Mr B's face and felt his pulse. "Don't excite him please Kiria Konstantinou. You've set his pulse racing and he really can't take these sudden changes in his state."

Dina respected the nurse but she respected her own needs more at this moment.

Dimitris's words echoed back to her. Ask him outright.

Okay, she would but first she had to water the balcony plants and have a cigarette to calm her nerves. It was no good pretending otherwise. She was afraid of what she might hear; what she didn't want to hear from him. She wanted to believe he was totally innocent and there was some other explanation of the photo. The photo. She crossed into Mr B's study, retrieved it from the drawer and slipped it into the pocket of her housecoat.

"Pano, I need to water the plants and see to a few things, then I'll come and sit with you when you've rested." Dina checked Mr B from the doorway. He had already fallen back on his pillows exhausted.

Dina opened the back door and began hosing the rubber plant and the winter jasmine climbing halfway up the wall, its tiny yellow flowers just pushing through. She lit her cigarette on the balcony that had served her well over the years, offering cool respite from her work. She had walked many times round to the front of the house and gazed at the lake as it changed its colours with the seasons. Today it was cornflower blue, rippling in the wind, framing the empty wooden boats moored together at the quayside. Brittle orange leaves fell from their branches into clusters, whipped by the fresh wind up against the tree trunks and legs of the abandoned lakeside benches. Dina squinted and spotted a grey squirrel hopping its way along one of the denuded branches. Every so often it would stop, its tail vertical. She wondered if this was perhaps for safety, to secure a better vantage point just as she had done as a soldier when preparing for ambush. But the squirrel then camouflaged itself somewhere behind the remaining foliage.

Gathering resolution Dina sat down next to Mr B's bed. She watched the deep cleated lines stretch themselves as his eyes opened into a smile. Without giving herself time to reconsider, Dina pulled the photo from her pocket and held it up to Mr B. His smile faded. She could see he was confused. He beckoned her to pass him his glasses from the side table and she helped him sit up against his pillows. The photo trembled in Mr B's hand. He peered closely at himself and the crowd before letting it go in hopeless surrender. It lay on the white sheet. Silent evidence of his past.

"Tell me then, Pano"

Mr B removed his reading glasses and laid them on top of the photo. Dina noticed how his hands shook and how the shock of discovery showed on his face.

"Where did you find it? I didn't know there were any left." His breaths were irregular. His cough cut into the silence between them.

Offering the glass of water up to his lips, Dina did not let her eyes stray from his. "In the drawer of your bureau, in your study. Vassiliki asked me to put some invoices back there and I saw it." Dina thought she detected a faint smile on Mr B's lips. His eyes fluttered then closed momentarily. She felt as if there was a battle going on inside her head. Her compassionate self wanted to reach out to him in his shock and discomfort but even stronger, from somewhere, she found her self-interest taking control. A terrible hollow gasping followed his cough and Dina moved towards Mr B placing the oxygen mask over his nose and mouth. She realised that if she wanted to learn the truth she would have to be patient with Mr B so she waited until his breaths became regular again and she could remove the mask. The gentle click, click of the nurse's knitting needles came from the lounge. The sombre bell toll of Agios Yiannis was heralding another funeral. Dina's eyes rested again on Mr B as he began his story.

"Dina, I come from a proud royalist tradition, drummed into me by my father. It was him who forced me to take responsibility for our family business," he sighed and took breath, "Vassiliki would have been so much better at it. She loved that work but he wouldn't hear of his daughter running the business. She's always blamed me for that. He became ill and took to his bed. As the eldest son I had to prove my worth to him." He gasped for air, clearing his throat. "By protecting my mother and brother and sister. It's a heavy burden on a young man, to invest him with so much responsibility at an age when he should be enjoying life." A rattling sound came from Mr B's throat. Dina put the glass to his lips. He lay back against the pillows and swallowed. "But that's what war does. It robs us of our youth." He wheezed before coughing again.

"And it deprives sisters of their sisters doesn't it Pano?"

"I was elected mayor in 48' and the people who elected me knew I stood on a Y.V.E. platform. I wasn't ashamed of defending our beautiful town from the Left." His eyes searched Dina's momentarily. She shook her head in silence. "When I was mayor I oversaw the safe evacuation of children to Thessaloniki and Ioannina so the D.A. couldn't recruit them into their ranks." He took hold of the glass Dina offered him, spilling some water as he raised it to his lips.

Dina stared at Mr B. "I didn't want to believe that you were part of our defeat. Lie still a little. Don't speak just yet. I don't like the whiteness of your cheeks." He rested.

Click, click continued the needles. Dina got up from the bed and went into the kitchen. As she did so the needles stopped and the nurse's flat soled shoes shuffled into Mr B's room. Good, thought Dina, she can see to him better than me. She heard her cajoling Mr B for exerting himself again but she didn't feel any guilt, only determination to coax him through his story. She stirred her coffee and rinsed the spoon under the tap, feeling like a change had come about her. She cared about one thing at the moment and that was to make sure Mr B lived long enough to tell her everything. How had she become so ruthless? She didn't like herself very much.

"Dina, I'm not proud of what we did to *andartes* like you. We did it because it was the only way. We rooted out families like yours."

"Like mine!"

A nod from Mr B. "You would always harbour one another and yes I…I did execute *andartes* in front of the town hall."

Dina took a deep breath. The nurse had moved Mr B onto his side. Dina thought he resembled a whimpering dog at that moment. His eyes pleaded forgiveness. "Some of them tried to run, but never the women, so that when the bullets hit them they fell into the lake and next morning…" Dina watched as Mr B's whole chest heaved as if it would burst. "Next morning the whole town could see for themselves that our words hadn't been hollow" Another bout of coughing racked the bedstead. Dina sat frozen.

Mr B grasped her hand. "You and I, we both know that to win a war you have to convince the undecided." She slid her hand away from under his. "More water, please Dina."

She hesitated. "Would you have granted them water if they'd been gasping like you? No! I don't need you to answer. I know you wouldn't. You didn't." Mr B was a dying man and as he sipped at the water, Dina realised how easy it would be to take advantage of his vulnerability. Wasn't she doing that anyway?

"The photo was in the local paper. They said it was the first time a public official had lived up to his promises. Dina, this was more praise than my father had given me in his whole lifetime and I just lost my head in my need for that respect."

He was gasping for breath but all Dina could think of was him enjoying himself murdering her comrades and as she pictured the scene at the lake's edge she felt her fury grow and explode. "You showed no mercy, you bastards. You didn't even give them the choice of prison! Who gave you the right to execute innocent villagers because of their beliefs? If I'd been there I would have killed you with my own hands." She was shaking. She could do it now. Why not have her revenge for her family and lost comrades. What did she have to lose? Her hands jerked in an involuntary movement. She saw the fear in his eyes. Had he read her thoughts? But she wanted more from him.

Dina's voice peaked with rage, bringing the nurse scurrying into the room while Mr B tried to find breath. She cast an accusing glance at Dina. "Please Kiria Constantinou, you know his condition. Show a little respect to a dying man, for pity's sake. Go and calm yourself down!"

Dina left, not trusting what she might do if she remained. She went out to the balcony and with fumbling hands she lit up her cigarette, igniting her anger in the process. So her suspicions had been right and Vassiliki's warning also true. She had come fairly close to marrying a collaborator without even knowing.

She felt impatient to get back to Mr B's bedside because she wanted to hear the rest. This wasn't the full story. She approached the nurse at his bedside, surprised at her own boldness.

The nurse collected some towels and made her way towards the bathroom. "He really needs to rest you know. Encouraging him to talk isn't helping him."

Dina walked along side her. "I understand that you have your job to do Kiria but I'm afraid I still need some answers and I'm prepared to wait till he's awake and more comfortable." Dina felt calmer in the company of another woman who spent her life caring for people like she did. Although unspoken there was a common understanding of the everyday that engendered mutual respect. She sat on the edge of the bath watching the nurse wash her hands and scrub her nails, methodically working the nailbrush around each fingertip.

"Your job must be hard especially at times like this."

"Times are always like this Kiria Constatinou. They only call me when it's terminal."

Terminal. The word had a brutality to it. Dina winced. There was something about the knowing of the fact. If you didn't know it was coming death would just happen. Dina thought that was a better option. Memories of torture flooded her mind. You knew what was coming the second time round. Much worse than the first. Too much knowledge could be painful. "Do they ever upset you? Your patients I mean."

"Oh yes, there have been a few times when I've allowed myself to get too close, drop my guard you know. All against our training of course."

Here was another woman who knew all about training. "What about this patient?"

"This one, well! He's a sweetie isn't he? He must have been a real looker when he was young."

Dina grinned. "Yes quite a catch as my daughter would say. But nurse, I wanted to ask you. How long has he got?"

The nurse turned off the tap and shook her hands in the sink before choosing a clean towel from the rail. "A month at the most."

CHAPTER FIFTEEN

"'Save our Children' they said on their posters. In the winter of 1947/48 they accused us of what they called Paedomazema – the collecting up of the children. They said we abducted them from their parents and in some cases that we raped them. They brought in the UN. But there were already thousands of our children in Communist countries over our borders and a lot of them were with their parents or they'd been born there."

Mr B was weakening fast. He could say no more than a few words before gasping for breath. Dina sat beside him, attentive but determined, firing questions as she had once fired bullets at the enemy.

"Did you have a hand sending in spies into Albania?"

"Yes." Mr B's head drooped, whether in shame or exhaustion, Dina didn't care.

"And what did they bring back to you from Vitsi?" Dina heard the door open and close, presumably the nurse returning from the shops.

"Vital information about Vafiades' band." The old wooden carriage clock on Mr B's dressing table struck the hour, causing Dina to glance over. Since embarking on her questioning she had become focused, single-minded and the chimes of the clock were an unwanted intrusion.

"That he was planning an attack on two fronts." The last two words faded out of Mr B's mouth and he closed his eyes.

Dina waited. The ticking clock reminded Dina that she should be cleaning by now but cleaning seemed trivial in comparison with this. "Are you asleep Pano? Shall we stop for a while?"

Mr B's eyelids flickered. "No. Just...what was I saying?"

"You were speaking about Vafiades."

"Ah, yes. His plan was to take both the Florina and Albanian roads."

"How much did you pay those traitors?"

Mr B snatched greedy breaths. "They weren't."

But Dina didn't let him finish. "Ah! No, maybe not in drachmes."

Mr B made no answer. Dina sighed, twisting her hands together. "How could you? Those scum!"

"Some people would say they saved our town."

Dina grimaced. "Like they say about Van Fleet. "Did you personally know Van Fleet?"

"I met his deputy." Mr B appeared to try to breathe through his nose but he couldn't take in enough oxygen. His mouth opened wide in panic, his chest rising and falling in fast spasms.

"Yes." She thought of Van Fleet's statue standing tall by the lake. The American reminder.

Mr B nodded, fear in his eyes.

Maybe he anticipates my next question, thought Dina. "Was it your responsibility as mayor, to ensure the town lights were extinguished for blackout?"

Mr B shuddered. "How?" Pause. "How do you know that?"

"Never mind how I know Pano. You failed in your responsibility didn't you? One of our shells hit the hospital killing two nurses because those lights were still on."

"And you blame me for their deaths?'

Dina swallowed. "One of those nurses was my little sister Lela."

Mr B wheezed, stunned by Dina's revelation.

"You know as well as I do they wouldn't be dead if those lights had been off. Even the Americans were asking why they were left on. Why Pano?" She saw his discomfort but she felt no compassion at that moment. She was unrelenting.

"Because we feared they would loot the place." Maybe Mr B sensed her anger; maybe he was afraid of her at this moment.

Dina watched as Mr B grimaced in pain as he tried to push himself higher up in the bed. Again she did not help him. "So you were willing to put your own nurses and soldiers there at risk because you feared a few hungry people would try their luck in Kastoria?" Emotional memories of her younger sister flooded Dina's thoughts. She sat looking at Mr B with tears in her eyes and a heavy heart. By what twist of fate had she been employed all these years by the man who was indirectly her sister's killer?

"Dina. I'm truly sorry for your sister's death. Yes, it was my responsibility. You have suffered so much loss but…" He indicated water to Dina.

It would be so easy to pay him back here and now. Why wait? He was dying anyway. In that moment their eyes met and Dina knew she couldn't do it. This wouldn't be in the name of any cause, greater than herself. It would be pure revenge, pointless, dark. It would haunt her for the rest of her life. No. There were already enough ghosts. Feeding him the water, Dina watched Mr B's moistening eyes. He took tiny sips, while she held the straw steady, Mr B's hands now too shaky to hold a glass. He pushed her hand away gently. "Enough."

A honey coloured morning light had entered the bedroom, followed by a strengthening autumn wind that had loosened one of the window shutters from its latch so that it banged and squeaked. Dina left the bedside, opened the balcony door and re-fastened the shutter to its wall latch. She noticed little patches where the green paint was flaking away from the slats. Below, in the narrow side street, the leaves scratched at the cobbles in a mad frenzy.

Mr B stirred. "It was for Greece. Whatever we did, we did it to defend our town and country from those communists next door."

Dina had heard this kind of pleading before and felt no more sympathy for it because it came from a dying man than she had when it was first used during the Resistance years. "But we were Greeks as well Pano. What do you think would have happened to Greece if it hadn't been for ELAS? So, you didn't want a communist led Greece but you didn't want a Nazi one either did you? Because without us that's what you would've got."

"I don't know what to say."

Dina brought the oxygen mask towards him and laid it gently over his nose and mouth. "There's nothing you can say. Your actions have said it all. It was a long time ago. She would have been forty-five now, probably a grandmother like me." Dina let out a deep, despairing sigh. "It's the waste of life though. So young. Just like Maki. Oh God! I don't want Evy to grow up in a world like ours was then – to be robbed like that, of those closest to you…but." Dina suddenly felt her self control crumbling and she cried openly and deeply. "Instead, what have I done? Her mother's not going to live to an old age. Evy will still be young when my daughter dies and let's face it the world isn't much better now than it was then."

Dina felt the hand of a dying man trying to console her in her sadness - a small gesture but one she would remember in time.

"You can't blame yourself for that Dina. Please." He paused for breath. "Your granddaughter will grow into a fine young woman and you'll be proud of her, as she will be of you." He flopped back, exhausted.

Dina studied him. Mixed feelings of hatred and compassion competed for space in her heart. It would be easier if she could just hate him. She was supposed to hate them wasn't she? The trouble was, she didn't feel like he really was her enemy. Once, yes but now? His eyes were closing.

Dina rose from her chair quietly and stood watching Mr B. She had learnt all she needed to know. The rest, if there was more, would be detail that did not interest her. He had been honest with her. What more could she ask? She walked slowly from the bedroom, closing the door gently as she left. The sound of water running in the bathroom brought Dina back to reality and the nagging reminder that she still had to wash the floors and sort out the laundry.

The nurse was washing some underwear in a plastic bowl in the bath. She straightened up, putting her hand against her back, when she heard Dina enter the bathroom. "Ach! All this bending over will be the death of me. Morning Kiria Constantinou. Is he sleeping?" She glanced at the watch pinching her plump wrist and then smoothed down her crisp white nurse's dress.

Dina's fingers wee fidgeting in her pocket. Time for a cigarette. "Yes, I think so and please just call me Dina, We don't need to be so formal do we?"

The nurse looked like she was considering this proposal as she might a suggestion to alter the dose of a patient's medicine. Her round, rosy face reminded Dina of the religious paintings of winged cherubs suspended in heaven that hung in Kiria Dabas's house. "I suppose not. Dina it is then. I'm Sophia."

"Sophia. Good. Now that's agreed I'd better get on with what I'm paid to do. I'll start on the lounge floor." Dina was still fiddling with her cigarette packet, trying to beat the craving.

"Oh! I forgot to say that Kiria Vouyoukas is coming early today and she asked me to tell you to get out the rugs since the weather's changing."

"I would have done it anyway. Did she say what time she was coming?" Dina now knew there was no hope of resisting the cigarette; it was already sliding itself free from the packet as if it had heard the name Vassiliki and fixed itself between her awaiting fingers.

"No, but I got the impression she wanted to see you."

"Yes, I'm sure she does!" Dina left the nurse nodding to herself in judgement as she watched Dina disappear onto the veranda.

Vassiliki's entrance was embroidered by her usual hyperboles. Dina counted three, including her fur backed gloves, even before she had sat down in exhaustion.
"It's freezing out there!"
It's October, thought Dina.
"Those cobbles have crippled me!"
We'll see.
"Good morning Dina." Vassiliki stood before the hall mirror, miraculously now cured of her handicap, licking the tips of her fingers before she applied them to her backcombed hair.
"Morning Kiria Vouyoukas."
"Did the nurse give you my message Dina?" Vassiliki collected her handbag and proceeded into the kitchen without waiting for an answer. Flinging open the door, she snapped her lighter with a brutally purple nail and bared her throat to the heavens as she inhaled. Dina avoided doing the same, glad she had only just put one out. She took the step-ladder to reach the highest cupboards in the second bedroom, easing the plastic covered rugs towards the door and tipping them out onto the floor. The smell of naphthalene showered the room as they splashed in their plastic onto the marble floor. Dina swore under her breath as the last rug proved difficult to reach and she almost lost her balance on the ladder. Before she had time to get down and try from another angle, Vassiliki was standing holding on to the bottom of the ladder. "Careful! We don't want any other casualties in this house do we?"
Dina twisted her head round and looked down on Vassiliki. How she would love to roll out the next rug and aim

it at her perfectly arranged hair do. She grappled with the plastic and finally released it together with a fine dust that unavoidably settled on Vassiliki. "Sorry for the dust. I can't get them down any other way."

Visibly angered by Dina's casual approach, Vassiliki abandoned her to the unsteady ladder and went in search of her comb. Dina chuckled as she rolled the large rug into the lounge with her foot. She had begun to feel sorry for the nurse who was receiving her instructions from Vassiliki. Then Dina remembered she hadn't yet swept or washed the floors. She couldn't lay down the rugs until she had. Hoping Vassiliki would not notice that she was behind in her tasks, Dina flew into the kitchen, retrieved her broom from its cupboard and began sweeping the lounge floor. The black marble was beautiful to look at but a menace to keep clean, every little spot showed up, displeasing to critical eyes.

Dina opened the veranda doors, immediately letting in a stream of cool, clean air blowing down from the mountains. September, with its balmy temperatures, had long gone, given way to the keen, fresh days of late October that brought with them a sharper edge. Leaning hard on her mop, Dina made arc shapes as she wielded it across the floor then swirled and twisted it between the legs of the glass cabinet and chairs. Humming one of her favourite songs, Dina found she was able to forget her sadness. Who was it who had said work was the best antidote to sorrow? Well, whoever it was, she agreed.

Deep in thought, Dina stood on her cloth foot- pads and slid her way across the floor like an ice skater.

Suddenly Vassiliki was in front of her, barring the way. "It's getting late to be polishing now isn't it Dina? Why are you so behind today?"

Dina checked the grandfather clock. "It's only eleven Kiria."

"But I noticed the laundry hasn't been taken and you haven't made a start yet on the kitchen cupboards." Vassiliki perched herself on the arm of the settee.

"Yes. You're right. I am behind today. I'll speed up." Dina was hoping this would be the end of the conversation but it was clear that Vassiliki was going nowhere just yet.

"Well, yes, do that but what I want to know is why? Now that my Panouli is unable, it is me who has to pay your wages and I think I have a right to ask you."

Dina saw that her escape was clearly not going to be so easy. "I was late arriving today Kiria. Dock it from my wages if you want." There was challenge and resignation in Dina's voice and she was hoping her answer would be enough.

Vassiliki rose from her perch. "Well that's strange because I asked the nurse and she said you had arrived at eight-thirty, so what's happened to all that time?" Vassiliki planted herself in front of Dina again. There followed a silence as Dina considered her next move.

"We were talking together – about your brother Kiria Vouyoukas and the time simply went without us realising it." It was Sophia's voice.

Dina's eyebrows rose in surprise.

"May I remind both of you that you are paid to work here, not to gossip!" Vassiliki straightened her oyster shaped skirt and left the room, followed by two pairs of eyes.

Touching the nurse on her arm, Dina smiled. "Thank-you Sophia. You saved my life!"

"But don't ask me to do it again. You have to understand Dina that he's dying and all this talk doesn't help him and if she found out you'd been tiring him like that and getting him to explain whatever it is you're so interested in, she would probably sack both of us."

As she skated on her floor cloths Dina thought about what the nurse had said. It was unlikely that Vassiliki would sack an indispensable nurse when her brother was in his last weeks. The same could not be said about herself, she realised. She could not count on her wages from here for much longer anyway and once Mr B had passed away, the house would be sold and her services no longer required.

Dina shook her cloths over the balcony. A light rain, coaxed by the wind, had begun to drive diagonally onto the front veranda and low clouds, hovering over the distant peaks of Grammos, now hid the late morning sun. Dina was drawn to the strange bruised colour of the sky created by the storm, and she remembered how once, what seemed a very long time ago, a battle raged below where the clouds hung. Some of the wind-blown leaves from nearby branches were stopped in their flight by the iron railings of the veranda and stuck to them as if glued. Dina shivered and closed the doors against the new season.

As the winds blew and the skies darkened, the nurse patiently tried to offer the straw up to Mr B's mouth but he pushed her hand away. He was succumbing under the weight of effort. The water spilt over the glass, dampening the sheet and Mr B fell back against his pillows. "Just take it all away, will you. I told you...I'm not interested." His raised voice brought Vassilki rushing into her brother's bedroom, her hands white with flour.

"Oh Panouli mou! Whatever is it little brother?" Fussing around the pillows, Vassilki spotted the damp sheet. "What's happened nurse? Why's the sheet damp here?" She smoothed Mr B's forehead, frowning. "Have you got a temperature? Nurse! When did you last check my brother's temperature and pulse?"

The nurse abandoned her knitting and flew to her patient's bedside, feeling his temperature for herself. "I took it only an hour ago Kiria Vouyoukas. He doesn't have a temperature."

She checked his pulse, all the while staring angrily at Vassiliki. Mr B mumbled something that neither woman could understand. Then, like a hawk spotting its prey, Vassiliki's dark brown eyes fell on the black and white photograph lying on the bedside table. Forgetting her earlier concerns over her brother's care, Vassiliki snatched up the photo and marched into the kitchen where Dina was cleaning cupboards. A bowl of freshly cooked spinach was cooling under the open window and a wooden rolling pin lay beside it. Vassiliki had been preparing to roll out pastry when her brother's voice disturbed her.

"Where did you find it?" Vassiliki confronted Dina with the photo.

"Where you left it for me." Dina replied as her head disappeared into the depths of the cupboard.

"And you've been interrogating a sick man, a dying man, my brother!" The pitch of Vassiliki's voice rose after each statement. So exaggerated were her movements, Dina imagined she could have been on the set of an opera. "I wouldn't call it interrogation Kiria Vouyoukas. I think I know enough about that not to inflict it on anyone."

"But you got what you wanted did you? Are you satisfied that you've weakened him and probably brought his death nearer?"

Dina had been slow. She had not seen this coming. "You wanted me to find that photo didn't you? You knew I would confront Pano with it because you knew how much I needed those answers. I can just see you laying the trap for me! You wanted me to find out what he was really like so I wouldn't want to work here anymore. Imagine how you would have felt if you had married someone and then found out that man had killed your sister!"

Total confusion showed on Vassiliki's face as she mouthed the words married and sister.

Dina threw her cloth into the sink. "Ah yes! He didn't tell you then? He asked me to marry him. I'm sure that surprises you doesn't it? Your brother married to a cleaner. An *andarte*. A Leftist. Oh what a nightmare for you. But I turned him down."

"I can't believe it! My brother asking the cleaning woman to marry him! You're lying. You always lie and you've infected that nurse, got her to lie for you. Why would he want to marry you anyway? What could you offer him?"

The truth, Dina thought, is that she couldn't have offered him much except care and friendship but that was all he was asking for.

Vassiliki blew cigarette smoke in Dina's face. "What's all this about a sister? I didn't know you had one."

"I had two." Dina saw no pity on Vassiliki's face, no recognition of what she had just told her. If she has any feeling in those bones, thought Dina, it's not for humans.

"Those partisans of yours who flooded back into our villages after their army was disbanded were responsible for the food shortages and starvation. People like you should be ashamed to call yourselves Greeks. You are not patriots. You forced children over the borders into Eastern Europe, tore them from their mothers' sides, never to be seen again, just to spread your propaganda. And you! If you didn't want God, King and family why didn't you cross the border with them? Why did you stay here if it's so bad?"

Dina smiled. "If I only want one of those three don't I qualify?"

Vassiliki snarled, unable to think quickly enough to match the blow.

"But no Kiria Vouyoukas! Those parents you're talking about preferred to lose their children to safety than allow them to stay in villages burnt to the ground by your battalions. It was you who burnt our villages to stop us recruiting and in the process you didn't care who you killed. And another thing! Many of those parents knew their children would get a better education over the border than they would in our villages. There was nothing left for them. Your lot made sure of that."

"Well, whatever you got, you deserved it, you and all your sisters! I'll get the truth from my brother. You're a lying Communist traitor! How dare you question my brother like you did when you should have been cleaning this house! Why, I've been too easy on you. You've been taking advantage ever since Pano became ill." Vassiliki's voice rose to a screech, bringing the nurse running into the kitchen. But Vassiliki ignored her and carried on. "We should have got rid of you a long time ago but now I'm in charge there'll be no more mismanagement. He's always paid you too much anyway. Well, today you can take your last wages from me and you'll never set foot in this house again."

The nurse tried to intervene, gesturing to Vassiliki to keep her voice down for her brother's sake. But this plea had the opposite effect and she shouted even louder. "Here. Take this. Go on, get down on your knees, you're used to that." Five hundred drachma notes fluttered to the floor, coins echoed as they hit the tiles. "Now I'll get the truth." And she marched into the sickroom.

Dina wanted to murder Vassiliki. She looked at the rolling pin but the nurse's glance levelled at her was enough of a deterrent. Then, from the bedroom the two women heard a frail attempt to shout coming from Mr B's throat.

"You're...you're a bad woman Vassiliki. You've taken that from father." Mr B was half out of his bed, the covers thrown back in disarray. Mustering all his strength and anger, he glared at his sister as he held onto the bedpost to steady himself. "Don't treat her that way. Have you no shame? She's never done anything to you."

"Yes, she has! She was turning your head. Tell me it's not true about the marriage proposal." Despite the fact that she was talking to her brother, Vassiliki had not once lowered her voice.

"It's true." Mr B fell back on the bed. Vassiliki made no attempt to help him or pull his covers up around him. The nurse approached and took over. Vassiliki was clearly stunned by his answer and remained, for once, speechless. She stood staring at her brother. The nurse brought the oxygen mask and sat beside him, mopping his forehead.

Nobody spoke but the rain continued to beat at the windows.

Vassiliki returned to the kitchen where Dina still stood, her wages scattered across the floor. They glanced at each other. Lighting her cigarette with a trembling hand, Vassiliki looked at the floor. "You can finish the cupboards and then go. If you ever enter the grounds of this house again I'll have my husband arrest you for trespass."

As Dina went down on her knees many thoughts ran through her head but shame was not among them. She had done nothing wrong. Lucky for her, perhaps, that the nurse had been in the kitchen or she may have seized the waiting weapon. There was no way of knowing now. Neither did she feel humiliated. Dina reckoned that to feel humiliation a person had to have some respect for their persecutor. She picked up the coins, retrieving one or two from where they had rolled under the table. The notes were short by five hundred.

Pocketing her money, Dina walked silently to the hallway and put on her coat. She could hear the nurse talking softly to Mr B and then her name being called. It was him. She moved swiftly into his room and stood at the foot of the bed.

"Dina, my little bird. I'm so sorry. I want to apologise for my sister. She had no right."

"Shush Pano! Don't exert yourself. It really doesn't matter now. I'm leaving."

Mr B touched the nurse's arm. "Please, Sophia. Could you leave us for a few minutes?" The nurse pressed his hand and left.

Dina moved round the bed and took Mr B's shrivelled hand in hers.

"Dina, I need to ask you just one more thing?"

Dina nodded.

"Forgive me?"

Dina hesitated, concentrating her gaze on Mr B who seemed to have become very small now. "I'll try Pano. Good-bye." As Dina released her hand from his she felt its brittleness and wondered how such a large, joyful man could have become like one of the fragile ornaments she dusted every day.

Sophia met her at the front door. "Well, Dina, I shall miss your company, short-lived as it was." They hugged.

Dina turned her inadequate collar up against the weather and smiled back at the nurse. "Bye Sophia and, thanks."

As she closed the front gate Dina looked up at the house in all its splendour and felt sad in her stomach as if she was saying farewell to an old friend.

CHAPTER SIXTEEN

> *"Even In 1974 when my husband was working for Esso-Pappas in Saloniki it was still illegal to strike. The leadership of the union are all secret police anyway and that makes it really hard to get other workers involved because they're not stupid. They know they're still being watched."*

How could she ever have doubted his role? He had been as active in the *Emfilio* years as she had. Fragments of past conversations occupied Dina's thoughts. Vassiliki had warned her, even planted the evidence where Dina would find it. Dimitris had challenged her to confront Mr B. No sympathy there. Then there were her own arguments with Mr B and his evasive answers that had made her suspicious, the political bantering, the keen interest he showed in her past, followed by his strange silences. He had managed somehow to get her to reveal things about her past that Dina had always kept locked away. But try as she might, enemy or not, Dina could not hate Mr B. She had spent too many hours in his house, cleaning for him, enjoying themth she felt because she was being treated with respect.

She remembered her first visit to Mr B's, after his wife's death, the house in chaos, all the signs of neglect that accompany a broken heart. Dina's predecessor had fled after the first week, disgusted at Mr B's behaviour, leaving Dina to inherit months of dirt and dust.

Events had happened so swiftly yesterday that Dina could only now begin to think about their significance. She had known that Mr B's illness was terminal and that the Friday would come when she would no longer catch the 41 bus over the hill and walk beside the lakeshore before starting work in his house. She wouldn't see Mr B again, lean over the front veranda and watch the seasonal shifts in the lake colours, enjoy her morning coffee overlooking the back garden with its cedar and lemon trees. She would of course occasionally have reason to pass by the house, perhaps when out walking with Evy on a Saturday but she wouldn't be returning. That routine would cease. Had ceased.

Freedom beckoned to Dina. Income nudged her. Family needs nagged at her. She felt restless. How could they cope if she only brought in four days wages? That would mean something being cut from the family budget at a time when food prices and rents were increasing. The landlord had already warned them of increases last year. Dina thought there was little chance he would forget or take pity on them. No landlords were that generous. She was worried about Rena's worsening health. Perhaps it had been selfish of her to refuse Mr B's marriage proposal. Accepting him would have put an end to the tedium of the weekly struggle to stretch their wage packets in so many directions. Still, Dina considered, sometimes the sacrifice is too great.

She told herself to slow down, stop worrying and then things would just happen; turn out right. But she could never quite convince herself of that when she was faced with a choice between buying Rena's medicine or enough mince to give the family a decent meal. She ran through the food list in her mind. They could do without the wine but then Nikos would rant and swear and end up going to the ouzeri with a good excuse, coming home with empty pockets. Could they cut down on bread? Unimaginable! Maybe she was being extravagant with the oil when she cooked. She knew that was untrue. Luxuries didn't really play much of a role in their family. What would constitute a luxury? Dina asked herself. If this government had to specify what they considered luxuries and what were essentials for life, I wonder what they would come up with? Well, it's clear they can't do without their yachts, they need them for their holidays in Skiathos, so that makes them essential doesn't it? Whereas for the likes of us, our luxuries would be a night out at the *taverna* when they release one of ours from one of their stinking prisons. Dina's list had turned into a venomous snake, coiling itself round her stomach until it was a tight knot and she felt sick. No, there was nothing she could cut. She would have to find another house to clean on a Friday.

The next week slid away and although a friend had recommended Dina's cleaning skills to another household, she had heard nothing. On her way home from Kiria Dabas's apartment she stopped off at the kiosk in Ermou Street and bought the local newspaper to search for jobs. From behind his glass window the kiosk owner chatted with Dina about the cold weather, the proposals to build a new highway and the fact that his youngest daughter had just given birth to his fourth grandchild – all boys, he said joyfully, and that he'd make a football team of them yet. Dina smiled as she dropped the coins into his jar and picked up the paper. "Congratulations. Don't forget though, that without your daughter, there wouldn't be any hope of a football team!"

The man emerged from the darkness of his kiosk and sat on the stool outside, flinging his *koboloi* round the fingers of one hand while the other brandished a cigarette. "Bah! Women. As if my wife would ever let me forget that!"

Dina waved goodbye with her newspaper, declining the offer of a winning lottery ticket and continued down the hill, all the while feeling the cold wind slicing through her coat so that she held the newspaper in front of her like a sacred shield.

The smell of grilling fish wafted from the fish *tavernes* as Dina crossed the square beside the lake.

White swans gliding on oily feathered stomachs across the water don't mind the cold and damp but they make me shiver.

Across the street from the *tavernes* stood the *kafeneon*, its long glass windows stretching round the corner so that customers, mostly men, could enter by one door and exit from the other.

Very useful. When their wives come in search of them through one door they nip out the other.

Glancing through the window, Dina could see the men of the town clustered round tables, intent on their games of *tavli*, while they sipped at their coffees and solved the problems of price inflation and industrial unrest. Some wore dark glasses. They all smoked.

They resemble actors on an espionage set.

One of them stood up and scraping his chair back, made his departure, mumbling *kali oreksi* to his fellows as he negotiated the step down from the *kafeneon* door. He clutched the family loaf of bread in its paper bag.

Forget it at your peril. She smiled.

Once back home Dina skimmed the newspaper, searching the ads for any cleaning jobs but there were none. Then she turned the page and found herself looking at the Marriages, Births and Deaths announcements.

His death announcement stared out at her from a neatly typed box, its letters elegantly rounded.

In loving memory of Panos B – 1902-1974
At his home in Nikis Road, Kastoria,
On November 20th 1974
Our loving brother and uncle passed away quietly in his sleep
You will remain in our hearts forever
Your ever-loving brother Spiros, sister Vassiliki, brother in law Alekos
Nephews Yanni and Thanassis & Niece Virginia
Burial and service 4th Dec, 12.00 at Agios Zacgharias, Pefko

He's finally gone.

Dina read the words a second time and appreciated their poignancy. They described the man. He had been a loving brother and uncle and he would remain in their hearts forever.

I will remember him too but not for the same reasons.

I haven't got used to Fridays yet. I still feel adrift, without a house to clean.

Attempts to forgive Mr B seemed a more difficult struggle than she had imagined. No sooner had she begun to feel magnanimous towards him than her mood would change into anger, even hatred at what he had done. In her darkest moments she saw his slow death as vengeance for all her dead comrades. Now she felt that Mr B's death represented more than just his mortality, in a physical sense. She had seen too many deaths to feel great sadness, yet at the same time she was not exactly cut off from her feelings. There was a certain distance now, both physical and emotional. Reading the words of his death announcement was like reading about the death of some prominent character in a novel. A character who had followed an expected path rather than taken risks but nevertheless an eventful life.

Laying the paper down, Dina stared at the floor. What did she want to do? She asked herself. Well, she had only been the cleaner, that was true, but she had been more than that to the man who had just died. She wanted to pay her respects to Mr B's family and in normal circumstances that would be a perfectly acceptable thing for a housecleaner to do. But Dina thought her circumstances were anything but normal and she hesitated to make arrangements to venture into Mr B's house given Vassiliki's parting words. Resentment bubbled up inside Dina. Why was she worrying about paying her respects to a family of monarcho fascists – a brother who had tortured and murdered her comrades and a sister who had thrown her out the house and threatened her with trespass if she returned? Who, in their right mind would even consider returning? And yet Dina knew the slavery that resentment could bring, leaving a bitter taste in the mouth and an unfulfilled heart. It wasn't the Greek way, to ignore someone's death, even if it had been imminent. She could, of course, send a card, flowers even, thereby avoiding the need to actually go to Mr B's house. But Dina wanted to see the inside of the house again, just once more. She loved that house, more than any other house or apartment she had ever cleaned and there had been many. Shocked at the realisation of how attached she had become to the house Dina tried to convince herself that it was because it was easier to clean due to its layout and fine workmanship, rather than any sentimental reason. But it wasn't just that. She had felt at ease there. Accepted. Knowing about Mr B's past made it possible for Dina to understand why he had accepted her as an equal in his house, because despite their opposing values they had each, in their own way, devoted themselves to a cause greater than self interest.

Having lived through the same war years as Dina, Mr B had understood the force of that legacy, like a tornado whipping up everything in its path and leaving nothing intact, everything changed. So she had cleaned his house diligently week by week, as if she were cleaning her own.

The shrill ring of the phone suddenly demanded Dina's attention, waking her from a reverie of sadness and resignation. It was Dimitris, his voice normallly deep and calm, now elated. "We had a big turnout Dina."

Dina was struggling to understand what he was talking about, her mind still on Mr B's death. "What?"

"Come on Dina! What's the matter with you? I'm talking about the demonstration today. We filled the park. The bus drivers blockaded Alexandrou so they could hear the speeches. Karamanlis may have legalised us but he won't buy us off!"

Dina's response was unusually vague. "Oh, sorry Dimitri, what did you say?"

"Dina. What happened? You don't sound yourself today?"

Dina sat down on the small wicker chair. "I'm distracted. You know my employer, Mr B, he died a few days ago. It was expected and I'd like to go and pay my respects to..." She was forced to think about who she wanted to pay her respects to. To Vassiliki and her police husband? To Mr B? He was dead. She didn't believe in an afterlife. No. She wanted to pay her respects to his memory and to the house. That was it.

"Ah yes. The one you were fond of. Well, my condolences to you for your feelings of loss. It's you that matters Dina. Ketty and Aris are having a small get together tonight. It's their anniversary. She asked me to phone you so here I am. Why don't you come along and we can talk. Ketty was asking about you the other day. She'd love to see you. I've got to go."

Dina sat for a few minutes cradling the receiver in her lap.

She hadn't even made a start on the day's dinner but that was no great tragedy as she only had to heat up leftovers from yesterday's bean soup, add a few more carrots. Nikos would moan. He didn't like eating the same meal two days running but that was tough. He didn't have to make five hundred drachmes stretch as far as she did. She heard Rena coughing in her sleep. She would go on like that until she woke herself up.

As Dina levelled coffee into a small aluminium *briki* she thought about what an important role chance had played in both her own life and consequently that of her daughter. Here she stood, fifty one years of age, pretty much physically able, except of course for her leg, having survived napalm attacks, air raids and ambushes while her poor daughter had been born, gone to school and ended up in a washing powder factory where her lungs were under attack. Take the company to the courts, friends had encourageded them, forgetting that affording legal fees was out of the question for a family of their means. A grand idea, thought Dina, but not for the likes of us and anyway, she had never heard of an industrial court compensating a worker for injury or neglect. Those kinds of results happened abroad, not in Greece.

The coffee boiled up. Dina poured it into Rena's favourite green cup. Carrying it through to her daughter's bedroom, Dina heard Evy's excited little voice bursting before her as she arrived home with her father. She was chattering about her new friend, begging Nikos to allow her to come over to play and Nikos, as usual, was deferring the decision to her mother.

Dina smoothed Rena's hair back from her forehead, an almost automatic movement she always made to wake her daughter. "Did you sleep any better today my love?"

Rena rolled over onto her back and put her own hand to her forehead. "I was sweating again! It's November and I'm sweating mama and this cough. I'm so tired of this cough. I just want it to stop."

Dina recognised the impatient child's voice in her daughter, the same voice she heard from Evy when she was hungry or tired. "Here my love, drink your coffee. I think we'll have to go back to the doctor and see if we can get some better medicine. That stuff you're taking doesn't seem to be doing much good does it?"

Rena sat up and reached over for her coffee as Evy bounced into the room ready with her question. Clambering up onto the bed she gave her mother a kiss and snuggled up beside her. "Mama, can my new friend come and play this week?"

Rena cuddled her daughter. "And what is the name of this new friend who you want to come?"

"Angeliki." Evy was clearly pleased with herself for having pronounced her friend's name correctly. She smiled. "Mama you're hot. Why are you hot when I'm cold?"

"Because mama's got a bad cough and you should have a jumper on. *Yiayia* will bring you one. Did you know that your friend's name means little angel?"

Evy's eyes opened wide. "She's lucky then. Why didn't you call me that name?"

"Here, put this on Evy." Dina held out a bright yellow cardigan. "I need to get on with the dinner." Rena could explain about angels.

As she scraped the carrots, Dina thought about Rena's medicine, the doctor and the cost of it all and determined that she would have to search harder for Friday work. Maybe when she went to Ketty's tonight someone would have a name for her to follow up.

Dina wondered if other women were like her when they cooked and cleaned. All the concerns of the world seemed to pass through her mind as she chopped, scraped, washed, stirred, tasted. She had solved many of the world's greatest conflicts by the time most meals were on the table. And as for cleaning, that seemed to be the most fruitful time for the real meanderings of her mind – a time to imagine herself in positions of power, able to change all the things that were wrong in peoples' lives, sweeping her broom across the floor just as the cartoons of Lenin had shown him sweeping the globe clean of imperialism.

But until then… Dina ladled bean soup into four bowls. "Come on children. *Fasolada* and feta."

Nikos made a face. His daughter tried to copy it.

Ketty's apartment was in a smart new block, set back, high up above the Athens road. Her lounge looked to the lake from the west giving glorious views of the sun rising from behind the peaks of Korissos opposite. Dina enjoyed her walk although she would have enjoyed it more had she been warmer. The November night- time sky was clear of clouds and the stars seemed to be winking at her as she looked up at them. The bitter wind that had blown through Kastoria earlier in the week had dropped. Dina felt stillness all around her. Wood smoke curled up from the chimneys of the old village houses dotted about on the hillside. They were burning pine logs. Dina caught little whiffs of the intoxicating resin as it wafted down towards her and brought back memories of her own family house and the daily routine of collecting firewood and chopping logs. Yes, she thought, the sights and smells of the village are very inviting but the reality of the day-to-day struggle kills any romanticism of peasant life. Her father had been right and she always remembered the lines he had read to her from Chekov. *"There is peasant blood in my veins and you cannot astonish me with peasant virtues."* She needed to make sure Rena learnt them as well.

Dina admired the shining glass door of No 3 Galileo Street as she waited for Ketty's voice over the intercom. As it came she greeted her and pushed on the giant brass doorknob that gave her entry into the mirrored hallway, adorned with rubber plants in huge clay pots. The lift took Dina up to the second floor, giving her time to look at herself in the mirrored walls and wishing she hadn't.

Ketty and her husband were good friends of Dimitris's. Ketty worked as a clerk at the bus ticket office and had invited along two friends who were drivers. Ketty gave Dina a big hug and kiss and Dina was immediately pleased she had made the effort to come along.

"Dina! Where have you been hiding yourself for the past months? We haven't seen you since Laki's engagement party." Ketty took Dina's coat and hung it behind the door. "How d'you like it? Isn't it better than Omonia?"

They passed through the hall, into the lounge. Dina's eyes swept across the apartment. "It's beautiful Ketty, much better, even if it's a bit of a walk from town."

Dimitris jumped out of his chair and embraced Dina. "Dina. I'm glad you came. Meet Vangelis and Petros, two of the bus drivers from the strike committee."

Dina shook hands and accepted the small glass of wine held out to her by Ketty. She was looking at two men who were complete opposites of each other. One, the elder by many years, was short and fat with a ruddy round face, shiny red cheeks and a ring of grey curly hair that grew round the bald centre of his head. When he smiled he bared more gum than teeth. At this sight, Dina's eyes moved willingly to the other man, young, tall, with an angular face, high cheekbones and reddish hair. She thought he looked more Albanian than Greek. What Dina also noticed was the one feature they shared in common – they both wore shabby, once black trousers, now shiny from wear and jackets that had seen better days.

"So, they've allowed you to form a strike committee? That's progress!" Dina was heartened by what she had heard.

Vangelis shook his head and laughed. "We're not giving them the chance to stop us. We need to act before they send one of their bureaucrats from Saloniki."

"What's the strike about?' Dina felt very out of touch with such things in her town.

"They're refusing to pay compensation to drivers who take on an extra shift when one of us is ill."

"You mean you work for nothing then?"

Vangelis smiled. "Exactly Dina. We love the job so much we refuse pay." They all laughed but they all knew it was far from funny.

The men resumed their conversation with Ketty and her husband. Dimitris turned to Dina. "Dina, you need to get out more. You're looking pale and worried." He lowered his voice. "How about your phone? Any change?"

"Yes. Since she got rid of me it hasn't done it again. I think she called him off."

Dimitris smiled. "She's called him off just like her lap dog eh? So what else is worrying you? Are you grieving over that Mr B's death?"

Dina considered the question. She always considered Dimitris's questions. "Not exactly grieving Dimitri. I've told you how I enjoyed working for him but you were right about his past – it was worse than I'd expected."

Dimitris offered Dina a cigarette. "Why worse? What did the bastard do?"

Dina told Dimitris about her sister and Mr B's part in the tragedy. He listened intently, making noises through his teeth every now and again. He poured them both more wine and crashed their glasses together. "Dina. To his death and better that way. Don't lose sleep over a man that could do those things. Save your worries for the present, not the past."

"But we did things that were wrong as well Dimitri. Don't you admit that?" Dina lit her third cigarette. She had already exceeded her self-imposed ration for the night.

Running his fingers through his thick, greying hair Dimitris sighed, blowing the smoke upwards to the ceiling. "Yes, of course I do but on a scale of atrocities which side would win?" He paused. "You can't answer those particular types of questions without reference to the general. Think about it. What was their overall aim? To stop us recruiting, bring back the king and for the Americans to get a foothold in our country. Your Mr B was part of all that and he was probably as dedicated as we were to stopping him."

Dina sighed. "Yes, and they managed all of those didn't they? And look where we are now? Perhaps he treated me well because he felt guilty – anyway, I'd like to think that."

"So, what's your problem now Dina? He's gone. Is it the work?"

"Well, yes, that's a problem for sure. But I still feel I'd like to have the last word over that sister of his."

The glint in Dina's eyes and sharpness of her voice as she thought of Vassiliki's treatment of her, was not lost on Dimitris. "Oh I can see the old fighter in you yet Dina." He chuckled and pulled her closer to him.

"Yes. She's still here. I wanted to go back to the house but under the circumstances I don't think I could. It would look like I've got no principles."

"Now you're talking. Here, more wine."

"But I do want to pay my respects, in the normal way. I did work for him for two years."

"Then go to his funeral. She can't stop you turning up there can she? Was he a local?"

"From Pefkos." Dina helped herself to the bowl of *fistikia* at her side and passed it on to Dimitris.

"Then go and damn the woman. If that will get rid of your obsession then go to Pefkos, make your peace and put an end to your agony." Dimitris cracked a shell with his teeth.

"Yes, yes I think I will go." Dina looked over at the others. "But not if your friends here go on strike. How will I get there without the bus?"

Petros, the younger of the two bus drivers, looked over at Dina and smiled. "Don't worry Dina. If we're on strike we'll find a way of getting you there, I promise. It's not something I'd want on my conscience, stopping someone getting to a funeral."

Talking with Dimitris had helped her, as always. Dina had made her decision. Ketty disappeared into the kitchen so Dina took the opportunity to join her. She looked about the fitted pine kitchen, with its marble topped units and matching table. "This looks fantastic Ketty, your move looks like it's been worth it. Did Aris do all this himself?"

Ketty put a large oven dish of tomatoes and potatoes on the table. Leftovers from lunch. "Yes. Most of it. It saved us a lot of money. "

"Well I think you've done it beautifully. It feels warm and looks so clean everywhere."

Ketty laughed. "Coming from the top housecleaner that's a big compliment! I know it's an awful way to think of it but the truth is if Aris's father hadn't died and left us his house we'd never have been able to buy this. We'd still be in Lefki in that old ruin."

"Ketty, Dimitris said you might know someone who needs a cleaner on Fridays, only that's the day I'm without work and we really need the money."

Ketty manoeuvred thick chunks of feta from a plastic container onto a plate. "Ach Dina, I understand how hard it must be for you. Dimitris told me about your daughter and I've put a word in for you with one of the furriers who works for Lakounis."

Dina's mind lingered on the name for a moment and then remembered the shop she had stepped into in a mad moment. "I know him. I went into the shop and tried on one of his furs."

Ketty turned in surprise. "Well done Dina!"

"I was only trying it on. He had it in the window and Ketty d'you know how wonderful it felt?"

"Of course I know. I made Aris buy me one when we inherited that money from his father. He didn't want to, said it was a waste but I promised I'd never ask him for another coat if he let me have this one. I love it. I love the idea that a bus clerk can weat a rich woman's fur."

Dina smiled. "I'll agree with you there. It always looks so good on you. Well, I took it off again pretty quickly. He was obviously annoyed that I'd wasted his time. D'you think he would refuse me a job because of that?"

"Who?"

"Kirios Lakounis of course."

"Was he in the shop then?"

"Well he helped me try it on. A short balding man with a fat stomach and a red face."

Ketty laughed. "No.That's not Lakounis. That's his assistant. Kirios Lakounis is younger, quite an attractive man and tall with a good head of hair. He set up his business a couple of years ago. His father died and he started it up again. Apparently it's doing very nicely. Well, now his family have joined him and of course they'll need a cleaner. I think there are three children." Ketty and Dina carried the trays into the lounge and invited the men to eat. Ketty handed out plates. "Nothing much, just usual leftovers. Make the most of it, if the strike goes ahead we'll be living on *fakies*."

Aris laughed. "Nonsense woman! I'll be shooting us a boar or two. We won't starve." He put his arm over his wife's shoulder and Dina felt that pang of sad regret that she always felt when she was with a happy couple.

CHAPTER SEVENTEEN

"I knew lieutenants, second lieutenants, battalion leaders, all women. Don't tell me women were only employed on logistics tasks. They were on the Front Line and they used their weapons and that included the nurses if they were called on."

The yearly snows had started the night before Mr B's funeral, feathering the ground and rooftops of Pefkos with tiny crystals that froze overnight. The day dawned with more threatening, heavy pink snow clouds that finally burst in the afternoon. It was only two o'clock but the purple, pink and grey colours of the sky created a sense of dusk.

Dina walked with apprehension through the giant entrance of Agios Zacharia and made her way swiftly and silently down the chilly aisle until she came to the last row of occupied pews. Several people glanced sideways and shuffled up to make room for her. Finding a path between the mourners in front of her Dina's eyes rested on the black bulk of the priest swinging his censer methodically, sending smoke signals through the congregation as he chanted the psalm. As priests go, she thought, he didn't have a bad voice, not as monotone as some she had heard.

Sniffles from the front pews were bounced back at Dina by the grey stone pillars of the nave. She could make out Vassiliki's form standing at the front, flanked on either side by her policeman husband and brother. Everywhere she looked Dina's eyes were met with a sea of black, broken only occasionally by the yellow flickering of the candles lighting the nave and altar. She shivered under her thin coat, cursing the penetrating, silent cold that worked its way into her bones. Then they were all crossing themselves while Dina's arms remained paralysed, unwilling and unable to do the same. She was thinking that for the unconverted, a journey into this church would scarcely tempt them to a change of heart. This place was almost a ruin, its dark wormed beams and icy stone slabs underfoot failed to offer any warmth or comfort to its bereaved congregation. What solace did the tiny slit windows offer? Too high up to cast any light on the dark surroundings.

The priest chanted the dismissal prayer and people began filing towards Mr B's open casket to look at him for the last time and kiss the icon on his chest.

Because she was at the back of the mourners Dina had a good view of people as they moved from their seats towards the casket – Vassiliki swathed in her fur coat, carefully dabbing one eye with the corner of her handkerchief so as not to smudge the mascara, her free hand herding the children forward. Mr B's brother Spiros, head bowed, looked distraught, followed by Vassilik's husband, smooth in his grey suit and black tie, his hair sleeked back with gel. Dina could just imagine him in an interview room, leaning back in his chair, cavalier fashion, while he fired questions at the accused. When her turn came Dina bent over the fine cedar-wood casket. "Goodbye." She whispered. "I'm still trying to forgive you but you'll have to be patient." She watched, shivering as the last of the mourners paid their respects and made way for the priest to anoint the body with oil. Surrounding the casket there were silver jugs of white lilies, their pure light contrasting with the sombre, heavy wood and grey stone of the church.

Thank goodness she had worn her fur boots, even in these she needed to keep wriggling her toes to keep her feet warm. They walked silently to the cemetery where Mr B was finally committed to his grave and only then did Dina begin to cry, not only for him but for all the people she had lost over the years. People were clutching onto one another to steady themselves going down the crumbling steps. Dina began by going towards the edge of the steps where she reckoned the risk of slipping to be less likely. Her arm was suddenly clutched from behind. Dina turned and saw Sophia, the nurse, smiling at her.

"I'll hold onto you and you hold onto me!" Both women laughed as they trod gingerly down the steps and collapsed hysterically in a heap at the bottom.

"Ach Sophia! It's good to see you again. It's taken a funeral to make me laugh." They had reached the crumbling walls surrounding the churchyard. Other mourners were gathered, rubbing their gloved hands together and stamping the frozen ground beneath their feet. Dina could see Vassiliki standing beside a black Mercedes, gloved fingers waving a cigarette around in the air as she spoke.

As an uninvited guest Dina didn't want to be seen by Vassiliki. She had taken care to pay her respects to Mr B after his sister had left the church. "I'm going to walk a little way up the road to keep warm until the bus comes. D'you want to join me Sophia?"

Sophia nodded. "Let's go before our feet freeze to the ground."

Six hundred meters below them the icy waters of the river Aliakmonas bubbled and slithered their way down the hillside, small frozen ponds forming at the edges in places where the river had spilled over its banks. Dina leant over the wooden fence and stared down at the river through the threadbare beech trees. She hadn't expected to come back to the Grammos valley and look again upon the same waters that had kept her alive almost thirty years before.

"Beautiful isn't it?" Sophia's voice was carried on the waters below her.

"The last time I walked this Grammos road my feet were sore and blistered from the nails sticking through my boots and my socks were more holes than wool. We were exhausted and miserable. Hunger makes you miserable as well as thin." Dina stopped to light a cigarette.

"But what were you doing here? You're not a local." A sharp wind whistled through the pine trees, dislodging clumps of snow from their branches.

"We'd been on a sortie to find food and clothes in the village but we didn't find them so our spirits were low. They expected us to return after three or four hours but in the end it took us all night. The wind had blown the snow into drifts up to our necks and we kept losing the road. See, even now it's getting hard to see it." Dina indicated with her arm. "In 1948 I was a wireless operator with the 11th Division in the Democratic Army. Now you know why I was so secretive about my past."

Stopping in the middle of the road, Sophia stared, wide eyed at Dina. "Ah, now it begins to make sense."

"The winter of '48 was very cold, especially up here but at least with snow we could always melt it down to drink and wash our hair, not like the summer months when our lips split from thirst. We got next to nothing from the village here, just a few oranges, barely edible, and a packet of flour that had already been attacked by mice. We found a donkey in the field there and of course we took him to help us carry the provisions that we were hoping to get. But we didn't very often come away with much. They'd usually beaten us to it. It wasn't the villagers. They would have given them to us but when the government soldiers started evacuation they made sure they left nothing behind. Those soldiers! Sometimes I think they were as bad as the Germans."

"Were there many of you?"

"Only five, one on horseback who carried the machine gun and four on foot. When we set out from the village the sun was still shining and one girl was saying 'come on let's sit a bit in the sun' but our platoon leader, I forget his name, said 'no, not in the sun. Walk!' And those who disobeyed and stayed were badly frostbitten. You see what you have to do is rub your bare feet with snow and you don't get frostbite but if you try and warm them, that's fatal. Many of our comrades came home after the war with missing toes and fingers. And they've had no help from any government, including this one."

Sophia nodded.

"Anyway, as I was saying, we continued up this road. You'll see, it becomes a hill soon. They let me ride the donkey, as I had to carry the weight of the wireless. We called him Voice, for reasons I'll tell you later. The light was going from the sky and the clouds were there over our heads again. It's no use trying to shelter in that weather because it just snows and snows all night, like it did last night, and you'd never arrive if you did that so you just had to keep walking. When you're moving at night you can't have any lights, for obvious reasons, so we used to pin a white piece of paper on our backs so the comrade behind could see where we were going. But that doesn't work when you're in snow up to your necks, then a piece of white paper's no use at all is it? D'you know how your legs ache after you've been lifting them up and down for hours to wade through snow that deep?"

"Mine are beginning to feel it just walking this far."

"Ach Sophia! But I was young then and somehow you don't have much fear when you're young do you?"

Sophia looked up at Dina and smiled. "I don't imagine you did."

The two women were coming to a small stone bridge. They looked over the side into the rapid waters flowing beneath them and Dina stretched down to snap off an icicle from under the bridge. She held it up to Sophia. "Beautiful isn't it? Look at all those tiny shapes and patterns in the ice; you can't see them unless you study it this close. But we had to be careful with these as well! If you're dying of thirst, never suck one of these, in these freezing temperatures, not if you want to keep your tongue. It's easy to melt one if you have the heat but we didn't often have matches. Come on; let's keep walking. It's uphill from here right round this bend. And just look at it! Still the same old road. It hasn't changed in thirty years but they've sent a man to the moon and assassinated a president and us Greeks, we got rid of another dictatorship didn't we?"

They had reached the brow of the hill. "Look at these big black pine. So dark. We sheltered a bit under those; they're so closely packed together in some places the snow can't get through. I think that forest saved my life Sophia. Suddenly they opened fire on us, from somewhere, we didn't know, we couldn't see anything. The snow was falling so thick then you could hardly see the road ahead anymore. We ran into the forest. The donkey couldn't move fast. He must have been tired as well as starved. One of our platoon was shot in the shoulder so we dragged him under the trees for shelter. Poor boy, I can't remember his name but he was in terrible pain. The bullet had lodged in his shoulder blade. If that had been me they would have hit the wireless and that would have been even worse as we wouldn't have been able to wire for help." Dina stopped and smiled. "I know what you're thinking Sophia. How can a wireless be put above a life? Am I right?"

Sophia perched on the gate leading into a field. "Okay. Yes, it did cross my mind. You sounded so different when you described that. Like you were someone else. I suppose I've only ever seen you as a cleaner at Mr B's."

"I know it sounds cruel and heartless but when you're in a war, when it's one life against many you have to sacrifice the one – without a wireless we would all have been lost. Anyway, luck was on our side, he survived. We bandaged him as best we could but we weren't equipped with the proper first aid box. We were on a sortie for food not a full-scale manoeuvre. We got deep into the forest where it was really dark before we stopped for breath. Then we took up our positions behind our guns and waited. My comrade Emilia was ordered to leave the wounded boy and help load the machine gun."

"Why?"

"You know, when you were ordered to do something by your platoon leader or your captain, you didn't argue, you got on with it because you respected their position, their experience of battle; they were always someone who had more experience than you."

"Men you mean, they were always men who had the experience."

"No Sophia, we're not just talking about men. You're very wrong there. I was given orders many times by a female platoon leader. Don't listen to anyone who tells you that we women were only nurses and…"

Sophia spun round. "And what's wrong with being a nurse?" Her naturally rosy cheeks had become red with the cold air.

"Oh come on now. You know I didn't mean that but after the war, you know, they didn't believe a lot of us women and they wrote lies saying we were just stretcher- bearers or messengers and that we didn't fight on the front line. Well I was on the front line myself in three of our biggest battles and so were a lot of other women."

"Allright Dina. I believe you and I respect you for it." Sophia took Dina's arm and pulled her closer. "Come on. Don't make me your enemy."

Dina leant into Sophia's shoulder and sighed. "Ach I'm sorry Sophia. It's all come back to me here with such a rush. I feel like I'm reliving it here in this place again. You talk about respect, well, we women brought respect and cleanliness to the Democratic Army as much as that was possible. The men valued that even if they didn't admit it."

"That's men for you. So, go on, you were in the forest."

"Well they did come after us but we had the advantage as we were already entrenched but I'd been ordered to keep going forward until I could get myself onto higher ground to wire our base camp. So I tried to get Voice to move. He seemed a bit reluctant and went on more at his pace than mine for what seemed like hours. The trees had thinned out so the snow was falling on me again. Then suddenly I heard the whistle of a mortar and that awful thud that always follows.

The next thing I knew I was rolling down a steep slope, dirt and snow in my mouth and then landing at the bottom with Voice on top of me and the wireless set buried. But the amazing thing was that the shell had missed him as well! Thanks to Voice I was unhurt but I was trapped under him so I couldn't do a thing. Then, you know sometimes in those really serious situations, you just see the funny side of things, as if you were watching yourself. And I couldn't stop laughing and I think Voice's way of joining in was to bray to the heavens. He opened his mouth, bared his huge teeth and let out the loudest high-pitched noise. My belly was aching under his weight. I couldn't reach the wireless set. I was just helpless. I tried to shift his weight, to make him stand but he had better ideas. But it was his voice that really saved us. My platoon had heard him. Thee mou, I was so warm under that donkey I didn't want to get up myself when they arrived. Of course, I was the joke of the platoon for a long time after that. It was the wireless set that came off worst, all cracked with a broken aerial. Being able to laugh a little was such a relief for us. It helped us get through that long, cold night."

Dina and Sophia began to head back, sliding down the winding road, its sides now moulded into huge curves by the repeated snowfalls. The river flowed more mysteriously in the fading light of late afternoon. The birds flew to their nests.

Dina linked her arm with Sophia's and tugged her forward. "Come on, let's run a little to warm up." They reached the bridge and saw their footmarks, still imprinted on the snow from their ascent. An occasional sprinkling of soft snow unbalanced itself from the black skeletal branches of overhanging trees and landed in the river with a gentle splash. The women's' boots crunched the snow underfoot. "You know Sophia, it's done me good to come back here and share a bit of my life with you. I can see how wild and beautiful this place is now."

The old blue bus was waiting for them in the village square, its engine rattling under the bonnet like the wheezing cough of an aged, bronchial man. It belched out black, muddy diesel that smudged the little hillocks of snow surrounding the exhaust. The driver paced around his bus hunched against the cold with both hands buried deep in his jacket pockets. He skilfully manoeuvred a shrinking cigarette between his yellowing teeth as he greeted Dina and Sophia. "Come on Kiries! Your carriage awaits you".

Dina laughed. "I'm glad your strike didn't go ahead or we might have found ourselves walking. If only it was a carriage and we were princesses eh Sophia? What d' you think? Shall we ride to the palace in this carriage or shall we order another?" They laughed as they clattered up the steps and sat down in the two front seats. The sign in front of them warned passengers not to speak to the driver.

The driver climbed into his seat and promptly lit another cigarette before pushing the long wobbling gear lever into place. He put his weight behind the big steering wheel as he turned the bus and checked the two women in his mirror. "I was near to sending out a search party for you both. Where did you get to up that godforsaken road in weather like this?"

"Oh but it was beautiful up there and anyway you weren't here when we left the church. " Dina rubbed her window clear with her glove. She wanted a cigarette but having Sophia beside her was an effective deterrent.

"Did you give him a good send off?"

"Yes. Very respectful and a lot of people." Sophia pulled her coat collar round her neck. "Any chance of some heating driver?"

"*Ella*, Kiria. You know these old things take their time warming up." He half turned to the women. "Unlike my wife." He roared.

The company continued bumping along the narrow road in silence for some minutes. Sophia had begun to doze but Dina was hungry for the view down into the frozen valley. As they rounded the sharp bend into Nestorio the driver leant out his window and greeted the furrier who was shutting up shop for the day – a tiny flat roofed building with his name and trade on a tarnished wall plaque. Dina had always liked this village with its *kafeneon*s clustered around the central square. She peered into the brightly lit interior of the largest *kafeneon* where the old village men sat around in their woollen caps sipping coffees and swinging their *koboloi*. It looks really warm in there, thought Dina. But the grey metal paintwork around the windows was peeling badly and the sign over the door was missing several letters, all of which told Dina that the owners hadn't made their fortune selling coffees and ouzos. No. Life looked more of a struggle up here in the villages.

A dogfight on the opposite side of the square distracted Dina. Scraps of leftover food had been thrown out by the owner of the *taverna* and within seconds two dogs were upon a chicken carcass, tugging it in opposite directions between their jaws. They set off the sentinel cats waiting in dark alleyways until someone threw a stone and they scattered, barking and spitting into the fast approaching night.

An aproned woman came up to the driver's window and gave him custody of an old cardboard box held together with string. The woman wagged her finger at the driver and gave him instructions for safe delivery. "Yes, yes." He consented, bored with the duty but resigned to its inevitability. He started up the bus again and they moved off in jerks as he juggled with his cigarette packet and gear change.

Dina closed her eyes and rested her head back against the seat. She felt good about herself, having declined the driver's offer of a cigarette for the second time but her peace was broken by the radio he had switched on. He swore at the news and switched it off again in an angry fit. "If there weren't Kiries on board the air in this bus would be blue by now; that lot are fit for nothing. Ach! They can all go to hell!" The bus beads and mascots fringing the windscreen, shook their way backwards and forwards each time the tyres bumped over the potholed road and the driver's poster of his favourite football team swung to and fro by one ragged corner.

"What happened with your strike then?" Dina had given up her search for peace.

"It's been put off while more negotiations as they call them, go ahead. It's all talk, talk, talk nowadays and then we get a pittance at the end of it. That's what I mean Kiria. They've got the nerve to tell us they're spending our taxes, that we break our backs paying to them every day, that they're spending them on defending us against that lot."

Dina reckoned that he had nodded towards the east although the way the roads wound round the foothills meant she was unsure of her sense of direction. "You mean our neighbours?"

"Who else? Now, I don't trust them anymore than the next Greek but what exactly have they done to us at the moment eh? Tell me that!"

"Nothing." Dina glanced sideways at Sophia who was now awake. "It's just an excuse anyway – they've got the money to pay you more, it's just you're not their priority. Isn't that right?"

The driver exhaled his cigarette smoke out between his teeth in a gesture of disgust and threw the stub out of the window. "They told us to hold back on action till they've tried more negotiations as they call them, so we're waiting, just like we always are."

As they approached the town with the lake on their right, Sophia turned towards Dina. "I'll be getting off before you. Dina…there's something I need to tell you before we say goodbye. Before he died Mr B called me into his room and asked me to do something unusual. He said he was asking me because since you'd left there was nobody else he could trust. He asked me to witness his signature on a change he made to his will. I don't know what that change was and nor would I expect to be told but he took this very seriously and asked me to make sure I delivered it myself, by hand, to the solicitor, which of course I did. He swore me to secrecy, except for you. He said I could tell you if I ever saw you again."

Dina looked at Sophia in surprise. "Me? Why me?"

"I don't know but I suppose it must mean it's got something to do with you!"

CHAPTER EIGHTEEN

"Between 1971 and 1973 I was involved in the London Night Cleaner's Campaign. These women cleaned office blocks in the City of London. They campaigned to join the Transport & General Workers Union. By doing that they challenged the white, male, trade union complacency. Night cleaners received less pay than day cleaners, no Sunday bonus, no holiday pay, no security and could be sacked without notice."

Sophia's parting words had stayed with Dina and she couldn't put them aside. She considered they could only mean one thing, that she had been named in the will. Then she told herself this was ridiculous. The mystery excited her. She believed Sophia seemed trustworthy. She would have told Dina if she knew more. Dina had tried phoning the nurse but there was never any answer. She would like to speak with her again because she felt there was a bond between them born out of their care for Mr B.

As she pushed her mop backwards and forwards, Dina thought how modest her family Christmas celebrations would have to be. Rena was out of work and sick. For Nikos, like all building workers, it was difficult to find work in the winter months. Severe weather in Kastoria made sure of that. So Dina's wage was their only security. Not that she really cared much about Christmas; it wasn't like celebrating a new year but it was more for Evy that she felt sad. Still, maybe they could afford a small tree to decorate and she would do a deal with the butcher, who was, after all, a distant relative. He could afford to sell her a turkey a bit cheaper without losing his business.

Dina rested her weight against the mop handle and surveyed her work, sighing; a long stretch of a sigh. Miss Dabas's apartment never seemed to scrub up as well as the other houses she cleaned. Maybe it was the poor quality of the floor tiles or just that she always cleaned it on Mondays and on Mondays she had little enthusiasm for anything. If she looked at the same floor on a Friday it would probably shine and smile at her. Not that anyone was going to see it anyway. Miss Dabas was hardly there and always spent Christmas with her parents in Athens.

While she sluiced the soapy water down the sink, Dina watched the bustling street below her; people coming and going from doorways, buying, selling, and gossiping. The peel of the bells at Agios Nikolaos echoed across the street. It was the funeral toll, announcing another death. Not another one, thought Dina. The cold must be killing them off!

At the same time an argument had broken out between two rival Christmas tree vendors who had both installed themselves on the corner of Mitropoleous. A tree had toppled over into the road in front of an oncoming car whose driver had abandoned his vehicle. "For Christ's sake, what's the matter with the two of you? D'you want to cause an accident?" His hands raised in the air, gesticulating towards the road. The two vendors looked at each other. "You're to blame!" Shouted one to the other. Seeing his chance the driver grabbed the tree from in front his car, shoved it into the back seat and drove off laughing.

"Bah! You idiot! Now we're both worse off. Why don't you take your scrawny trees to another pitch instead of crowding me out and driving away customers?" The fatter of the two men puffed out his chest, put both hands in his pockets and planted his feet a decent distance apart. He was not moving. From lower down the street the nut vendor had caught sight of the dispute and begun to drag his trolley towards the men, its chimney belching out little puffs of sunflower seed aroma.

Dina chuckled. This was an entirely different view of life from the one she used to study from Mr B's balcony. The smell of grinding coffee beans teased her nostrils as it was fanned up towards her by an ice edged breeze. She inhaled, licked her lips and closed the window.

Miss Dabas had left Dina a Christmas card sandwiched between the salt and pepper on the kitchen table.

It read:
To Dina,
Wishing you a Happy Christmas
And a
Peaceful and Prosperous New Year 1975
Marilena Dabas

Miss Dabas always left Dina dainty sweets or leftovers from the numerous parties she went to. This week it was sugared almonds and she had placed an extra thousand drachmes for Christmas inside the little net *koufeta*. There must have been a wedding or christening, thought Dina as she popped one into her mouth and filled the *briki* with water to make herself a coffee. The tip was welcome. It had come at exactly the right time and renewed her trust in Greek humanity. She felt really grateful to Miss Dabas because she knew she wasn't a wealthy young woman. She must have been tempted to spend the money on other things, like new clothes or going out to a *taverna* with friends.

Sophia's words slipped themselves into her thoughts again. She let her mind wander into surreal pictures of thousand drachma notes fluttering from a turquoise sky above Mr B's house. The coffee boiled over, leaving a bitter, burnt tang hanging in the air. Abandoning her break, Dina decided to change the bed linen instead. She didn't like it when her mind took her to places she couldn't control and then left her with the consequences. She set to work, fervently stripping the pillowcases and sheets.

Miss Dabas had such beautiful sheets. Each corner was shaped into a finely hand-embroidered rose, deep red silk stitching, so smooth and even that it resembled velvet.

Pressing them against her cheek Dina almost conjured up the perfume of the rose. Miss Dabas had told Dina that they had been intended for her dowry, given to her by her grandmother before she died in the hope that her granddaughter would soon secure a husband. That was three years ago, Miss Dabas was now twenty four, enjoying her sheets and still unmarried despite her parents best efforts.

As she smoothed the sheets rhythmically across the bed Dina was thinking how little progress Greek women had made since she was young. Here was a perfectly happy, educated young woman who was continually reminded that she could not be fulfilled until she married and had children and what was the end result of all this? The poor thing was becoming depressed, having to go along with the matches arranged periodically by her parents in Athens. Why didn't they just leave her alone? They all acted out of selfishness really, pressurising them to marry and then once they'd jumped through that hoop they started on the baby bit.

Dina flicked her feather duster along the slats of the shutters and locked them for the holiday. She thought of her own life, never relying on a man, never depending on one economically, nice as that would have been at times. Oh for the companionship and love and intimacy! That was the worst thing. But she had survived without a man. Ach! She shook her head from side to side. Women were their own worst enemies sometimes! Kiria Mavros, her next-door neighbour, was always bleating at her two daughters to get married and the youngest not even twenty-five yet.

Sometimes Dina thought it was so that women could punish their daughters for having put them through the traumas and trials of motherhood. It would soon make them realise and appreciate their mothers. But then in the rest of Europe and America it seemed, the women were revolting and saying no, demanding equality. Dina's years in Yugoslavia had opened her eyes to the way a country could treat its women equally. Yes. They could teach Greece a thing or two. She'd heard that even in England, where she'd always assumed things went on peacefully, there had been a big campaign to unionise the women night-cleaners who cleaned big office blocks during the night. God, she wouldn't fancy doing that! Cleaning people's houses in the day was one thing but having to work all night and be finished by the time the offices opened in the morning was much worse. The more she thought about women and men the more questions popped into Dina's head. What did women really want? Equality? But who with? Men? Surely not! There had to be a better aim than that. But the funny thing was that when she was fighting alongside men in the *Emfilio* they'd always treated her as an equal. There was nothing the men did that she couldn't and didn't do and that was war. Would they have to go to war again to get equality?

    Dina emptied the small rubbish bin into a large plastic bag, tied its ends and put it out onto the balcony, making a mental note to take it down with her when she left that day. She shivered in her thin nylon overall and retreated quickly into the kitchen.

    So why was it different in war -time? Katerina had talked sense when she said they should make the most of their time in the Democratic Army and that war, terrible as it was, brought opportunities for women that they wouldn't experience again. Dina stared down at her old shoes despondently. But look! Where had it all got them? That equality had evaporated like a puddle in the Cretan sun. At least it had in Greece. Women's views were more often than not ignored and wages, well! Women's wages were a joke. Maybe it would change with the generations. Yes. That was it! Dina shook off her shoes and pulled on her boots, ready for treading the cold pavements home. It was a generational thing and eventually the older attitudes would die out. But even as she put on her coat and wound her woollen scarf round her neck Dina had doubts about this last possibility.

The good thing about Miss Dabas's apartment, thought Dina, was that she could clean it quicker and it left her in the centre of town to do any shopping on her way home whereas Mr B's was a much longer walk to the bakery. Here we go again, she realised, I'm thinking about his house again, comparing it with this. Dina locked up Miss Dabas's and dropped the keys into her pocket. She decided to approach the tree vendors for a price but on closer inspection, changed her mind.

"No wonder you haven't sold any! They're not exactly full bodied are they Kirios? Look at these little thin branches. You've uprooted them too young."

The fat vendor glared at Dina and then began to fold up his table as if her words had struck the decisive blow to his disappointing day. Dina knew very well that they were stolen trees but she was hardly the type of person to inform on the men. People had to make a living as best they could.

Large ominous clouds had begun to form over the hills to the west. More snow was on its way. Dina could smell it as surely as she could hear the wails of the women coming from the nearby churchyard. Crunching the frozen clods of snow that had riveted themselves to the pavement underfoot, Dina left the bakery with two fresh warm loaves pinned against her chest. Dina broke off a large chunk of crust that she chewed and savoured all the way to the bus stop. A wave of mild satisfaction and relief rolled over her. Monday was looking better than it had five hours ago.

And it got better. That evening Ketty appeared at Dina's door with a fresh black spruce for Christmas. She carried it over to the window. It left behind it a spicy perfumed trail in the air. Evy jumped up and down as if she was on a spring, her arms flapping at her sides. Her eyes became two huge green saucers speaking her joy and anticipation. Dina hugged Ketty. "Thank you so much Ketty. We really appreciate your thought don't we Evy?" Dina scooped the child up into her arms.

"It smells like the forest we went to. Is it from your forest *aunt*?"

Ketty beamed at Evy and pinched her cheek. "Ach! *Kardia mou.* You're a little beauty aren't you, just like your granny here, same skin and eyes." Turning to Dina. "The boys will go mad for her before you know it."

"Evy, aunt Ketty lives near the forest but it's not her forest. Shall we decorate the tree tomorrow when we've bought all the magic decorations from Kirios Gavras?"

Evy wriggled herself free from Dina and clapped her plump palms together. "Yes, yes, *yiayia*! Can't we go now and get them?"

Dina threw her hands up in the air and shook her head. "At eight in the evening when you should be in bed already? No, no. Say goodnight to aunt Ketty and go see your mother. She's waiting to read you a story. Go on. I promise you we'll decorate the tree tomorrow; now off with you, you little minx." Evy waved her hand and tore out of the room.

Ketty sat down opposite Dina and smiled. "Isn't she lovely? Oh Dina you're so lucky having a beautiful grandchild like that. It's something I'll never have." Ketty's eyes had filled up.

Dina had never seen her like that before. She had always seen her as a woman with a purpose, always busy planning and organising other people. Now she saw a glimpse of some deeper secret. "Let me get you a glass of wine or a cognac Ketty."

Ketty dabbed the wet mascara from under her eyes. "Sorry I'm a bit emotional; it's that time of year. I'll...I'll tell you all about it some time Dina but not tonight. Now, I'll have that cognac but just a small one, don't go pouring me a big glass or I'll fall over going home."

Dina admired Ketty as she crossed her shapely legs and adjusted a brown tweed skirt. Ketty was a slight woman, much like herself, thought Dina, but she dressed with taste and care. She wore a black crew neck jumper under her fur coat, set off by a string of elegant pearls round a throat that was remarkably free of lines for a woman of her age. Dina liked Ketty a lot but she felt old sitting next to her. Ketty kept her coat on. Dina was ashamed of her cold flat. They didn't have guests that often.

"Anyway, Dina. That tree isn't the only good thing I've brought you tonight. I've some good news as well. Starting in the New Year you have a job on Fridays at Kiria Lakounis' house. She wants you for five hours a week and she'll match whatever wages you get at the moment. Don't consider that generous, she's just so loaded it won't matter to her."

Relieved, Dina took a big gulp of cognac. "How can I repay you for what you've done for me Ketty? Thank you again; that's the best news I've had in a long time."

"What are friends for? I said I'd try. Give me a piece of paper to write down her address and phone number."

Dina rustled around on the table and found an empty envelope. "Does she want to meet me before I start?"

"No. You come recommended to her." Ketty stubbed out her cigarette and wrapped her coat tighter around her.

"I'm sorry about the cold – these old heating systems are useless in this weather but I suppose we get used to it."

Ketty patted Dina's knee. "Don't you worry about me I'll be fine. I always feel the cold a lot anyway. That's why I wear this all the time." She indicated her coat, a rich brown fur. "Once you put on one of these you'll never be able to take it off. I bet Kiria Lakounis has got a few of these in her wardrobe." Ketty giggled mischievously. "Maybe you could slip one out without her noticing."

Dina stared. "And lose the job before I've hardly started? Don't be mad."

"Well! She's got so many she probably wouldn't even miss it."

Inside Kirios Gavras's shop at Christmas time was like a fairy's grotto. Purple, red and silver lights twinkled from the four corners, fading silently on and off. Small cardboard boxes containing trinkets and big glittering baubles were set out on the counter, impossible for a small child like Evy to miss. She moved back slightly in hesitation when the owner suddenly leapt through his door and peered at her from behind a pair of dark rimmed glasses. Dina felt her grandchild pushing shyly into her side, hiding her face in Dina's coat. She stroked Evy's mass of tangled black hair, smiling at Kirios Gavras. "Now she's afraid to touch them."

The shop-owner pushed his glasses further up his big nose and leant back away from the counter, beckoning Evy to come forward. She relaxed her grip from Dina's side, her eyes flitting from box to box. "That one and that silver one there and the little gold star. Can I have those *yiayia*?"

"Well I'm sure the Kirios here will put them all into their own special box for you won't you Petro?" Dina winked at him. "And how about some tinsel to drape over our lovely tree? Shall we have some of that too?" Then Dina's eye spotted the small white dove nestling in its own box. "Ah, look Evy, look at the beautiful dove. We'll put it on top of the tree for peace."

"And the white snow *yiayia*. We need the snow."

"We'll have to go to another shop for that my love, the one that sells shampoo for washing your hair and we need to do that tonight."

CHAPTER NINETEEN

"Those of us who were still alive fought the last battles of the Emfilio on Grammos and Vitsi mountains, close to the Albanian border. Some of us found ourselves in the People's Democracy of Yugoslavia, Albania, Bulgaria, Czechoslovakia and USSR. Some have never returned to Greece."

"The language of childbirth knows no country"

Dina leant against an old peeling pillar, relieved that another Christmas was over. It hadn't been as frugal as she had feared. Her cousin had come up with a turkey at a reasonable cost and Rena had been well enough to cook it. There had been wine, at least for Nikos, and they had all put their money together to buy Evy a doll's pram. But even so, she was glad it was over for another year. And now, she mused, it was almost 1975 and they were no better off, life didn't seem to get any easier. Wages were barely enough to live on. Dina bit the inside of her lower lip and spoke severely to herself. That was defeatist, depressive talk and on New Year's Eve of all nights.

She was standing in her neighbourhood *taverna*, her left hand cupping her right elbow while she smoked a soothing cigarette. Having re-dyed her hair, Dina at least felt renewed in one sense even though the evening had not started as she would have liked. She was intolerant of her own dark thoughts when they crowded her head but trying to chase them away with positive ones, never did any good either. Wary of making any resolutions for the forthcoming year, Dina's thoughts slid into her new Friday job, wondering what Kiria Lakounis would be like as an employer and if her wardrobes would really be full of furs from her husband's shop. Wicked woman, she berated herself, thinking about Ketty's remarks. No. If she was ever going to get her hands on a fur it would be honestly.

Then the music began and as usual when she heard the voice of Faradouri rousing the whole *taverna*, she began to feel better. The strength and commitment of Faradouri's voice awoke emotions and broke through all the feeble doubt hiding in her heart. And not just in her heart. She watched the effect it had on her neighbours and friends as they bellowed the chorus, their eyes shining with tears. The music was so compelling that even the children were tempted away from their games to emulate their parents. Plumes of purple cigarette smoke fused into a haze- like cloud overhanging a valley, where below the people revelled, forgetful of their year, bad or good, singing, dancing, all animation.

Dina watched Ketty threading sideways in her direction, holding a carafe of wine high up above her head. Because it was New Year's Eve, the *taverna* owner had covered the old rickety tables with fine red cotton cloths and provided his customers with olives and *tsipouro* to start their evening. Ketty set the wine down and drew up her chair, her golden brown hair swept onto the top of her head and fixed with a red ribbon.

Dina filled their glasses. "You look wonderful. You should wear your hair up more often Ketty. You look like royalty tonight!" Dina and Ketty didn't really know each other very well but Dina admired the woman's assertive and yet warm manner. She was clearly a brilliant organiser in any situation. She found it very easy to talk to Ketty and she had already been a great help to Dina.

Ketty laughed. "*Thee mou!* Don't say that. What's your secret then Dina? You've got more energy in your little finger than most women of your age have in their whole bodies. Now. Tell me how you do it. Where d'you get your spirit from?"

Dina considered the question. "I don't know. I suppose you're born like that to some extent. The rest, well, maybe what happens to you when you're young has something to do with how you carry on later, you know, how you handle things in later life." Dina swallowed her wine, reconsidering her answer. "But you know Ketty, I'm not always spirited. Sometimes I'm down. Really down. I felt a bit like that tonight. If it hadn't been for the likes of Farandouri I don't know if I'd have stayed here."

Ketty smiled. "D'you think your time in the D.A. was a big part of it then?"

Dina had never told Ketty herself about her part in the civil war but she would have heard it from Dimitris. "Maybe. Well, I had to grow up pretty fast. We all did and then losing Maki…if I'd been at home, if we hadn't been at war I think it would have been much harder. At least the war meant I could focus on something outside myself. I did that. I just buried myself in the war. It became everything to me. Nothing else mattered. My only existence was there in the mountains and I didn't care if I lived or died after Maki went. It was the years following that were the hardest."

"What did you do Dina? Where did you go?" Ketty moved closer to Dina to hear more clearly over the singing and shouting.

Hesitation must have shown on Dina's face as Ketty added. "Don't think I'm prying Dina. If you'd rather not talk about it…"

"No. It's okay. It's almost 1975. Tme I was able to share those experiences without being afraid. It's Rena's birthday next month. She was born in 1949 in Yugoslavia. I crossed the border and gave birth two days later."

"So you were still fighting while you were pregnant with her? That must have been hard Dina." Ketty smirked. "How did you get the uniform on?"

Dina pushed Ketty's elbow. "Trust you to think of clothes at a time like that! Forget the uniform. Ask me how I ran from the ambush in Grammos with an ancient Russian rifle slung over my back and ended up in a frozen ditch."

"Go on then, tell me."

They had lifted her as gently as the unusual circumstances would allow. Three men, hesitant, sensitive to their predicament. It was, they had all agreed at the celebration after, a very delicate situation. Delicate. The word was emphasised in drunken humour but in a language foreign to Dina. Long and hard they had searched their heads and scratched their shaven scalps but in vain. None of them spoke Greek but one of them, a young boy no more than seventeen, offered the word to Dina in his best French. Afterwards, when she rested in the hospital in Skopje, her new daughter in her arms, Dina was lucky enough to find a doctor who spoke French and Greek. "Delicat". He said smiling. "You were in a delicat situation. *Lepti katastasi*".

"Aha!" Dina chuckled, recalling the men's faces when she had first stared up at them from the depths of the ditch. "I certainly was doctor."

That same ditch had sheltered Dina from the random bullets whistling past in both directions but she knew it couldn't hide her from the air attack that would inevitably follow. Sombre thoughts filled Dina's head as she lay, wedged sideways, the only comfortable position, her rifle ready to defend herself. Who was she kidding? One shell on target and she wouldn't know any more. She would have liked to have given birth before she died. One life; her own life. She was expendable but two? Why should her unborn baby die as well just like her father had done?

'Pull yourself together woman', she had said to herself. 'This is no time for tears.'

Then miraculously, they had appeared above her, peering into the abyss, disbelieving of their own eyes. One remained above while the other two scrambled down to Dina. She still aimed her rifle at them, unsure of their allegiance. But she had no resistance left in her body and they lifted her as carefully as they could, passing her up like a body rising from the grave, to their comrade waiting above. They gave Dina water and the remains of the bread they were carrying and then debated how best to carry her to the nearest railway tracks. But Dina insisted on walking, believing herself to be exhausted rather than in labour. They escorted her, the youngest taking her rifle so that she travelled as lightly as possible.

In this way Dina and the ragged band of soldiers flagged down the next train headed for Skopje. The old wooden wagons rattled and swayed under Dina as she tried to sleep. The assembled crew of war weary soldiers had done their best to make room for her and gave up their coats willingly but the bitter February winds sliced their way through the slatted floors of the wagon and made hissing noises. Years later Dina could still remember some of their faces. The shrunken faced boy who coughed his lungs out in bursts of three. In his discomfort he tried to be respectful to Dina, moving to the edge of the wagon, propping himself against the sliding door like a spare metal post. Dina had hoped it wasn't tuberculosis. She didn't fancy the idea of going through a war only to die of a disease like that.

She recalled the men as they averted their eyes from her, probably embarrassed that they could do nothing to make her journey more comfortable. Several of them were her compatriots. To be able to talk in her own language had seemed like a luxury to Dina. The men had joked, sotto voice, about some of the Yugoslavs on board. How they idolised Tito. That kind of worship was unhealthy, they had argued. No one person could hold all the truth. There had to be a variety of views for a real socialist society to work. They weren't convinced that going to Yugoslavia was going to a better place, like heaven or something. What they wanted was to stay in their own country. To be valued.

. Even so, another insisted, the Yugoslavs had helped their Greek struggle and what were they doing now if it wasn't opening their borders to the Greek refugees?

For a few hours Dina had managed to convince herself that the twinges she felt came from her old shrapnel wound but both her legs were numb from the cold and the sensation was a vague aching coming from her back and encircling her waist. She was only twenty-five yet she felt she knew more about war and death than she did about life. Giving birth was something she hadn't had time to think about or to fear. But now the twinges were changing to dull pains Dina was forced to accept she may be in the early stages of labour. The thought frightened her more than any of the battles she had found herself in, more than lying in the ditch waiting for her own death.

Her train lumbered and chugged into the crumbling Skopje station, emitting huge clouds of steam like an exhausted runner flinging himself at the winning tape. The pains came every ten minutes now. Unknown hands lifted her high above the crowds swarming off the train onto the platform. She could hear men shouting in the language she didn't understand and then she was bundled into the back of a truck, howling every time the pain struck her. How wicked was this pain! Worse than any shrapnel hit. Deeper than all the stitches she remembered being sewn into her hand wound.

Then, in a white room, echoes, women's voices. At last women's voices and female hands smoothing back her once black hair, now white. White hair on a twenty-five year old woman. But they had seen it before. The shock of bad news, fear and trauma preyed on young *andarte*s like Dina and from one day to the next their beautiful hair could turn white. They reminded her how she had shouted and screamed in her own language during the birth but it didn't matter to them because the language of childbirth knew no country. They understood her pain and followed it through with her until little Rena shot out. "Just like a bullet", they had joked afterwards.

Dina cradled her daughter in her arms, searching for traces of Makis and finding them in her eyes and shape of her tiny nose. She studied her daughter as if she was a rare work of art and she cried, releasing more than just the birth experience. The three wise comrades who had saved Dina's life, gathered around her bedside and made cooing noises at the baby. And they had each brought a gift. Hand knitted, baby white bootees, three sizes too big; a thick chunk of the best feta. Dina hadn't eaten feta for many months. Her mouth watered at the sight of it. The young one brought her a warm red woollen hat that he planted proudly on her head, stepping back to admire it. She squeezed the men's hands, tearful, overwhelmed by their kindness.

She realised that she had arrived to stay. Yugoslavia was where she had landed, like a migrating bird. It was up to her to make it her home for as long as necessary. She wasn't alone any more and she adopted the responsibilities of motherhood as she had taken up arms – with conviction and trust in herself. But one thing she always knew in her heart was that she and Rena would return to Greece. What she didn't know was that it would take them twenty two years.

"Ach! You poor thing! What you went through. And you come out of it all alive! Little Rena, how did she survive through that? No wonder you can face things as they come at you now."

Dina was being reminded of a time that she would rather forget but it was too late because Ketty's questions had already set free the painful memories.

"Rena was born with a weakness because of that she took on the burden of my soldiering and now look at her; because of me she was a weak child and now she's even sicker because she's had to work in that factory. I haven't really done her any favours by giving birth to her have I Ketty?"

Moving closer, Ketty took Dina's hand tenderly in her own. "Now then, don't you ever blame yourself for what those bastards do every day to millions of workers in their factories. You ask Rena if she'd rather she hadn't been born and you know the answer. And another thing, your children are proud to have a mother who risked her life liberating our country, standing up against those bastards! Come on Dina! Stop denying yourself what you deserve. You'll see, in times to come they'll write about women like you." Ketty poured them more wine and pushed a handkerchief in front of Dina. "At least you have a child and grandchild."

"You said that before Ketty. So, tell me. Why haven't you and Ari got any?"

"Some would call it bad luck but I call it deliberate botching, revenge against a woman who refused to do what she was told." Ketty folded and refolded her paper napkin into squares. "I got pregnant at seventeen, said no to marrying the boy who was responsible, ran away to Saloniki and was unlucky with an abortion. It left me unable to conceive, such a mess he made of it. That butcher! Called himself a doctor!" Ketty took a gulp of wine to drown her anger. "My family had promised me to the baker's son, huh! Michaelis was his name. My mother had already filled a trunk with her stupid starched sheets and my grandmother's woven rug, a couple of our goats as well, for my dowry! I imagined that life often and you know Dina, the biggest dread was the inevitable pregnancies that would have followed one after the other, child after child, never leaving the village, always having given birth or about to become pregnant again, year after year. And now! What I would've given for one of those pregnancies but it's too late and I've had to live my life differently. But Ari is a treasure. We've got each other and our friends and comrades. There's still a lot to put right in our union."

Dina nodded and gave Ketty a hug. "We've both of us got our grief Ketty and you're right, there's still a lot to be done. You've done a great job with the bus workers. It's obvious you're the organiser there."

Ketty smiled and raised her glass to meet Dina's. "To women, like us, everywhere."

Meanwhile, hysterical children, abandoned by their parents, were lobbing firecrackers out into the narrow street, scaring even the feral cats that roamed the alleyways in search of scraps.

" There was no chance of me being sent back to fight on the front line because I'd had three victims in my family and when you'd lost three members of your family you weren't allowed to go and fight. I went to Buljkes, an *andartes* camp in Yugoslavia and I spent my time sewing clothes while Rena was little. They had wonderful nurseries for the children. They would put ours to shame here, even now. Then I got a job in a factory weaving thread for rugs. We worked so hard we raised the production levels and the local women resented us a bit for that. That's when I had my hand operated on. This one". Dina held out her right hand for Ketty to see. Between her thumb and forefinger a deep silvery scar still stretched her skin. "The worker behind me drank too much; he used to referee our Greek football team. I took over his machine for him and the Gestapo woman behind let go her machine and the thread broke. I put my hands up to protect myself and the thread wrapped itself round both my hands. It caught my overall, we didn't have dresses then. I don't know how I found the strength but I managed to stop the machine. Then I woke up in hospital to see this ugly scar."

Ketty patted the scarred hand and sighed. "At least they saved your hand Dina."

"Yes so I could spend the rest of my life scrubbing and polishing with it!" Dina took another gulp of wine. "It's time we had more of this." She stood up from her chair and waved the empty wine carafe at a passing waiter.

Ketty speared an olive with a toothpick. "Tell me more Dina. Were the Popular Democracies all they were made out to be? I've heard stories about their education system and everything."

"You saw women driving buses, trains. It didn't seem to make any difference if you were a man or woman. Rena had good schooling. She would have gone on to study engineering would you believe it! And then when we came back here, to our homeland. What a joke! She ends up in a factory working on a conveyor belt." Dina felt her hatred mounting. "If we'd stayed in Skopje we would've been better off and healthier and probably happier than here. What do we offer our kids, eh Ketty? An education system that's so corrupt you can buy your way into the top if you've got the money. Otherwise forget it."

"D'you wish you'd stayed there then? D'you regret coming back?" Ketty grabbed the waiter's arm. "Bring us some pork and potatoes before we faint will you please, *paidi mou?*" The waiter nodded and put the wine carafe down on the table.

Dina smiled at Ketty. She could see how she got things done in her workplace. "No Ketty, I could never regret coming back. I would never have seen my mother again. This is where I belong. It's just that I get mad when I see the possibilities here, the beauty. Most of us never get to enjoy it. I seem to have spent my whole life fighting against the odds, trying to do what's impossible."

"Maybe that's your destiny eh?" Ketty downed her glass in one gulp and refilled it, her voice becoming faintly lyrical. She grinned at Dina and coaxed her into another glass of wine. "We need to eat something or we'll be under the table before midnight."

"Looks like you're nearly there already. Go on then, pour me another."

CHAPTER TWENTY

"It sometimes seems like we had more equality between the sexes then, you know, during the Emfilio because whether you were a man or a woman wasn't the most important thing, not when you faced hunger and maybe your last day. Who knows? We lived each day and no more. When the war was over those of us who could, went back to our homes. But I don't think it went back to normal for most of us ever again. Yes, we ended up doing the same old cooking, cleaning, caring but we never forgot those times, the excitement all mixed up with fear and I don't believe there's a woman who doesn't sometimes wish she was back in the mountains. Don't misunderstand me, I don't mean the horror, the killing. But maybe you will think I'm romanticising it."

"Did you know Dina, that our ancient ancestors chewed dill to keep themselves awake during the interminable speeches of senators or when they had to sit through long plays at the theatre?" Kiria Lakounis was preparing to entertain guests that evening and was mixing her ingredients in a large bowl.

Dina was searching for the sack of chickpeas, one of many on the huge larder floor. She stood upright, rubbing her back, when she heard Kiria Lakounis. "I imagine they must have needed it. That's all they seemed to do, sit on their backsides for hours!"

Kiria Lakounis giggled. "I think my guests will need it tonight if my husband starts on one of his political tirades. I prefer to 9numb myself with wine before he starts." She slid the dish into the oven, washed her hands and retreated to the balcony to pluck some thyme from a large terracotta pot. As she moved she left a trail of expensive perfume.

The larder was so huge and full of all sorts of foodstuffs that Dina's slight form was swallowed up among the sacks of pulses, vats of olives (harvested from the Lakounis own olive groves) and bottles of red wine.

Tall, almost regal, Dina thought Kiria Lakounis was everything that Vassiliki was not. Just look how she carries her beautifully cut clothes, she said to herself as she studied her from the larder door. But when Dina had the opportunity of looking deeply into her employer's face she saw a strange loneliness in her candid brown eyes. It was as if she went through all the motions of being a perfect mother and housewife and was never found wanting but that she did it all without conviction. She entertained when her husband's position demanded it, which was often, and she put on the most sumptuous displays of food that Dina had ever seen, most of which she cooked herself. She tended to all four of her children's needs. This surprised Dina. She had imagined that such a wealthy family would employ a nanny but it seemed that Olga Lakounis preferred to do it all herself.

"I like you Dina, you make me laugh." Olga Lakounis grinned. "I look forward to you coming on Fridays. It's good to have an ordinary, decent person to talk with."

Ordinary, decent – Dina was glad she was decent and ordinary. Therre was a comfort in being appreciated and thought of as ordinary. She also liked Olga Lakounis. "Well, thank-you Kiria Lakounis, I enjoy coming here to your beautiful home and if I've made somebody laugh in my day then I reckon I've done a good thing."

It was a coincidence that the Lakounis house was at the far end of the same road as Mr B's. Dina had been told it was the largest house in Kastoria but she still preferred Mr B's and missed its familiar smell and feel. Lately she had put Sophia's words out of her mind but now, as she polished the rich walnut banister, they came back at her and she felt slightly disappointed that the talk of his will had all come to nothing. Sophia had disappeared.

The broad wooden staircase looked like something from a film to Dina. If she stood still and waited she could imagine a glamorous star like Audrey Hepburn in My Fair Lady come gliding down those stairs, her long white gloves poised over

Dina's glossy banisters. Dina had bent down to pick up her bucket and on straightening up found herself looking into the eyes of Kirios Lakounis who had just come through the front door. So this was Olga's husband. Dina saw him freeze on seeing her. A startled, trapped rabbit. She would have introduced herself but he appeared so uncomfortable with her presence that she didn't. Ketty had been right, Kirios Lakounis was not the man in the fur shop but somehow she had a strange feeling that she knew this man from somewhere. His hesitation was only brief and he was off down the corridor, heading for the kitchen. He carried a black briefcase. Very important looking, thought Dina. A rotund man in a dark, expensive suit, his thick black hair greying at the temples. Each step of his newly shined shoes made a squeak as he crossed the marble floor.

It wasn't until she was ankle deep in crumpled white sheets in the laundry room that it came to Dina. He was the man in the square. His face had been half hidden by the branch of the tree but it was him. And the briefcase! The whole scene played back to her as if it had been yesterday and when she remembered, she wished she hadn't. Kirios Lakounis had clearly forgotten his briefcase as he hurried across Dina's local square. The woman running after him and trying to catch him up was the woman in the beige trouser suit. Her first thought was surprise. With a beautiful wife like that why on earth did he need to visit prostitutes? This was followed by anger. Bastard! She felt her position in the house had been compromised, knowing something like that with poor Olga around. In that moment Dina hated men.

Olga Lakounis liked her sheets starched white. Luckily for Dina this meant piling them into bags and handing them over to the delivery man from the laundry so all she had to get on with were the rest of the family clothes. Sometimes, when she cleaned the room of Olga's eldest daughter. Dina would be faced with little heaps of clean clothes that had been discarded from their drawers and left on the floor for Dina to pick up. On this day, while she was still angry with men, Dina made the decision that she would leave Athena's clothes on the floor.

"Our last cleaner did it. She was a nice, kind woman!"

"And I am also a nice kind woman but I am a cleaner not a slave."

Fifteen-year-old Athena shifted her feet apart, putting her hands on her hips. "I'll have to tell my mother in that case and you'll be sacked for not doing your job."

I'll probably be sacked anyway now, thanks to your father. Dina thought of Kirios Lakounis and what he might do to prevent his wife finding out what he was up to.

"Tell your mother. I think she will agree with me *paidi mou*."

Of course, Olga Lakounis did agree with Dina.

Later that evening, while Dina was enjoying a coffee with her feet up, her thoughts returned to Olga's husband. Her anger had abated by then and she was more able to think of things rationally. It was true. She had defended that woman to her female neighbours. Now it seemed that her justification for the woman's activities had been perhaps a bit too generous. Her new employer was a wronged woman and she felt a definite loyalty to her but it also didn't seem fair to put all the blame for that sort of activity onto the other woman. Surely the man had some responsibility in all of this as well! Why were men so dissatisfied with their lives? Women just got on with it and took the good with the bad but men…they seemed to like women one of two ways, either as a thing to buy or to keep imprisoned at home to bear their children. That wasn't the way she had been treated in the war. So much for progress!

The following Friday morning, Dina began her routine at the Lakounis house by washing up after the usual breakfast chaos of four children. Olga Lakounis was buttoning up the coat of her youngest child, eight year old Thanasis, in preparation for his walk to school. The January snows had fallen steadily that year, the temperature rarely rising above freezing. Thanasis stamped his feet, impatient to be outside, treading the depths of the newly laid snow. He pulled his mother towards the door, leaning back so that he was at a diagonal angle to her.

"Okay, okay. We're going my child. See you later Dina. I'll probably be a bit delayed because I have to pick up books for Athena."

"Enjoy your walk Thanasi." Dina plunged her gloved hands back into the washing up bowl. She liked the youngest Lakounis child. He reminded her of Evy, full of a spirit of adventure and curiosity.

The cold of the marble floor penetrated the thin soles of Dina's shoes. Her feet shrivelled. Next week she would keep her boots on indoors. As she was about to turn on the radio for some company, she heard a noise, like a squeak. At first she was afraid it might be a mouse that had found its way up from the cellar but then she sensed something human, familiar. She turned round to face Kirios Lakounis hovering in the kitchen doorway. Dina was shocked. She had believed herself alone. Kirios Lakounis moved forward.

"Kiria, we need to talk."

"Oh! Do we?" Dina stood there, her rubber gloves dripping water.

"It's just that…I know what you saw and your opinion of me is probably…"

"It's really none of my business Kirios Lakounis. I'd rather not."

Kirios Lakounis straightened his dark grey tie. Dina noticed he looked younger than he had when she had first encountered him last week. "But you did see me, you don't deny that?"

Dina shifted awkwardly from one foot to the other. Both her feet were now numb. "No. How could I deny that? It's my local *plateia* and I know the people who live round there."

"Well then, I think I may be able to sort this out to satisfy both of us. My situation is, how can I say?"

"Delicate?" Dina offered, beginning to sense what was coming.

"Yes. Exactly. You understand completely that for a man in my position, my wife, nobody must know about my…"

"Your visits to the prostitute!" There. She had said it.

His face darkened. "I don't like to think of it like that but anyway what I want is to repay you in some way. I thought perhaps, one of my furs?"

What she wouldn't have given to be wearing one of them now. She felt so cold today. How could this be happening? To think, a fur coat, her own, for nothing! No. Not for nothing. Everything had its price. "So, if I understand you right, you're offering me one of your furs if I say nothing about what I've seen? Well, you needn't stoop so low Kirios Lakounis. Cold as I am I couldn't accept your generous offer. I'm not about to tell your wife what you do when you're away from her. I respect her too much to be the messenger of news like that."

They hadn't heard the front door.

Kirios Lakounis stood there, a frightened man. Dina wanted to go from the room but there stood Olga in the doorway, her face ashen. "News like what Dina?"

Dina's heart pounded. She needed a cigarette. "Please Kiria Lakounis, don't ask me. This is none of my business. I'm sorry."

"You've nothing to be sorry for Dina." She turned her head towards her husband. Dina saw the contempt on Olga Lakounis's face. "If it wasn't for our children I would have left you years ago and now you stoop so low as to try and bribe my cleaner. How could you Aleko?" She slammed the kitchen door, trembling. Avoiding her eyes, thought Dina. He can't look at her through that guilty conscience.

Dina decided she would not stay in the room a minute longer. If she could have blocked her ears and eyes she would have done. It was only mid morning and she had plenty of cleaning yet to do. The beds needed stripping, the rugs beating and then the floors would have to be swept and washed but somehow Dina just couldn't bear the idea of remaining in the house. She made a hasty decision to go home, darted out the kitchen, grabbing her coat on the way. She would take whatever consequences awaited her.

Leaving so abruptly was something Dina had never done to an employer and she turned her reasons over in her mind as she walked along the promenade beside the frozen lakeshore. It was so cold that the tiniest branches of the trees overhanging the lake had frozen into brittle glasslike splinters, suspended downwards like stalactites.

She really hadn't wanted to get involved in a domestic scene between husband and wife and she doubted her ability to remain neutral when she knew all her sympathies lay with Olga Lakounis. But she also felt tainted by the offer Kirios Lakounis had made to her. It was an insult, made worse because it was as if he knew how tempting that fur would be to her, the poor, shivering cleaner. Dina was so preoccupied by her thoughts that she nearly forgot to buy bread. She was greeted with a 'you're early today Dina,' from the baker's wife who was already putting Dina's usual loaf in a bag. But Dina was in no mood to talk and anyway she would have to make up some ridiculous story. She returned the woman's curiosity with a smile and continued along the Orestion promenade. She always grimaced when she saw the old bent road sign, its black arrow and the words: Towards Florina and Albania. Who in their right minds would want to go to either?

It was turning out to be a bitterly cold start to 1975. Dina felt herself cowering under the cold even though the sun had come out and the sky cleared of its voluptuous clouds. Walking home meant that at least Dina could appreciate the beautiful sculptures made by the freezing of the lakeshore. Even the gnarled, sprawling tree roots were frozen solid onto the promenade. The lake lay there beside her as she walked, still, deep, cobalt blue in the middle, its edges frosted like a framed painting. A lone, long necked swan glided alongside Dina. She took pity and lobbed it an end piece from her loaf of bread. Plummeting half its neck into the depths, the graceful creature resurfaced with the bread secured in its orange bill. The gentle splash made by the swan's head as it dived was the only sound to break the brittle silence.

Worried by the consequences of her hasty departure, Dina sat down on a bench to light a cigarette. Her nerves were getting the better of her. She needed calming. But it was far too cold to stay sitting down, beautiful as the lake was. She gathered her bag and continued home, left from Orestion into Olympou and onward towards Kalithea Square. It seemed to Dina that few people were out today unless they were compelled. To occupy her thoughts as she walked she considered the possible reasons for going out, apart from work of course. Top of the list would have to be to buy the daily bread and possibly newspaper (for men), secondly children had to get to school, thirdly street vendors, poor souls, had to do their business outside in all weathers. Rounding the corner of her street she ran out of reasons and interest but noticed a solitary mother pushing her child on a swing in the playground and that made her fourth reason. She peered again at the woman and realised it was her, the woman in the beige trouser suit. And at that moment Dina felt sorry for her, not angry, not resentful, just sorry she should have to make her living like that. Then she closed the door on the cold outside world.

That same evening Olga Lakounis phoned Dina. It wasn't the phone call she had dreaded. "Dina, I'm very sorry you had to witness that scene this morning. It wasn't fair on you and it was despicable of my husband but that's nothing new where he's concerned."

Dina heard bitterness in her voice. She wasn't expecting an apology from her employer, more like a dismissal without wages for an unfinished day.

"Please Dina. Come back on Friday, don't desert me. That's the worst thing you could do. I can't cope with it all, not with the children and the house."

"Yes Kiria Lakounis, I'll…"

"I'll double your wages. I…"

"I said yes, next Friday." Dina didn't want her to change her mind.

"Oh thank-you, thank-you Dina. I'll make it worth your while."

Dina felt she should ask something, at least how Kiria Lakounis was feeling! After all, she had suffered a terrible shock. "Are you all-right Kiria? I'm sorry I walked out. I don't make a habit of doing that sort of thing. I was concerned for you though."

"Yes. I'm fine thank-you. Having the children, they don't give me time to think about it. They're my salvation!"

Dina found her voice incredibly calm for a wife who had so recently learned of her husband's cheating. Not just any cheating but paying for it. Dina thought that made it worse. "Well, if you're okay I'll see you as usual on Friday Kiria."

"Thank-you again Dina. Bye."

Poor woman! Poor women. Dina felt sorry for the two of them. They were both wronged in their own way.

CHAPTER TWENTY-ONE

"During Ethnikofrosini (National mindedness) the dictators banned all the things I liked, for example mini skirts, long hair (on men), beards (on men), some of my musician friends performed Theodorakis's music but that was also banned. I loved foreign literature but it was hard to get hold of it in translation. Sometimes we had visits from people in England and Holland and they brought us books and films. But you had to be able to read English."

The bus was late. Headlines announce the release from prison of two members of the Lambrakis Youth Movement. Dina studied the two haggard faces peering at her from the newspaper photos. She wondered how they had looked before their imprisonment and torture. The report gave their ages as twenty-two and twenty-four but they looked nearer forty. Then she saw the names and realized the younger one was Dimitris's son. *Thee mou*, he looks as old as his father. The poor child.

What have they done to you Laki?

The bus arrived. Dina dropped her coins into the slot, took her ticket and clasped the handrail. She read that the two men had been n prison for four years and that the only charges finally brought against them had been for fly posting. Leaning over her shoulder an elderly man shook his head in response to the article.

"Think of that eh! Four years for advertising a meeting. And they don't say why they didn't release them last year. This so-called New Democracy doesn't stretch to free speech does it?"

Dina was heartened by the man's words. She was not alone in her distrust of the new government. She noticed other passengers reading the article and before long was caught up in an argument that divided the bus between the government supporters and its opponents. Neither side allowed the other to finish a sentence before plunging in with ultimate truths. Dina was as animated by the arguments as any other passenger.

Someone at the back of the bus said that one of the faces was Dimitris's son. Noises of disbelief flew from open mouths.

Dina seized the opportunity. "Yes, he's right. It is Dimitris's son. He'll be overjoyed at his release. It's well overdue." There was a silent collective nodding even from the pro-government side of the bus. Good, thought Dina. Human pain goes deeper than political divisions. "And listen to this bit." Dina prepared to read to the bus. "At first the prosecutor, Yannis Hadjidakis, tried to bring an additional charge against Lakis Garganas and Sotiris Nambouris of being students of the occupied Law faculty of the Polytechnic in 1973 but this charge was dropped as at this time being a law student could not be said to constitute a crime." There was a second collective eruption. A pregnant woman with a small child beside her began to rise from her seat in preparation for the next stop.

She addressed the bus. "But they should continue by saying that instead of inventing a crime that was laughed out of court they reaped their revenge by slaughtering my brother and many like him. Lakis Garganis is a lucky man today. My brother was not so lucky."

Dina paid attention to the woman's solemn expression, inherited by her son who peered out of hollow eyes and clasped his mother's hand tightly. The bus shuddered to a halt, its passengers silenced by the words of the unknown woman. They murmured their condolences to the memory of an equally unknown brother. The child was scooped up into the air and planted at his mother's feet. Dina remained silent, affected by the woman's lament. The joy she had felt for Dimitris had evaporated and she was left with the television image of the tanks and troops flattening the gates of Athens Polytechnic in November 1973 as she watched in disbelief.

But for that woman who just got off the bus it was a reality. Dina's two voices spoke to each other strongly. Imagine if they had been able to televise my struggle! What images would have been brought to the people? Like those pictures of Vietnam and the naked children running away. At least we were spared that indignity.

But what do we achieve by exposing people, children, to the horrors of war? Do we hope they will understand better why their loved ones are killing each other? Are we trying to shock them into a promise that they will never send us to war again? Or is it that we have just lost the respect for human life so we make death into another type of entertainment? The questions came but not the answers.

Saturday night. *Plateia* Omonia. Dina sat in the Mantziaris *tavern*. The long centre table was draped with the customary white paper cloth. Dimitris was celebrating his son's engagement and it was the same day the government had announced the trial verdicts. There was silence as everyone's attention switched to the television behind the counter. The barman turned up the volume. An oily haired newsreader greeted his audience with a smile and then assumed a serious expression as he began. *"Breaking news in what is being described as a triumph for the Greek people. On trial at last, those with primary role in the dictatorship; for their role in torturing dissidents and for their brutal suppression of the student occupation of the Athens Polytechnic in November two years ago. Brigadier Ioannides, former head of notorious military police, has been given a seven-fold life sentence for his role in the Polytechnic killings."*

Shouts of 'seven isn't enough!'
"Only death is enough."
"Ioannides, we want you dead."
"Death to Ioannides."

"Let him eat his own family like he ate ours."

They stamped their feet in unison and lobbed obscenities at the newsreader. Then one of the grandmothers struggled to her feet and shouted louder at the screen than the others. "Stop ignoring us will you!" She waved her arthritic forefinger at the television. "Come on let's see what you're really made of. We'll take you on any day won't we children?" There was an uproarious cheer and more than one glass forced into her hand. The collective anger evaporated into uncontrollable laughter. The grandmother was lifted high into the air by her two grandsons and then placed carefully down again when someone reminded them of her frailty.

The joy and celebration of the news rang out of the open doors of the taverna. The waiters were kept busy with demands for more retsina and extra plates of chips. Men tapped their knives against wine glasses, impatient to get their word in, while women in full flow, defied all attempts at being cut short in mid-sentence. The company were so engrossed that they even failed to pounce on the plates heaped with souvlakia when they appeared, as if by magic, at both ends of the table.

On one side of Dina sat Dimitris. His son, Lakis, sat on the other. He was keeping his fiancée close to him. What's the matter? He asked, seeing her tears. Nothing, she replied. She was just so very happy. He kissed her on the cheek and popped a piece of meat into her open mouth. Dina watched them. Ach! What it was to be young and in love. So much caring, attention, total indulgence. What she had missed. But someone from the other end of the table was on his feet and proposing a toast to the couple. Long life to you both and strength for battles yet to come. They all crashed glasses. Dina rose to her feet and hugged Lakis and Alexandria, entwining arms to drink.

Alexandria was a tall slim girl, her long legs crossing themselves elegantly as she attempted, in vain, to pull down her party dress to a respectable length. As she did this she bent her head forward, sending her black mane cascading over her face. This innocent movement had already attracted the eye of her grandmother who sat opposite. Dina noticed the look on the woman's face; very judgemental, putting unspoken pressure on the young woman because she dared to defy convention.

And where would we all be now if we had followed like sheep and done as we were told? She and I both know how dangerous grandmothers can be especially when they vote the way she does.

Dina admired Alexandra's engagement ring. The only piece of ornamentation on theis girl, Dina mused, is her unusual pearl ring that she occasionally strokes as if reassuring herself it's really hers. Dina had warmed to her. She resembled one of the girls in her battalion, Aleka. Dina remembered her name and her long, thick black hair that used to take three hours to dry even on a hot summer's day. Then Alexandra's father was laughing and joking and thanking Lakis for taking her off his hands. The volume of the music was turned up and some of the table began singing rebetika songs. No sooner had the copper *karafakia* been refilled than they were empty and handed back to the waiters.

Dina sat down next to Dimitris. "It's good to see Laki looking so much better now Dimitri. He's put some weight back on. Alexandra must be a good cook."

Dimitris cupped her hand in his. "Yes, she waited those four years for him. That's love isn't it?" He held her hand in a secure grip and studied her eyes.

"A modern day Penelope waiting for her Odysseus. They make a handsome couple don't they? I'm so proud of that boy, Dina. I can't tell you." Dimitris had tears in his eyes. He raised his glass to Dina. "To our health and especially you Dina. My old faithful comrade."

"But Penelope wasn't some dumb wife who thought of nothing but her husband's return. She was wise and cunning wasn't she? All those presents she managed to get from her suitors when she lied to them about marriage. Ach! I love all that history of ours. If I promised marriage to you Dimitri, would you bring me all those gifts?"

Dina had drunk a few glasses of wine by this time and she was relaxed. Dimitris had become unusually silent but she didn't notice.

The tavern was now heavy with smoke. Drunken, out of tune voices were attempting to accompany the bouzouki player. Dimitris led Dina onto the dance floor and they plunged into the middle of a Hassaposervika dance. Dina was whirled round by Dimitris. His hand was never far from her waist. Hardly able to catch her breath she shelved earlier thoughts and abandoned herself to the challenges of the dance floor. The circle closed and she was propelled into its middle. Amid roars and clapping she spiraled down, then up, her steps nimble and swift, her arms reaching high, her hands coming together as she spun herself round. More cheers and whistles from those still seated at the tables, then the circle opened for her and another dancer took the centre. Immediately Dimitris was scooping her away from the circle, carrying her in his arms, out into the night. She hadn't felt this alive since her soldier years.

Later the music changed. The thirsty players took a break while one of the waiters hastily manoevered a tape into the music system. A second waiter tied a red sash around his waist to match that of his colleague and they stood, facing the exhausted customers, one arm outstretched either side, the other resting on each other's shoulder. Kicking and bending forward, backward, their audience was now resuscitated with wine and grapes. They clapped in tune. Then the boss, Spiros, a short, square man with a balding head and a waxed moustache, stomped from the kitchen to dance alone. This was an authoritative male dance that sent Dina and the older women in the company into choruses of 'bravo *levendi*' and 'again!' Because, although they did admire his dancing as well, what they really liked was his sturdy black trousered legs and his broad chest heaving under his pristine starched shirt. Having downed his beer the second waiter then dragged one of the tables into the middle of the floor and placed a chair on top of it. Spiros took a brief bow and a sip of his wine, mopped his brow with a handkerchief and began his showpiece.

The children had been gathered from all corners of the tavern and retrieved from the pavement to watch the spectacle. They stood, mouths agape, as he straightened himself up, hands stretched out either side to balance his body and presented himself to the audience, taking one of the chair legs between his teeth and lifting it into the air. As if this wasn't enough, he treated them to the impossible by repeating the trick, this time with the table leg. Up went the battered old table, gripped in the vice of his upper and lower jaw as he staggered to maintain his balance. Beside themselves with disbelief, the children screamed and shook their heads, the older ones asking their drunken parents how it was done. Evy flew into her mother's arms, her long white dress billowing round her ankles, its ribbons undone.

After some time the clapping subsided and Spiros took a seat at one of the tables. Dina dabbed Evy's forehead. "Sit still for a while or you'll get a chill from the draught." Rena was coughing from the excitement and smoke. Not a healthy place for Rena but Dina knew it was more important for her daughter to enjoy life while she still could.

Raven haired flower girls circled the table with buckets of wilted gardenias balanced on their hips. Dina rummaged in her purse for a few coins and picked out a white gardenia that she planted behind Evy's ear. "Now all the boys will know you as the one who smells of paradise."

Lakis beckoned Dina over to sit at his table. He was with some other young university friends. "I saw you dancing Dina. You and my dad make a great couple on the dance floor."

Dina's face felt hot and she didn't know what to do with her hands. "Give me a cigarette would you Laki?"

They were debating the continuing Turkish occupation of northern Cyprus and the Greek government's naval build up in the Aegean. They wanted Dina's opinion. She listened to the enthusiastic words coming from the lucid tongues of the young group. "It's a simple choice." She found herself saying when she was more composed. "Keep up the opposition or give in, retire to your homes and bury your heads in the sand."

One girl banged her fist on the table and nodded in agreement with Dina. She had spent five years in America learning about great leaders like Malcolm X. She had even spoken to Angela Davis at a rally. "The only way forward", the girl continued, "is the armed struggle."

Dina baulked at the mention of the armed struggle. Where had it got them? A lot of dead brothers and sisters, heartache and sorrow. And yet, here was that question again. What was the choice? Dina decided that choice was a misleading word. People didn't seem to have a free choice. It was more like they got to choose from a menu already decided.

A fair haired Ionian boy was arm in arm with Lakis, their heads together in loving friendship. "But be careful Laki, remember what I told you. If you take the lead in this they'll have you back inside within days. They're waiting for any excuse to nab you again and this time you'll go down for longer if they can pin any organizing on you." Lakis nodded in understanding. "I know brother. I know the risk."

Dina watched him and thought how he was like his father, resolute, not afraid of taking serious risks. She spoke to the group. "They'll do to you what they've done to prisoners through the ages. D'you know that in England the Suffragettes were force-fed and then released to recover, then, just when they thought they were safe, they rearrested them. They called that the Cat and Mouse Act." The group listened intently, their heads nodding with drunken attention.

"And they're still doing it now, in Northern Ireland. I was reading a copy of the British newspaper my sister brought back from London and they're reporting forced feeding of republican prisoners in Long Kesh. It's like a concentration camp." This from a very young girl who looked to Dina to be no more than fifteen. The group remained silent, in deep consideration of the state of the world.

"Well, I say kill them all!" A curly haired Adonis staggered to his feet and headed for the toilet.

"And does he really think the Turks are so different from us? They're not all Muslims. No. They use religion to try and divide us but in the end the ordinary Turk has to earn a crust just like we do. Just think about it *paidia*. Who was it who actually made the decision to invade our side of Cyprus? Was it your brother working in the FIX brewery? Was it hell! Was it Dina's Rena coughing her guts out in Omex Hellas?" Lakis hung his head down in despair.

Dina tousled Lakis's hair and sighed. "Ach *paidia*. Come on now, no more moping. That's what they want. For us all to go back home and close our doors on the world. Come now, we're here for a celebration and my wine's run out. Waiter!" Dina waved the *karafaki* in the air. "Let's have some more dancing. Someone put something lively on. The night isn't over yet."

CHAPTER TWENTY-TWO

"The women livened up the Democratic Army. The girls started to clean up the children and the women were respected for that. They also boosted morale with their songs"

"In EPON I was a lieutenant. One minute you were deloucing a child's head and the next loading your gun."

Friday morning and Kastoria lay bathed in white. The town even smelt of snow. A heavy downfall throughout the night had silenced the normally noisy streets. Doors closing, car tyres rolling, human steps on the pavements, voices calling out, dogs barking, all were muffled, as if wrapped up in one big blanket.

Olga Lakounis swung open the heavy back door for Dina, beckoning her in and out of the newly gathering storm. Dina shook the snow from her coat and hung it in the porch. Her boots however, would remain on her feet this week, even though her toes were wet through. But the kitchen felt warm and Kiria Lakounis had coffee ready.

"Sit down Dina, you must be frozen. How do you take your coffee?" Kiria Lakounis strutted about her kitchen, busy, focused, but still that elegant stride. Under the apron her black skirt shaped to her slim hips.

Dina drew a chair up to the table and sat down." Thank-you Kiria Lakounis. *metrio* please." She was grateful for the rest. Her feet were tired from walking. Her war wound was nagging all the way down her leg today. Kiria Lakounis handed Dina her cup of coffee and poured herself one. She unravelled a pack of cigarettes from the depths of her apron pocket and joined Dina at the table.

"Cigarette?" The wind was driving the snow against the window, making gentle splintering noises as the crystals stuck to the panes.

Dina hesitated. "Just the one then. I don't usually like to start before I've done any work." She felt slightly embarrassed sitting down with her employer and accepting her hospitality, especially since she had left the house untouched the previous week.

Kiria Lakounis cleared her throat. "Dina, I know it was embarrassing for you last week and I'm sorry you've become involved in my mess of a marriage but there are a few things I want you to know, for your own peace of mind, apart from anything else." She blew the smoke through her carefully painted mouth. "You see, it's not that I didn't know about my husband's infidelity. I had to learn to put up with that after only a year of marriage. No. It didn't come as a surprise. I knew he'd got some mistress in Saloniki but what I didn't reckon on was the filthy bastard paying for it with some local *poudana*." She spat the last word.

Dina flinched. A woman of Olga Lakounis' class wasn't meant to use such words.

"Doing it right here under my nose, in a small town like Kastoria! Did he really think he wouldn't get found out? Huh! If he wasn't so pathetic it would almost be laughable. He comes face to face with you in his own house and gets the fright of his life." Dina watched her smile broaden as she leaned back in her chair and shook her head.

"I'm sorry Kiria. I wish I hadn't seen him, then none of this would've happened."

"Sooner or later someone else would have spotted him. His carelessness is what really hurts, you know, the children – he doesn't even think of his children."

"It must be really hard for you Kiria. I can't begin to imagine how you must feel knowing these things and having to live with them. But why, why do you continue living with them?"

Olga Lakounis stood up and paced the room, her arms folded. She stared at the frosted window, now covered with ice crystals. "I have to think of my children. He won't do that. I have to make sure they have the best. They deserve the best. They're my life. If I left him what sort of life would they have? He's the one with the money. As his mother always reminds me, her Alekos married beneath him." Her face scowled as she emphasised the word. She turned from the window to face Dina. "But don't imagine Dina that I take this without getting my own back. No. If I wanted I could ruin him by this, by exposing his mockery of our marriage. He depends on me throwing dinner parties for his business cronies who come to buy the furs. I'm his appendage. I complete the picture he presents to the world, like a presidential first lady. *Thee mou*! You see Dina, I have to use this situation to my advantage and make demands on him, mainly for the children but I would be dishonest if I didn't take some of it for myself. As you can see I like nice clothes, furnishings. I like to spend my summers in our house in Thassos with the children – all that costs money and he's paying!"

Dina stubbed out her cigarette and stood up. "Kiria, I must get on with the house. I've a lot to do and I'd feel more comfortable doing what I'm paid for. I feel very sad for you."

Kiria Lakounis took Dina's elbow. "Before you start Dina, I want you to come with me." She led the way to her bedroom and flung open the massive mirrored door of her wardrobe revealing a row of fur coats and jackets, rich and dark, hanging next to each other in one luxurious line. Kiria Lakounis picked one out and held it up to Dina. "It's amazing! You're almost the same size as me." Dina opened her eyes wide. She stood there, her hands hanging by her sides. "Come on then! Let's try it on you." She felt as if she was at a fitting, being swivelled round and tugged at by a dressmaker. She became as a child, doing what it was told, knowing it was for its own good and found her arms had threaded themselves through the lush wide sleeves of the coat and Olga Lakounis was pulling the lapels gently together in front and turning Dina by her shoulders to face the mirror. "There! Just look at you now." So Dina looked at the woman she saw in the mirror, swathed in deep brown mink and she liked what she saw.

"Maybe it needs taking up a little. I'm a bit taller than you but otherwise I'd say it was a perfect fit. Just take it into the shop and Kostas will do it for you."

Dina spun round, hugging the coat close to her, then stopped and looked at Kiria Lakounis. "Are you offering this to me Kiria?" She could barely believe she had the cheek to ask her employer but she had to be sure. "To keep?"

"Of course to keep. Look at my wardrobe! I have plenty of choice don't I? I won't go cold."

Dina remained in front of the mirror, hugging the coat close to her. "It's beautiful but why? Why are you giving me this, especially now, after…"

"After what? Dina, don't blame yourself for anything and as for leaving last week, think no more about it please. I want you to have the coat because you deserve it and I respect your integrity and loyalty to me. You didn't know I heard most of what my husband proposed to you and yet you rejected his attempt to bribe you. I haven't met many people that would do that, especially someone who really needed what he was offering. No! That coat belongs on your shoulders Dina. I give it to you gladly."

Dina stood. Her eyes had not left the mirror. Dina Constantinou covered head to toe in mink. Blink twice. She was still there.

"Ah Kiria! It's like being in a hot bath. I can't believe it! The way it makes me feel, all cosy." She was smiling and crying at the same time. "Thank-you Kiria, thank-you. I accept."

Kiria Lakounis rested her hand on Dina's shoulder, running the fur through her fingers. "And I thank you Dina. You came highly recommended to me. I haven't been disappointed."

Slipping out of her coat, Dina folded it over her arm. "And now Kiria, let me get on. Your house won't clean itself."

Wringing out her cloth into the bucket had never been such a joyful action for Dina. She hummed and sang and swirled the damp cloth round the base of each bed leg, picturing herself walking home, carefree, snug in her coat whatever the weather threw at her. She wouldn't care. Making up the beds she took special care over the folds at the four corners and gave the pillows an extra plumping. Each of the bedrooms in the Lakounis house had beautiful parquet flooring. Dina admired how perfectly one block fitted into another as she manoevered her wide sweeper. She couldn't hang the rugs out on the balcony as snow was still drifting in, piling up and up outside the glass doors. How badly the day had started. She had been filled with worry before arriving but now she was so excited about her walk home that she hardly noticed what she was doing. Of course she knew her job so well she didn't really need to think.

Standing amidst the clean, soapy smell of newly ironed laundry, Dina worked the iron up and down the length of one of Kirios Lakounis's shirts. Every so often she replaced the iron on its end stand while she sprayed the shirt with water. All the creases disappeared under the puffs of steam as the iron did its work. Dina only hung each shirt on its hanger when she was satisfied that every crease had been pressed out. Kiria Lakounis had provided her with a stool to sit on but Dina could never get a good enough grip on the iron if she was sitting down so despite the ache in her bad leg she continued the job standing up. Shirts, children's trousers, white vests, handkerchiefs, tablecloths, all one big, lopsided pile. She didn't much like the idea of ironing his shirts, considering what misery he was causing but what could she do? The idea of boycotting Kirios Lakounis's shirts appealed to Dina as she zigzagged the nose of the iron between the buttons, all the way down the front like a slalom course. She wanted to scorch a hole in it. Instead she eliminated all the creases and hung it up in line with the others that decorated the walls of the laundry room. Occasionally, as Dina laboured through her list of jobs, she would remember the coat; her coat. And the prospect of her journey home became something to look forward to. For once, she wouldn't shiver.

People were undpredictable. She didn't care what Dimitris said. There was always the possibility of people changing, including herself. Dimitri might call it softening but maybe she needed to soften. Maybe he did as well. Who would have thought a woman of Olga Lakounis's standing would show such generosity towards a cleaner. Some employers would have sacked Dina for walking out as she'd done. She knew this well. She'd worked for enough of them in her time. One had sacked her on the spot for letting slip that she bought her vegetables at a stall owned by a KKE sympathiser, another because she had found a smear on the hall mirror. The Lakounis household was pleasant to work in if only he wasn't part of it. As long as their paths didn't cross it was fine. She wondered if that would be the end of his visits to the nameless woman in the beige trouser suit or would he have the nerve to continue as normal?

She heard the children arriving home from school with their mother, banging doors, screeching, pattering feet above in the kitchen. It was nearly two o' clock already. Dina scooped up the pile of ironed clothes in her arms and climbed the stairs slowly. She placed the laundry on the hall table so that she could sort them into piles for each bedroom. "Athena." She called. "Come and take your clean clothes to your room. They're ready here." Athena came running, arms open.

Olga Lakounis followed her daughter into the hall, arms folded, a smile on her face.

"You know Dina, she never obeys me like that, not until I've asked her three times and even then only with a moan! What's your secret? How d'you do it?"

Dina smiled. "There's a way of giving orders with respect. Children sense that from an adult. It's really that simple." Thanasis had arrived, pulling at his mother's skirt and whining for food. Olga Lakounis stroked his fair, curly hair and he purred.

"And you learnt that from having only one child. I haven't managed it with four!" It wasn't a question so much as a statement of surprise. Dina's reaction was guarded. There would be nothing to gain by telling Olga Lakounis of her time as an officer in EPON, how she had run an orderly camp for the children evacuees, training them, comforting them. Sometimes burying them. How they were ambushed at Platamon bridge and the tall, fair girl with plaits down to her waist, quite like Athena, how she didn't get lice in those plaits! A brave girl who forced the younger ones to sing to keep warm but couldn't protect herself from the bomb that struck the beech tree, splitting it down the middle so that all the fragments came down in a shower, cutting deeply into both her legs.

"I must get going Kiria Lakounis. There won't be any bread left."

Olga Lakounis took a wad of notes from her pocket and handed Dina her day's wages. "Sorry for keeping you. You've already done more than you need to today. I'm really very happy with your work Dina. Thank-you." Dina was putting on the fur coat. Olga Lakounis stroked its deep pelt. "Enjoy your coat Dina. Keep warm. That's an order!" They smiled at each other. Something important had been achieved.

Dina closed the kitchen door behind her and stepped out into a blizzard. She felt that Fridays at Olga Lakounis's house wasn't going to be so bad after all and she was already forgetting her old employer. Reaching the lakeside promenade she couldn't resist twirling round in the snow, her furry arms outstretched either side like an ice skater. Homeward bound school children stared and giggled at her as they trotted past, their small backs bent under heavy bags of books. But Dina didn't mind being stared at. Her coat was her armour.

The coat didn't disappoint her. She was so excited by it. The baker even came out from behind his counter, holding his floury hands in the air. He put his cheek against Dina's fur collar, making a contented growling in admiration. "Eh! What have we here then Dina?"

"*Ella* Laki, my usual please. I may look like a princess but I'm still in need of bread!"

The baker smiled and dived behind a shelf of trays to retrieve a large round loaf that he slid into a paper bag. Dina pushed her coins across the counter and hurried out with a '*kali oreksi*'. Laki made moon eyes after her.

Back at home Dina showed off her coat. Rena pawed it. Evy hid under it. "You should see her wardrobes! Full of coats just like this one and the dresses! You wouldn't believe one person could have so many clothes. We couldn't fit even one of her wardrobes in this whole flat of ours."

Rena took a few steps back from her mother and surveyed her. "You look fantastic mama. I think it could be shortened a little. Is she a tall woman, this Kiria Lakounis?"

"Yes. Slim and tall and very beautiful." Dina went to look at herself in the hall mirror. "Uhm! So you think it needs taking up too? That's what she said."

Rena joined her at the mirror. "Yes, just a little. Does she have any more of these she wants to get rid of?"

Dina laughed. "You never know. If I work well for her and please her she might feel generous enough to push another one my way."

Evy was jumping around, rubbing her cheek against Dina's coat. Rena coaxed her away. "Come on Evy now. Let *yiayia* sit down and rest. She's been working hard. We can set the table for food together. Come and help me get the knives and forks and then see if you can put them in the right places."

Evy followed her mother into the kitchen and waited while Rena handed her the cutlery. She looked down at her hands. "So that's a knife and a fork each, for you, me, *yiayia* and *baba*. Where's *baba*? Is he coming soon?"

Rena sighed. "Yes. He'll be back soon. His stomach will lead him." Rena saw her daughter's eyes open wide and realised that she had taken her words literally. Evy stuck out her small stomach and marched towards the table.

Nikos arrived as the three of them were sitting down to eat. Rena had begun dishing out the baked fish. He noticed the fur coat draped over the armchair and whistled.

"Do we have a royal guest today or have you been hunting illegally?"

Dina tucked a paper napkin under Evy's throat. "I'm the only royal visitor you're likely to see in this household. You'll have to make do with me I'm afraid. But I came home today feeling lucky so don't ruin it Niko."

Nikos protested, throwing his arms in the air. "Did you steal it then?"

"Of course I didn't! My boss gave it to me for good service and because she took pity on me, shivering in that threadbare old thing."

Nikos looked at Dina in disbelief. "Just like that? You must have a very unusual boss. Tell you what Dina. I could do with a boss like that. Does she have any jobs?" He downed his drink and banged his glass back on the table. Sometimes Nikos and Dimitris resembled each other, maybe years in the Party did that.

Dina didn't react to his anger. She knew how humiliated he felt not to have any permanent work. "I know it's rare but she really is very kind and it wasn't exactly difficult to accept when she had so many."

Rena glared at her husband. "Ignore him mama. You have every right to a coat like that. If anyone does, it's you. Niko, pass the bottle please. You're not the only one at this table who drinks wine."

Dina had considered telling the true story behind the coat but decided it was better kept to herself. She did feel a loyalty to Olga Lakounis and above all other considerations was her need to keep the job. Nikos should bear that in mind, she thought, at least as long as he was out of work. She expected Nikos to go into a rant about wealth and injustice; he was the type who was prone to moaning rather than doing anything. Dina found this the least appealing of his characteristics but he remained silent, too busy eating and drinking and angrily breaking off pieces of bread. Rena was chatting optimistically about her health, how the new medicine seemed to be working and Dina breathed a sigh of relief. It was news they had all been hoping for. She was looking forward to her afternoon nap, being alone with herself and her thoughts. Today had been a good day. Her eyes began to close with the thought of her bed.

"You go on and rest mama. I'll do the dishes. Come on Evy. Take this for mama. There's a good child!"

Dina decided to do as she was told without argument. Olga Lakounis had been right. She had done double the amount of work today and she was feeling it now. She closed her bedroom door and flopped onto the old feather eiderdown. A wall of drifted snow blocked all light from Dina's small bedroom window. Mid afternoon may as well have been night time.

As her head touched the pillow Dina's eyes closed and she drifted off. Many colours and people came to her in her dream, all flying across azure skies dotted with fluffy white clouds. They flew like blown leaves, some upside down, others sideways. Some faces she recognised as comrades from the past. Uncle Stefos sat on a bale of hay in his field. He smiled at her. The three wise comrades smiled down at her from a balcony in the clouds. They were cradling Rena between them. Her mother and father were there, standing in their little garden full of geranium pots of orange and pink. Even Mr B was waving at her from his front veranda. And all their faces were turned to Dina, all happy, grinning. Dimitri's was the face closest to hers. It was beaming. Dina was laughing. Why was she laughing? Was it at something or with someone? Her mouth was stuck in a grin. Her jaw ached. As she awoke she was left with a heavy feeling from the dream, like it wasn't a dream at all. Allowing her head to rest flat on the pillow, Dina gradually opened her eyes and blinked at the ceiling but she remained still. She knew she was back in reality because she could see the crack in the ceiling and the corner of flaking plaster next to the window that the landlord still hadn't repaired. She shifted her gaze as she heard the rattling of a cup and saucer getting closer and closer and her daughter's face above it.

"*Ella* mama, wake up. I've brought your coffee and I forgot to give you this. It came this morning." Rena handed Dina a smart, creamy envelope addressed to herself. Dina studied it. This wasn't cheap paper, more like parchment. She read her typewritten name and noticed the business frank but it only said 'office'. "It looks a bit official mama. What have you been up to eh?"

Dina turned the envelope over.

Rena made her way towards the bedroom door. "Anyway. I promised Evy I'd take her round to Angeliki's. You stay where you are for now. It's the warmest place."

Dina pushed herself up against the pillow, drew the eiderdown to her chin and tore open the letter with some concern. What her eyes read then, made her wonder if she was really still in her dream world. She studied the letter. Official. Short but courteous. Almost congratulatory in tone. She pushed it away from her in disbelief like a precious thing she couldn't look at in case it disappeared. She took a sip of coffee and the letter was still there, staring at her from the folds of the bedspread. Temptation won her over. Dina's shaking hand felt the edge of the thick rich paper and she peered at it a second time, blinking. She took a deep breath. What am I still doing in bed? Where is everyone? They had all gone out. No-one to tell. Dina was left alone with a mounting euphoria. She threw back the covers and grabbed the letter. The words in clear black print were the same words she had read before. She had almost expected them to be changed. Was it a joke? If so, what a mean joke to play... and why? Then she remembered Sophia's words.

CHAPTER TWENTY-THREE

"In 1945 we in ELAS were forced to surrender our weapons at Varkiza. It was Velouchiotis – he was commander of Roumeli ELAS who refused to recognize the surrender. And he was right. But Zachariades threatened anyone who resisted. Aris Velouchiotis was a brave man and he defied orders, returned to the mountains and a lot of us followed him. I did. He always distrusted the British. He called them 'those great allies who divide up continents' and when they tried to dig him out each one of us were proud to step forward and say 'I am the Capetanios! No surrender.' But with those same weapons we had surrendered, they hunted us afterwards."

A.T. Sofoulis　　　　　　　　　　　Maria's House
Solicitor　　　　　　　　　　　　　4 Nikis Road
15 Mitropoleous　　　　　　　　　　Kastoria
Kastoria

15th January 1976

<u>Confidential for the attention of Kiria Constantina Venetiadou</u>

Following the death on November 20th 1975 of Mr B of Nikis Road, Kastoria, my office has been instructed to inform you that the same deceased has named you in his will as sole heir to the above property.

The relevant documentation is held at my office and I would be happy to offer you an appointment at your earliest convenience so that we may complete our legal duties.

Signed
Alelxandros Sofoulis

Pacing the lounge floor, Dina clutched the letter close to her chest with a shaking hand.　What a convergence of feelings were flooding her body. Disbelief, fear, joy, excitement, suspicion. Dina had to speak to somebody. She was so animated that she flung open her front door in the hope that there would be somebody in the hallway but promptly closed it again as a bad idea. She seized the phone. Sophia. What was her number? Dina stubbed out her cigarette and dialled. Nothing this time. Not even a ring tone. The line was dead. She had tried many times to make contact with the nurse but with no result.

Finally, unable to contain her excitement any longer, Dina flung on her coat, stuffed the letter into her pocket and left. She had walked the length of her street before she knew where she was going. It was Friday evening. Dimitris, Ketty and other trade unionists would probably have retired to the *taverna* after their weekly meeting.

Propelled by her need to share her good fortune, Dina could not have predicted the stunned reaction her appearance would receive. She shook herself free from her coat as if she had worn it all her life. Ketty's eyes followed Dina and then the fur. "Dina." She said with wide-open eyes. "You really did steal one!"

Dina sat down. She clutched the envelope in both hands, resting them on her lap. She didn't respond to Ketty's question. Instead she yanked the letter from its envelope and waved it in front of Dimitris. "Read it Dimitri! Read this, so I'll know I'm not dreaming."

He took the letter from Dina and read. She watched his reaction, his eyebrows rising into a furrow. He called the waiter for more wine and a glass for Dina.

"Well? What d'you say? Isn't it my lucky day?"

Ketty took the letter from Dina and read. It then went all round the table from hand to hand. The wine arrived. Dimitris poured Dina a glass and refilled others. They raised their glasses. Dina felt all their eyes on her. "To Dina." He said. "Soon to be a wealthy property owner."

Although they all chuckled, Dina suddenly felt a little uneasy. As if she was under scrutiny. Dimitris's words hadn't exactly been the ones she was expecting but Ketty grabbed her arm while she read the letter. "Dina! Can you believe it? Leaving you his house! God! You must have made some impression on this Mr B. Was he in love with you?"

"There are other motives for giving aren't there Ketty?"

Another member of the group cut in, laughing, joking. "Come on Dina. Tell us what you really did to get this result."

Dina didn't laugh. The youth who had made the crude comment wasn't even well known to her. She felt a little offended, downing her wine in one and looking him in the eyes. "I worked like a slave for him, cleaning his house." She jabbed her forefinger at the letter lying on the table. "This house. I worked miracles on this house, that's what I did comrade...I don't know your name."

The youth was reduced to a humble silence.

"Hah! Bravo Dina. I've never seen Spiros speechless before. Come my son. Don't cross this Kiria here. I'm warning you, she has fire in her." Dimitris lifted Dina's glass and tipped it to her lips following it with a kiss.

Ketty repeated her question to Dina.

"Actually Ketty, he did ask me to marry him at one point." She watched their reactions, open mouths, dropped jaws. "But I said no. I wasn't in love with him."

Ketty was shaking her head. "And you never told us before. Did you tell anyone?"

"Yes, of course I told Rena. She was disappointed but you know...I didn't surrender my principles along with our weapons at Varkiza. How could I marry someone I didn't love?"

"Plenty do." Said someone.

"That's what my Rena said."

"Well, it paid off anyway Dina. He clearly thought the world of you to leave you his house." Dimitris cocked back his head and patterned the ceiling with smoke rings.

He's jealous. Dina looked at Dimitris.

"I think he felt guilty as well. I'd confronted him with his past and he'd admitted it to me. I think this was his way of trying to make peace with me, with our cause."

"What about his past?" Asked Spiros.

Dimitris turned to him. "He was mayor here and leader of Defenders of the Northern League."

"So you worked like a slave for one of them did you?" The youth again, raising his head, getting his own back at Dina for her last challenge.

She studied his unlined, inexperienced face. "You know. It's like this my child. Some of us never had the choices we would have liked in our lives. D' you think I had an ambition to become a cleaner all my life? Cleaning up after other people? Seeing how they lived in their big houses, touching, tasting what they took for granted all their lives? Do you think I enjoy being paid a pittance for my work every day? And let me tell you this, so that you can remember my words when you've grown a little wiser and taller. He wasn't a mean employer and he showed me respect. You wouldn't know but that's important to a cleaner. We don't always get that from our employers. And you know why he was respectful? Because he understood what commitment meant. I think he began to change his mind about what he'd done in 48'. That's my guess anyway. People can change you know." Dina paused to drink more wine. "Think about it! Otherwise what hope is there for humanity eh? We've got to convince people to change their way of thinking if we're every going to finish the job we started in 47'." The table nodded in unison. Spiros had been silenced again. Dina began to soften towards him.

After all, she thought, he could be my son. "You're not from round here are you?"

"No."

"From Athens?"

"Yes."

"Are you a student?" She asked him kindly.

"Yes."

"Polytechnio?"

"Yes." He looked down at the floor, resting his elbows on his knees, his head of black curls swinging.

Dina laid a hand on his shoulder and dropped her own head, putting them at the same eye level. "Let me guess. You lost some close *palikari*s in 73'?"

The table was silent momentarily, and then Ketty spoke. "Yes he did. Dina's right. We have to keep fighting, for their sakes. They didn't die for nothing. Come on my child. We know how you feel. Don't be so confrontational with us. We're your comrades not your enemy. Here." She pushed his wine glass towards him. "Drink and be happy. The struggle continues!" Their glasses met. Spiros smiled. Tears like a baby. Dina watched.

Dimitris looked seriously at Dina. "You're going to have a bit of a problem with that sister of his aren't you? I don't imagine she's going to take this news well do you?"

Dina stared at the table, its old knotted wood battered and uneven from years of use. "I hadn't thought of that to tell you the truth Dimitri." All the joy was draining from her, leaving an empty ache. Had she celebrated too soon? Unpleasant memories of Vassiliki came back to her. She felt irritated by Dimitris's comment although she knew what he said made sense. "Thanks Dimitri! You could've saved that warning till tomorrow."

"Sorry. It's just that I fear this may not be as straightforward as you'd like it to be. People usually leave their property to their relatives not their cleaners! I'd hate to see you hurt."

He was holding on to both her arms and looking down at her from his tall height. They were standing outside the *taverna*. Their breaths were picked up by the freezing air like smoke signals.

"I feel you're disappointed in me Dimitri. Did you expect me to refuse the offer of his house? Have I let myself down?"

Dimitris smiled and moved closer still. "No I don't see it like that. I think you deserve what he's left you. Before your news I was preparing to ask you something but now it seems..." He let go of her and hung his head. "It seems irrelevant."

"What's irrelevant Dimitri? What are you saying?"

"I'm saying that you and I, we should move on from our old comradeship, move on to something more."

Dina stood very still even though she wanted to shift her feet to warm them. Now it was her turn to look up to Dimitri. "You mean?"

"Yes. You must realise by now how I feel. How I've felt for a long time."

Yes. She thought. Yes I did realise and I did nothing about it. The way her body had responded to his when they were dancing was a signal to her and she did want his attentions. She wanted him to put those solid arms around her. That's why she loved her fur coat so much. Wearing it felt like she was being held by a man like Dimitris. Not like Dimitris. Dimitris himself. And there it was. A dawning of the possibility that she had feelings for this man. Not just comradely feelings. Desire. There it was. Effortless. She thought back to the times when Mr B had laid his hand on her arm and when he had looked at her in that different way. Mr B had called her a wiry bird and what had happened was that he had unfrozen her wings so she could fly.

"Yes." Was all she finally said. She moved to go.

"Is that all you're going to say?"

She touched his arm with her gloved hand. "It's all I can say at the moment because although you're right it's never that simple." And she walked away towards the lake leaving Dimitris standing while flakes of snow sprinkled from an angry sky onto his greying hair.

Dina knew it was the truth but she'd hardly had time to consider the implications of her inheritance. So, in this way, her doubts started and wouldn't leave her for the rest of the evening. She had begun her evening so joyful and light, now she said goodnight to her comrades with a heavy heart. What if this all amounted to nothing? What if she had told Rena and Nikos? And imagine little Evy hearing the news that they were moving into a big house overlooking the lake. Dina swept the image of disappointed faces from her thoughts and decided she couldn't tell them about the letter. It might never become true. This was so cruel. She would have to go to the solicitor's office to get some answers. She saw Vassiliki's face grinning. It was a sight she had hoped never to see again. And what about the reaction of her comrades? Was Dimitris trying to tell her something when he described her as a wealthy property owner? He wasn't usually sarcastic but had she been so caught up in the thrill of it all that maybe she had missed his meaning. The more she dwelt on the evening the more she felt there was a decision to make where before there had been simple hope and joy. She had thought the decision had been made for her but nothing in her life ever seemed to be that simple. She wondered if she had made a fool of herself or had she just appeared naïve to them? Maybe they wouldn't trust her anymore! They could turn their backs on her as if she had changed sides. Ah that would be so stupid.

The wine was probably helping her paranoia, if it was only paranoia. Her thoughts started going round in circles. She became dizzy and had to sit down on the nearest bench. Pulling her coat around her and thanking the host of twinkling stars above for its warmth, she breathed in the icy air very slowly and deeply. Then, when she had steadied herself, she scooped a handful of snow from the branch of an overhanging tree and sucked at it. She hadn't drunk enough water in the *taverna*. Now she was paying the price.

When she arrived home, Rena was waiting for her. It was late. She opened the door to the flat before Dina had chance to put her key in the lock and looked parentally at her mother who was a little unsteady on her feet. "Mama! Where have you been? It's midnight and we didn't know where you were. I left you safe in bed and now I find you drunk. What's happened?"

Dina couldn't help gigglling at the tone of her daughter's voice. It was like hearing herself. Rena pulled her mother into the hall and started to take the coat from her shoulders. "I'm not drunk for heaven's sake! It's only a little wine. I'm not a prisoner am I?"

Rena frowned. "More than a little by the look of you. Who've you been with?"

Dina flopped down in an armchair. The effect of the wine was beginning to wear off and her worries returned. She closed her eyes and rested her head back against the cushion. "With Dimitri and Ketty and some others at the *taverna*. I didn't want to stay in on my own tonight so I joined them."

Rena sat opposite her mother. "Just like that eh? You don't normally just go off on a whim like that. With him again! Why him mama? You could have had Mr B and all his wealth but you let him die."

"I let him die? You know nothing my child"

Rena's eyes opened wider but her mother was already pushing up out of the armchair. She hesitated and then did something she never did. She lied to Rena. "It was Ketty's birthday and they rang me. I'd forgotten. Now, if it's okay with you I'll go to bed. I'll need to sleep off this wine."

Leaving the room, Dina could feel her daughter's eyes still penetrating her. Had she been convincing? She couldn't be sure. At that moment she didn't care but she knew her daughter wasn't stupid and would, at some point, remember the letter.

I must make that appointment, Dina whispered to herself as she fell asleep. And the snow started again, showering the window, at first with little gusts then with giant flakes.

Mitropoleous was a long winding street, home to many and assorted small shops and businesses. Dina counted three solicitor's offices on her walk up the hill before she found Sofoulis. The offices squatted above a hardware shop that sold expensive stainless steel saucepans and catering equipment for *tavernes*. Dina peered into the shop window, spotting gleaming utensils, frying pans, pots that she would have loved to use at home. But you had to have a big kitchen for things like that! Where would she put them in their tiny basement!

She entered the solicitor's from a rickety side staircase, not really living up to the gold plaque fixed to the wall, thought Dina. She knocked the clumps of frozen snow from her boots before beginning her climb up the stairs. A stray dog was passing, its ribs sticking out under a mangy coat. It tried to follow Dina up the stairs. She stamped her foot, sending it loping away to sniff at more promising doorways and bins. The staircase walls were painted a peppermint green. Faded, second hand prints of Greek islands probably unknown to many of the inhabitants of Kastoria, clung lopsidedly to the walls.

Dina knocked gently on the frosted glass door behind which she could see a light and a human shape moving about in a blur. Nobody came to open the door. She knocked again, harder. The shape began to move closer until the door rattled and opened to give Dina her first glimpse of who she imagined to be Kirios Sofoulis. He stood there facing her, breathing heavily from the exertion of opening the door.

He doesn't move from his chair very often, thought Dina.

"You're supposed to just walk in without waiting so you don't disturb my concentration Kiria. To be effective in my work I must focus very closely."

"Oh I'm sorry Kirios Sofoulis. I'm Dina Venetiadou. We've got an appointment now?" Dina offered her hand but the obese man in front of her just stood looking down at her. Shiny creases in his cheap suit jacket expanded and shrunk at each breath he took.

"I'm not Kirios Sofoulis. I'm his clerk Kiria. Kirios Sofoulis will be back shortly. Please sit down." And he planted himself back in his wooden swivel chair, lit up a cigarette and pawed the pile of papers on his desk. Dina took in the office surroundings to pass the time. It reeked of cigarette smoke. Stale. She shuddered, removed her coat in a protective move, looked around for somewhere to hide it but there was no place free from the cloying smell of cheap Sante cigarettes, a smell that would last for years not months. The windows had never been opened. Dina had once smoked the brand herself but was persuaded to change by Rena's doctor who had himself just been weaned off them. The phone rang. The clerk swore at it before picking it up and breathing smoke into the receiver. Dina imagined the caller choking at the other end of the line. His voice rose into an angry growl. Dina thought she would be happy for this man to remain a clerk in the office but never to defend her in a court of law.

Dina was a little surprised that this was the solicitor chosen by Mr B to deal with his legal matters. She would have imagined a grander suite of offices in somewhere like Alexandrou. But then again, she thought, Mr B wasn't so predictable as a person once you had got to know him. He would have had his own good reasons for choosing Sofoulis. Dina looked at her watch. He was already half an hour late. She was bored with sitting down so she walked over to the window, noticing the grime that had accumulated on its ledge. Apparently her restlessness annoyed the clerk who swivelled round and glared at Dina. "Please Kiria. I have important work to finish here and your pacing up and down the floor makes me nervous!"

"Well I'm sorry for that but if your boss was on time I wouldn't have to bother you like this would I?" Dina continued to look out of the window and noticed a man getting out of a taxi outside the shop below. He was smarter than his clerk and his overcoat was of a quality wool. "I think your boss has finally arrived. I'll stop annoying you now." She sat back down in the chair she had been allotted and smoothed back her hair. Then she began to feel nervous at the thought of the impending interview. The door burst open and Kirios Sofoulis appeared. As Dina had thought, he was much more refined than his clerk and one could clearly see how this man had made it to the top while the other would remain where he was for the rest of his life.

"Kiria Venetiadou I'm sorry to have kept you waiting. Please accept my apologies. I had an urgent case to attend to in Veroia that I could not avoid. Please come into my office."

He ushered Dina into an inner room and indicated an ancient leather chair in front of his desk. This room was just as musty as the first one. Kirios Sofoulis was greying gracefully, showing remnants of a once very handsome man with high cheekbones, not unlike those on the faces of Mongolian fighters she had seen in a history book as a child.

But this man had brown eyes, large and puffed and Dina thought that somehow his features weren't matched well together, as if they had been assembled wrongly. He offered Dina a cigarette, took one for himself and stretched over his desk to light hers. Dina sat patiently as he shuffled his papers in an effort to find the correct file.

He cleared his throat as he opened the file and contorted his face. "Uhm. Uhm. Here is the problem." He peered at Dina as if to ensure she was ready for what was coming. Dina felt her fist tightening. "My letter to you stands as correct Kiria but unfortunately there is a complication that I had not foreseen."

Dina fidgeted in her chair. "Does this complication happen to be the deceased's sister by any chance?"

The phone rang. Kirios Sofoulis ignored it. "Well, yes, as a matter of fact it is. Kiria Vassiliki Vouyoukas. She has decided to contest this part of her brother's will."

"Ah well! I suppose I was warned. I should have known it was just a nice dream." Dina sighed and began to gather up her handbag in preparation for leaving.

"But where are you going Kiria? Don't you want to hear the details of the case?" Kirios Sofoulis looked almost aggrieved.

Dina was now standing up, her bag over her wrist. She had brought her best black leather handbag. She hesitated. "Is there any point?"

"Kiria Venetiadou, please." He swept his hand towards the chair. "Please sit down and listen to what I have to say. This is not a closed case yet. Greeks contest wills all the time but that doesn't mean they succeed."

Dina sat back down. "Well I suppose it's not surprising. I'm not family am I?"

"That's not the basis on which she is contesting this though. She is alleging that her brother wasn't of sound mind when he changed his will in this way. She is even hinting that he was coerced into signing." Kirios Sofoulis raised his eyebrows and stared at Dina, both hands resting on his desk in front of him.

Dina looked at his large hairy hands, a gold wedding band gripping tightly round the fleshy fat of his finger. She frowned and looked up. "But that's nonsense! Mr B had been completely sensible until his death. There was nothing wrong with his mind."

"Were you with him until the end Kiria?"

"Well, no…I wasn't. She sacked me." Dina hung her head down in shame at her own description. The idea just didn't sit happily with the pride she had in her work.

"By she you mean?"

"His sister. Vassiliki. She told me to go and never come back."

"Then how do you know of his mental state?" Kirios Sofoulis lit another cigarette.

"Because Sophia would have told me. She was with him at the end."

The phone rang again. "Christo, for the sake of your father, answer the bloody phone and switch it over to you when I'm with a client!" He drummed the edge of his desk with his fingertips, one of which Dina spotted, was ginger from nicotine. "Uhm. And you know this for definite?"

"Yes. I know Sophia. She told me about his last hours when we were at his funeral. He'd asked her to witness his change of will by signing but she didn't know what change he was making. That's all I know Kirios Sofoulis." There was a silence in which Dina felt she should be adding something, anythingt. She looked awkwardly down at her battered old boots, all her joy draining away. This man really had nothing to offer Dina, no solace from the reality of the fact that she, a common housecleaner had less right to Mr B's house than his blood relatives. Kirios Sofoulis cleared his throat and looked kindly at Dina. She felt his eyes on her and she instantly suspected pity. Her dignity put her on her feet. She was ready to go once again.

"It's her word against the nurse's you know Kiria. And all I can say is that, of the two of them, the nurse is the more expert on health and medicine. Mr B's sister has no proof that her brother was not of sound mind." The solicitor was now standing as well.

Hugging her coat in her arms Dina moved towards the door. "Will it go to court?"

"Yes. That would be the normal procedure and if the nurse testifies I think we could win your case." He propped himself on the corner of his desk and smiled. "That is, if you want what is legally yours!"

In that instant, Dina felt supported, that this man was truly on her side and it boosted her. There were some good people. Kirios Sofoulis took her coat and held it open for her. "Thank you. Can you give me a little time to think about this? I mean, not a lot of time, just a day or two."

"Of course, but no longer. We have to execute the will within three months of the deceased's death. If Mr B's sister contests this in court and there is no defence, she will automatically regain her brother's house. The nurse, you see, is critical."

Dina nodded. "Yes. Yes, I understand what you're saying but I'm not sure I can find her."

Kirios Sofoulis brought his palms together. "There I can't help."

Each stair creaked under the tread of Dina's worn soles. She hung her head low and imagined she resembled the dog she had earlier sent on its way with her toe. Bright sunlight blinded her as she stepped down into the street again. The sky had cleared itself of snow clouds for the first time in weeks, replacing them with a canopy of winter blue. A good omen, thought Dina but the sky's not going to find Sophia for me.

CHAPTER TWENTY-FOUR

"Cleaning houses for a living isn't so bad. It's better than cleaning the body of one of your dead comrades"

Dina didn't know where Sophia lived or if she was even still in Kastoria. Their last conversation had been on the bus after Mr B's funeral. Dina remembered Sophia saying that her work prospects in Kastoria weren't good but she had never said anything about leaving town. Where to start? Dina was in doubt again. Even if she found Sophia and she agreed to give evidence, it didn't mean Dina would win. Vassiliki would hire the best barrister, or whatever they were called. She would probably ask her brother to employ one from Thessaloniki or even Athens. The barriers mounted up in her mind like road blocks. But she had to act now or forget about what might have been.

Acting now was all very well in theory but when there were dishes to wash, a pile of ironing to do and the bed to make, acting became difficult. Dina never cut corners in her cleaning. It wasn't in her nature. Cleaning was an art and had to be finished to perfection. That was how she had built her reputation and she couldn't afford to start putting it in jeopardy. She breathed hard as she spun her cloth round in widening circles on the wooden table until it shone and her elbow ached. If Sophia was to be found it was because she was meant to be, not because of any elaborate search party or investigation. Taking a step back, she rubbed at the wood again where she had spotted a small smear. The light beamed its rays onto it. Dina cajoled herself. She sounded like some clairvoyant.

She made the decision during her coffee break. After Miss Dabas's she would go to the nursing agency in 11th November Street and ask about Sophia. Making the decision put her mind at rest. It was like her sorties back in 47'. Once the first foothill had been claimed, the rest seemed less daunting. As if her leg had ears, her old wound started aching. Dina rubbed at it with all the strength of her thumb and forefinger to get the circulation flowing again. She had spent too long on her knees today, buffing up the floors for the imminent visit of Miss Dabas's mother. Well, she wouldn't be disappointed with these floors. Let her try and find a dull piece of wood or a speck of dust anywhere in this flat. Dina spoke to herself as she scraped the remnants of food from the plates of last night's dinner party and then slid them into the soapy water. As she washed the dishes, she stood on her good leg.

Melting snow dripped from the wooden eaves of the older town houses. Gutters and drainpipes gurgled with the sound of running water and people were
treading their way less carefully along the uneven pavements that had been frozen for months. Balcony doors were beginning to open because they were no longer blocked by mounds of snow. Dina was encouraged by these sights. She felt the town awakening after its hibernation, in hope and preparation for spring.

After Mr B's, this sink was Dina's favourite viewpoint. Whoever designed this kitchen knew a lot about housework and the pleasures of observing the world below. Dina thought about the daily rituals involved in her working life; watching others go about their tasks was a necessity if you wanted to remain sane. Cleaners were a solitary lot but windows made it possible for people like her to feel connected to others, even if it was at a distance. The youth in the *kafeneon* came to her mind. Was he so naïve as to believe anyone would choose to spend their life doing this? She shook the remaining trickles of water from her rubber gloves and dropped them onto the draining board. A proper education. That would have been her wish. Filling her days with learning about foreign countries and peoples, understanding her own ancient culture, making sense of the literature under the watchful eye of a dedicated teacher. What a luxury that would have been. Indulging her imagination day after day. A rich life, richer by far than any material wealth. But that would never have happened. The war changed everything for many people. It put a stop to the mundane and brought instead the extraordinary, diverting the course of people's lives forever.

The nursing agency was about to close as Dina squeezed her way through their door, in search of information about Sophia. They didn't know her whereabouts. She had taken her last week's wages and said she would not be available for a while. When they asked her for how long she was evasive, replying that she did not know. They suggested the name of another nurse who might be able to help.

Dina was directed to a street not far from the agency. An aproned grandmother opened the door to Dina with a smile that quickly turned into a frown. "Ah. I thought you were the plumber. The tap's leaking and the floor's suffering." She peered more closely at Dina over the top of her glasses.

"Good morning Kiria. I'm looking for Zoe. "

"What has the girl done now? Has she been in trouble?"

"No no Kiria. The nursing agency sent me. They said Zoe might know where I can find someone I'm looking for."

"Well she's at the shops now. Would you like to come in and wait? She shouldn't be very long but then again you never know with the young women of today. She's probably gazing in some fashion shop window for clothes she'll never have."

Dina hesitated, unsure if this was all just a waste of her time. But then again, what else was she going to do? There were no other leads she could follow to find Sophia. So she stepped inside, carefully wiping her feet on the doormat. "Thank-you, yes I'll come in and wait if you don't mind. "

The two women introduced themselves and Dina was treated to coffee and homemade halva. They chatted politely for half an hour before the conversation turned to religion. Dina had not missed the large gold crucifix resting on the grandmother's chest. As the woman rambled on about the new priest at her local church Dina studied the icons dotted around the walls of the living room where they sat. She was relieved when she heard the front door.

"There you are Zoe. There's someone here who needs to speak to you." Zoe turned out to be young. Probably not yet twenty, thought Dina.

"The nursing agency said you might know where I can find Sophia. They said you and she were friends?" Dina waited anxiously.

Zoe looked down to her shoes. "No. I don't know Kiria."

At this point the grandmother took control, lifting the young woman's hair away from her face. "And what are you hiding young lady? You know very well you can't fool your old grandmother."

Dina was grateful the grandmother had stayed in the room. She waited, not wanting to impose herself in someone else's house. She could see Zoe was blushing. She felt awkward. She had ruined the peace of the household.

"Kastania." Zoe looked at her grandmother as she spoke. "Kastania is where she might be but I'm not sure. I know her father's in a village somewhere and she mentioned that one to me."

Before Dina could speak the grandmother flew in again. "Then why in the name of our God did you lie when the Kiria here asked you if you knew?"

The girl blushed deeply and sighed. "Because, *yiayia*, she asked me not to say a word to anyone and I didn't want to let her down. And now I have."

"Now listen to me child. Your first duty is to the Lord and you will not lie even when someone asks you.to. Do you understand? *Thee mou* what will become of our young ones if they don't respect the Lord's teachings."

Dina looked from grandmother to granddaughter. She didn't have time to get tangled up in a row about religion and youth. "Do you know where Kastania is?"

"Somewhere on the road to Veroia I think." Said the grandmother.

"Well Zoe, thanks for telling me. Did Sophia say why she was leaving Kastoria?"

"No, not to me but she didn't look very happy about it."

"How do you mean?"

"Well, as if she was doing it because she had to. That it wasn't something she wanted to do because the agency had given her another patient and I know she needed the money."

"Don't we all my girl! Now if we're finished here Kiria I need to get on with the food."

Dina moved towards the door. "Yes I'm sorry for keeping you and thank-you for your help Zoe."

The grandmother disappeared into the kitchen cursing the lateness of the plumber.

Dina took the opportunity to whisper into Zoe's ear. "And I'm sorry you had to tell but it really is very important to me that I find her."

She would have to try Kastania. It could be a wasted journey but that was a risk she had to take if she wanted to get to the end of her story.

She trod her usual road towards home, bothered by what she was going to tell Rena about an unexpected, mysterious journey in search of someone her daughter had never met. Tomorrow she would have to call Kiria Theophilos to excuse herself from work. She composed her explanation in her head as she crossed over to the sunny side of the street so that she could feel the heat on her face. It was a premature, weak sun but it was still welcome. As she walked at her usual swift pace down the hill Dina opened her fur coat at the front, letting it flare out on either side. She would say that a second cousin was very ill and Dina, the sole surviving relative, was obliged to visit her. Nobody would argue with that explanation. Dina's journey would cost her a day's pay. She did have a cousin in that area so she could really visit her. That would make it only half a lie. She had consoled herself a little but Rena would take some convincing. She couldn't bluff her way past her daughter.

"You'll just have to trust me, your mama! You know I wouldn't be doing this if it wasn't important for all of us."

Rena was hollowing out peppers with a spoon. Then she stopped and turned towards her mother, gesticulating with the spoon in mid air. "But why can't you trust me with whatever this secret is mama? Of all people you can't even tell me the truth."

Rena's feelings were hurt. Dina wanted to tell Rena the truth but as a mother she also felt the pangs of wanting to protect her daughter from the disappointment that could so easily be the result of her quest. She stood up, removed the spoon from Rena's hand and put her own hand where the spoon had been. Their eyes met in a deep stare. "Rena, my little one, please let me do this my way. I've thought about what I'm doing."

"But mama, it's all so mysterious – going off on your own to visit Dora after all these years of silence. Is it about us going back to Nestorio? Have you changed your mind?" Rena's eyes widened, expectant. "Is it something to do with Dimitri?"

Dina caught the look on her daughter's face. It re-affirmed for her why she had to be so careful not to raise her hopes. "No. Not about that." She sighed.

Lunch was a quiet affair that day. Dina was subdued at the thought of her journey tomorrow and she could see Rena was sulking. She planted a kiss on Evy's perfectly curved alabaster neck. "Come on now. I'll read you a story before our nap."

Before sleep took her Dina heard Rena crashing the dishes into the sink.

CHAPTER TWENTY-FIVE

"You think you've forgiven but then you remember something very bad or you see it in a magazine or on television and you start hating all over again. I think you just have to keep trying and that's all you can do."

Daybreak, Tuesday. Sharp gusts of wind curled round the corners of the bus station, nipping at Dina's ankles. Curious glances were aimed at her. She imagined she must look conspicuous propped up against the coffee kiosk in her expensive fur coat. Ladies who wore such clothes weren't usually seen loitering in draughty, oily bus stations. The sun was beginning to break through the small high windows around the station roof. It picked out puddles of oil on the floor that shimmered like polished metal. Distinct smells filled the meeting place of buses leaving and arriving, of people waving goodbye and welcoming their loved ones. Bitter roasting coffee, fresh *koulouri* rings, vapours from bus engines being revved up by frantic mechanics, fumes from decrepit exhausts as they belched out of the station.

The sounds of men coughing from the depths of their nicotined lungs and the cackling tones of women who looked a thousand years old, thrusting bunches of lavender under the noses of the occasional, early season tourist. Dina was amazed at how successful they were in hawking their wares, thrusting coins into the pockets of their heavy woven skirts and grinning their crooked thanks. She had a premonition that the woman she had been watching would approach her. She made ready a few coins to put into her palm. In return she was blessed and promised eternal prosperity. Dina saw the funny side of her situation and chuckled. Accompanying the gypsy was a small ginger skinned girl. Life on the road, sun and dust layering themselves on top of her filthy clothes. Dina took pity on the child. She was about Evy's age but her black curls were matted around her face. She noticed the weary, life worn look in the girl's eyes as they followed the journey of the *koulouri* passing from her fingers to her mouth. How could she enjoy her breakfast while this pair of hungry, dark eyes stared up at her? Dina handed the remains to the girl who fell on it before her younger brother had chance to realise what had happened. Theirs was a tough world. She watched the girl devour the *koulouri* ring in seconds and then get a clip round the ear for not leaving any for her brother. She considered buying another one to give to the tiny, malnourished boy but this would only invite a family feud.

Dina's bus was beginning to load. Passengers handed over their suitcases and cardboard boxes to the driver who shoved them into the baggage hold under the belly of the bus. Dina walked over to Bay Four, happy to escape from the gathering of gypsies she had somehow managed to attract. Gesticulating in front of her was an elderly widow bound up in black skirts and a holed woollen cardigan. She was having an argument with the driver. He refused to allow her to bring her cockerel on board. She pushed forward, cockerel under arm, he pushed back, barring her way up the steps. She waved her ticket in his face. She had bought a ticket, she told the driver. What more did he want?

"You have a ticket Kiria, your cockerel doesn't!"

People began to load their own bags. Dina just wanted to get inside and sit down and really she thought, if she was honest, she didn't want a live bird flapping up and down the aisle while its owner slept like an infant. She had seen it many times and blamed the bus company for its inconsistent treatment of villagers coming and going from the town. Some drivers turned a blind eye to the livestock issue, others, like this one, wouldn't allow it under any circumstances. The other passengers were becoming irritated at the widow and her bird and one man, a suited city type, proposed to the driver that they take a democratic vote as to the fate of the cockerel. Then they could all get on their way. He had an important meeting in Thessaloniki at eleven that morning. Dina saw the driver's expression. He was considering the idea. She had already decided to vote against. Thank Christ Evy wasn't with her or she would have been heartbroken by her grandmother's lack of sympathy. The driver finally climbed down the steps. He addressed the passengers gathered around the Bay. They were threatening to carry the widow off to the ticket office where the manager could deal with her. The driver explained to her that he didn't think there was anyone who wanted her bird on the bus with them but to show her that he was not an unfair man he would take a vote. Did the widow really know what a vote meant?

"All those in favour of this cockerel boarding our bus, raise your hands." The driver stood importantly, hands on hips, his years of driving represented by the deep creases on his forehead. No hands were raised. The widow refused to let go her bird in order to raise her hand. "Okay. All those against!" All hands shot up.

"What's she going to do with it?" Dina heard someone ask. Nobody had thought of that.

"Are you boarding this bus or not Kiria?" The driver cajoled the widow as she continued standing at the foot of the steps. He hooted the bus horn and revved the engine as a signal for departure. Dina settled into a window seat near the front. She could hear the woman screeching to the world that she couldn't abandon her cockerel. What would become of it? What would her husband say when she returned empty handed? In her distress she had forgotten she no longer had a husband. Dina began to feel sorry for her. A live animal was worth a lot to a villager and she felt a little ashamed that she hadn't supported her. Then, as she was considering what to do about her conscience there was an almighty squawking and fluttering. The widow had released her charge into the depths of the bus station and it had been immediately set upon by a stray dog. The dog snarled. The cockerel flapped its wings and tried fluttering up onto the nearest beam but only managed to land on the bonnet of another bus. People were shouting. A party had formed to attempt the capture of the bird.

Cackling to herself and masticating her gums, the widow hobbled up into the bus. They reversed slowly and then lurched forward towards the entrance of the station. The last sight Dina caught was of a man lunging towards the escaped bird with the pole of a child's shrimping net. Then they were off, accelerating up the road. It was still only seven o'clock. The widow sat opposite Dina and when she turned her face towards the aisle, Dina saw a small tear trickle down her leathery cheek as she slept. Dina collected a few coins from the passengers and placed the money in the widow's pocket without even waking her.

The road from Kastoria emerged between bright green cypresses, dark pines and thick red earth. There had been landslides as the snow began to thaw, leaving great mounds of soil dotted about the road. Giant grey boulders lined the edges of the road, ice still visible in their eroded crevasses. It had been a long time since Dina had travelled outside Kastoria and she felt excited. If nothing better came of her journey, well, at least she could think of it as an adventure, like she was some kind of sleuth on the trail of a wanted person. And she did want to find Sophia so that she would be put out of her misery one way or another. The old bus rumbled happily along the pot- holed road until it began to climb higher, past Kozani and into the hills overlooking the Aliakmonas, far below. Then it struggled, especially round the increasingly sharp bends. Dina was peering down at the river again but unlike at Pefkos, here it meandered wide and proud. Far over to the south -east she could pick out the snow capped peaks of Titaros and Olympus, towering up from the plains.

Another argument broke out. This time the widow and a young woman occupying the seat in front of her were engaged in a tug of war with the sliding window. As quickly as the young woman pushed it open, the widow forced it closed, complaining of bitterly cold draughts that would be the death of her. In the end, the young woman gave way and fanned herself with a magazine borrowed from the suited man who was paying her respectful attention. The driver checked the widow in his mirror, asking where exactly the widow wanted to be dropped. His question elicited a few mumbled suggestions and subsequent laughter from other passengers. She finally creaked down the steps of the bus at her village – *Levendi*. Dina smiled at the name. A fitting name for a village of women like her. Dina watched her as she bent her way up a rough, cobbled footpath before disappearing into a cluster of beech trees. She probably faced a lengthy walk but she was hardy, they all were, all those village women of a certain generation. She had made Dina feel young again.

The driver informed Dina that Kastania was another half an hour. She pictured the widow's face when she emptied her pockets and discovered her fortune. Her head lolled back against the seat, rolling with the motion of the bus. Dina felt her eyes succumbing under the weight of their lids.

"Your stop Kiria." The driver was calling from his cab.

"Kiria. This is Kastania." The young woman was gently tapping Dina's shoulder to wake her.

Dina opened her eyes and jumped. "*Thee mou*! I was dreaming. Are we here?" She gathered up her bag and coat. "Thank-you driver. I forgot to ask what times do the buses pass returning to Kastoria today?"

"Every two hours. The last one passes at eight."

The bus struggled up the hill and disappeared round a bend leaving Dina in a shroud of dust. It was mid morning.

The sun was well risen and Dina felt its early spring warmth. She looked around her and headed for the first building she spotted, a poor villager's house set back from the road and surrounded by a rusting wire fence. Two black dogs strained their muscled necks over the fence, breathing frantically with open, salivating mouths.

"Get away with you! Shut up." Dina had never liked dogs having been bitten by a stray as a child. She picked up a stone from the path and held it tightly in her palm, just in case she needed to defend herself - an old childhood habit learnt the hard way in her village. The dogs deterred Dina from attempting to open the gate. "Hello. Is anyone at home? Hello!" She heard a door bang and a woman appeared on the veranda. She stepped down and came towards Dina who cowered at the fence, a good distance from the dogs.

"Good morning Kiria. Are you lost? Did you get off the bus?" The woman smiled at Dina and folded a pair of plump arms over her large stomach. Miraculously, the dogs had become silent at her arrival.

Dina relaxed a little. "No. Well, I might be. I don't know Kiria. Can you help me? I'm here looking for someone – she's a nurse, Sophia, about forty -five. I was told this was her village."

The woman chuckled and caught a stray hair that had been swept over her face by the gathering breeze. "Now that's not as easy as it sounds Kiria. There's quite a few of them here, on account of the church you see." She nodded her head backwards. The bell tower rose out of the pines on the hill above the village."*Agia* Sophia . D'you see? That makes it more of a difficulty then."

Dina saw how much the woman was obviously relishing the unusual attention she was receiving. "Ah yes! I see what you mean…but anyway I'll have to make a start somewhere. They're not all that age and they're not all nurses surely?"

The woman scratched her head. "True enough! Better you ask at Manoli's."

"Who's he?" Dina was becoming impatient. This woman clearly wanted to spend the rest of the morning making Dina work for her answers.

"Baker. Everybody passes by him sooner or later don't they?"

"And where is he?" A cigarette would be wonderful but Dina held off. Women seen smoking in public didn't go down well with villagers.

"In the *plateia*, where else? You'll smell him before you see him."

"I thank you Kiria. Good day. *Kali oreksi*." As soon as she reached the road Dina lit up a cigarette.

The woman had been right. Dina smelt the baker's before she entered the village square. Apart from three old men clustered round a metal table and more stray dogs, the square was empty. It felt strange to Dina that she was walking into an unknown village in the morning on a day when she would normally be scrubbing floors. She had a sense of freedom, of being out of place, unaccountable but also a little scared about what to do with such feelings. This caused her to be more hesitant. She still held the stone in her hand, taking no chances. She knew how unpredictable village mongrels could be.

Manolis had a pale creamy face, like a pudding. He wiped his hands on his floury apron. "You're not local are you? I've not seen you in here before Kiria." He was studying her fur coat.

"No Kirios I've come from Kastoria in search of a woman called Sophia, a nurse, about forty five years old." Dina looked in his face hopefully.

Manolis saw her hope. "So! Forty five, Sophia, a nurse you say?"

"Yes. D'you know her?"

"Now let me think." He sat down on a chair and beckoned Dina to do the same. She gladly agreed. "There's Eleni up at Lodger – she's got two daughters, one of them would be about that age but you never know with women do you – present company excepted of course Kiria."

"Thank you. You were telling me about Eleni's daughters?" Dina felt warmed by the closeness of the big ovens and removed her coat.

"That's a beautiful coat you've got there Kiria. They don't trap them like that round here." He leant over from his chair. "May I?' Without waiting for a reply he stroked the pelt and nodded his approval. "Excellent."

Dina felt the same surge of impatience she had experienced with the woman earlier. "You were saying? About Eleni's daughters?"

"Ah yes, Eleni's youngest is Sophia but I never heard of her being a nurse. Last time I saw her she was big with her fourth child. Three daughters they've got so we're all praying for the son." Dina thought of Ketty's story.

Manolis took a packet of cigarettes from his apron pocket and offered one to Dina. He leant over to light hers. "So I don't think that's the Sophia you're looking for." He hesitated and grinned. "What's she done then, this Sophia?"

"She hasn't done anything Kirios! It's too long a story to tell now. Please don't think me rude but it would be a really big help to me if you could think where I could find her."

"There's old Grigory's daughter. She's about that age and I think she was away doing something like nursing but then her name's Georgia not Sophia."

A young woman had entered the shop from the back, catching their conversation.

"She calls herself Georgia, *baba*, but she's baptised Sophia on account of her grandmother! Don't you remember the trouble that old witch caused them? I don't blame Georgia for not wanting her name."

"Kiria, my daughter Penelope." Manolis gestured towards the young woman. "She bakes the best *Tsourekia* this side of Kozani"

Dina smiled. "Then I'll have to come back in a month or so! What does she look like, this Georgia?"

"On the plump side, good colour in her cheeks, natural curls, doesn't stand any nonsense that one but she has to be a saint to put up with old Grigory."

"Where can I find Georgia?"

Penelope was about to answer but her father cut in.

"But there are two more I can think of. There's Sophia over at Mavrona but she's more like sixty, not wearing well that one. She's grey, doesn't colour her hair like most of them." He quickly glanced at Dina's hair.

"And who is the other?"

The baker stood up to serve a customer who had come into the shop while they were talking. He retrieved a large square dish from one of the ovens and handed it over to the woman who had come prepared to carry it home with her own oven gloves. Cinnamon and tomato steamed up from the dish. Dina's mouth watered. She nodded her greetings to the woman.

"Eh Kiria Chrissoula, know any Sophia here? Nurse? This Kiria is looking for her." Manolis moved out from behind the counter.

"Eh? What d'you say? I can't hear you. Come closer for a cuddle." She giggled, nudging him with a threatening elbow.

Manolis went round to her good ear. "I said do you know any nurse here, name of Sophia? This Kiria is looking for her."

"Me? No, no nurses. They do nothing but make you worse. Plenty of Sophia's but no nurses. Now the real *Agia* Sophia, she was the one. Our dear, true Sophia." The woman almost tipped her dish over in her haste to cross herself at the mention of the saint.

"Never mind Kiria. I'll be on my way now Kirios. Can you point me in the direction of Georgia's house?"

Penelope rushed forward, eager to help. "I can show you Kiria."

But her father intervened again. "No you won't my girl. You've got bread to take out and don't forget aunt Olga wants that cake ready by two."

Penelope's mouth puckered at the corners and her beautiful dark lashes swept down in disappointment.

"Straight over and left at the telephone office. First house up the passage, faded green shutters. Say Manolis sent you. Here, give them a loaf from me, save her coming down for it." Dina took the bread and another for herself. The day already felt too long.

Taking a deep breath she stood looking up at the house.
Is this it? Have I finally found her?

The passage was darkened by a large chestnut tree. Old olive green paint had long ago started cracking away from the wood of the shutters and the once white walls were covered in mould. Vines creeping across from the adjoining vineyard strangled the smaller oleander bushes and a rusting gate hung lopsided on one hinge. At least there were no dogs this time.

Dina's knock was timid as if she didn't expect any answer. An old man's rasping cough responded. She jumped. Then quick footsteps approached the door and it was flung open. Sophia at last.

At first she tried to close the door on Dina but Dina wedged her toe in the doorway. "I haven't come all this way to go home with no answers." Her tone was determined. She surprised herself. And she waited, her toe stuck in the doorway and Sophia's red face looking at her. Dina could hear the father calling out to his daughter, asking her who it was and why she didn't close the door. Good, thought Dina. The pressure will force a decision from her. She was right.

"How did you find me?"

"It wasn't so hard but it's taking my time and time is loss of money for me."

Sophia opened the door. Her father was hobbling towards her. "Who is it? Who is it? Let them in or say goodbye but don't stand there letting in the draught."

Dina removed her toe but waited.

"You'd better come in."

She entered a village house. Dark. Small windows. Thick, cold stone walls. But in the corner there was a warming wood burning stove. "Sit down Dina."

"Thank-you Sophia. I won't keep you. I'm sure you know why I'm here."

Sophia sat opposite. Dina thought she looked healthy. A little plumper than the last time they had met.

"I imagine it's about the will."

"Yes. You know she's contesting it so I won't be able to inherit the house and…"

Sophia stood up. "Sorry. I haven't offered you anything. You must be tired after your journey. Coffee?"

"Thank-you. That would be very welcome Sophia." Dina glanced around the room while Sophia disappeared behind an old curtain. Her father took the opportunity to introduce himself. Dina stood up to offer him her chair out of respect. She judged him to be a very elderly man with a harsh cough. They shook hands.

"Come a long way have you Kiria?"

"Yes. From Kastoria."

The man smiled and wagged his finger at Dina's coat. "Ah yes. That explains the beautiful coat you're wearing. Old Lakounis still trading down there is he?"

Dina was surprised. "You must mean the old Kirios Lakounis. No, he died but his son took over the business of course. I'm their cleaner."

The man nodded his head before replying. "Well. They pay you in furs then eh?" He chuckled at his own joke.

Dina smiled with him. "Kiria Lakounis is a very kind woman. She could spare one of her furs." He continued nodding as he made his way out of the room.

Sophia appeared again with the coffee. "There. Some biscuits as well."

"So. As I said, Vassiliki is claiming that Mr B was mentally unsound when he changed his will and you're the only person who…"

"She paid me."

Dina's eyes widened. Why hadn't she thought of that? Of course. It made sense that Vassiliki would try and buy what she couldn't get any other way.

"She paid me to leave Kastoria. She said I'd be doing my father a favour by coming back and being his nurse." Sophia smirked. "I'd like to see her giving up her life to go back to her village. I never saw her spend much time with her brother when he was sick."

"She didn't."

"So she paid me the equivalent of a year's nursing wages and I promised not to return to Kastoria."

Dina sighed. Sophia had told her the truth but would she be prepared to do anything more? The clock on the wall allowed Dina another half an hour before she had to leave to get her bus.

"What would you like me to do Dina?"

It was sweet to her ears. Dina felt warmed by Sophia's words. "Testify that Mr B was of sound mind when he changed his will. You could also tell the court that Vassiliki had paid you to leave. I think that would just about finish her, don't you?"

Sophia stood up and warmed her hands in front of the stove. "Do you think I'll have to give her back her money?"

Dina realised this must be a consideration for Sophia. She didn't see any signs of wealth in this household. "No. I don't see why you should give it back."

"Dina. I feel bad about what I did. Taking that money and helping to prevent you from getting what Mr B wanted you to have. I haven't been principled in all this. I don't know what I was thinking. To tell you the truth, if you hadn't come knocking I don't know if I'd have ever gone back. Not that I enjoy village life. It's fine if you're eighty years old or you never left the place but for me…"

"Tell my Rena that. She still thinks village life is better than the one we have in the town. She doesn't see the hardship." Dina checked the clock again. "Sophia I need to go to get the bus. What's your answer?"

"My answer is yes Dina. I'll testify. Your courage coming here has inspired me to do the right thing." She moved towards Dina and held out her arms. Dina allowed herself to be hugged. She sunk into Sophia's hug allowing the relief to take over.

There weren't enough minutes in her bus journey for all the thoughts crowding Dina's brain. Until now she had been able to forget about her last meeting with Dimitris. He hadn't been in touch and who could blame him. She couldn't tell him what he wanted to hear. She had watched and listened to his reactions to things she said about people and she didn't like them particularly. She certainly didn't agree with him on a number of political issues and she knew in her heart that she would never rejoin the Party. It was easier for him. He was a man. Widows of her generation from the villages weren't expected to marry again and it was unthinkable for Dina to imagine the alternative. Yes, if you were a young woman, living in Athens but not a fifty year old grandmother from an Epirean village. And anyway, their love was built on memories of a time when they were different people. That could never be enough.

Finding Sophia had allowed Dina to have hope. The risk had paid off. She ignored the potholes in the road that caused her bus to bump and bang every few minutes. She looked out the bus window, noticing the village houses as they sped by. But the veranda she saw as she closed her eyes was the veranda at Nikis street and there she was again, standing on it looking lovingly across at the lake.

Sophia kept her word. Events moved fast, at least they moved fast by Greek standards. Vassiliki came back into Dina's life with force like a passing whirlwind spitting out its venom as it did so. Dina was prepared for Vassiliki's hatred and resentment. She had never expected to be accepted by her. She didn't respect her brother's wishes. Dina thought that Vassiliki very probably would never be able to understand why Mr B really wanted his cleaner to inherit his house. *She may strut about with her authority but really she is not a wordly woman. I am not educated. What I know I have mainly learned through my life experience but I know more of the world than she will ever grasp. It's as though the lens through which she* sees the world is rigid. Things are black or white. If you're so stuck you will never be able to open your heart to the possibility that you may be wrong. I can look back at my soldier years and admit that there were times when we did the wrong thing. On some occasions we demeaned ourselves by bringing ourselves down to their level, the level of the enemy. That, I believe now, was a mistake. Dimitris wouldn't agree but there it is.

Vassiliki can only interpret her brother's actions as betrayal of family loyalty. She is like a limpet clinging to the slimy rock of the monarchists. Her anthem is family and nation but in reality what does family mean to her? She didn't understand anything about her brother especially his disintegration after Maria's death. Where were the hours she should surely have spent at his bedside when he was dying? It had been left to herself, a cleaner and Sophia, an agency nurse. Fine talk of family loyalty. And as for nation. Vassiliki's notion of nation was a country cleansed of all dissent. Total control by an unelected cabal. Dina nodded to herself. Her life would have gone on pretty much as always if Mr B hadn't changed his will and if she hadn't found Sophia or if Sophia had refused to testify. Then Dina would have let go of her dream.

Will you forgive him now? Sophia had asked. Dina had given it a lot of thought. Such a big gift was Mr B's way of saying he was sorry for his actions in the past especially those that had caused the death of her sister Lela. She had to ask herself if she would have forgiven him if he hadn't changed his will. Was she just saying *yes please, I want your house for myself and family and what you did in the past stays in the past. I'll forget about it because I have this house?*

No, she would never forget. Not one thing. But did that mean she would never forgive? The gift of Mr B's house didn't cancel out his leading role in the horrific events of the past but it did help. He must have known it would help Dina but it was also as if, by leaving his house to her, he knew he was leaving it in safe hands. He hadn't trusted his sister and he was right. Dina was glad she had never told him what Vassiliki was planning to do with his house even before he died.

She wanted to give Dimitris her wonderful news but she didn't. There was something telling her it wouldn't be received with joy. Instead of telling him she imagined how he might react. Maybe making her feel guilty for accepting such an inheritance. Why? Because socialists didn't inherit wealth. They opposed the system that thrived on it. But in her mind Dina reasoned that it was a gift and a peace offering from a man she was still trying to forgive. That was all she had promised to do.

EPILOGUE 1989

"When ordered, the soldiers didn't raise their weapons towards the girl in the red dress. Evangelitsa she was called. Twenty years old she was and she sang as the officer was forced to raise his own gun and execute her. You might think of these as good stories but I've lived them."

The researcher shifted in her chair and sipped from a glass of water. She looked deeply into Dina's eyes then scribbled onto her pad.

"Did I tell you yet about a young one called Bligouris? It was 47'. We didn't have any food and it was the eve of Easter. We decided to go down from the mountain to find bread. Our company was joined by comrades from two or three other platoons. Bligouris was married. His wife was a Captain in another brigade. He was struck by the beauty of the land around him and the weather. It wasn't snowing and it wasn't cold. The sun and the flowers had come out so we felt enthusiastic. And d'you know what Bligouris said? He said, 'Eh, *paidia,* if I get killed now, bury me here! Look at the weather Death has chosen, how the grass is growing green and the colours of the mountains.'

And we went back to our camp with some food given to us by the villagers. We couldn't sleep in the villages. That would've been putting their lives at risk more than they were anyway. And many times we found ourselves far away from any villages. Those were the times when we went hungry. We'd eat anything we could get our hands on but there weren't many of us who were good enough marksmen to shoot a moving rabbit or a bird. And I've told you about the atrocities they committed in the villages already. We tried not to make them an easy target for our enemy."

"The villages you mean?"

"Yes. The villages."

Anne didn't attempt to fill the silence. Her eyes wandered over to the lake where some ducks were waddling in single file along the boating jetty. A pleasure boat, full of tourists, was steaming its way across the calm water. "It's like a painting, so beautiful!"

Dina sipped her coffee. "Yes. Since I've been in this house I see beauty everywhere. If I didn't know better I'd believe my eyesight was improving instead of getting worse." She laid both hands on her knees and looked down. It was a movement that always helped her to refocus.

She resumed. "We had taken up position on a hill but we failed to secure it from the West and that's where they came from and the first bullet fired, Bligouris fell, without a battle, nothing, just like that." She flung out her arm. "Gone. Dead! Someone called out his name but it was like an echo to me. I sat down on a rock, trembling. I couldn't believe what had happened. Our Captain said, 'we'll take him comrades and we'll bury him there where he wanted.' And we didn't know how to find his wife. She was on another hill, about five miles away. One of our unit volunteered to go and break the news, I forget his name. I was glad it wasn't me. Anyway, d'you know what happened? Such coincidence! While our man was on his way to the wife's unit, one of their comrades was coming to us with the sad news that she'd been killed. Think of that! But we said, at least neither of them had to hear that tragic news about the other, at least they were spared that heartbreak. And you know, thoughts like that gave us comfort then. We fell on anything that softened the blows and lightened our hearts."

The researcher nodded. At that moment a large black dog came shuffling onto the veranda, panting its way towards Dina. She patted its head. "This is Pano. I named him after the man who left me all this. He's slow and he plods around and he's a big presence in our house, just like Pano was. I used to be frightened of dogs but when we moved here my granddaughter begged us for one, so I gave in and got over my fear at the same time. I always think we can overcome most of our fears if we really put our minds to it, you know, when there's another force like a child really urging you to change. Old Pano was a puppy then." She held the dog's chin towards her. "Now just look at you, you silly old thing." The dog panted, its mouth wide, almost smiling at Dina. "Excuse me a minute while I give him some water." And she disappeared inside with the dog on her heels.

On her return Dina placed two glasses of water on the table. "Here. Drink this. Do you like vanilia? I always like it on a hot summer day."

"Now. Let's get on. I was twenty-three in 47'. We had all our lives in front of us but it was as if we had lived everything inside those two years till 49'. Battles day and night. Walking freezing, crazy from lack of sleep. Some of us fell in love. We danced and sang and some had better voices than others.." Dina chuckled.

"Could you sing me one?"

Dina's face creased in laughter. "I've got no singing voice my child but I could try a very simple little rhyme that was told to me by my *yiayia* when I was a girl and I wanted to adopt all the cats in the neighbourhood." She saw the delight on the researcher's face and cleared her throat. And Dina sang in a trembling, shy voice.

> *Once upon a time*
> *A cat went to a dance*
> *And she didn't dance well*
> *And they cut off her tail"*

"That's it! As you can hear, they don't have much heart for cats in our villages but it's one of those rhymes you always remember like you remember the smells and tastes of different places you've been in your life. You've probably travelled to lots of foreign places but me, all I know are the mountains and villages around here and Skopje of course. That's a regret I have, not to have seen all those places they show now on television. But that's now."

"You said that some of you fell in love. Is that what happened to you?"

"Yes I fell in love before I actually went to the mountains and I married there but my daughter was born in Skopje."

"And your husband? Do you mind telling me how he died?"

There was a silence as Dina stared at Anne. It was a reasonable question but she was aware that even now she was trying to avoid saying the words. "I…" She swallowed. Her throat had suddenly become very dry. "I tell you what. You can write this down. First use of napalm in the mountains of Grammos 1949. My husband was one of the first victims. He could very well have been on another mountain but as luck would have it he was on Grammos. We underestimate how much of a role luck plays in our lives. But even if he had lived I would still be here talking to you and we would still need to remember."

Dina lit herself a cigarette and leant her head back against the sun lounger. "I'm afraid I never managed to give these up. It's good you never got started *paidi mou*. Sophia never gives up telling me off either!"

"Sophia?"

"She's my nurse. She lives here with me. I'm lucky. I've got Sophia and Olga Lakounis who I used to clean for. Olga lives along this street. When Mr B died I was lucky to be recommended to Olga and so my Fridays were spent at her house instead of here. We became friends and she looks out for me now. She gave me my precious fur coat and I still wear it. Every Christmas she insists on inviting me round for drinks and *mezedes*. But it's thanks to Sophia that I have this wonderful house. But that's another story and it's not why you're here. Now, you wanted to know about the government soldiers. One time, I think it was in Alivitsa in 48'. We were dug in on one side of a big chasm, between two huge rocks and they were on the other side. They threw us food and we talked. We even knew one another's names. 'Good morning girls, hello. What are you doing?' They would ask. We told them 'today we're eating, (we imagined real food).' And they would reply, 'leave it out! We know you're starving. We know you haven't got any food.' And they threw us bundles of bread and cheese sometimes. Many times they told us, 'hide! We're starting the machine gun.' Many times they gave us information, 'tomorrow they'll start bombing. Where will you go?' We answered that we would go wherever we were ordered but we wouldn't tell them, naturally. We were in the mountains, we had to fight, nothing else. But soldiers weren't all the same you know. There were some very hard, fascist types but there were also some democratic ones who helped us, like those I've mentioned."

A sudden gust of wind swept across the veranda, billowing the sun canopy above the two women, lifting the cigarette butts and sprinkling the ash into the air. Dina pushed herself up from her seat to attend to the mess. "It's the warm August air that blows upfrom the Ionian all the way over the Pindus."

Dina rushed back with her dustpan and brush. "Sorry but I just can't leave a mess, I have to see to it right away. It's all my years cleaning and looking at dirt and untidiness. As soon as I see it I feel like I'm at work and need to finish the job. Now, where was I?

"The soldiers."

"Ah yes. Some of them were so harsh, bloodthirsty. They were the ones who would kill you, even if you were from the same village but I was lucky. I met a lot of young boys who didn't really know why they were there, in the mountains.

Often it was simply because they knew they would be fed and clothed properly whereas if they joined us that would be a luxury. And some of my comrades did die from starvation.

One of the good comrades I remember was Mitsos. He deserted from the government army and joined us. He was from the officer's class as well so he was educated. He came to fight with us, a fine young man. He ended up in Moscow, a scientist and still there, last I heard."

The force of the wind had subsided to a gentle flapping on the fringes of the canopy. Dina fanned herself with a folded newspaper. It was getting towards midday. The sun overhead was at full strength. Dina watched a dove landing on a branch of her favourite chestnut tree overhanging the lake. She pointed it out to the researcher, beckoning her to walk across the wide veranda to get a closer view of the lake. "This is my view, day and night. I watch the lake change colour with the light and the time of year. You see now how it soaks up the brightness from the sun so it almost looks like a sheet of ice. Then when it comes to late afternoon, before the sun sets, it gets deep and dark like saphire. I bring my coffee out here when I've had my afternoon nap. You wouldn't believe how many hours I probably spend just gazing out at the lake and the mountains. I never get enough of it!"

"Oh, I would believe it Dina."

"Then there's the autumn colours. Ah! There's no describing those, you just have to see them. You'll have to come back in October to see what I mean. The smell of the air in that month is fit for bottling. We have a lot of wood fires here, on account of all the forests nearby, so you can smell the wood-smoke any time of day. Some of the older houses still use wood stoves to cook with but I prefer the luxury of my electric kitchen and d'you know how easy it is to clean!" Dina made a circular movement with her right hand. "Two minutes and it's done. Come and see my kitchen. I don't mind showing a guest my kitchen because it's like an old friend I've known for a long time and it has seen a lot of action and words flying around it in its time."

They walked into the house, across the lounge, now stripped of its winter rugs. The walls of the kitchen were like vanilla ice-cream. Pretty saffron coloured curtains framed the window above the sink. Dina opened the back door that led out onto the balcony. "See. This house has light surrounding it on all sides. To the front we have the lake and the mountains. To the back we have the trees and hills. My favourite tree is the sweet almond over there." Dina leant over the balcony. "And that lovely cedar in the middle, it smells wonderful."

Anne sat down at the small kitchen table. "Dina, when I last visited you there were some things I didn't get round to asking. Do you ever think about the cruel things done by your own side in the *Emfilio*?"

"Yes of course I do. I still think about them today. Those pictures never disappear but I have changed a lot in some ways since then."

"In what ways Dina?"

"I still believe we were right to resist this, this Americanisation we're now beginning to see in our country. And I think in years to come, when I'm no longer around it will be even more obvious what their interests really were in Greece. But I didn't go along with the Stalinists because I never imagined Greece to be like Russia and anyway people are right when they say he was just another dictator. Look what's happening in West Germany now. It looks like things will get better for those poor people in East Germany."

"You mean if they open the gate and knock down the Wall?"

"Well, yes. I mean, they're all Germans aren't they? But to go back to that time, well, you know, when you're in the middle of a war and you've committed yourself there's no question of being right or wrong. You don't have time or energy because every choice you make can result in dying or living not just for you but for others, children included."

Dina sat down and plucked a golden nectarine from a large wooden bowl. She cut it skilfully like a surgeon then sliced the fruit and pushed the plate towards her guest. "Eat, my girl! They're the most tasty and juicy at this time of year. You won't find better."

"Thankyou. But now, when you look back, do you have any regrets about your life?"

"Regrets! Ach *paidi mou.* Who doesn't have regrets?"

The researcher dabbed fruit juice from her lip and smiled.

"The point about regret is what you do with it. I could become bitter and only think about the life I might have had with my husband. Dwell on all those corpses, the hunger and yes, the atrocities committed on both sides. Or I could say to myself you did what you had to do at the time. We didn't have a lot of choice. Me, personally, I could have stayed in my village and probably survived, maybe not."

"Was it worth all the sacrifice?"

"I don't think I know how to answer that but I do know one thing. War isn't the answer. It brings more trouble and the ordinary citizens are the ones who pay."

"Did you actually kill anyone when you were a soldier?"

"I did."

After they had finished, Dina led them into the lounge. She stood in front of the large marble fireplace and picked up a black-framed photograph of a young, dark haired girl. "This is my little Evy." She smiled at the photo proudly. "Not so little anymore!"

"She's beautiful. She was a small child when I last saw her."

"And you have a child now, I hear. *Na sas zeisei*".

"Thankyou, yes. I have a son. Well that's mainly why it's taken me so long to return for the rest of your story Dina. That and work."

"Ah yes! Work. We have no choice in some things."

Dina turned to the photograph. "My granddaughter. We're very proud of her you know. She started at the university, in Thessaloniki this year."

"She looks just like you Dina, the same colour eyes and hair."

Dina saw that Anne was looking at the photo next to Evy's. "You remember my daughter Rena. She left us last year."

"I'm so sorry Dina. What a lovely picture. You must miss her so much."

Dina smoothed the photo frame and planted a kiss on the glass. Her hand shook a little. "Yes.I do. Her husband married again but he still pops round to see me. Evy looks so different now, so grown up, I really need that picture of her there. All I wish for Evy is that she never has to see the same horrific things as I did then. Ah! We've got such high hopes for our Evy."

"What's she studying?"

"She takes after her grandmother in more than just her eyes and hair. She's studying Political Science and Philosophy." Dina replaced the photo and picked up a small velvet box. "And this…this is my medal. I don't show it to people very often. Well, most people wouldn't be interested." The medal was small. The years had corroded its silver surface and the red ribbon it was attached to had become frayed and thin like tissue paper. "This is my Electra medal. They gave it to all of us women who had fought on the front line at Grammos. It doesn't look much but it means a lot to me." She rubbed the surface with her thumb but was distracted by the pain in her leg.

She flinched as she sat down in the chair. The researcher jumped up to pull the footstool nearer. "Thank-you dear. It hits me sometimes, just like that – no reason. But it's worse in the winter with the damp and cold." She rubbed her leg forcefully. "They can't do anything. It's my circulation, as a result of all that time dipping in and out of freezing waters. At least I managed to keep all my toes and fingers, which is more than can be said for some of my poor comrades." Dina gazed out through the veranda doors towards the mountains beyond the lake then closed her eyes but the beautiful scene opposite could not wipe out her memory of the blackened, swollen feet and comrades struggling to aim their weapons with missing fingers. She opened her eyes again and sighed. "I think I've covered everything now. I feel a little tired. Please don't be offended but I get to a point and I just don't want to remember any more and talking about it makes it worse."

"I understand and thank-you for giving me so much of your time. I respect and admire your courage and you've been so generous in sharing your memories with me. You've given me a lot of your time. I'll leave you to rest. I hope this hasn't upset you too much." Anne stood up. Dina was struggling to do the same. "Please, stay where you are Dina. I can show myself out."

But Dina used Anne's arm to push herself up. "What are you saying? Nonsense my girl! I can't let a guest in my house see themselves out." And she hobbled to the main door, all the while clutching onto the researcher. The two women exchanged a tearful embrace. "Go well, *paidi mou*. I'm glad that someone is interested in my past. Do what you can."

Anne made her way down the steps to the wrought iron gate where she turned to wave. Dina raised her hand and then closed the door.

Dina remembered the first time Anne had come knocking on her door. How she had given her a hard time, saying she'd rather forget about it all, sending her away. She was glad now that she had changed her mind. And now, all these years later she had been able to finish her story and close the book on those unspoken years. She was proud of her memory. It may not always have been accurate. She could have confused the date or month when certain events actually happened but at her age she thought she had earned the right to be a little confused sometimes.

Dina felt restless after the researcher had gone. She wandered back out onto the veranda and took up her usual position in her chair and for some reason a conversation between herself and Mr B came back to her. It had been about the difference between a house and a home. These four walls were a real home. She felt that if Mr B were still alive he would have approved of the way Dina had made it her palace.

There had been a time in her life when she appreciated the warmth and shelter offered by a camouflaged dug out. How quickly people learnt to take things for granted and get used to their luxuries, like television and video. She remembered the scenes of children in Africa dying from AIDS and the Live Aid concert. That was four years ago and they were still dying. And here she was feeling sorry for herself. But talking with the researcher reminded her of the value of human life. And she had been able to sift out some of the happy memories as well as the tragic

She sipped her water and lit a cigarette. There was time to get a quick one in before Sophia came back from shopping. Occasional voices echoed from the cobbled steps at the side of Dina's house. People returning home from work with set jaw lines, worried brows, still affected by the jobs they had just left. In contrast, little children at play by the lake, their joyful voices carried on the breeze. From here Dina could sit and watch and hear everything without getting involved. She thought about the time when Evy was small. They had such fun. How determined she had always been to enjoy her granddaughter because Rena's childhood had been so different - a harsh beginning in a foreign land.

She dozed then woke with a start. Something was nagging at her. Dina went into the lounge and switched on the television to watch the lunchtime news. Mitsotakis of New Democracy was speaking. She grimaced when she saw his face. Just think of that, she seethed. An alliance with them! Liars!

Dina slapped the arm of the settee. Is this what we fought for, old comrades sharing privileges with a conservative government? What a sell –out! She wondered about Dimitris. Since KKE had been included in the coalition government she didn't see much of him. His face appeared on television programmes and magazine covers but ever since he had become an MP, a 'proper politician', he called himself, he seemed to have left Dina behind, just like his past. He had merged with those same politicians who had once denounced and hunted them.

Like he's been drinking and chatting with them forever, she said to the television screen. Good job I never rejoined his sell-out Party. He told me people don't change but just look at him. Ach Dimitri what are you playing at?

She turned off the set in disgust. He would appear on her doorstep at some point. He still brought her poppies on Mayday. She flopped back into the settee. Her hand found its way into her apron pocket. She had forgotten to put her medal back in its box after showing it to Anne. Stroking the frayed ribbon, she began crying and her tears flowed for all the experience of her life. She didn't apply any brakes. Old Panos came to lie at her feet, all the while looking up at her with large, worried eyes.

Later, when her tears had finally dried, Dina replaced the medal in its box and carefully positioned it back beside Evy's photograph.

The clock struck two. Lunch was going to be late. All her routine today had been disturbed. Dina stopped in the middle of the lounge, slapping her palm to her forehead.

"Thee mou!" She uttered in disbelief. "For the first time in my life, I forgot to buy the bread.

GLOSSARY

Agapi mou – My love

Andarte – guerrilla fighter/partisan

Alithia – truth/it's true!

Babas – Father

Barba – Uncle

Briki – Metal coffee boiler with handle

Ella – Come on!

Enosis – union of Cyprus and Greece

Emfilio – Civil War

Eleftheri Ellada – Free Greece

Fasolada – thick bean soup

Fakies – thick lentil soup

Fistikia – Pistachio nuts

GSEE – General Confederation of Greek Workers (ΓΣΕΕ)

Hafies – Spies

Halvopitta – sweet pie made from halva

Kafeneon - Cafe

Kali mera – Hello/Good day

Kali oreksi – Good appetite

Kiria/Kirios - Mrs/Mr

Koufeta – small bunch of sugared almonds wrapped in net given to wedding guests

Kerkira - Corfu

Kerkirean – from Kerkira (Corfu)

Koboloi – Worry beads

Kokkinisto – Rich beef stew made with red wine and cinnamon

Kounavia – Type of wild weasel found in Greece

Kourelou – cotton rug of many colours

Koulouri – round crispbread with sesame seeds

Levendi – Braveheart/warrior

Mamma – Mummy

Metrio – Medium Greek coffee

Mezedes – Hors D'Oeuvres / Tapas

Na pas sto diabolo – Go to the devil

Na sas zeisei – may h/she live for you

Paniyiri – Greek village festival

Paidi/ia – Child/Children

Paidi mou – My child

Palikari – brave young man

Panayia mou – My Virgin Mary

Plateia – square/piazza

Poudana - whore

Prodotis – Traitor

Souvlagidiko- stall selling souvlakia (kebabs) and othe fast food

Stefania – round flowered head wreaths crossed by priest during marriage ceremony

Taverna – Greek restaurant

Tavli – Backgammon

Theia – Aunt

Thee mou – My God

Tiropites – individual feta pies made with filo pastry

Trata – Small fishing boat

Tsipouro – strong white spirit distilled from grape seeds

Tsoureki – sweet Easter bread, plaited or round

Yiayia – grandmother

Visinada – cherry juice

S.O.E. – Special Opeerations Executive – WW11 British organisation that conducted espionage and sabotage against the Axis powers. It was specifically set up to aid local resistance movements and was very active in Greece.

Y.V.E. – Defenders of Northern Greece (Monarchofascists)

EDES – National Democratic Greek League

K.K.E. – Communist Party of Greece

ELAS – National Popular Liberation Army

JUNTA – the Colonels' military dictatorship established after 1967 coup

Farandouri, Maria. Singer/political and cultural activist/PASOK MP 1989

Rigas Ferraios – Name taken by youth wing of KKE after popular Greek hero

Van Fleet – US general who supervised the Greek government army's operations against the Communist Democratic Army in final campaigns of 1948/49

Varkiza – the Varkiza Agreement when ELAS surrendered their weapons to the British in 1944

Averoff – notorious prison, burnt down in 1971, where resistance fighters and communists were tortured and held during German Occupation 1941-44.

Markos Vafiadis – ELAS capetan, later c- in- c of Democratic Army during Civil War 1947-49

Metaxas – General John, Greek dictator 1936-41

Karamanlis – Greek P.M.
 Leader of New Democracy 1974-79/1984-1989

Rebetika – Urban Greek folk music

Zeibekiko – Greek folk dance originally danced by one person

Hassaposervika – Originally the dance of the butchers of Constantinople

Bougatsa – Greek pastry made from semolina, custard, cheese or mince

*From the Greek song by Nikos Ksilouris
On A High Mountain (Ο Αϊτός)

Σε ψιλό βουνό
Σε ριζιμιό χάρακι
Κάθεται 'ενα αϊτός

Βρεμένος, χιονισμένος
Ο καημενός και παρακαλεί
Τον ήλιο ν' ατάτειλει

Ήλιε ανάτειλε- 'ηλιε ανάτειλε

Ήλιε λάψε και δώσε
Για να λιώσουνε
Χιόνια από τα φτερά μου

Ήλιε ανάτειλε-ήλιε ανάτειλε

Liam Allen PCSO Rural team
                 Combrooke
5   Nr Kineton
Rest day - 7am - 4pm
101   Ex 4600
email   Liam.Allen1@warwickshire.police.uk
722 40645

Printed in Great Britain
by Amazon

39255909R00185